DEATH OF A CURE

A Thomas Briggs Novel

STEVEN H. JACKSON

TELEMACHUS PRESS

DEATH OF A CURE

Cover Art Design: Telemachus Press, LLC
Cover Art Illustrations:
Copyright © istockphoto.com / Rich Legg (Background)
Copyright © istockphoto.com / Stephan Klein (Chalk Outline)
Copyright © istockphoto.com / David Wilson (Police Tape)
Copyright © istockphoto.com / www.bubaone.com (Caduceus)

Edited by: Sophia S. Michas and Dr. Fred Tarpley
Published by: Telemachus Press, LLC
Marketing and distribution provided by: Yorkshire Publishing

ISBN: 978-0-9841083-0-5

Printed in Canada

10 9 8 7 6 5 4 3 2 1

IN MEMORY OF MY BROTHER

Timothy Douglas Jackson

September 16, 1959 to January 11, 2007

An unfortunate side effect of hope is deception.
— *Anonymous*

DEATH OF A CURE

PROLOGUE

We know them as humanitarians. Of this we are sure. We are certain; their calling unimpeachable. They have forsaken success in industry and in government that was surely theirs just for the taking. This personal sacrifice is for us but, more importantly, for those we love. They are servants of a greater good. In return, we entrust them with our time, our talents, and our money — all we can give. They move the hearts of our children, our friends, and our coworkers all of whom enlist sponsors who contribute even more money based on miles hiked or biked along traffic-laden thoroughfares. We look to them to lead us from the heartbreak — the overwhelming emotional devastation that cripples us as our lives derail when someone we love is struck down by a cruel and life-robbing disease. We hold them to a higher standard. They are better. We need them to be. They are the caretakers of our hope.

But is our dream of a cure really their mission? Have we been deceived? Could it be a cruel duplicity, a personal deceit, phenomenal in its audacity, yet nothing more to them than an evil means to a selfish end? A falsehood perpetrated against the trusting, abetting positions of power; our hope blinding us from the truth. Have the lifestyles, the position, and the money become their true motivation? Have they come to see the disease, our enemy, as their benefactor? How far would they go to protect the enemy?

Would they kill?

CURE PREVENTION

Just moments before his death, Dr. Ronald Briggs had been alone standing behind his desk, about to call it a night. Someone, once a friend though now an enigma, entered his dimly lit office. The semi-automatic pistol looked menacing in the light cast by a desk lamp. Although the hand that held the weapon was not large, its grip was sure. The gun was steady and its aim unwavering. The two stood motionless as they faced each other.

"I'm not ready for a cure." It was a simple statement. Briggs waited for more, for the excuses, the rationalizations, but none were offered. Personal agenda had superseded that of the organization, of the mission. A fact suspected was no longer concealed.

Briggs had not been surprised by the sudden appearance in his office and only a little by the gun. He quietly replied in a resigned, uncharacteristically tired voice, "How long has it been since you really cared for those who believe in us? Did you ever?"

Ignoring his question, the intruder gave a quick command. "Give me the backup disk you made this afternoon. I know you have it with you."

Without looking, Briggs reached slowly into his lab coat pocket and produced a DVD sandwiched inside a scratched yellow plastic case. It contained the new material, pivotal information that would become part of this week's backup — the documentation of his recent success in the search to find a cure for CID. He laid it on the desk next to him. The light from the oversized lamp captured the pistol and the yellow case in its circle. There was no immediate move to retrieve it, to take from the world this vessel that held the secret to CID's inner workings and the blueprint to render it impotent.

The voice, icy-cold in its resolve, spoke to Briggs again, "It doesn't have to be this way."

His adversary was partially concealed, hidden in the shadow, with only a hand and the gun it held in the direct light of the lamp. Briggs couldn't see an expression. He couldn't examine the face for some weakness to exploit. If only Tommy were here. He had no concern that his brother would share his jeopardy; that he too would also be in danger. No, not for a moment because Tommy would know what to do. Their roles would reverse; there would be no jeopardy, no danger. The junior brother would take the lead stepping in front of Briggs as he had done twice before. He would then somehow, with some swift, frighteningly primal action, end this as easily as Briggs knotted his bow tie. Tommy would momentarily expose a part of himself, his true self, to his older brother — a part that Tommy worked hard to keep under control, out of sight, even from Ron. Especially from Ron.

Instead of that hopeful scenario, Briggs floundered for what to say, his emotions selecting simple words in response to the challenge, "You mean you're not going to kill me?"

"You may have left me no choice, but it's really up to you. I know your secret. The one you keep from us, all the while thinking that you are so much smarter than everyone else." In the voice he heard something that he had never heard before. The words not simply spoken but sneered with contempt, with a meanness, a hatred, that seemed strangely to bring pleasure, so unlike the carefully maintained persona. For the first time Briggs was afraid. The evil side was the reality: everything else a facade, a mechanism sufficient to deceive both the naive as well as the sophisticated.

"I don't know what you are talking about." Briggs offered the accusation destroying hope.

"Save it for your staff and the summer interns. The great Dr. Briggs, so perfect in every way. I know what you really are, so don't try and take the moral high ground with me. I know about your little girlfriend. I know your plans to steer development rights to SynapTherapies. I know about your sweet little inside deals with CNEG." The words, the indictment, should have been spoken with some emotion, but they came in a calm monotone. These words had been rehearsed.

"The cure is worth more than anyone's reputation," he answered back with just the beginnings of defiance in his voice, almost as if he had forgotten the pistol aimed at his heart and his complete belief that it would be used.

The deceiver advanced toward him, the gun projecting a virtual force driving him back to the open window. The familiar and usually comforting sounds of the city street seemed louder than normal, the pavement below somehow closer.

"I guess I was wrong. Exposing you and the ruin that it would cause not only to you and to your new friend won't be enough. I can erase the data, but I can't erase your mind."

The words were practiced, uttered without emotion, a conclusion foregone. Nothing Briggs could have said would have changed the actions about to take place. Others had decided his fate. Even so, his adversaries could take false comfort later that an effort had been made to prevent his death. But in the end, there had been no choice. No other outcome had been acceptable.

Backing up, Briggs felt the windowsill as he moved against it — there was nowhere left to go. He closed his eyes. He waited for the gunshot that never came. His surprise, at what came next, complete.

* * *

Falling twenty-four stories takes just seconds. Yet in those brief moments, he did not experience fear even though he knew his fate with exacting certainty. Instead, an image quickly filled his mind displacing the outrage that had been his constant companion for more than a year. It was that of a patient, a young girl in Texas named Connie who had CID, the disease that had been his life's work, a professional and personal passion. The girl was memorable for her character, her courage tested by CID's painful and deadly progress. Then, the youngster's comforting presence, surviving for just a moment, quickly faded.

As physically paralyzing as the moment was, the last thoughts of Briggs's life were those of sad acceptance. He had come to know that his colleague, his sometimes mentor, was capable of amazing treachery. His employer was an institutionalized sham betraying the trust of the innocent. Ignoring the deceit and duplicity around him as he closed in on the cure had seemed the right thing to do — the high road. The route he had always traveled, following without exception to his own words of advice he had given to Tommy when he was young and looked to his big brother for guidance. "Just do what's right. Let the world work out the rest." A simple rule.

Tonight his guiding principle had only enabled the enemy, emboldened to greater atrocities culminating in this moment — his death. More significantly, more important than his own life — the death of a cure.

* * *

The emergency response team was capable and quickly arrived on scene. There was, however, little for them to do. A body falling from over 200 feet has attained almost one-half of the speed of a skydiver at terminal velocity. Dr. Ronald Briggs hit the concrete sidewalk face up at more than 60 miles per hour. The blunt trauma impact to his head, his back, and his torso complete, death was instantaneous. Real life is unlike children's cartoons — bodies do not bounce. The crumpled form of Dr. Ronald Briggs lay still in the cold Manhattan night as advocacy's evil benefactor triumphed again.

HOUSE CALL

There had been a collision last night involving a nuclear attack sub traversing the Spratly Islands in the South China Sea. She had been on a spy mission, an unseen interloper, silent, deep and watchful among the already suspicious. The *USS Hawaii*, a very new Virginia class submarine, was damaged yet remained operational. The *Hawaii* had not collided with another vessel. The top of an uncharted seamount had violently interrupted her at 3 a.m. resulting in multiple injuries. Due to her sensitive location, she remained submerged limping toward the safety of a repair facility.

The *Hawaii's* benthic misadventure had been reported up channel from the Commander, Submarine Forces, U.S. Pacific Fleet, and then down a different, little known channel to our team not found on any publicly disseminated, military organization chart. We don't have a fancy acronym identifying our inter-service unit made up of specialists from all of the military branches.

At least one critical injury required emergency surgery beyond the skill set of the onboard talent. The Navy needed me, Lt. Col. (Dr.) L. T. Briggs, USMC, delivered aboard unnoticed, tout de suite. Successful covert insertion providing medical, scientific, or engineering support was our group's stated mission. Successful extraction, covert or otherwise, was my personal goal.

Prior to this sortie, each of *Hawaii*'s crewmen had to sign a document that not-so-gently reminded them about the penalties for sharing certain aspects of their Navy life. Penalties pointedly described with words like "treason" and everyone's personal favorite, "mandatory prison sentence without the possibility of parole." The sensitivity was due to the *Hawaii*'s presence in the Spratly's. She was not an approved visitor by any of the contentious parties claiming sovereignty over the island archipelago and its tremendous, yet mostly untapped resources. I learned this in my briefing — I signed the same papers and, like the crew, I didn't get a copy either.

Another member of our team rotating with me through Yokosuka on Tokyo Bay, Major William Sanchez, U.S. Army, assisted me with the next step of my assignment. Billy's specialty was weapons of mass destruction, or more correctly, the destruction of weapons of mass destruction. He joined me at our office and helped me gather equipment that our group had cached at Yokosuka. Billy made careful note of what was being removed from storage and would email his list back to our replenishment team. While this was yet another example of the mighty military paperwork monster, it was a necessary one due to the nature of our assignments. When we take equipment on a mission, it almost never makes it back and one of us might need to requisition the same stuff again next week.

My jump gear for this mission was a standard low-altitude airborne issue round canopy and harness. I looked sadly at the fancier parafoil wing chutes in the adjoining locker.

"No parafoil?" Billy asked. They were much more fun, but the jump wouldn't keep me in the air long enough to make the steerable rig worthwhile. Not to mention the fact that there would not be any point of reference to steer to.

"Maybe next time," I replied.

The assembled SCUBA gear was fairly standard, open-circuit dive equipment that any sport diver would have recognized. Being a somewhat responsible steward of the taxpayer's money, the fancier re-breather would remain behind.

"No re-breather?" Billy asked with an even greater look of pain on his face. It wasn't needed. No one would see my bubbles in the dark, and I wasn't going to need the extended time underwater offered by the more expensive toy.

"Maybe next time," I again replied, rather lamely.

"You wouldn't impress a Kabukicho b-girl with this shit," he said disgustedly, referencing the local red light district and the fact that the tools that had been selected were less than futuristic.

"Maybe I can get by on my good looks," I offered hopefully.

Giving me a lopsided grin, Billy shot back, "Not likely, Marine."

Getting the jump and dive gear together had taken us less than twenty minutes. The surgical tools and meds would take longer. As a military doc, I travel with a fairly complete collection of diagnostic tools and medical supplies. For this trip with anticipated abdominal surgery, more would be needed. I was probably taking four times the surgical instruments and pharmaceuticals than would be required, but there would not be the luxury of sending out for more after getting aboard the sub. Better to err on the safe side. Billy was no help assembling the medical gear, but it didn't stop the stream of sarcasm as he noted my removals from the cache. From my personal locker, I grabbed a couple of fatigues without any markings that would identify who I was or what country I was from and a small bag holding a razor, toothbrush, and such.

On rare occasion to help with an insertion, we have Special Forces, or an overwhelming regular military presence, escort us into enemy country. Given the fact that we are typically without operational support, everyone in my group takes personal safety seriously, and like all of my peers, in my previous life I was one of the gunslingers. There has been more than one occasion where, if I wanted to live through the mission, I had to become one more member of the fire team and not just the doc along for the ride like so much freight. Most everyone in my group has had similar experiences. Because of this hypersensitivity about my personal safety, the next thing to be packed was a Beretta Model 96FS decocker chambered in .40 S&W carrying eleven rounds, ten in the clip and one in the pipe. Billy added four spare clips holding ten more rounds each. The weapon did not come from storage — I already had it on me. In addition to the pistol, I slipped in a couple of other surprises. Sharp ones.

Billy nodded approvingly as if finally some good decisions were being made. "I don't trust the bubbleheads either," he joked. "All that time at sea might make your skinny ass look way too mermaid-like!"

I wasn't so much worried about defending myself in the sub although some strange things have happened to me in friendly places, as I was about an unplanned emergency diversion interrupting the insertion. Of course, if I did end up in a hostile environment, the sidearm might not be enough, but it was all that could reasonably be packed. I was certain that once aboard the sub everything brought in with me would become visible to others and a shotgun would raise eyebrows. Submariners could be an overly sensitive bunch. Must be the weeks on end without seeing the sun. I wasn't going to share Billy's mermaid comment with the crew.

We packed it all in one of our standard, olive drab canisters. The canisters were cylindrical, almost five feet long and about a foot in diameter. They were sealed when closed and would keep out ocean water or desert sand. They also had a pointed end and could penetrate a jungle canopy or the roof of any third-world hut — we had had a couple of embarrassing incidents to prove that. If you weren't careful, you could over-pack, making them incredibly heavy. The one feature they did not have was built-in luggage wheels.

I emptied my pockets into my personal locker and pulled on another set of the nondescript fatigues. My transportation arrived, and the driver helped me carry the canister and the rucksack containing my jump and dive gear to a small truck. Billy watched and worked hard at staying out of the way. He had defined his assistance as limited to note taking and the provision of verbal abuse. There was no mention in his job description about lifting and hauling. We drove a short distance to the flight line where I boarded a C-17 Globemaster transport aircraft.

The loadmaster looked at the canister knowing that he and my driver would have to haul it aboard by hand. He shot me a look, and I knew what was coming.

"Is that your kit?" he asked with more than a little attitude. He also conveniently forgot the "sir" due to the fact that my jumpsuit did not have rank insignia. I was sure that he knew that I was an officer, but I let it slide.

I glowered back, the best defense being a good offense. "Yeah, just the rucksack and the tube."

It was obvious that he preferred cargo, even 70-ton, M1 main battle tank cargo, provided that it could roll itself aboard. The luggage wheel idea was building a following.

I said goodbye to Billy, and soon the bird was buttoned up; the sole passenger (me) was safety-briefed, and the take-off accomplished, all with little fanfare. The six-hour flight in a noisy transport gave me plenty of time to be alone with my thoughts.

* * *

I could do this 1,000 times and would still experience some anxiety just prior to the big moment. Only James Bond is James Bond. The rest of us are considerably less cool.

I was going in alone — we almost always operated alone. This would be the fifth time I had parachuted into the ocean and knocked on the door of a submarine but only my second time at night. The night factor added significantly to the degree of difficulty, but it wouldn't get me any sympathy from my boss, Gen. Marlon F. X. Fitzhue, self appointed protector of the entire free world.

Mentally, I rehashed what had been learned from my previous underwater sub insertions. After carefully considering the objective, a good plan had been developed. I was well trained and had more than a little experience at this sort of exercise. Even so, I went over every detail I could think of that might operationally affect my ability to get safely aboard the sub. All of that took less than the first hour of my trip leaving me a lot of time to kill. At this point, the worst thing to do was to over analyze the task at hand. Fixating on the upcoming jump and dive for the next five hours would only cause needless anxiety.

My brother, Ron, entered my thoughts as he often does when I'm about to do something he would consider dangerous. What would he say if he could see me now? He would try to hide his concern behind a forced laugh and let me know, as he had countless times before, that his younger brother had not really moved beyond adolescence. The excitement in his life was limited to the view through a microscope with an occasional, tense skirmish in the boardroom. He would tell me that the excitement in my life could get me killed! I would answer back that someday his boardroom buddies would kill him with boredom. He was supposed to call me last night, and I hadn't heard from him. There would be a message from him waiting for me upon my return from the mission.

* * *

The rear cargo ramp slowly opened. I was more than ready to get this part over with knowing that my heart rate would settle down the moment I left the aircraft, even more so after getting under underwater.

When the time came, the loadmaster yelled, "Now!" and slapped me on the back. Standing bent over behind the canister containing my gear, I pushed for all I was worth and followed the five-foot long tube out into the dark space engulfing the fast-moving aircraft. The fine print promised that my static line would stay attached to the plane, automatically deploying the parachute. Although the aircraft was less than 500 feet above the Pacific, there was nothing to see during my freefall in absolute darkness — no, my eyes were not shut, just useless. They would be of little help until actually underwater and then only after putting on the dive mask.

There was just barely enough time to throw my arms and legs back into the hard arch position drilled into me many years ago by my jump instructors when suddenly I was just about stopped in mid air by the opening parachute. Almost instantaneously after the chute had opened, another less-than-subtle yank on my body pulled at me when the canister reached the end of its tether. I think I gained two inches in height. There was an overcast completely blacking out the stars and the moon. With no light above the horizon to give me a frame of reference for up or down, it was impossible to tell how far it was to the surface. The luminous hands of the altimeter fixed to the aluminum mount on my chest were barely visible. The loadmaster and the now empty transport plane long gone.

The downward pull from the canister relaxed as it impacted the surface, floating momentarily. Hitting the water hard somewhere next to it, I was forced under by my downward velocity better than fifteen feet. The time had come to pull the regulator from its holder, put it in my mouth, breathe in some bottled air, and clear my ears. Removing the dive mask from its pocket, putting it on my face, and clearing the water from it came next, followed by extricating myself from the parachute harness. My eyes stung from the salt water.

Be cool, Tommy.

The canister followed me down like an obedient pup. At thirty feet, all was peaceful again even if it was still very dark. Thirty feet had been chosen because it was deep enough for the ocean to be still yet not so deep that the eighty cubic foot tank would get quickly sucked dry. Pulling the homing locator out of another pocket marked a key moment as without it, finding the sub would be impossible. The beacon was coming in strong.

I swam in the direction indicated by the glowing pointer. After about 250 feet as measured by my kick count, the beacon emitted an audible alarm – the *Hawaii* was close. Turning on my dive light while descending to eighty feet as instructed, I set off in the direction of the sub. After swimming another seventy feet, I saw the submarine appear suspended motionless in front of me. My position was near the bow on the port side. Turning right, my slow and measured kicking brought me along the length of the sub just over the curving deck.

Moving aft until the sub's underwater entrance, the lock-out/lock-in chamber, was encircled in the illumination of my dive light left me with mixed emotions. Getting aboard the sub would be a relief, but at the same time, I was going to have to enter the air-lock that was not only a claustrophobia-inducing crypt but also the only part of my short journey that was completely dependent upon the actions of others – something I dreaded even more than the small, dark, enclosed chamber. Opening the outer hatch required actuating the release lever and lifting the cover. Pulling the canister towards me, I pushed it into the open hatch and followed it in. Standing next to it, my fancy fins folded up and out of the way. Reaching up and pulling the hatch shut secured the locking mechanism. After banging on the inner hatch with the butt of my dive knife, I could hear the sound of water rushing and knew that the crew was draining water out of the chamber. Even though the water level descended around me, I kept the regulator in my mouth, breathing normally. Well, as normally as you can breathe when trapped in a steel crypt watching your air supply diminish. Respiration rate may have been up a touch. I just don't like small spaces and may have closed my eyes.

The wheel in the inner hatch started to turn and eventually the inner portal opened dumping the last couple of gallons of seawater. An officer in a working uniform looked curiously in at me as the regulator dropped from my mouth. Having no idea what he was thinking, my words were less than poetic.

"Hi," I said. OK, maybe it could have been more eloquent. It was a strange entrance, but it wasn't a Neil Armstrong moment, even if it wasn't your typical house call.

SKI REPAIR

"Nice of you to drop in, Colonel." He had been working on that one. "I'm Johannson, the exec. Welcome aboard!"

By "exec," Lt. Cmdr. Gary Johannson had meant that he was the executive officer and the second in command of the boat after the captain. Subs are always boats, never ships. Submariners, those who for reasons known only to them, volunteer to be sub crewmembers, are particular about the distinction. I've never asked why, but you will get a guaranteed correction if you say ship. The ones I have met are even funny about the pronunciation of the word *submariner*. It is always *sub-mare-in-er*, never *sub-marine-er* — important stuff in the realm of the bubblehead. Personally, I thought that the version with "Marine" in the middle sounded best.

Johannson was a big, tow-headed Swede who probably made cranial contact with many of the low-hanging spaces aboard the sub. He wore a perpetual, ear-to-ear grin and seemed to be one of those eternally cheerful guys. Or, maybe, he was just happy to have the doc who could fix his shipmate aboard and ready to get the job done. I get that a lot except from the occasional bad guy who doesn't want me fixing anyone.

I was happy to get out of the wet gear and get a fresh water rinse. All of this occurred in the torpedo room with cold water starting out in a hose aimed at me and then draining through a grating to somewhere out of sight below. The sub's crew didn't seem concerned about where the water was going so I wasn't either. After toweling off and breaking the canister's waterproof seal, the dry storage area inside provided underwear, fatigues, shoes, and socks. I retrieved my traveling medical equipment leaving the remaining personal items in the canister. Smiling guy that he was, Johannson had still scrutinized every item as it came out of the canister. He instructed the two seamen to take the rest of my gear to his cabin where I would be bunking on a cot between him and the chief engineer. I wondered if the sidearm would still be loaded when I next saw it? Johannson quickly led me to the sickbay. Don't know what happened to the canister; I never saw it again — another piece of equipment loss to explain. Later, my unloaded pistol and four empty magazines would magically reappear, stuck in the top of my medical bag. Maybe the rounds ended up in the canister.

Along the way we passed through the crew's mess where a cup of hot coffee was pressed into my hands, and then we proceeded along several brightly lit passageways. The boat did not have the small, claustrophobic feel of its diesel-electric predecessors. Although we passed only a couple of seamen, both of them seemed very curious about the newcomer, even though they knew what I was here to do. This changed as we got near the sickbay. There was a lot of activity as well as some very serious faces.

"How many are on the final injury list?" I asked.

"Thirty-nine requiring more than a band-aid or aspirin. Everyone aboard is probably a little shook up in some way. We hit hard and slid to a stop without any warning," Johansson answered quietly. "Had the boat been ten feet deeper, we'd have struck the side of the mount instead of grazing the top, and we would all be dead." For the first time, his face lost its customary smile.

He recovered quickly. "But now that the United States Marine Corps has been kind enough to send us "Super Doc" straight from the heavens above, we are saved! Thank you, Jesus!!" exclaimed Johannson immediately regaining his happy demeanor while channeling some departed Southern preacher. He then started loudly singing "From the Halls of Montezuma" announcing our arrival. He got a lot of the words wrong.

Sickbay was overflowing even though most of the injured were being treated in their bunks. Dr. Orr and some volunteer medical support were in constant motion, moving back and forth from patient to patient. I was introduced to Lt. (Dr.) Raymond Orr and his ad-hoc team of very committed helpmates. I told the lieutenant to forget the rank, and we quickly became Ray and Tom. He was happy for the informality; he was happy that I was here; he was a lot happier than he had been at anytime in the last 24 hours. In my personal life, I almost never have this effect on people. Maybe my disdain for the bubbleheads needed re-thinking.

Electrician's Mate 1st Class Terry Kawalski, "Ski" to his buddies, was doped up pretty good, and though he was pale, he did not seem to be in much pain. Stripped to the waist, he had a large bandage wrapped around his middle. Ray handed me his chart with the notes that had been made since the accident. You could read not only his medical but also his military training in the record. The make, model, and serial number of the generator were part of the package as was a description of the lifting eye that Kawalski had fallen upon. A sketch of the steel eye and the metal flange on the piece of equipment that had pierced the abdominal wall was included. Ray suspected that the spleen had been damaged and required removal. Had the injury fully trashed the spleen with subsequent hemorrhaging, Ray would have attempted emergency surgery on his own and probably gotten away with it.

Having decided that he had some time, he did a very smart thing and waited. Buying time bought him options — I was the option selected. From Kawalski's vitals, some testing, and my own evaluation, it was obvious that we had to look inside.

Planning for spleen removal surgery required patient vaccinations for pneumococcus, H. influenza, and meningococcus, the protocol for a splenectomy. Ray helped me prep Kawalski and get him under. My new junior doctor friend would monitor his vitals and play anesthesiologist/assistant surgeon while I did the cutting. Due to the trauma, we performed open surgery. Upon inspection, it became quickly obvious that the damaged spleen had to come out, and it did without much fuss — it's not difficult surgery. Disconnecting it from its arteries allowed me to remove it by cutting it free from the ligaments holding it in place. We sewed the abdomen back together, giving Electrician's Mate 1st Class Terry Kawalski a scar to scare his future grandchildren. Yet it was not the basis for a Purple Heart as he was not injured in combat. Unless some significant complications arose, Kawalski would, after some recovery, once again do whatever it is that 1st Class Electricians Mates do aboard nuclear submarines. Hopefully, I would be long gone before he regained the energy to tell me what that was. I noted to all of the medical team, and to a few members of the crew within earshot, that the Marine Corps had once again bailed out the Navy — everyone could sleep soundly. Even though some serious eye rolling ensued, my little joke was all the assurance that the onlookers needed to know that their shipmate was going to make it. There wouldn't have been any kidding around if I had any concerns. The good news would spread quickly along the submarine jungle telegraph.

We safely returned the patient to one of the three fixed litters in the little sickbay, the other two occupied by injured seamen. It was time to chase Ray out and send him to a bunk of his own.

"Go get some sleep, Lieutenant," I ordered, a colonel once again.

"What, and leave the safety of my crew to a Marine?"

While pushing him out the door and into the companionway, I was updated on the more serious patients in a rapid-fire verbal volley. Finally, he gave in, waved a resigned thanks, and with a junior officer dragging him by the shirt sleeve, moved off in search of sleep. He was a good doc — the crew had been served well and they knew it.

I checked on the other two patients in sickbay — they would keep. The executive officer had been hanging out in the companionway relaying updates on the surgery to the captain whom I still had not met. Johannson led me around the ship to see the other injured sailors. We used the excuse that it was too easy to get lost. There was no need to verbalize what we both knew — not a great idea for a stranger (even a brother officer) to wander about a nuclear sub without a keeper — at least until they got to know me a whole lot better.

After seeing and evaluating all thirty-eight of the remaining injured, a process that took over six hours, I was satisfied that the *Hawaii* would suffer no fatalities. Sharing this with the captain seemed like a good excuse to meet him. Johannson (who had become Gary to my Tom) led me to the officer's wardroom. The sub's skipper, Commander Richmond, would be along soon.

Planting my butt in a booth, I declined coffee but accepted orange juice. Ray walked in looking a lot better and well rested. He thanked me — my 45th since my arrival on board. I said, "No problem" for the 45th time and off he went to check once again on everyone that I had just seen.

Commander Mike Richmond silently appeared and faced me. He was short like my brother but more laid back like me. After introductions, I received my 46th thank you, this time from the skipper. I had never met Commander Richmond before, but it was obvious that he had something to tell me and was uncomfortable with whatever it was.

"Colonel, I have been in touch with COMSUBPAC, and I have some news. You have a brother, Dr. Ronald Briggs, in New York. Is this correct?"

It could only be bad news. Family matters are not passed along to me, or any members of my group, unless the news is really, really bad and then only if the basic mission has been completed. The sick feeling that had started way down deep in my gut was expanding. I was working hard to control my breathing and could feel my skin get cold.

"Commander Richmond, is my brother dead?"

TRANSIT

Richmond told me that he had no details about Ron's death. Three days after my jump into the Pacific, we rendezvoused with a surface combatant group in a less embarrassing part of the Pacific. One of the ships was an amphibious assault vessel with a large medical staff and impressive facilities. I supervised the transfer of nine of *Hawaii*'s most injured to the larger, though probably not better, medical quarters. After turning the cases over to the new docs, it was a short hop by helicopter to a carrier.

The transport back to Yokosuka seemed to take no time at all. I was dispatched as part of the cargo aboard a twin-engine turboprop. The base chaplain, a stranger to me, filled me in on what he had found out about Ron's death, which wasn't much. The official line was that he had jumped from his office window.

It was going to be a long, butt-numbing trip from Japan back to the United States. At the best of times, travel like this is an endurance contest. Some people have told me that I can be a surly traveler. This, of course, is simply not true. I'm a prince of a guy – just ask me. In my current situation, I wasn't sure what was going to be worse, the travel or actually arriving in New York. Looking forward to the reality of a life without Ron, his death not yet an emotionally accepted fact and even worse, death by suicide, was physically and mentally draining, leaving me feeling hollow and removed from everything around me. Being half the world away had somehow made it seem unreal. I was sure that coming face to face with the funeral, Ron's work associates, and dealing with his condo in Manhattan would remove any barrier that my subconscious had constructed keeping me from finally dealing with the fact that he was gone. No matter how long the trip to New York would be, it would go too fast.

I quickly arranged for emergency bereavement leave and then purchased a last-minute, first class seat from Tokyo to New

York on an Asian-based airline that I had used extensively. The price made me think that I was buying into the airline, not just renting a seat. At least this airline's idea of service actually included service. What a concept. On a 747 they would have over forty flight attendants and a purser. In first class, the ratio was one flight attendant for each six passengers. If you inadvertently lifted an eyebrow, one would magically appear by your seat. In my case, an aisle seat — 3B.

This particular airline amused me. All of the flight attendants were females between eighteen and twenty-four years old. They all had the same body size and shape — diminutive, a size one dress. There had to be a factory that made them somewhere, an assembly line where small, always smiling Malaysian ladies came off a conveyor belt. I don't know what the airline did with them when they turned twenty-five. Maybe they went back to the factory for refurbishment and smile reconditioning. They were consistently shy, and I had noticed on all of my fights with this carrier that they had peculiar names. Not peculiar because they were Asian, but rather because their names were American. That is, American circa 1950. The two attendants waiting on me on this flight had name tags displaying, "Mabel" and "Ethel." Stopping Mabel, I asked her what her real name was. She became very uncomfortable and nervously looked around before answering me.

"Airline give me name."

"So, what is your real name?"

She checked up and down the aisle again and whispered something very exotic that slipped off of her tongue without effort.

"Why can't you use your real name? It's very pretty," I quickly added.

"Airline does not want to offend Americans."

Amazing. "Americans could use a little offending," I said, maybe a little harshly. I enjoyed a quick fantasy about taking apart the ancient oriental bureaucrat who had traveled to the States fifty years ago and was the official "re-namer" due to his worldly sophistication. I was a surgeon — I could take him apart.

Eyes cast downward, she wasn't sure what my words meant and was still nervous about being overheard. As she moved away, I smiled at her trying to change the mood and then, making sure no one could hear, I said thank you and did my best to use her real name. She smiled back. It was a very large smile on the face of a very small lady.

I focused on trying to sleep. On this flight, I did not have it in me to make any more small talk with the flight attendants or anyone else. The only thing needed was sleep. Sleeping on a plane is usually never a problem for me. Sleeping anywhere at anytime is never a problem for me. For transoceanic flights, the airlines have made first class a very reasonable place to sleep. The seats fold down flat and make up a bed with a little divider between you and the rest of the world. Still, tonight it wasn't working.

I got up and walked the length of the aircraft a couple of times. This is something I seldom do although I should. Long-distance flyers can get clots in their legs if they remain too sedentary. Everyone should get up and walk every four hours and drink lots of water to stay hydrated. Returning to my seat and electing not to watch the movie caused me to fend off another visit by a flight attendant. This time her name was Mildred, checking to see if anything was needed, was the movie playback working? Finally, I'm not sure when, I fell fitfully into a world full of bad dreams, reliving the moment when I was told that Ron was gone, over and over again.

* * *

The two Briggs brothers were physically about as different as two brothers could be. Ron was small in stature, trim with a high energy level set to a constant boil. He always sported a bow tie and wore a spotless white shirt that was never unbuttoned. I was more than a foot taller, wider at the shoulders than Ron and was considerably less driven than he was. I have never been able to get Ron to go either hunting or fishing with me. The pace would have placed his sanity in jeopardy.

We were, in spite of our personality differences, very close. As the only two children of wealthy parents, we have had little to worry about financially, allowing us to develop diverse interests and careers. Most of this we owed to our dad. He was not going to let us rest on the family laurels and made education and making something of ourselves the priority — a distant, boarding school priority, but a priority none the less. Demonstrating considerable good sense, Mom stayed out of our father's way when it came to the establishment of personal goals. When I was eight years old and Ron was a senior in college, our parents were killed in an auto accident. Ron finished college and entered medical school — one of the good ones.

My little big brother was a truly great doctor, scientist, and philanthropist, and my pride for him was genuine. It was because of Ron that my military career was re-directed to medical school and residency. He was, however, the really gifted physician; I was a mechanic — a fixer. In spite of his exuberant nature and fast pace, he had the intrinsic patience necessary to see scientific experimentation through to a successful end, with him pushing every step of the way. I struggle finding the patience for long-term anything. Even though I usually look like I am half asleep, I am restless and impatient with the world. Ron is the nice guy; I can't suffer fools for very long. As a doctor, I learned surgery so I could fix problems and move on. Ron shared funny stories with his friends. I shared waterfowl hunting techniques. Ron pursued science and the cure to one of mankind's most debilitating diseases. I pursued girls and the next mission — mankind was on its own.

After prep school and college with frequent visits from Ron, I entered the Marine Corps as an officer candidate, my engineering degree doing little to impress my drill instructors. Six months after training began, I graduated and was placed in command of my first platoon as a freshly minted 2nd lieutenant. My road to adventure started with a lot of growing up. Thirty-nine soldiers and a platoon sergeant were rightfully suspicious of my leadership abilities. I learned quickly and had a very experienced platoon sergeant to keep me out of trouble. Through a couple of lucky breaks, I was selected for Force Recon training — the Marine Corps' special forces. We thought we were truly the baddest of the bad. After all, the regular Marine units view themselves as equals to the other service's special teams. Force Recon was a cut above that.

Two tours of running with the best of the best made me just about the world's biggest pain in the ass — but Ron still put up with me. On one visit while recovering from a training injury, Ron leaned on me one more time about medical school. We made a bet about the pre-admission test, the MCAT, which I would have to take to get accepted into medical school. The rules were simple. I had to try my best, take a prep course, and if I scored above a mutually agreed upon number, I had to give med school a chance. If I scored under it, Ron would leave me alone and happy with my fellow jarheads. Answering the 146 questions took over four hours. I scored two points above the target.

Having presented my commander with my MCAT score, the military was happy to have me in medical school. I took a temporary leave of absence and promised to return. The government offered to pay for my tuition expenses and even continue my then-1st lieutenant's salary in exchange for some more of my life after graduation, internship, and residency. Declining as I didn't need the money and even though I planned to return to the military, I wanted to keep my options open and not extend the period of my indenture. After a one-year internship, a very respectable surgical residency at an institution where Ron was well known accepted me into their program. Although he never admitted it, Ron must have intervened on my behalf.

Returning to the Marine Corps as a newly promoted captain and the only medical doctor in the corps, I gave up the "snake eater" life for surgical tours in forward Army and Navy medical units where eating snake would have been a way to improve on the cuisine. The work, however, was rewarding, and maybe I was finally growing up. News of my impending maturity must have made it to the senior members of the Marine Corps. Fortunately for me, they stepped in and rightfully put a stop to that evolution. Two years after serving as a military surgeon, the corps requested, strongly and with several not-so-veiled threats, that I volunteer for a billet in a new group comprised of officers from each branch of the military which had combined front-line skills with medical or science/engineering specialties. It turned out to be the best thing that could ever have happened to me. For the last six years, my position happily blended my two military lives. I was one of five docs in the group, and the only one who knew what "Semper Fidelis" meant — the rest being stunted in their development, as they did not have the benefit of being a Marine. This was something that I reminded them about regularly. In addition to my surgical skills, my new command added some crash courses in internal medicine and infectious diseases/bio warfare to my resume. Ron was a big help with these add-ons helping me in our almost daily phone calls.

The satisfaction of base-level curiosity had kept me in the game during medical school and residency. It had been the same with engineering in college. For me, finding out how things work takes the work out of learning. However, without Ron's constant support, my time at USAMARID learning about bacteria, viruses, and genetics would have been a nightmare. I hoped that my training had adequately prepared me to evaluate what Ron had been up to.

All of that seemed like it was a million years ago. Losing Ron made everything else insignificant. I struggled with the facts of his death. Suicide? Why would Ron kill himself? There had to have been an accident. He would never have taken his own life. I was sure about this. How could I be wrong?

L.A. BOUNCE

Missing my connection in Los Angeles caused me to spend the night. Waiting for the shuttle to the hotel, I had to laugh at the civilian attempts at airport security. While standing at the curbside, I watched the TSA approved "Rent-A-Cops" chase off a young wife attempting to pick up her husband. She was driving a minivan with two kids in car seats in the second row. Her blonde hair was tied back in a ponytail. She made several loops around the arrival level before the hotel shuttle arrived, and with each trip she was becoming more stressed, probably concerned about her husband's late arriving aircraft. Her driving was becoming impatient as she mingled with the other stop and go traffic.

Lining the curb, at least fifteen cabs long, was a taxi stand with very little activity given the time of night. Every driver in view had a turban wrapped around his head. One was beside his car on a prayer rug facing, to the best of his knowledge Mecca, with his forehead touching the rug and his butt pointed skyward.

Let me understand this: "Suzie Homemaker," with kids in tow, is forced to circle the airport while the middle-eastern cabbies wait unmolested by the front door. Now I don't want to practice any "profiling" as the bleeding hearts put it, but this was somewhat beyond stupid. Next time I want to blow up an airport, I'll wear Islamic garb and show up in a cab filled with explosives while I pray next to it. My earlier plan to disguise myself as a suburban housewife, complete with kids, was obviously a bad idea. Approaching the uniform, I stated the obvious.

"You know, the population at large would have some degree of respect for you guys if collectively you had more than one brain cell."

"What? What's the matter with you?" he asked.

"There's no guarantee that Blondie in the minivan isn't a terrorist, but most would lay better odds that Achmed over there just might be."

"He's got a hack's license. They can wait next to the curb if they got a license," he recited from the rulebook.

"Background check comes with the license?"

"I don't know."

"You checked to make sure that the driver is really the license holder?"

"We don't have to do that!" he yelled at me, his mouth hanging open at the end of the sentence. He was getting irritated and was about to lecture me on the perils of interfering with his important security-related duties.

Fortunately, my hotel shuttle arrived before an arrest was made. After a short ride, the hotel loomed into view, and I checked in. Falling to sleep, images of terrorist taxi drivers chased my older brother away from me.

* * *

The next morning I stumbled, jet-lagged back to LAX for the final leg. By the time the plane landed at NY Kennedy, I wasn't any better rested. I made my way to baggage claim without seeming to be of special interest to anyone. While waiting at the baggage carousel, another of the traveling public's strange group behaviors revealed itself. Almost all the passengers think that it is necessary to stand right up next to the moving baggage carousel. When their bag finally revolves around to them, they almost kill each other pulling it off the belt due to the fact that they are jammed in side by side, the over-packed bags kinetic energy weapons.

It always seemed to me that if they just stepped back ten feet, not only could they see their bags more easily, but when the time came to retrieve the luggage came, they could step forward and pull it out without knocking anyone senseless. The even more stupid behavior is that of parents standing right at the carousel with all of their small children next to them. I am sure that when I brain one of their little angels, they will be ready to bring suit.

I waited for my single, medium sized bag, looking for an opening in the wall of bag grabbers like a halfback sizing up the defensive line. Pulling my bag out and not beaning one of the lemmings was difficult, but I managed not to put anyone in a hospital.

Walking away, it became clear to me: I had officially become a pain in the ass. Even to myself.

CONDO

Moving quickly from the baggage carousel to the taxicab stand, I tried to stay in my own little world and not interact with anyone. It's a mind game that men play when dealing with stressful times. Stay focused on the tasks at hand and try to make yourself feel good because you are accomplishing something, no matter how trivial. Keeping a hand over my billfold pocket for obvious reasons, I stepped through the crowds of people. One thing you can count on in any airport is that people look everywhere except where they are walking. You can get run over while a passenger is looking up at the electronic gate signs, looking for a bathroom, looking for a shoe shine stand, looking for an airline agent, looking for a place to buy one of those Hollywood gossip magazines that they just can't live without, looking for their connecting gate, or looking for the friend who is supposed to pick them up. Looking everywhere except in front of them. Looking everywhere except at me — the guy they are about to crash into. They can't stop to look. They must keep going. They are travelers.

I nearly tripped over a dog recently released from baggage. He was looking desperately for a place to release the water that he drank during the flight from the cute little bowl molded right into his cute little airline kennel. I was looking at all the people not looking at me and not paying attention to the lower-to-the-ground life forms, not expecting there to be any. Sorry, guy. Hope he made it.

Heading for the exit door and not the entrance door, although that did not appear to be an issue for many of my fellow travelers, I managed to avoid religious conversion — twice.

On the way to the exit, the public address system warned passengers not to accept rides from "ground transportation" solicitors inside the terminal.

It repeated over and over again. It was interminably warning those from out of town, the incredibly naive, "Please do not accept offers of ground transportation while inside the terminal. This activity is illegal and is not permitted by airport authorities."

Before getting to the door, I was stopped three times by unlicensed cabbies trying to get my business. I bobbed and weaved around a sea of drivers hawking their "illegal and not permitted" services. They obviously had not been listening to the announcements. Probably couldn't hear them over the racket they were making trying to hustle business.

It seemed to me that if this activity were really "illegal and is not permitted," then it wouldn't take much for the airport authorities stop it. The gypsy drivers were not hiding what they were doing in the slightest. A determined Cub Scout trying to get his "Crime Stopper" Merit Badge could have nailed two-dozen offenders in ten minutes. Like all travel security for the masses, it was a facade, hiding the truth in lies propped up by bureaucrats and politicians in an effort to make the taxpayers feel safe.

The unseasonably hot and humid New York night reduced the efficiency of my perspiration/evaporation-based personal cooling system. I was going to sweat a lot for nothing. The forecast was for cooler weather starting tomorrow. City cool and crisp was better than city hot and sticky.

There was no wait at the taxicab stand, and thus began the most dangerous portion of my trip from the *Hawaii* — the cab ride into midtown. My driver, Farouk, headed off for the Manhattan intersection closest to Ron's condo in the mid 70's and Central Park West. Forty dollars plus tip later we arrived. Farouk didn't attempt conversation, and he didn't try to rip me off. Farouk was OK in my book. I silently wished him luck as he made money to send home to his family in whichever of the 'stans he was from.

Walking the last 100 meters to the building where Ron lived, had lived, I was let in by a doorman whom I vaguely remembered from my last trip. He remembered me.

"Hi, Colonel," he said. This impressed me as I wasn't in uniform. "Sorry about your brother. He was a friend to everyone here."

I read his nametag. "Thanks, Antonio. I think that a lot of people will miss him." Like most guys, we were struggling trying to talk about an emotional subject while still being the men we thought we were supposed to be.

"If you need anything while you are here...."

"I'll let you know. Thanks again."

I made my way across the marble floor to the security desk where a spare key was provided by a guard. Maybe fortunately, I didn't know the lady at the desk. After producing identification, it was determined that I was on "the list." I wondered for a moment who else was on "the list." Finding the correct bank of elevators, I went up to the eleventh floor and then left down the hall a short distance to Ron's unit.

New York, actually no large city, will ever be a comfortable place for me. I like the outdoors with lots of room around me and without the crowds. I like to see people coming up on me. When the door shut, I felt the relief of sanctuary away from the busy streets — at most, a temporary sanctuary. The good feeling was short lived as I looked around the room. It was Ron in every way and reminded me again of my loss. We had had some good times here. Not a wasted space anywhere. Everything was neat and orderly. Although this was not our family home in Boston, the condo was a pleasant enough place to be during the workweek, especially when you consider that it was in the middle of four million Manhattanites. Ron commuted home on weekends taking the Amtrak Acela Express from Penn Station in Manhattan to Boston's South Station. Always the egalitarian, a quick ride on the Boston subway known as the "T" got him near the large house and compound that we still shared. The New York condo was certainly better than a hotel for as long as Ron needed to work in the city. Probably a good investment also — Ron didn't make dumb financial decisions. Our family home in Boston was my only connection to permanence. Ron used to tease me that it was only a place where I stored my back tax returns. I thought of it as more than that, a little more than that.

Throwing the comical number of locks and latches on the typical New York apartment door made me feel appropriately insecure. The condo had two guest rooms. One was actually for guests, and although he wouldn't admit it, Ron kept the other one just for me. He encouraged me to leave clothes here so I would not have to pack as much when visiting. As usual, the sheets had been flipped, and the towels were fresh. My big brother always tried hard to make me feel at home. I'm sure that I had never been properly appreciative. He'd overlooked that.

Although tired, I still was not ready for sleep. Travel makes you tired. It wears you out, all the while disrupting your sleep patterns. So I roamed the place looking for something that would help me understand why he would take his life. Other than the master bedroom and the two guest rooms, there was a large kitchen with an eating area, a formal dining room, a living room, and a large den. This place had set him back a big bag full of shekels. The furnishings were contemporary and expensive; at least I thought they were. I'm not much of an interior decorator, and I have been informed by a lady friend of mine who works for the FBI, that my taste is "mostly in my mouth." She thinks that is very funny.

Ron liked to cook and was good at it. The large kitchen seemed to have very professional looking appliances. Not an area of expertise for me. The expansive dining room had a table that seated ten with a view shared by the living room out onto Central Park. A little to the north, you could see the Jacqueline Kennedy Onassis Reservoir in the daytime from here. Whenever I was in town, Ron planned some gathering and invited people he wanted me to meet. He was constantly trying to fix me up with one woman or another. It used to amuse me to see how long it would take after the guests started to arrive for me to figure out who my intended was for the evening, if not longer. Most often the poor girl was way too sophisticated to ever want anything to do with me. This realization would come to her after only getting to know me just a little. Doctors are supposed to be classy; frequently I disappoint. I did manage to shock him a couple of times by having my dinner date stroll out of my bedroom the next morning and become my breakfast date. Not knowing that his brother had had an overnight guest, he would stumble over every word, and by watching him you would think that he had never scrambled an egg before.

After checking the master bedroom and closets, I finally made my way into the den. I had saved this for last because this was the place we used to enjoy together most of all and the place that would remind me of what I would be missing. We'd spend late nights tinkering with whatever project he had going on. The small shop-like atmosphere was a great place for a couple of brothers, each working hard to show off to the other; Ron still trying to be the teacher and me trying to prove what I knew. On one wall, each sitting on its own shelf, were the radio controlled model helicopters that Ron built and loved. We would take them to the park and fly them like two little kids. He would make me fly them first as I had actual experience with the real world versions of the models. One of the shelves was empty, and I wondered what had happened to the bird that was supposed to be there. Maybe it had crashed. That had happened more than once. It made me think, "Why had Ron crashed?"

Turning in, my last thoughts before going to sleep were why hadn't Ron communicated whatever problem he had to me? Even worse, suppose he had been trying to and the message hadn't been received? Sorry, big brother.

MIDTOWN

I awoke hungry — an indicator of a good night's sleep. After a quick shower and a shave, a seven-block walk brought me to a delicatessen that Ron and I had been to several times before. I found the deli without losing my way. Once having been somewhere, I can always find it again. This is especially true if the place serves up a good meal. One thing that New York City does well, although it's not enough to make me fall in love with the place, is breakfast, and Arno's Deli did it better than most. I walked in and was quickly seated, quickly ordered, and quickly served. The food was good, there was a lot of it, and I took my time eating while observing the street through the restaurant windows. I did not sit right next to the window. I never do. It may be occupational residue seeping over into my private life. It may be just my belief, but you can be paranoid, and people can still be out to get you.

I had emailed back and forth over the last several days with the funeral parlor holding Ron's body. My instructions to them were to do nothing other than safeguard the body and await my arrival. They had asked twice, but I intentionally did not tell them the specific date of my planned arrival in New York, just that I was on my way from the other side of the world. Not wanting anyone from Ron's office to know of my arrival plans either, I was staying below the radar. It wasn't that I did not trust any of his coworkers. I didn't know any of them well enough yet to not trust them. That would come later. What I wanted to do was get on the ground and talk to the police without any help no matter how well intended. If I had reached out to the CID Society, last night I would have been met by a car service, chaperoned around, and overly assisted. I didn't want a minder.

My first stop was the 17th Precinct Headquarters on East 51st between 3rd Avenue and Lexington placing it four blocks north of the CID Society offices. A patrolman from the 17th was the first to respond when Ron died. Finding this out had not been easy. While in Yokosuka, I spent most of my available time before the flight to New York on the telephone. It began with calls to the New York City Police Department general information line, followed by a struggle through several voice mail jails before finally getting to speak to a human. The lady at the other end of the line was surprisingly helpful and was able to identify not only the precinct and its location but also the names of the detectives assigned to the case.

Even though Ron was obviously dead at the scene, protocol dictated that he had to be taken to N.Y.U. Medical Center. The ambulance driver did not hurry as Ron's fate, while not yet memorialized, was already known with certainty. No reason to wreck the rig, or worse, add another casualty to tonight's list. Ron was pronounced dead at the emergency room and then taken by ambulance to the New York City Crime Lab for assessment and establishment of the cause of death. It was normal for the body to go to the city facility, as the cause of death was not natural. I wanted to speak with the detectives, Sento and Broon.

The 17th was easy to spot. There were two dozen patrol cars parked diagonally in front and flags on either side of the steps leading up to the door. I took the short flight of stairs two at a time. Walking over to a counter and asking for either of the detectives, I was instructed to wait in the lobby. In less than five minutes, and to my surprise, the precinct commander appeared.

He introduced himself, "Dr. Briggs? Jim O'Dale. Wish we were meeting under better circumstances."

I made an appropriate response and shook his hand. We made small talk as we took the stairs up one flight and walked to his office. The precinct was already busy with phones ringing and multiple meetings taking place around us in the bullpen that we crossed. He made some reassurances about sharing with me all that the police department knew about the incident. He didn't call it a suicide. O'Dale seemed genuine in his concern for me and about the circumstances surrounding Ron's death. If it was an act, it was a good one. I was about to learn that he was the real deal. It was no act.

"I knew your brother," he said quietly. This surprised me, but it answered my question about his motives and explained why he had met me and not the detectives. "I met him on several occasions when I made official visits to the CID Society offices. We got to know each other and even had dinner a half a dozen times. I hadn't seen him in a month or so, but the fact that I can't pick the phone up and get him on the line leaves a hole. I know that my relationship was nothing compared to yours. He talked about you all the time. Again, I'm truly sorry."

Ron was incredibly friendly with everyone, but he would not have gone out to dinner with O'Dale without holding him in some regard.

He continued, "I'm very glad that you stopped by. If you feel up to it, I'd like to talk about our investigation and see if you can add to what we know," he said.

This was looking much better. "Absolutely, Captain. Whatever I can do to help and I don't want to wait. I'm sure that time is a factor in any investigation."

He looked a little uncomfortable as he responded, "You know, I've worked a lot of suicides. This city takes a lot out of some people. Sometimes when you look into it, you can believe that this man or woman was completely capable of taking his or her own life. However, many of them have been real surprises. Many more than you would think. You know, the guy was just not the type. His family and friends are shocked. It gets easy for a cop to turn a deaf ear. But in your brother's case, and maybe it's because I knew him and I liked him, I was shocked. I caught myself saying all the same trite things that we routinely hear. How he wasn't the type, he had everything to live for, what a waste. Probably the same things you have been thinking. So, although my guys are telling me that it looks like a suicide to them, I'm keeping it open as a possible murder for the time being based solely on a personal belief. All we know so far is that Ron went out the window that he normally kept open this time of the year. There doesn't seem to have been a struggle in his office, and no one has come forth with any information that might indicate that anyone wanted to kill him."

"Captain, I've asked myself a thousand times if my personal belief that my brother could not have killed himself was just another example of what you described — I'm just a shocked family member. I'm trying hard to be objective, but I'm not buying it. Not yet at least. The frustrating part is that unless a killer is found, the default is that he killed himself. Not the ending that I want to this."

"It's a process of elimination," he patiently explained. "We identify everyone who had opportunity and look for motive. If we can't connect opportunity with motive, suicide becomes the official verdict simply because we have nothing to take to the D.A. As far as opportunity goes, I have a list."

"A list?"

He produced a manila file folder from his desk drawer. "Here, these are all of the people that were in the building when Ron died." He still hadn't said murder or suicide, keeping his options open.

"The ones highlighted in red are CID employees. The ones highlighted in green are employees with other building tenants. The group in yellow, the last group, are the visitors. What can you tell me about anyone you see on the list?" he asked.

I looked at the list. Due to the fact that it had happened after normal business hours, the list was not long, even given the size of the office building. There were eleven names in red and about seventy-five in green. Then I turned the page and saw the visitor list. It had over a hundred names on it.

"How did you get this?" I asked, as it was more than just a copy of the visitor log from the security desk.

"It's from the building security log. Everyone who works there has a radio frequency identifier tag that they carry. It's called an RFID. They are picked up by the system as they pass by the security desk going into and out of the building. Visitors must sign in. We added the manual visitor log to one generated by the computer tracking the RFID's. There is a hole. Almost no visitor signs out even though they are supposed to, and as they don't carry the RFID, they aren't recorded by the system either. They just walk out the door. So, most of the names on the visitor list are people who had come and gone. I've got Sento and Broon running down the visitors trying to eliminate those who had left the building. I'm sure they think it's a waste of their time."

"I recognize a couple of names on the red list. Ron had made some passing comments about his co-workers from time to time. I don't see any names here of people that I have met in person."

"Anyone on that list a problem for him?" Captain O'Dale asked.

"Ron's style was super optimistic and 'everyone is great,'" I replied.

"Yeah, I got that from him too. He would have been a great guy to work with."

"I can only think of a couple of times when he let a little frustration come through. Once he complained about some woman who was a peer. Kind of like the chief of staff to the CID Society president. I can't remember her name. She rubbed him the wrong way. There was also an outside researcher who tried his patience. I don't recall her name either. In neither case did he mention any specifics. I figured it was just normal work politics and on that day he had had a belly full."

"That's probably what it was. Are you planning to go to his office?" he asked.

"Later today or tomorrow morning."

"I can't officially let you look at or have this list. But then again, the copy you are holding might not make it back into this folder — we don't log copies," his eyes narrowing as he spoke.

I folded the list length-wise and slipped it into my inner jacket pocket. He didn't comment.

I asked Captain O'Dale, "How can I help?"

CRIME LAB

I left the 17th and headed straight south and farther downtown by cab to the city crime lab. O'Dale had called the coroner's office to alert them to my impending visit. He told them to expect me — he didn't ask if it was convenient. I liked him more and more.

There exists a popular misconception about forensic detective investigation. It is a misconception based on the number of television shows about forensic investigators and the role that crime labs play in bringing the nefarious to justice. People seem to believe that each and every crime in America somehow has a forensic budget allowing for countless lab tests and unlimited technician labor. Amazing science depicted with animated 3-D renderings of the trauma affecting the victim's insides along with special software that only exists in the minds of the show's writers, will expose every criminal. It's just not that way.

A simple bit of arithmetic tells the truth. According to the city budget easily found on the Internet, New York's Crime Lab has an annual, departmental operating budget of just over twenty million dollars. Let's be conservative and suppose that only one-third of that is fixed costs to maintain the physical plant, pay the administrative staff, and service the fancy equipment. It's probably more like one-half, but I'll be kind. That leaves about thirteen million dollars for the science-based labor and consumables — the direct costs associated with solving crime. Now consider just the major crimes that Gotham's five bureaus have to contend with: Murder and Non-Negligent Manslaughter, Forcible Rape, Robbery, Felonious Assault, Burglary, and Grand Larceny. New York City reports over 200,000 major crimes per year. What it comes to is sixty-five dollars per crime. Sixty-five bucks doesn't buy you a lot of scientific testing. Sorry to disappoint.

In reality, the preponderance of the budget gets spent on the high-profile cases that get district attorneys favorable mention in the press and on TV. I suspected that Ron's case did not have the requisite profile elevation to warrant any excessive allocation of resources. He was a prominent physician and scientist, but without a push from above, not much was going to happen at this lab. Not a big leap in logic. Numbers don't lie.

The Crime Lab did have the basic dodge that his body was so damaged impacting the ground that there was little to do other than blood and other body fluid chemistries. An assistant coroner, Dr. Philip Michaelson, met me. He introduced himself with a bored voice and did not offer to shake my hand. He led the way to a conference room near the lobby.

"Although I am sorry for your loss, Dr. Briggs," he said mechanically and with a strange emphasis on 'Dr.' almost as if he did not believe that I was one, "I'm not sure that I can offer you anything." His tone did not sound like he was sorry about anything other than the fact that he had been ordered to deal with me.

"What do you know?" I asked, still being the nice guy that I know myself to be.

"It should be obvious to any doctor that the blunt force trauma from a fall like that would have killed your brother instantly. The impact to his head was fatal and the immediate cause of death. The blood loss from the compound fractures and internal damage would have killed him quickly even without the head injury. There was nothing for the E.M.T.s to do if the reason that you are here is that you are considering a legal action against the city. We did the full line of blood work and found no trace of drugs or alcohol," he added with finality at the end in a way to imply that our meeting was over. I thought briefly about causing him to experience first-hand the effects of blunt trauma or maybe a compound fracture — possibly a femur?

"I want to see the report," I managed while controlling my voice and looking at the file folder under his arm.

"It will be released later. Releasing it to you now would violate our protocol. As it is, this is most unusual. We never speak to family members. We only share our findings with police department officials and members of the D.A.'s office. We made a significant exception for you." His tone had further degraded as he was making it clear that he did not like those who violated protocol — significantly or otherwise. He was getting close to having his protocol shoved up his ass. He just didn't know it yet.

"Dr. Michaelson, I've traveled a long way to be here. I'm sure that I am not up on your procedures and will apologize for any inconvenience that my visit has caused."

I moved closer to Michaelson, step by step, and spoke quietly to him in a calm monotone. I caused my face to harden and continued to lean closer to him. He began to back up, matching my movement. The first looks of alarm were registering on his face.

Speaking as I continued to move toward him, he was becoming increasingly aware of my violation of his personal space, and that was becoming a problem for him, a major problem, especially for a New Yorker. "But, let me help you understand what I am not going to do. I am not going to call my friend at the 17th, I am not going to call the mayor's office, I'm not going to call a press conference, and I'm not going to call for Divine intervention. What I am going to do is call on your sense of humanity to help out a fellow physician and the brother of a fine man recently deceased. I plan to help you give me the report that I have politely asked for. I should mention that my plans are always successful."

The entire time I kept closing in on this worm, I stared at him with unblinking eyes that were fixed on his. I leaned over from the waist staring him down, getting closer and closer. He seemed to shrink two jacket sizes.

He quickly offered the file to me. I noticed that it was now a little sweat-stained. Imagine that.

"Here, take this!" he stammered and tried to back further into the corner. It was amazing how helpful he had become. I was regretting all the terrible things that I had been thinking about civil servants. I took the file and smiled at him.

"Thanks. Do you want me to come back?"

He shook his head vigorously.

"Then I think we should keep this little meeting just between us."

I could tell he agreed whole-heartedly by the energetic way that he was nodding his head. I left the building.

I still did not know exactly what to think about Ron's death. My gut was screaming at me that he did not take his own life. At the same time, I wondered if I was too close. Could I possibly be objective?

As much as it was great to have a battle-hardened, precinct commander on my side, I wondered if he could be objective either. He had become Ron's friend, and even though he was obviously tough and experienced, Ron could have been fooling all of us while living with something terrible. He was perfectly capable of keeping something very bad to himself and not burdening others. He was perfectly capable of thinking of himself as not needing the help of others. Arrogance — it was a family trait.

I needed help. As I exited the building and stood on the street corner, I decided that it was time for one of the Briggs brothers to avoid the arrogance trap. I needed someone who had investigative skills, who was experienced in police work, and who didn't know Ron. I needed someone that I knew well enough to know exactly what his words meant, not what he might mean, right when they were spoken. I needed someone I could trust. Someone I could trust about police investigation procedures. The problem was that I couldn't trust her about us — me either for that matter. It was only due to Ron's death that I was back from my temporary assignment in Asia designed to put some space between us — my design, not hers.

I knew exactly who that person was and was certain I could enlist the support I needed. It was, however, a call that I did not want to make. After hesitating for a minute and gathering my thoughts, I pulled the number out of my brain without having to search for it in my cell phone and dialed the Hoover Building in D.C. Tapping in the extension when the robotic voice directed me to do so correctly routed my call.

"Special Agent Rigatti," she said. Her voice was her 'official FBI' voice but with an interesting European accent.

Here we go. "Marilena? It's Tom."

"Thomas, where are you?" she asked softly. "Are you back in the country?" She didn't sound angry or even cool to my call. She had every right to be.

"I just got to New York late last night."

"It was in the *Post*. Tell me what you know?" She did not offer the same automatic apology that everyone leads with when you have a loss. In her mind, Ron was gone. She was concerned about the present and me. Being sorry about an event that happened almost a week ago didn't help. It was her way.

"I met with the police earlier this morning and just came out of the crime lab. I need to go to the funeral parlor to make arrangements." Talking about my recent activities let me dodge the emotional question, at least for now. She would not be derailed for long.

"What have you learned?" she inquired.

"Competent people have shared facts with me. In my pocket is a list of people who may have been nearby when Ron went through the window — either of his own free will or not. I have some second hand, rudimentary forensic information. I have a major internal struggle going on about whether or not Ron could have killed himself. I am not having any internal struggle with what I will do to the person who killed him if I discover that he was murdered."

My last two sentences were indicative of my relationship with Marilena. There were very few people that I would speak to this way about what I was feeling. She was on a very short list, a list recently reduced in number.

"Knowing you, Thomas, I imagine that you will be very direct in your investigation. Even more so than usual given the anger that I am hearing."

"Yeah. Direct." I smiled as I thought about Michaelson.

"If your brother was killed, you might back his killer into a corner," she warned.

I wasn't sure why this would be a problem. "Works for me. I'll join him there. Briefly."

"You are already making mistakes. You don't even know if you have an adversary, and already you are underestimating him. Successful police investigation is based on probing and follow-up. This is not a military action. Blunt force will not work — at least not at this stage. The time might come later for confrontation to elicit a response. I hate to disappoint you, but that probably won't be necessary. You need to be the benevolent doctor and brother. You are only here to pay your final respects and deal with his affairs. Don't let people see you as a threat. Get them to talk to you. If Ron had a killer, make him comfortable with the knowledge you have accepted his death as a suicide. Let any overconfidence be his, not yours."

She was right, of course. That was why I had called her. I knew she would be right. She would say what I needed to hear. She would tell me what I needed to do.

"I'm not good at subtle," I said.

She laughed and punctuated each word, "Now there is an understatement!" After a moment and back on an even keel she said, "You will have to adapt. When do you go to his office?"

"Tomorrow morning. I don't have an appointment. I'm going to drop in unannounced."

"Call someone and let them know you are coming. Let them be prepared. Don't push. Not yet. Please."

I was quiet for almost sixty seconds. She did not interrupt my thoughts and let me take the next step.

"I need help."

She replied without hesitation, "I will be there tomorrow."

VOLUNTARY HEALTHCARE ADVOCACY

Michaelson had not called the cops. I had been standing in front of the crime lab building in plain view for over twenty minutes while talking on my cell phone. So far, the local law had not arrived and arrested me. If he was going to make an official complaint about me, I wanted to get it over with and not wonder whether or not there would be a later interaction with New York's finest when I returned to the condo.

I walked a few blocks to a place I know at 19th and Park that serves a great steak. It was time for lunch, and I had worked up an appetite. Intimidating civil servants will make you hungry. This wasn't my first time. Others have told me that I lack respect for my fellow professionals. Well, sometimes, maybe.

The restaurant was a typical New York, high-end steak house. In spite of the brilliant white linen tablecloths, well-trained serving staff, and quality beef, it was a noisy and raucous environment. The kind of place where you could sit a table in the center of the maelstrom and be alone with your thoughts. It must be the combination of noise and high ceilings because if you had a companion, you could have a reasonable conversation that would not be overheard at the next table. My kind of place. There was a lot to see going on around me. I was invisible to all but the waitress.

After lunch, I set a fast pace and hoofed it sixty or so blocks back to the condo in Central Park West. A fast walk helps me think. It also helped settle the protein infusion that my gastrointestinal tract was trying to accommodate. I had been correct in telling Marilena that I had some facts, but they had not even begun to answer my basic question — could Ron have taken his own life? What else had I accomplished today? I had a new friend in a command position at the police department. I had a new enemy at the coroner's office. A balanced day. I might need

O'Dale to bail me out if Michaelson grew a backbone. A low probability concern.

Arriving back at Ron's — I still thought of it as his place although title would pass to me soon enough, I started up his desktop computer in the den. My plan was to use the rest of the day to do a little research before going to his office tomorrow. Not knowing much about VHAs, the type of organization that he worked for, was something that needed rectifying. I knew even less about the CID Society in particular. A definite hole in the intel.

I checked my email knowing that Marilena would be sending me flight info. I had to log into my email provider's website and use the browser to check my mail as I had not installed my personal email account info on Ron's computer. She was arriving tomorrow afternoon on a shuttle from Reagan to LaGuardia. I noted the airline, flight number, and arrival times before responding to her that I would meet her in baggage claim. We had each other's cell numbers for real time coordination.

At first read, her email was innocuous enough. However, a more careful review was a little troublesome. After citing her flight info, she added a short paragraph.

> *"I'm glad that you called me, and I would have been very unhappy if you had asked someone else for help. We will resolve this together.*
> *Always, M"*

Marilena was the bureau's liaison to our group. We had worked several operations together; me in the field and for the most part, she had remained in the command center. She had surprised me because unlike her predecessor, she had actually come to our base of operations and twice participated in the field. The guy before her was a voice on the phone constantly demanding an update. She was highly competent and the first Fed that we didn't want to shoot. It did not take her long to earn everyone's respect.

We had become good friends and enjoyed each other's company. The problem was that we had started to become a little too attracted to one another. I put a stop to our extra-curricular involvement after it had progressed to dinner and dancing. Work relationships are off the table for me. I am by no means a saint when it comes to the boy-girl thing, but I was never going to screw up my job with an in-house relationship. Explaining this to Marilena was awkward, and when the after-work contact abruptly ended three months ago, she became a little frosty. We never really moved beyond her irritation and my fear. The best we had been able to do was to strictly limit our interaction to work. Skipping town by volunteering for the western Pacific rotation hadn't helped.

My call for help with a personal issue had changed the rules of engagement. With our recent history in mind, her final paragraph was disconcerting. Or, maybe I was just reading too much into her words. She did not know how hard it had been for me to pull away from her, and even worse, to do something that would make her mad at me. It had been close — scary close. This Marine was going to have to be on full alert to keep this professional. She had me outclassed, outnumbered and outgunned. If I weren't careful, Marilena would alter my life in a big way. A life that I am extremely happy with, thank you very much.

Putting Marilena's image aside — not an easy thing to do — I started my investigation into VHAs. A VHA is a Voluntary Healthcare Advocacy organization. It is organized for tax purposes as a "not-for-profit" with a specific focus on something to do with healthcare, usually a chronic disease. The VHA is the advocate of those who suffer from the disease. It provides community, develops resource to fight and hopefully cure the disease while providing comfort and assistance to those who are afflicted. Some examples are the American Cancer Society, the American Heart Association, and the Juvenile Diabetes Research Foundation. They raise money employing many methods from high-end, society-style philanthropy to organizing street-level events like sponsored bike rides and walks. The latter method was the most effective, yet the high-society approach got the press. Some of the money raised would be used for research to find a cure, some would be used for programs helping constituents, and some would be used to run the business.

And, it was a business. I knew that Ron's shop, the CID Society, raised millions of dollars a year. What I didn't know was the exact amount or how it was spent. This was where I got started, this was all I knew about VHAs, and it was a little embarrassing. You'd think that as a doctor, I would have been well versed in healthcare advocacy. Or, at least, a little less ignorant about the topic. In some ways, I'm just not a great doc. I tried to feel better about this. If you ever find yourself hanging in your parachute harness under a jungle canopy while bleeding out from a gunshot wound, I'm the best doc you will ever meet. Yeah, this happens to everyone sooner or later. No sale — even to myself. I'm pretty sure that I'll never be a servant of the greater good helping out the masses.

I'm just OK at traveling the information super highway even though my job has made me become somewhat Internet savvy. I made a few unintentional exits and wrong turns. Using a search engine requires some intuition that you only get with experience, although some people seem to have the gift from day one. A couple of my prior experiences were memorable, disturbingly memorable. Once, I had to find a repair shop for a small inflatable boat. Never use the word "inflatable" in a Google search. Ever.

The first thing I discovered was that the not-for-profit business is very big business. The phrase "not-for-profit" had always made me itch, definitely a genetic inheritance from my father who was the ultimate capitalist and proud of it. However, after looking at a few of these multi-million and even some multi-billion dollar charities, I might have to rethink my assessment. It seemed that generating a lot of revenue while not officially showing any profit (but still keeping a lot of the money around for later use) was the name of the game. The not-for-profit name was definitely a misnomer.

The not-for-profit world seems to be divided into two camps. The first is the healthcare-related one whose morally lofty goal is the defeat of some terrible disease. The second is the "anything but healthcare-related." These groups are not so pious. In fact, they come right out and argue without apology for some parochial cause, be it gun rights, looking out for retirees, defending an indefensible industry, religious conviction or political action. In both arenas, healthcare or not, the stream of cash from the legions of believers is incredibly impressive.

The not-for-profit business segment has gotten so large that it has become an industry in itself. I even found multiple sites that rated charities, allowing donors some understanding about where their money was going. A line of business was based solely on the fact that there were not-for-profits in existence. They were collectively referred to in the pages I was reading as the "Watchdogs." The largest and most followed Watchdog had a rating system. Out of curiosity, I checked and saw that Ron's VHA was awarded three out of four stars. I wondered how important that was and what it meant to the CID Society?

I looked more closely at this site to see how they determined the number of stars to award a particular not-for-profit organization. It seemed that the mechanism was objective and that was good, but it relied on only one source of information. That was bad even to a non-financial type like myself. The sole source was the yearly tax return filed by the not-for-profit — the Form 990. Although I don't know anything about charitable organization tax compliance, it seemed odd that they looked only at a tax return. There was no examination of the management team, the efficacy of the sponsored research, the constituent programs or the functional areas. Growing up in my dad's house and hearing the annual shouting matches in the evening as he argued about the annual report on the phone was the basis for my concern. He would browbeat the accountants until the financial data were categorized to his liking. I wasn't so naive to believe that in this high-dollar world of the not-for-profit that the same accounting voodoo wasn't rampant. Money is the source of all political power and how you report it is what keeps the palace walls in place.

I downloaded a couple of representative Form 990s from some charities that I knew by name. Reading a few of them left me even more certain that any analysis based solely on their tax return was going to be worth very little. The financial statements were similar to the ones that I saw in commercial financial reporting. As I have admitted, I am no financial expert, but Ron made me look at a lot of the stuff the family owned and did his best to explain it. There were some significant differences between the not-for-profit reporting and the commercial reporting I was more familiar with that I needed to learn about.

The other area about VHAs that interested me was how they funded research to find a cure for their disease. Almost universally, the mechanism was the award of a financial grant.

The word *grant* was not new to me. Before coming to work at the CID Society, Ron was an academic M.D. involved in neurology research. His labs lived and died on grants. The grant was their lifeline, their oxygen supply. Applying and re-applying for grant money was a big part of his life. Schmoozing the organizations that had the grant money for award was his second life. On a couple of occasions, when he was coming up short on grant money, our family would become an impromptu grantor keeping some lab on life support. Ron always checked with me before using our money and acted like he needed my permission. I never gave it a second thought, did not need to know the details, and always trusted his judgment that it was money well spent for some good cause. We had more than we could spend by several orders of magnitude. It also assuaged my guilt about my personal philanthropic void — cheap at twice the price.

When I made my final exit off the Internet autobahn, I was surprised to see how late it was. My last thought before climbing into the rack was how glad I was that I wasn't an accountant. I had a nightmare about being trapped in a room with guys wearing green eyeshades. Did they still need to wear those things while sitting in front of a computer?

POST-IT-NOTE DNA

The guard looked at me, his eyes narrowing. "I don't know what you're trying to pull. Don't take me for an idiot," his voice as menacing as he could make it. His partner, noticing the exchange moved over next to him to add some stare and glare power without needing to know why.

"And I don't know what you are talking about," I replied while letting indignation creep into my voice. I had set the guard up. His help might be needed and one way to quickly get him on my side was for him to embarrass himself and owe me a little — I didn't have time to build the trust so it had to be stolen. Approaching the guard desk at the CID Society headquarters, I had mumbled to him that Dr. Briggs was expecting me.

"Dr. Briggs is dead," he said forcefully with a tone that implied that he knew it, everyone knew it, I knew it, and it wasn't a matter to joke about; or worse, part of some perverse subterfuge to sneak into the building.

"I don't need you to tell me that my own brother is dead," I rifled back with a preplanned response, pretending not to notice his partner and drilling my unblinking eyes right back into his.

"Your brother? I thought you said Dr. Briggs was expecting you."

"I said I was Dr. Briggs, and they were expecting me," I lied with a deadpan.

"Oh, man. I'm sorry. I'm really sorry. I'm kind of messed up about Ron, I mean our Dr. Briggs here. I'm sorry you lost your brother, man. I liked him a lot — we all did. He stopped and talked to us all the time. I guess I'm kind of touchy. The last thing I wanted to do today was offend Ron's brother."

He tried to get all of this out as quickly as possible, his words all running together. He wanted to put the offense that he felt responsible for behind us. His nametag read Wm. French, and he looked about fifty.

"Hey, it's not a problem. I understand. It's been a shock to everyone he knew," matching his pace, letting him off the hook. I lightened up, letting him know that it was an understandable error and more importantly his outburst was based on his genuine feelings for Ron.

"Ron is going to be missed by all the guys here. Whenever one of us had a medical issue, we could ask him about it. You know, is my doctor telling me everything? He told me this. What should I ask him? Especially if it was about one of our kids. A lot of the brainiacs that come through here don't give us the time of day. We know they look down on us. Ron always cared," he finished and looked away briefly.

"Would you mind if I came back some other time and we talked?" I asked. "I'd like to know more about Ron's life here and his friends. I have been away more than I wanted to, and I feel like I need to know more about his life here."

He lit up immediately with a huge smile. "Absolutely, I'm here everyday until 6 PM!" He paused and then said, "Hey, I remember you now!"

"Did we meet before? Do you go by Bill?"

"It's Will. No, I don't think we met face-to-face, but Ron talked about you. Man, he was proud of you. The stories he would tell us! His little brother, the Marine daredevil doctor!"

There was a title I had not heard before. I told him to call me Tom and that I would look for him sometime the next few days. He said he looked forward to it and confirmed it with a strong handshake. Compadres.

I headed off to the elevator with a new friend and feeling like a little more of a heel than normal. After I crossed Will off of my suspect list, I would apologize.

I exited the elevator and had the receptionist call Suzie Ling, Ron's administrative assistant. Suzie and I had spoken literally several hundred times. She had been the conduit between fast-moving brothers. She knew our birthdays, our likes, and dislikes, the state of our romantic involvements, and lots of other things that would have bothered me if I had not come to know just how great a gal she was. We had met at Ron's during dinner parties on three or four occasions.

We walked toward each other. This was her turf, and we were around her coworkers. I had planned to keep my greeting reserved so she wouldn't have to answer gossipy questions. She had other plans, and I found myself on the receiving end of a big hug, as big a hug as a five-foot tall lady can give (which in Suzie's case turned out to be pretty big), and then she pulled me down and kissed me on the cheek. She obviously didn't care about what anyone else might think. I should have known better.

"I'm so glad you're here!" she said with a genuine smile.

"Thanks — it's great to see you," I replied.

"Let's go talk." She set off down a hallway with me in tow.

We walked into a typical office setting. At least what I thought an upscale office should look like. I didn't spend a lot of time in them. A sea of cubicles opened up before me with private, hard-walled offices lining the perimeter and having windows to the outside world. There were squared-off columns holding up the ceiling that held calendars, clocks, and fire extinguishers.

The office had recently undergone a remodel that Ron had told me about. Suzie and I had joked about it on the phone. The big laugh among the worker-bees was management's efforts to make the environment more open with the big-dogs becoming accessible to everyone. The private offices had been built with a glass wall allowing everyone in cubicle-land to look into them. Paragons of virtue and responsibility sitting stoically at their desks locked in battle with CID. Each tableau a photo op.

Of course, the cubicles still had regular dividers pretty much keeping their occupants from seeing into the offices except when walking somewhere. It certainly allowed the higher-ups to keep tabs on the underlings as they went back and forth, clocking the length of their breaks. Ron had told me that a guest had walked into one of the glass walls, it had broken, and he was seriously cut in several places. Supposedly, and solely due to the accident, the walls were to be etched with some artwork that would alert the unsuspecting to the dangerous, transparent barrier. I wondered how much they had paid the interior designer for his nouveaux look into management/subordinate interaction combined with his lack of basic common sense. Several of the glass walls had been decorated in the interim with "sticky notes," little yellow squares seemingly suspended in air as a warning to unsuspecting pedestrians. Some of the goldfish had arranged their little yellow squares in patterns anticipating the upcoming adornment. Some of the glass walls sported a single yellow square, the insecure occupant bowing to safety without exposing him or her to artistic ridicule.

We passed by two dozen offices with the last ten or so having nameplates that ended in Ph.D. or M.D. Must have been the research team that reported to Ron. His office was the last one in that group. I involuntarily held my breath and followed Suzie inside.

My first thought was how was it that with all of my trips to New York, I had never been to Ron's office before? He had never been to my only and rarely used office at MacDill Air Force Base in Tampa. But then again, had he tried, someone would have shot him before he got there. I had not had that obstacle and therefore no excuse.

I looked around. I looked for signs of his inhabitation. He had spent enough time here. The room was larger than the others passed along the way. It was about twelve by eighteen with a single desk, a small conference table, and guest chairs that we dropped ourselves into.

"I'm going to pack up Ron's personal things. I just haven't had the heart to do it yet, and I've been using the excuse that you should get a chance to see it like he kept it. I'll get everything to you soon. I promise."

"I know you will," I answered back.

I looked around the room. Ron had stuff everywhere. Unlike his apartment, his work life was cluttered. The conference table would only convene a group of professional organizers acting out an intervention. Little stacks of paper, piles of magazines, mail opened and unopened, paper reports partially read, staff submissions for scientific journals awaiting his commentary, sticky notes attached to walls and his computer monitor, and a hundred other tasks that had revolved around the head of the Research and Clinical Trials Department were littered about. Perched precariously on a paper pile on the bureau running down one sidewall was a recently arrived gift basket with the empty note holder still inserted — the note gone and certainly awash with all of the other office detritus. Ron could have found it. He could have recited it without finding it.

The last thing I looked at, the object I made myself look at, the reason I had come, was the window. A desk lamp, too large for the desk but one that would have provided the light that Ron would have demanded no matter the decorating faux pas, blocked part of my view of the window. I stood up and walked next to the desk toward the window. It was tall. It was a slider. It lifted vertically, the bottom half sliding up behind the top.

"He always kept that window open. Even in the winter, it always had at least a crack. He liked the city noise coming in and said he needed the air." Suzie talked to me while looking at the floor, looking at the desk, looking anywhere but the window.

I looked closely at the window. You could see about five inches above the lower half in the casement sides the holes where some hardware had been removed. It was obvious that there had been some restraining device that would keep anyone from opening the window more than the width of your hand. Ron would not have given a second thought to taking this out. The fasteners would have made a metallic "plink" as they sailed unceremoniously into the trashcan.

Turning to Suzie, "I know he worked late. Would the window have been open then?"

"Yes, especially at night. Ron liked the cooler evening breeze."

"The sill is too high for him to have accidentally fallen through it." I had said it. She nodded. No accident. He traveled out the window purposefully, but on whose purpose? Suzie had not contemplated murder. She was uncomfortable but showed no fear about being here, about being in the office.

"When did you hear about Ron's death?" I asked.

"Not until the next morning. When I got here, there were police up and down the hall. They asked me some questions. About his schedule the day before, you know, his last day. I was so upset that I really don't remember much. When they left, they locked the door and put that yellow tape across it. For the first time I was happy to be stuffed in my cubicle. I didn't want to stare at the yellow tape all day."

Her voice was labored, and her eyes were filling up. I turned my back pretending to study the window again so she could have a little privacy.

After a few more moments of studying the window, I walked across the room and sat at Ron's desk. His view into cubicle land was uninspiring. I understood the need for the open window. A little input into an otherwise stuffy sanctum. Some background noise was a desired intrusion. Looking back from the window to the glass wall, I could see that Ron's particular brand of 'sticky note' art preventing guest laceration was a diagonal array of multi-colored squares formed into the familiar double helix of a DNA molecule fragment. It looked like two or three base-pairs had come adrift and found their way to the floor.

Genetics. The focus of his life's work memorialized by 3M.

TOSSED

Suzie left me alone in Ron's office sitting at his desk and not really knowing what to do next. In this office, in any office, I am a stranger. I was in an investigation mode and struggling with my lack of detective skills and an anger that would not go away.

I needed an outlet. I needed a way to use the frustration bubbling inside. Some people talk about closure and how a funeral provided that for the family and loved ones. A funeral would do nothing for me; a waste of my time and not the way I wanted to remember my only brother. Until I was convinced otherwise, Ron had a killer. I looked forward to our meeting. Closure, yeah, I'd get closure.

I found the on/off switch on Ron's office computer and powered it up. Taking a chance, I entered the same password he used on his home computer. No surprise, the boot process continued. I was sure that Ron's office computer was only password protected because some network administrator required it. There was no place in my brother's world where someone would snoop or steal. Why have a password? Even the locks on his condo door had been installed by the previous owner. I think that Ron had forgotten that the locks were there. Convincing him to use a password on his home machine because it had financial information stored on the hard drive had been difficult. He relented, but only to make me happy. I made him change it each time I came to New York — a brother-enforced security protocol later synchronized with his office computer allowing for the memorization of only one password.

Clicking on his email program icon caused his in-box and mail directory structure to be displayed. His mail directories were the antithesis of his office. There were highly organized layers of file folders neatly identifying the collections of email stored within. The volume of email was amazingly large. He must get 1,000 emails for each one I get, and most of mine are spam. His email software was a part of a larger suite of programs that also managed his calendar, tasks, and contacts — a complete life manager for the busy executive. It made me itch. Hunting around a little I eventually found what I was looking for. OK, I cheated by actually using the "Help" menu and getting the promised help. I pulled down the "file" menu and scrolled down. Selecting "export" opened a dialog box and told the program to copy everything, calendar, contacts, email, task lists, notes, and it made a backup for transmission in the format that I hoped would do something for me later — not that I would bet my life on that. Anyway, I stored this file on his desktop and then emailed it to my personal account for retrieval later at the condo. I thought about sending it to Ron's personal email account and not mine, knowing that a record of the transmission would be on the society's mail server. I did not want to raise any flags and an email from his office email account to his personal account might seem innocuous. Office workers by and large have no idea that once an email is written and sent, copies of it tenaciously float around the info-space. Finding and getting rid of all of them is just about impossible. Just ask the multitude of greedy business execs indicted by their shareholders and prison-enabled by their email ghosts. I discounted the effectiveness of this subterfuge as the email would be time-stamped, a time and date when I had been in his office, not to mention a time and date well after he had died. Eventually, if anyone cared, it would be discovered that I sent it. Also, I did not want to cause problems for Suzie. This way no one would suspect that she had his password and had sent it using his computer. Better to keep the attention off of her and fingers pointed at me.

Looking at the folder names on his hard-drive was not much help as they were shortened to the point of being cryptic. There were also links to shared drives on the network. I was already pushing the envelope snooping around the data on his computer; reaching beyond that to his organization's network would be a greater infraction. As I considered whether or not this really bothered me, a shrill female voice spoke sharply from the doorway.

"Who are you? What are you doing in here?" she demanded.

Looking up, I saw a tall, angular woman about fifty years old. I was drawn to her hair. It was several shades of mouse burger brown with bright red streaks, cut short on the sides but with some longer lengths on top sticking up from front to back like you would see on the top of a rooster. She had both hands on her hips bent at the wrist with the backs of her hands making actual contact. She was bent slightly forward at the waist, glaring at me and waiting for an immediate response. Chicken woman in full rage.

Keeping my face neutral, I leaned back in the chair and crossed my arms. Waiting long enough to intentionally add some more heat to her internal pressure cooker, I finally replied, "I'm an official guest."

Her look didn't soften, but maybe one of the overworked facial muscles did relax. I'm sure it was more from some small measure of disappointment than from relief that she had not caught an actual trespasser. She contemplated what to do for about three seconds while her lips continued to press themselves into even smaller horizontal lines.

"You have to leave this office immediately. You might have been associated with *Doctor* Briggs, but that doesn't condone your presence in a private office. We can make a conference room available to you after we confirm your association with him, but you can't stay here, and you can't be rummaging about a society computer."

"Who are you?" I asked without showing the slightest sign of moving from the chair.

"Not that it matters, but I am Margaret Townsend, executive vice president."

I ignored her momentarily and casually looked at the computer monitor as if she had never spoken. The email containing the backup was already showing as "sent." I opened the "sent" folder and deleted the message.

"STOP WHAT YOU ARE DOING THIS INSTANT!" she shouted, fully enraged.

Leaning back in the chair, I put my feet up on the desk. "Are you planning to get any help or do you think you can toss me out all by yourself?" If I smoked I would have pulled one out and lit up.

Her eyes all but bulged out of her head, and her mouth fell open. "Then I'll call security," she declared.

"Are they armed?" I asked, stopping her retreat from the office.

"What?" she stammered — confusion mounting.

"Are they armed?"

"I don't know. What does that matter? They will arrest you for trespass."

"You'd better call the cops to help them out. Would you like me to call my friend Captain O'Dale, the commander of the 17th Precinct? I'm sure he'd be happy to send along a couple of uniforms to help you out. He seems very helpful," I deadpanned.

"Are you with the police?" she asked with a significant amount of caution creeping into her up until now demanding voice.

"Worse," I answered.

"Worse?"

"Yep. The military."

She stared at me, her confusion now complete.

"Don't sweat it, sweetheart," I said as I rolled out of the chair and stood up. "I'll go."

I walked the three steps across the office and looked down at her. She stepped back, fear replacing confusion. She was taller than most women and eye-to-eye with most men. My seventy-five inches, however, provided me with an elevation advantage. My eyes were unblinking and staring into her. She was used to having her height work for her as she dominated coworkers. This was unexpected.

"As I see it, your considerate reception has just saved me a stack of greenbacks," I said with a sarcastic tone and smile.

She had moved from confusion to total bewilderment. I was enjoying this. "I have no idea what you mean," she replied with a little of the huffiness returning with her retreat from the office.

"Then let me explain. You've just insulted a multi-million dollar donor to this organization. I'll let my chapter president know that because of you, Dr. Briggs's brother, THE OTHER DOCTOR BRIGGS, has elected to redirect his family's philanthropy. I'm sure she will make your blunder an agenda item at the next board meeting."

"Wait! Wait! I didn't know you were his brother! You must understand!"

"I understand well enough. The only thing I don't understand is how Ron managed to tolerate you."

I stepped through the door, executed a heel-turn that would have made a Paris Island drill instructor proud, and headed for the elevator lobby. Leaving Townsend speechless — probably a first — and standing in the hallway, she was clenching her fists, looking quickly left and right, and generally not knowing what to do.

I moved quickly by Suzie's cubicle. The commotion had drawn an audience. She, along with about twenty others, had stood up to look over their dividers. Suzie looked at me with a worried expression. I winked back at her causing her to choke back a smile. She quickly dropped back into the security of the cube like a prairie dog that had come up, quickly sniffed danger, and tactically retreated. The other prairie dogs followed suit.

Entering the elevator lobby, the receptionist was just getting off the phone with a pained look on her face.

"Dr. Briggs! Can you please wait? Ms. Townsend just called, and she wants to meet with you in her office. Please don't leave." Her words were quick and her face worried.

"She's summoned me? That's rich."

The receptionist was only partially successful at containing her amusement at my characterization. I didn't think that Townsend had a lot of friends in the worker ranks.

Before she could say anything else, I turned around and headed back from where I came. It would look like I was being a good boy and doing as told by the execu-bitch-in-charge-of-everything. As I rounded the corner, I was no longer under observation by the worried receptionist. Instead of continuing back to the executive offices, however, I opened the door to the stairwell, stepped through and moved quickly down the twenty-four flights to the lobby. At roughly five seconds per flight the descent was accomplished in two minutes. Pushing the lobby door open, I emerged next to the security area. Will was not at the desk, and his partner was engaged with someone else. I exited using the revolving door at the front of the lobby, turned right, and headed uptown. Confusion and frustration would again be a part of Margaret Townsend's day. I hoped she wouldn't beat up on the receptionist for not hog-tying me at the elevator. Don't worry, Maggie. I'll come back. Then you can really worry.

I had stirred the pot. It felt right, but I didn't know why.

CIRCUMVENIO INFRACTUS DEMYELINATION

It is an engineering marvel. Nothing in the known universe is as complex, as capable of carrying out so many chemical and physical processes in such a small yet mobile package. It is the assemblage of ten generalized systems that function together as one harmonious unit. It is self-healing, fragile, and yet highly adaptable over generational time. To most, the inner workings are a mystery. We each have one. We tend to take it for granted. The human body, ubiquitous, yet each one unique.

My understanding of the human body, while considerable when compared to most people not involved in medicine or health science, was still in my estimation primitive. There is so much left to learn. There are so many areas of medicine where we are just getting started.

Medical researchers today have determined that chronic disease often has a basis in genetics. Missing chromosomes, extra chromosomes, chromosomes with pieces damaged or duplicated or even swapped between chromosomes are the stuff of inherited disorders. Genes are also the tempering factors standing between you and environmental factors, good or bad.

The problem with learning about chromosomes and genes is that it involves the study of Deoxyribonucleic Acid, or DNA. Most of us have seen the pretty pictures of the interlaced, double helix. We may have further learned that the body's master program directing our development, appearance, and resistance to disease is laid out in the 3 million pairs of amino acids that contain our exact representation of the human genome. This all sounds highly organized with a very precise structure. Unfortunately, it's nothing like this. Immediately under the covers is chaos. There never seemed to me to be any organizational structure to DNA's contents. You will not find similar program subroutines gathered together based on function. The genes that regulate this or that are scattered about haphazardly, making any logical flow of program instructions impossible. A computer programmer looking at what is in a DNA strand would find neither an object-oriented approach nor a functional decomposition based upon a program's objectives. Calling it spaghetti-code was way too generous. As important as genetics is to medicine, and even though I made myself learn all that I could stand in order to be the best doc that I could, I was never going to like it. Give me a broken part to fix – that's a stand up fight I can win. Way too many of the gene boys remind me way too much of the sleazy intel operatives that we have to deal with. Nothing concrete, nothing you can ever depend upon, and a lot of excuses about the subtle complexity of their domain and how brilliant they are as the sleuths in this mystical world. I used to hear the frustration in my brother's voice when he would tell me about the difficulty in pinning down the actual science allegedly underlying some researcher's claim. He had the patience for it. I didn't.

I needed to find out the current state of research into finding a cure for CID. Due to the abbreviated stop at the CID Society headquarters, there was some extra time in the morning schedule. I walked back to the condo across midtown and around the bottom end of Central Park. Passing the towering buildings and by the perceived serenity of the park, I planned my next moves. Marilena was not due in for almost five hours. There was time to hit the gym and then do some research. My breakfast would hold me over; lunch was not a priority.

I changed at the condo and walked less than two blocks to the gym where we had a membership. The hour of exercise was divided into equal parts of cardio and weight training and made me feel human again. As I dressed in the locker room, I noticed that my cell phone had received numerous calls from the same number. It was the three-digit prefix for Ron's office. No surprise that someone at the CID Society was trying very hard to talk to me. The message-waiting indicator blinked ineffectively. I smiled and let it continue to blink.

After returning to the condo, I fired up Ron's home computer. I doubted that anyone would try to stop me this time. Launching his Internet browser allowed me to log into various medical sites that I use when I am in the field. In those cases, I am typically trying to learn more about a pathogen or a surgical technique to help me do my job. Today, I was going to look at a broader body of material.

CID had been a familiar part of my life even though no one in the family had it. We were not a high-risk group due to our lineage and resulting genetics. I had studied it briefly in medical school, again during my neurology rotation as a resident, and had learned much more from my discussions with Ron about his work. If there was a connection between Ron's death and his involvement at the society, I needed to know specifically what he was working on and whom he was working with. I began with a quick CID refresher just to set the stage. To do this, I turned off my surgeon-doctor thought process and replaced it with my lesser-developed clinician-doctor thought process.

To begin with, the human body is protected by a highly sophisticated immune system. The immune system interacts with all of the other systems in the body. It is our last line of defense and comes into play when something bad penetrates the derma or is unintentionally infused along with the air we breathe, the water we drink, or the food we eat. The immune system senses invasion and musters the defenders. I couldn't help myself. I always thought of the immune system in military terms — my own personal army, excuse me, Marine Corps. In my mind there are recon teams detecting and reporting incursion by enemy units into friendly territory. A command, control and communication system takes in the information and determines an appropriate response. Orders are sent out to build antibodies and white blood cells. The body's infrastructure cranks the troops out, puts them on the blood vessel transport system where they hook on and parachute into the battlefield. The speed of the response and the industry demonstrated by the immune system would make any Pentagon logistics planner envious. Landing at the front, the troops are fearless and launch themselves at the invaders with kamikaze-like commitment to the cause — defense of the homeland. The system was anything but simple, and incredibly effective.

Knowing a little about the immune system helps you understand many chronic diseases that afflict humans. There are hundreds of these disorders, from allergies to Lupus, some mild, some terrible, that cause the body's normally well-intended immune system to run amuck. The immune systems of patients afflicted with one of these diseases have decided that some healthy part of the body that is supposed to be there is really an invader with evil intentions. The immune system attacks that body part as if it were the enemy. Using my military analogy, headquarters receives bad intel and friendly fire starts taking out the good guys. With a chronic disease, the intel never gets corrected, and the self-inflicted damage goes on and on.

Some examples of autoimmune diseases that many people have heard of include Lupus, Rheumatoid Arthritis, Crohn's Disease, also known as chronic inflammatory bowel disease, Multiple Sclerosis or MS, Cirrhosis and Circumvenio Infractus Demyelination, better known as CID. Curiously to many people, HIV is not an autoimmune disease. In the case of AIDs, a virus infects the body, hides, mutates, and replicates as part of the host's DNA, and then attacks the immune system eventually reducing it to the extent where it becomes completely ineffective. The difference is simple: autoimmune diseases cause the immune system to attack an otherwise healthy body, the HIV virus attacks the immune system with the symptoms presenting themselves as an acquired immune deficiency.

The discovery of CID was made by a Greek physician whose name escapes me. He stayed close to his roots by giving the disease a Greek-language derived name. *Circumvenio* translates to "surround," *Infractus* means, "broken" or "impaired." *Demyelination* was his reference to the impairment mechanism that affects the nervous system. In other words, that which surrounds the nerves is broken due to demyelination.

The stuff that surrounds the nerves in our body is very important. When people talk about their brain, they sometimes refer to it as the "grey matter." Surrounding the "grey matter" is the "white matter." The "white matter" is called myelin. It is a fat-based material that insulates our nerves keeping them from firing off or short circuiting indiscriminately and not just when specifically ordered to do so. Demyelination is the loss of this important insulating material. Loss of myelin is also the cause of MS and believed to play a role in fibromyalgia. Unlike MS, CID affects both the central and peripheral nervous system — to my knowledge, it is the only neurological disease to do so. Further, it is strongly believed that CID has a genetic basis, but the onset requires some still to be determined trigger, either some other disease or an environmental factor yet to be discovered. It strikes only in the teenage years afflicting both males and females equally, but only those kids having some eastern European ancestry within the last eight to ten generations. The patients will live another ten to thirty years having symptoms not unlike MS before they die.

I was contemplating breaking into the society's network from the outside. After this morning, I was sure that any attempt from Ron's office would not be possible. Having highbrow friends in low places, this would not be a major problem. In the meantime, I would look around on the outside. I searched Ron's name and was amazed, and more than a little proud, at how many references there were to him and his accomplishments. Most of the publications, events, and awards were news to me. I wish he had told me about them.

It appeared that Ron had recently been collaborating with a research team in Boston at a prestigious institution. His principal collaborator was Caroline Little, Ph.D., M.D. and most of the rest of the alphabet. A recently published paper described the search for genetic markers shared by the patient and both parents. Real progress was being made. The paper hinted at the fact that the net result of this work would be the determination of the gene or genes causing susceptibility to CID. They would not have made this statement unless behind the scenes they were actually closing in on the genetic facts. Dr. Little's name was new to me. Ron had never mentioned her. He did, however, recently tell me on the phone that he had been having a hard time with a senior-level woman whose "ego was bigger than all outdoors!" Maybe he was referring to her. I decided that a visit to Dr. Little was in my future.

After poking around for almost two hours, I had to head to LaGuardia. Marilena was certainly capable of getting to the condo on her own — somewhere in all of that advanced FBI training, there must have been a section on high-risk, urban taxicab transport. Nevertheless, I had promised her that I would appear in person and planned to do just that. A part of me was also excited to see her as soon as possible and not wait for her arrival in town. That was the part that bothered me. I needed to have a firm talk with that part. I wrapped up my research for the time being and headed downstairs. As I bounced down the stairwell, I thought of CID, Ron's enemy, and his passion to end it.

CID is a tragedy for any family. The financial burden of the disease management and treatment is immense, the emotional toll on parents and child immeasurable. Ron was going to end this. He believed a cure was inevitable. He told me many times that in ten years, twenty at most, CID would become like polio: A part of history, not a part of anyone's future. With Ron's death, the odds of that outcome had diminished.

A LITTLE HELP FROM MY FRIEND

Antonio, the ever-friendly doorman, had arranged a car service for my trip to LaGuardia and back. He swore to me that the driver, conveniently his Uncle Ricardo, was “the only guy in New York City you can trust behind the wheel” and that “I was as safe as if I was in a church.” I elected not to tell him that once in Bosnia, I got shot at while in a church. The shooter had missed, and no one on my team had been injured. The church didn't stop him from shooting. I don't think he missed because we were in a church. My response prevented him from ever shooting at anyone, anywhere, ever again.

At 2 PM, I was in front of the condo and boarding the limo for the promised quick trip to LGA. My driver, “the only guy in New York City that you can trust behind the wheel,” looked to be about ninety years old. This did not bode well. However, looks can be deceiving, and in this case they were. For a guy thirty years into social security, he was spry and had a bounce to his step.

“Get you there in no time, Colonel!” he exclaimed with a bob of his head and a little louder than I thought necessary. I hoped that hearing was his only sense diminished by time.

“Thanks. We have plenty of time. No hurry,” I plead my case, not needing him to show off driving skills that began with the Model T. I needn't have worried. Ricardo drove carefully yet just aggressively enough to survive the urban combat that New Yorkers think of as driving through Manhattan. The car had a large passenger compartment, the kind where there is only a back seat and your legs stick out in front of you onto a small, carpeted lake. There was a well stocked bar with an ice bucket recently filled. The limo was clean and must have been equipped with extra sound insulation as it was very quiet. Ricardo, to his credit, left me alone with my thoughts. We worked our way to the east side while traveling north to 125th and then across the bridge to the Grand Central Parkway taking us right to the airport. Ricardo was right. The trip was quick.

He dropped me off at curbside and gave me a card with his cell. We were in a place where he could wait and not have to circle because he was a commercial vehicle. TSA's security failures are nothing if not consistent. I headed into the baggage claim area. Marilena's flight had been scheduled to land five minutes ago. I checked a monitor to further narrow down where she and her bags would magically appear. The flight status showed that her arrival had actually been a little early. She might already be in the baggage claim area. Just as I absorbed this thought, I heard a familiar voice.

"Hey mister, give a girl a ride?"

I turned and replied, "I don't know, lady; I got my reputation to think about. What'll people think?"

"Ha! Your reputation couldn't be hurt with an axe in the hands of an ambulance-chasing lawyer."

"Ouch! I guess the truth really does hurt," I said with a grin. Our mutual attempts at humor, while not ready for a prime time sitcom, had allowed us to reconnect and put off more serious conversation — at least for the time being.

She gave me the full 1,000-watt smile and replied, "Don't worry, being seen with me will move you back a little in the right direction."

"Thanks, I'll take anything I can get."

I looked at her hoping to see no more than the teasing eyes of a friend engaged in playful talk. There was more. She was studying me, looking for something else. Her divining and discernment skills were in overdrive. Maybe she was trying to measure the stress I had been under, maybe she was trying to figure out if there was anything more in my call for help than just the need for her professional skills, maybe I was reading more into her look than it deserved. I don't know. What does any man know about something like this? I was a complete believer that men are from Mars and women are from some other not-necessarily-parallel universe. Putting my inabilities aside, I was just glad she was there. Mostly.

There are many beautiful women in the world, but few who truly take your breath away. Marilena constantly caused respiratory distress, guaranteed among those fortunate enough to carry the "Y" chromosome. Although she stood only five feet four inches tall, she commanded attention. She was olive skinned and voluptuous, benefiting from her Mediterranean DNA, had thick auburn hair, and radiated an intensity around her that defied description. When she passed through a crowd or entered a room, she captured the thoughts of everyone in view. She had that ethereal quality of "presence" in any group. Marilena did not have to say much; she just used her eyes and posture to convey her attitude. I waged the first of many battles with my inner, lecherous self that I would have today. Stay focused, Tommy. Think Chicken Woman!

The hug we mutually started was one that you would expect between friends given that one of us had just suffered a terrible loss. Even with the difference in height, we fit together well. After what seemed to me like an appropriate time, I attempted to disengage. She held on a couple of seconds longer before stepping back to look me over again.

"You look good, Thomas," she said, offering an appraisal.

"I'm not the one everyone is looking at."

"Whatever are you talking about? I'm an FBI Special Agent — I blend," she said with a straight face.

"Yeah, right."

Her blending ability was hampered by the combination of classic beauty, truly exceptional curves, and the outfit she was wearing. The skirt was tight and cut mid-thigh. Her white blouse a trendy European-cut that was sheer enough and cut low enough to be extremely interesting. I did not kid myself that she had dressed just for me. It was her usual style. I had previously termed it "classy provocateur."

We walked arm in arm to the baggage carousel (wasn't I just here?) and watched her suitcase emerge. I grabbed it, and we headed for the door, other passengers parting the way. She had no problem playing the role of a lady letting me do the schlepping and door opening.

We got settled in, and Ricardo eased into traffic heading west back to the island complete with four million highly driven inhabitants. Marilena sat sideways so she could face me. It was a posture that only a woman could adopt. If I had tried it, I would have broken something on the first pothole. The limo's mini carpet lake was now significantly improved, having her silk covered legs extended upon it, slightly bent and tucked up a little as she perched on one hip, focused on me.

"Tell me," she began.

I reviewed in one fifteen-minute, nonstop dissertation my activities and observations, moments of brilliance and moments of bumbling, whom I had enlisted and whom I had angered, and the fact that I still had not resolved the basic premise that it was a suicide.

She looked thoughtful and surprised me by saying, "Not too bad. Although you were acting on instinct, some of the things you have done may give us something to work with. But first, before we poke at the hornet's nest anymore, we need to sit down and plan out the rest of the investigation."

"Does this mean you believe that there is anything to investigate? That Ron was murdered?" I asked, a little hopefully.

"I think we need to establish a working hypothesis that he was murdered," she spoke with quiet resolve. "Whether or not he was is not important. If he was, we will find his killer. If he took his own life, our investigation will point to that with a high enough degree of certainty to convince you. My personal belief from what you have told me about your brother and your history together is that he was murdered."

A small wave of hope came over me. O'Dale had said pretty much the same, but it had not had the same meaning to me.

"You really think so?" I asked.

"Yes. Experienced homicide investigators will tell you that anyone can take his or her life, surprising all those around, so it is not a good idea to base an assumption like this on subjective assessment of the victim's personality, perceived state of mind, or place in life. However, that is just what I am going to do because I am adding one important item to that list of non-measurable, non-quantifiable factors."

"What is that?" I asked genuinely hopeful that she had something concrete to end my emotional upheaval about Ron's death.

She smiled, made herself look as confident as she could, and said evenly, "He's been not only your big brother but also a surrogate parent — he was a surrogate for both parents. You are the most determined, truth be told, infuriatingly stubborn man I know. Giving up is not a part of your life. I did not know him, but I seriously doubt that it was a part of his. If he had only five percent of that quality that you have, he could not have ever considered suicide an option. I'm willing to make a bet that I think has great odds that familial DNA would have persevered no matter what the circumstances. And, beyond any challenge that he was personally facing, there is one issue that we cannot ignore. *He quite simply could not have abandoned you!* I know that you think of yourself as a tough guy, but in his mind you were still his little brother, the brother who would always need him. You were his first, his most important, and his last priority. If he had a problem that was taking him anywhere near a life-ending decision, his responsibility to you would have overridden any selfish decision."

"You don't think he would have kept it inside, tried to deal with it himself only to be overcome in some way?"

"Would you have reached out to Ron in that situation?" she asked.

"Yeah. Something that bad — no doubt."

"Why?"

"We didn't keep things from each other. When I was little, after our parents died, sure he protected me from a lot of stuff. But as we got older, we were always there for each other. I would have talked to him. Yeah, no doubt."

"So, here is your brother. A man in many ways not unlike you, with a natural, trusted outlet to discuss anything. A man who I am sure recognized in his younger, but no longer little brother, someone of tremendous resource who would join him in any fight without question or hesitation. He would have put aside ego and not hidden behind worries about being ashamed in front of you. He would have seen you as part of the solution. And he would have believed that there was a solution. I am certain."

There it was. Comfort did not begin to describe her words. It was what I had wanted to believe. It let me off the hook. Ron had not been trying to tell me something. He had not been trying to tell me that he needed me — that I had been too wrapped up in my own life to hear some quiet call for help. A call that had it come from me, he would have heard. This was what I had wanted to believe all along but needed to hear from someone else, someone smart and objective, and someone who wouldn't say it just to make me feel good. Someone who would tell me the truth whether it hurt or not.

"If it were a bet, what are the odds that you are right?" I asked, always trying to quantify things.

"Nine-hundred, ninety-nine to one," she replied without hesitation.

"That good?"

"Better."

She reached over and took my hand in hers. She held it firmly, looked into my eyes, and said, "The first thing you must do right here and right now is to believe in the memory of your brother. Regardless of the problem he may or may not have been fighting, he would never, under any circumstances, have willingly left you."

I looked into her eyes. The fire was there. She had hit the nail on the head. She had also validated my belief that I needed her help. Ron, no matter what he faced, would not have left me; an obvious fact that I had missed completely. I knew that in the days to come that Marilena would help me in many ways, but the most important thing she could have done for me had just been accomplished. Marilena — mistress of the obvious. My confusion had lifted. She could not have made the case over the phone. She knew this yesterday when we talked. She didn't try to sell it then, knowing that it had to be face to face.

To others, my brother might be gone, but for me he was back. Ron, I won't let you down. Better than that, we won't let you down.

APOLOGY

Ricardo delivered us to the condo without incident. He had that professional chauffeur approach to driving, limiting extreme movements of either the gas or brake pedal. Somewhere along the line, he had been to school and been taught that passengers should not sense any change in speed or direction.

When I got my driver's license in Boston as a sixteen-year old, our family driver and groundskeeper took me out for some refinement after experiencing my idea of automotive operation. He informed me, man to man-cub, that squashing my dates into the dash, car doors, or the floorboards would not get me a return engagement. Focusing on the hormonal aspects of driving got my attention. I had laughed at first but then discovered that he was dead serious about pretending that there was an egg between your foot and the gas pedal. Breaking the egg demonstrated bad form. An egg? I hadn't heard anything about the accelerator egg in Driver's Ed. Over two decades later, I had come to appreciate the egg, at least when other people drove, and I further appreciated the fact that Ricardo was egg-savvy. Further, I decided that Ricardo was now my New York driver. We swapped cell numbers. He seemed to like the idea of semi-regular employment. More probably, he was looking forward to seeing Marilena again. Her proximity would keep his testosterone levels at pre-ninety-year-old levels.

We arrived at Central Park West just as a rain shower had started. Three doormen raced to the car with umbrellas and provided a moveable rain canopy lest we start to dissolve in front of their very eyes as only the spoiled can do. They, of course, walked next to the over-sized umbrellas and never showed any signs of melting. Marilena made all the right sounds of appreciation and enrolled three more unsuspecting males into her personal fan club. They never had a chance.

Entering the lobby, Marilena stopped in mid-stride. She looked quickly around, taking the room in. I stopped and turned to her thinking that something was wrong. I scanned the room quickly, looking for the threat, yet seeing nothing or anyone out of place.

"Your brother lived here?" she asked.

"Well, not in the lobby. Upstairs."

Ignoring my sarcasm, she continued, "Not your average foyer." She didn't say "foyer" the way homegrown Americans do.

I looked again at the lobby that I had walked through a couple of hundred times. "What's the matter with it?" She headed for the elevator without answering me. I moved to catch up. One of the doormen had already summoned the lift, and the door was open as we approached. He wished us good day as he always did, the door closed, and up we went. Was I missing something?

I slipped the key into the condo door, and we entered the apartment. Marilena was looking around and wearing the same inscrutable look that she had in the lobby. She slowly walked through the unit, stepping briefly into each room. She didn't say a word. I stood and watched, having no idea what was causing her odd behavior. She made a second pass and studied the furniture and the artwork, still mute. Finally, she turned to look at the view eastward into Central Park, standing motionless. I left her to her inspection knowing that sooner or later she would come back to Earth — hopefully before dinner.

"Thomas, do you know what this place must have cost to buy? To furnish?" she asked, turning to me.

"Not really. I guess that the condos in this building are on the pricey side. We may have talked about it when he bought it," I answered.

"But your brother was a research doctor, not a practicing specialist?"

"Yeah, he was."

Then it occurred to me why she was struggling. Since I had met Marilena, I had never spoken much about my family background. I remember telling her that Ron and I were pretty much on our own, having lost our parents. I am sure that I told her that Ron was a neurologist and working in research. Never mentioning that our parents were well off, it never had become obvious as a lieutenant colonel could have easily paid for the things we did together; especially one having no visible significant financial obligations. Most of the time that we were together, I was in uniform, and when I wasn't, my choice in clothing was never "rich-guy" expensive. Additionally, whether we were in the ops center at the base in Tampa or in the field together, the work environment was unusual to say the least, and there would have been no way to correlate anyone's financial standing. Taking in what she had just seen, she was beginning to see that her on-again, off-again, hoped-to-be on-again boyfriend really didn't need his day job. I watched, as her features became a little sharper. Uh oh. When any woman, especially one who knows that she is pretty shrewd about sorting people out, thinks she has you classified, categorized, and pigeonholed, and then she discovers a major misalignment, it can go bad in a hurry. This is true even if the misalignment in her assessment is something where you were perfectly innocent. If, of course, you believe that any man can ever be innocent in any way, much less perfectly.

"Thomas, are you wealthy?"

We knew each other well enough that the question was not inappropriate. "Well, Dad did real well in a couple of businesses. Ron and I didn't need to borrow money for med school."

"Why didn't you tell me?" reading a lot more into my dodge than I wanted her to.

"I don't have money problems, so I don't worry about it, so it's not something that ever comes up, so there are always more fun things to talk about and that's really all there is to it." All the words in that sentence tried to come out at the same time. "If I was broke, you would have heard about it — probably a lot," I said trying to make light of the issue. She studied my face looking to see if I was being disingenuous. Deciding that I was leveling with her, she relaxed. I was out of danger for the moment. Still not time to get cocky. Until this was laid to rest, I had better demonstrate my sincere side. Unfortunately, my sincere side, much like the backside of a full moon, doesn't get a lot of sunlight.

"If we are going to look for motives behind your brother's death, you need to do a little better than that," she said with the beginnings of a smile. While her justification was true, and the smile told me that while I was a little off the hook, she still wanted to know for reasons that were more a part of her personal investigation of me. This was certainly an area missed in the initial FBI-trained, agent recon.

Money was a topic that I was uncomfortable talking about. It was obviously not a problem for her. At least asking about my family money was not a problem for her. I lived well but did not think an inheritance separated me from my friends or those with whom I worked. While I appreciated my inheritance, it was not how I measured myself. It was mine to spend, but it was family money.

As much as I would have preferred to answer in generalities, I knew she wouldn't give up without some level of specifics. I said, "Ron and I shared equally in the family estate. The total value goes up and down with the market, real estate, whatever. He stayed closer to it than I did. Last time we even talked about it, it was just over nine hundred."

"Million? Nine hundred million?" she whispered, eyes growing very large.

"Yeah," I shrugged.

"Oh, boy. I never knew. You never let on."

"Would it have made a difference?" I asked.

"It would have been nice to tell the lady you were dancing with — maybe," she said thoughtfully. "But then again, I can tell that it is an awkward subject for you."

"It's not that simple."

"Rest easy, Mr. Marine. I like the fact that you have kept this to yourself. I may have a little feminine curiosity about your bank-ability. It's a basic part of female genetics. But I like it even more that in all your boyish attempts to impress me, you never used your checkbook."

I wasn't sure where this was going. In an effort not to look like the decent guy she was describing and to keep things more in balance, I came back with, "I like to live well. I like not worrying about money. I'm not planning on giving that up."

It didn't work. I was out-gunned. She stepped closer, cocked her head a little to one side, smiled, and said, "That's good to know. I will not feel so bad about it when you buy dinner for me later tonight."

"Sure. Anywhere you want to go," I fumbled.

"I take it that the family home in Boston that you have mentioned is something more than a hovel?" she continued.

"Beacon Hill. Full-time staff. You can get a BLT at 2 in the morning." What the hell.

"Is that an invitation?"

My cell phone beeped at me — truly saved by the bell. Panic forestalled.

I usually check the caller ID before answering the phone. I figure that the caller, this goes for me too when I am calling someone, is making an assumption that we both can and want to talk right at that very moment. Maybe, when the phone rings, you just don't want to talk. Maybe you just don't want to talk to that person. All of this is OK with me. If I call you, and you just don't want to talk to me at that moment, don't answer. We'll talk later — no problem. But in this case, maybe as a way to derail the conversation with Marilena so that I could mentally catch up, I flipped that phone open as fast as I could. I dropped the phone and had to pick it up. Please, let the call still be there.

"Hello."

"Dr. Briggs? Are you there?" a voice inquired. It was a female voice that I categorized as "medium-female." It was not at either end of the female voice spectrum. The spectrum that is bordered by lilting soprano on one end and finishing out with a deeper, lustful timber at the other. It was in the middle. A medium-female. A medium-female whom I did not know. With my luck I had just stepped from the frying pan into the fire.

"Yes. I'm sorry. I didn't hear you at first." Marilena smiled at the lie that covered my clumsiness. Even better, clumsiness that she knew she had caused.

"I'm so glad you answered," my caller said with genuine pleasure. "This is Alison Montgomery."

The last four words brought me back to reality. I knew the name if not the medium-female voice. Alison Montgomery was the president of the CID Society and the person that Ron had reported to. I had never met her, but he had spoken of her often. She had been instrumental in getting him to leave his academic posting to run the Research and Clinical Trials Department at the society.

"Is this a convenient time to talk?" she asked.

"Sure," I said as I walked to the window and looked out. I looked toward the southeast, in the general direction of the CID Headquarters. I wondered if she was in my line of sight.

"To begin with, I want to express my sympathy for the loss of your brother. He was more than a senior member of our team. He was a true leader and my most highly valued friend at the society. Although I won't compare my loss with yours, we have both been separated from a great man. Please let me say that I am sorry again."

I made the appropriate thank-you for her sentiment and her kind words.

She continued, "Having said that, you can only imagine the pain and embarrassment I am feeling having learned the details surrounding your visit here today. To say that I was devastated is not an exaggeration in the least. I have just expressed my anger at the individual who asked you to leave your brother's office. I sincerely hope that this incident will not stand between you and me."

"I don't know why it should, Ms. Montgomery."

"I would like to meet you as soon as it is convenient and discuss an idea that I hope you will agree to."

"OK" I said tentatively.

"The New York City Chapter of our organization is having a significant social and fund-raising gala event tomorrow evening at the Plaza. Would you please come?" Without waiting for me to answer, she continued, "I will make arrangements to have you seated at the President's Table. It will be a very special evening with dinner, music, dancing, and will be attended by many people very important to the society. I sincerely hope that you will become one of them. I would very much like to start over and have you join us as my personal guest at this summer gala. Nothing is more important to me right now than making amends and getting to know you."

I thought about it for a moment. Not that I was going to say no, it was too important an opportunity to get inside to let go by, especially for petty reasons. Still, I had to push a little. After all, she had blended an apology with an invitation to a fund-raising event in the hopes that I would become one of those people "very important to the society."

"Can I bring a date?" Marilena perked up, her eyes drilling holes into me.

A short hesitation followed. Was she counting heads and thinking about whom else she had to displace at her table, or was she trying to decide if it was appropriate to ask who my date was? Either way, she recovered quickly, "Of course. I look forward to meeting your companion as well," giving me the opportunity to reveal "my companion's" name. I looked at "my companion" across the room where she had nestled into the big couch and winked. I wasn't planning on sharing her new designation with her given the nature of our interrupted conversation.

"I'm sure that she will be most pleased to meet you as well." Marilena smiled and shook her head mildly admonishing me to be nice.

After waiting long enough to determine that I was not going to be more forthcoming with a name, Montgomery said, "I'll have my assistant call you with the particulars tomorrow. But in the meantime, I look forward to seeing you tomorrow night. There is a reception at 7:30 PM with dinner an hour later. Our gentlemen guests will be wearing formal attire." The last part was absolutely the smoothest I had ever heard any woman ever tell a guy that he had to wear a tux. Truly impressive.

We said goodbyes and hung up. I looked at Marilena.

"How would you like to go to a black-tie event with me tomorrow night?"

"I would love to. You can buy me the appropriate evening gown tomorrow morning."

"Huh?" I gulped.

HIGH HEELS

Marilena walked into the living room where I was sprawled trying to catch up on current events. We talked more about tomorrow's society shindig and what we had to do to get ready. A more pressing event was dinner tonight. Earlier, I had carried her suitcase to the unoccupied guest room. She had been unpacking for the last ten minutes while I waited, listening to my stomach growl.

"Are you carrying?" she asked, inquiring if I had a firearm. I nodded back. She knew I was always armed. On a commercial flight I don't have to check my sidearm. I have the correct paperwork signed off by the correct government officials making this a non-event.

I looked over at her, taking my attention away from the evening news. The female half of the newscaster team was a fashion plate, her male partner a somber reflection of the day's events. I'm not sure why they call it the news. Every night they talk about pretty much the same stuff. Crime, corruption, man's inhumanity to man, and somewhere near the end, a human interest story of little consequence that is supposed to restore our faith that the veneer of civilization while thin, is still a barrier protecting us all regardless of race, color, creed, or national origin. They do, however, sell it all with a smile and practiced banter. We are supposed to believe that the light-comedy is extemporaneous even though the filler-talk ends just in time for the sponsor's important message.

Standing next to the window, Marilena checked her pistol. She ejected the magazine and then checked to see if it was full. Setting the clip on a table, she pulled the slide back making sure that an errant cartridge had not found its way into the chamber. She carried the weapon because the FBI made her. She had never fired a shot in the line of duty, or, to the best of my knowledge, never while on the job pulled the weapon out of its holster or handbag or wherever she was keeping it these days. It seemed to move around a lot. She wasn't afraid of it. I think she just hated the size of something she had no plans to use. There had been only one time when we were together in the field that warranted producing a firearm. She had left hers holstered, explaining to me later that one more gun, even one competently held by her, wasn't going to be any help. The semiautomatic pistol she carried, the only one I think she owned was a Glock 23 chambered in the FBI's minimum acceptable load, the .40 S&W. She didn't carry an extra clip. The FBI had abandoned the "9 millimeter" several years ago after a gunfight gone bad. During a shootout in Miami, an agent had attempted to hit the driver of a car by aiming through the windshield at close range. The bullet had not penetrated the safety glass. Later testing showed that to consistently get the lead through the glass, you had to have more firepower than the previously vaunted "9 millimeter."

Contrary to popular belief, today's FBI agent is more likely to be a graduate of a law school or a public accounting program. The job, while occasionally requiring physical or firearm skills, is more cerebral than physical. Still, Marilena had bucked the academic trend. Her education had been liberal with little exposure to debits, credits, notwithstandings, or whereas's. Like a lot of people raised in Europe, she had learned to speak several languages becoming fluent, articulate, and literate in seven that I knew about. Maybe there were more. I, on the other hand, massacre three languages and am simultaneously devoid of fluency, articulation, and literacy. American, a little Bostonian and just enough Mexican to get in trouble in a sleazy bar in Juarez are my three claims to linguistic achievement.

In addition to her language skills, she had the ability to handle delicate problems, minimizing embarrassment to all parties. European ambassadorial staffs expecting the ghost of J. Edgar Hoover to show up were always surprised and then put at ease when a lady of obvious European descent arrived representing Uncle Sam. She got results, earned respect, and was always in demand, keeping little problems from becoming big problems. Very frequently, she would get the initial call about an issue headed her way from a fast acting ambassador who wanted her involvement and not find himself saddled with your average, culture-impaired Fed.

Because the FBI had trained her in the basics of physical defense during her time at Quantico, her ability to protect herself from an overly amorous Belgian, Bosnian, or Brit was not in doubt. If Marilena had her way, she would not be armed at all. She forced herself to go to the practice range the minimum required by the bureau. She fully believed that in her assignment at the FBI she didn't need a weapon. For the last six years, she had been stationed in Washington, D.C. as part of the bureau's diplomatic liaison department. Agents in her department worked cases involving foreign diplomats and those crimes involving either the dignitary or their dependents. Her only additional responsibility was our team. The FBI had needed a liaison with us and somehow, somebody thought that all liaisons were the same, and her shop got the call. This was funny as my peers and I are about as far removed from the French ambassador as you can be and still be on the planet. Government-think at its best.

Just to tease me a little, she said with a smile, "Well, mine has all of its little bullets."

"All of its little bullets?"

"Yes. All of them," amusing herself with the obviously contrived, matter-of-fact response.

She said it this way because they were not just bullets, and she knew better. The lead bullet is only one of four cartridge parts, the others being the case, the primer, and the propellant. What you feed into the clip is a cartridge or, if you prefer, a round. She smiled as she looked in her bag knowing that the gun would get stuffed in the bottom under all of the other more important girl stuff. If a quick-draw could be defined as anything under three minutes and you could get someone to hold all of the junk that had to come out first, then she qualified as a quick-draw artist. Dirty Harriet she wasn't. Then there was the gun itself. She had chosen the Glock because it was ugly — a brutal-looking tool without any physical charm. This almost made hiding it justified. I had called it a "Block" on more than one occasion due to its squared-off sides and ultra-utilitarian look.

"Somewhere in your family are people from a country that makes very nice firearms, both short and long. I still don't know why a classy Italian babe doesn't sport a classy Italian gun." I said, thinking of my Benelli shotguns as well as my Beretta compatible with the FBI's mandatory load.

"There is nothing classy about any of the cannons acceptable to my employer that he wants me to hide on my delicate person," she said with some fake haughtiness. "I stand a far better chance of losing this damn thing than ever having to use it." The pancake holster in the waistband of my pants would prevent me from losing mine.

We left the condo and headed off to dinner. Riding the elevator down was contrary to my usual rules about not being in any elevator whenever you can help it. We could all use the exercise that the occasional stairwell offered. A quick assessment of Marilena's high-heeled sandals had eliminated the stairwell as an option. Exiting through the lobby brought out the night-team of doormen who had obviously been filled in by the day shift and did not want to miss the "looker" staying with Briggs. The fan club added more members. We would soon have enough for a New York chapter.

The restaurant I selected was only four blocks away to the south and deemed within range of shoes, even those with elevated heels, provided of course that an arm was available for support both to and from. I moved Marilena to my right side placing me between her and the street, as was drilled into me by my prep school mentors when I was in young gentlemen's training. She latched on, and off we went enjoying the cool evening, yesterday's heat and humidity having vanished.

We crossed the first intersection and moved less than ten paces along the sidewalk when I noticed a horse-drawn carriage in the street coming our way. Suddenly it stopped, the surprised driver reigning in the horse. A car's engine close to our side of the street revved up, loudly announcing its approach behind us. Moving as fast as I could, I turned toward Marilena and scooped her off her feet, my legs driving hard launching us both over a line of hedge bushes. We hit the ground side by side. The hedges, now behind us, were exploding out of the ground, some in pursuit as if they had minds of their own. Not stopping, I held on tight to Marilena and added to our momentum. We rolled entwined together across a small lawn rapidly changing places, left and right, top and bottom. Marilena was no longer a captive participant in an unplanned and painful detour. She rolled with me, energetically helping us move as one, away from the street. To my eyes the world had become a rotating panorama of sky, a smooth gray granite wall, green grass beneath us, and above, airborne bushes ripped from the ground frozen in haphazard trajectories. I tried my best to focus on that part of the revolving montage that was the homicidal car, now penetrating the defending foliage, determined to hunt us down and crush us. I took a sprinkler head in the back, the pain ignored as I did all I could to keep us moving. The car, revolving in and out of view, was closing on the immovable building that we were fast approaching — the stone facade had become a second hazard to life and limb. Fully through the hedge line, the metal beast was a blur of yellow, bumper chrome within inches. Marilena took the brunt of the final collision with the granite wall of the building. An inelastic collision — her head protected from the stone wall by one of my encircled arms, my elbow sending an electric shock up to my shoulder — nowhere else to go. Marilena was back against the wall and facing me. I pulled her into my body while pushing hard toward the stone, trying my best to protect her. Her eyes were wide with fear yet never closing as they remained fixed on the moving metal, her body rigid against me waiting for the crush of the car. The car turned — its course now parallel to us and the building that we were plastered into; wrenching more shrubbery into the air it moved back to the street, the granite's proximity scaring it away. I heard the retreating vehicle complain as it came down off of the curb in two metallic crunches — then it was gone.

REASSESSMENT

I took a quick physical inventory. Anxious inquiry hurried along the neural pathways to distant limbs. The internal sensory system quickly reported back that as far as the pain senders were concerned, the damage was limited to bumps and bruises. Knowing that sometimes an immediately life-threatening trauma can be painless, I turned to the external senses. With just the streetlights casting a dim glow, I could not see much of either of us. No help there. From experience I know that deep laceration, the kind that can cause you to bleed out, is often first detected by the sense of smell, the injury site not yet signifying damage with pain. Significant blood loss has a smell that is metallic. It is a distinctive odor that smells like copper sheet or tube that has just been sheared. Only after the smell will you will feel the slippery wetness of plasma and corpuscles confirming what your nose already knows. I didn't smell any new pennies, could not detect any leakage.

There would not be much to see of the car that had almost killed us even if I scrambled upright as fast as I could. I sure couldn't run it down even if it was still in sight. My concern was focused on Marilena and the possibility of spinal injury. If she had been seriously hurt, then care would be needed in the disentanglement process. It was time for deliberate movement, not adrenaline-driven flailing.

"Are you hurt? I spoke into her ear, not releasing my grip, not allowing her to move. She remained still, waiting for me.

"Everywhere," she said more in exasperation than in pain but with complete awareness. She wasn't fading on me.

"Everywhere is good. Can you feel each hand and each foot? Try them separately," I ordered, keeping my voice calm.

"Yes. I can feel and move each OK."

So far, so good. "I am going to slip my arm out. Be still. Try not to move." I managed to get my left arm out from under her shoulders, my forearm complaining where it had been the fender between her head and the granite. My elbow set off a new series of electric shocks. I managed not to pull her hair out where it had been trapped under me. Getting to my hands and knees, I got my little 9-volt LED light out of my pocket. There would be a bruise-outline of it later. Turning it on, I scanned up and down her body. Dress torn at the shoulder, destroyed nylons, one sandal heel bent at 90 degrees.

"Can I get up?" she asked, rather nicely all things considered.

"No," I responded without the niceness.

I used my hands to search for damage and was rewarded with two small exclamations of pain and one giggle that she tried to hide. I slid my hands under her, one at the rib cage and one at mid thigh. Gently pulling, she slid out on the grass away from the wall, and then I supported her head and spine as I rolled her onto her back. She tried to lift her head up as a first step to sitting. I stopped her with my left hand.

"Give me a minute," I ordered — no request. Shining the light to her face, I carefully checked each pupil — reactive and even. "I can't see anything serious, but you are going to feel it later," I said, my relief evident.

I helped her to a sitting position and brushed a dead leaf from her hair. She looked at me, "As much as I appreciate the professional concern for my health and the opportunity it has provided for you to feel me up, shouldn't you be letting someone do the same for you?"

"It's too soon for paramedics, and I'm pretty good at self-assessment." Her expression said that she didn't believe the last part, so I followed up with, "Don't worry, I'm pretty hard headed. I'm fine." She took the light from me and did her own inspection. Deciding that I wasn't going to pass out on her, she let it go.

My next concern was preserving the scene. My Beretta had shifted, and I moved it back. Looking for Marilena's purse I located it about ten feet away. I got up and retrieved it, not so much worried about some bystander lifting her wallet as I was about the Glock. By the time I had returned, she was on her feet looking at the tire tracks in the grass back to the street where the mud had left marks. Taking her purse, she removed her cell phone. With the camera function on, she held the phone in front of her looking at the ground.

"Not enough light here in the grass," she said, pointing out the deficiency of most cell phone cameras.

We moved to the sidewalk. Several onlookers had stopped and one reported that he had called 911. I thanked him. Marilena took several pictures of the tire tracks better illuminated closer to the street lamp. We looked at the hedges and couldn't find any car parts stuck in among them.

The first patrolman, excuse me, patrolwoman (patrolperson?) arrived and demanded to know what had happened. What had we been doing? Marilena sensed that my response was going to be at the very least argumentative and probably offensive. She produced her FBI badge and ID, both in a leather holder, and held it out to the beat cop for inspection, not collection.

"I'm Special Agent Rigatti," she spoke in her official, cop-to-cop voice. My friend and I were almost run down by a yellow cab." Her tone accusatory and setting the cop back as if the incident could have been prevented by better local law enforcement. Also, she must have seen more of the yellow car than I had. "We were walking on the sidewalk when it left the street."

"You jumped over these here bushes?" the uniform asked, incredulous.

"Yeah," I answered.

"Did you know the cab driver? Do you think it was intentional?" Both questions amazed me.

"No," I answered again. Marilena lifted one eyebrow a millimeter, maybe two.

"Did anyone else here see anything or get a plate number? A cab number?" she unenthusiastically addressed the small crowd and got blank looks and shrugs for her trouble. Looking back at us, she continued, "Well, almost a hit and run as you didn't get hit. Do either of you want to make a complaint or go to the hospital?"

We declined and she spoke into her radio. Her report to her supervisor seemed to have more to do with the property damage than us. By listening to the cop and given her lack of enthusiasm reporting the event, you would think that pedestrian rundowns were a common occurrence. Then it dawned on me — they were. I love this town.

We provided names, addresses, and contact info, and started back for the condo. So much for interdepartmental concern between New York's finest and the FBI, I was less than impressed. Once again I placed myself between Marilena and the street. This time, my head was on a swivel, looking for homicidal motorists.

We managed the block and a half without incident. The first of the night shift doormen popped out to hold open the entry. When he noticed Marilena's torn dress and one remaining shoe in hand, his eyes widened, and his mouth fell open. He didn't give me a first look, much less a second.

"Signora! What happened? Are you hurt?" he asked, his voice genuinely concerned. A definite improvement over the cop.

"We're OK. A car came up on the sidewalk and almost hit us," she explained.

"Oh, my God. We have a doctor on call. Do you want me to get him?"

"No thank you," she answered. "I have my own personal physician right here."

"Oh, yes. Dr. Briggs." He paused. And then, to me a little late, "Dr. Briggs, are you OK?"

And so it went all through the lobby, the hired help very concerned about the lady, a little about me. At one point, when we seemed to have the greatest number of worried attendants, Marilena looked at me with a devilish smile and said loud enough for everyone to hear, "You sure know how to show a lady a good time!" For the second time that night, I was concerned about my personal safety.

We made it upstairs to the condo leaving a small, angry mob of doormen defending the portal from assault, each wondering why I had not done more to protect the lovely Signora.

"Like some aspirin?" I inquired with a smile.

"Is that all you doctors know?"

"First year, first day, first class in med school," I answered.

"I think I am going to sadly throw this dress, one of my favorites, in the trash. You will buy me two tomorrow. Then, I am going to take a hot bath. Think you can keep any crazed drivers at bay until I am done?"

"No problem. We'll hear them gunning their engines as they come up the stairs. Give us plenty of time to barricade the door."

Off she went. I was going to let her use the single guest bath first and wait my turn. I didn't have it in me yet to use Ron's. Even though she had not closed the bathroom door, attempting to use the shower stall while she was in the tub would be begging for trouble. Anyway, I had something important to do, and I didn't want to wait.

I removed my pistol from the pancake holster and took Marilena's out of her purse. In the den-turned-into-a-shop, I unloaded and broke down each weapon. Her firearm, in spite of her previous commentary, had been recently cleaned and lightly oiled. A lighted magnifier allowed for a careful inspection of each piece making sure that there were no broken or bent parts. Cleaning and reassembly forced an even more careful examination. Once returned to a supposedly operable condition, I dry fired each gun. All joking aside about murderous cars coming up the stairs, I felt a lot better after I had reloaded.

Later, after a shower and having returned to the living room, I joined Marilena on the couch.

"Two questions," I said.

"And they are?" she responded knowing what one of them was, curious as to the other.

"Inept driver or inept killer?"

"Killer, and not so inept. He came close, very close," she said somberly. "By the way, thank you."

"Anytime."

"Whatever did you see or hear that made you move so fast? One minute I'm walking next to you thinking about how to take your mind off of your brother's death if only for dinner and then I am flying through the air. It wasn't until I was rolling across the grass with you that I saw the cab chasing us across the lawn."

"The traffic on Central Park West is one way. It's northbound and we were walking against it," I said.

"And."

"The car behind us was getting closer, and it was on our side of the street. He was at the curb driving against the oncoming traffic. The carriage driver tipped me."

"Not that I am complaining, but from that you acted? A car driving the wrong way on a one-way street?"

"My sense of self-preservation is highly tuned. Dying on the street in New York would be bad for my rep. I jump out of harm's way in a flash. It seemed convenient to take you with me," trying again unsuccessfully to make light of it. It's a defensive mechanism used by those of us in jobs that are sometimes dangerous. If you can joke about a close call, then you won't dwell on it to the point where the memory gets in the way.

"Do you agree with me?" she asked, referring to her belief that we were targeted and not just in the wrong place.

"Yes. The driver worked pretty hard coming after us after getting up on the sidewalk. He wasn't drunk. He managed to get between a fire hydrant and a phone pole on his way back to the street. He came as close to the building wall as he could given his speed. No, it was not an accident followed up by someone fleeing the scene."

"Not tonight, but tomorrow I want to see your list — the list of suspects that the precinct commander gave you. I want to compare it with whom you have been speaking," she said, back in investigator mode so soon after the attempt on her life. She was something else, tougher than she looked.

"What is your second question," she asked remembering.

"Are you still hungry?"

I was happy to hear her laugh. "You are thinking about food?"

"Yep. Gotta keep the old furnace fueled. Man can't live on unfulfilled promises of fine dining alone — he must have pizza!"

She laughed some more and said she would take care of it. Calling downstairs, she asked a member of her personal fan club how to go about "procuring a pizza." With an enthusiastic promise of "no problema!" our team of doormen got the operation underway with an energy level and attention to detail that would have impressed NASA.

Later, we drank ice-cold beer to wash down pepperoni and sausage-laced bread dough from a purported Chicago-style pizzeria conveniently located right here in New York City. We talked about anything but the problem we were here to resolve. Until we got some more answers, hopefully tomorrow, there was nowhere to go with that conversation.

She steered the talk to my childhood and my adult life with Ron. At first I thought she was trying to fill in the holes about me. But the more she gently probed, the more it became obvious that she just wanted me to talk about Ron. When the realization hit me, I surprised myself by continuing to do as she asked and not clamming up, having realized that I was being somewhat manipulated. It was comforting to talk about him to Marilena. I told her things that I would never have imagined myself revealing to anyone. The more I spoke, the more the anger inside of me diminished. She knew it would.

Hours later, neither of us wanting to be alone, we sat close together watching the late news. She had brought the comforter from her bed to the sofa. I had my arm around her as she leaned against me using me as a support and pillow. It wasn't sexual. It was simply two people staying close after a harrowing experience. Somehow the TV got turned off and two tired friends, having shared a very scary event, fell asleep. Security, different for each, enhanced by the other's presence.

FUNERAL HOME

It's an occupational side effect. I wake up in strange places, sometimes not remembering how I got there. You get used to it and the thought that some day you would have a routine way of life, secure by society's standards, is actually unsettling. I had briefly awakened twenty minutes earlier when Marilena disentangled herself and carefully moved from the sofa, immediately falling back to sleep as she slipped away. She had tried not to wake me — that would have been impossible. Now in the nearby kitchen, she was working hard at not making any noise. She couldn't, however, disguise the aroma of frying sausage. Given the way it smelled, I wouldn't have wanted her to.

Getting up required stretching out the kinks acquired from a night on the leather sectional and not on a mattress. My right shoulder a little sore from bearing up under the girl-weight throughout the night. I wasn't going to complain about that. I might, however, mention the collection of aches and pains that had emerged from our previous evening's gymnastics. There was still some numbness in my left arm where I had whacked the granite. I'd be happy when the paresthesia had departed.

Moving to my bedroom, I changed into shorts and a sweatshirt. After a quick trip to the shared facilities to brush my teeth, I walked into the kitchen. I was surprised to see that Marilena had changed into a USMC T-shirt complete with the picture of Chesty, the English bulldog, and, unless I was mistaken, it belonged to me. Due to its size, she was lost in it, and it made an acceptable cover up with the short sleeves coming down to her elbows. Still, when she moved, Chesty became very animated making it obvious that there was nothing on underneath. If the Marine Corps could film this as a recruiting tool, they would be beating the highly motivated, prospective enlistees off with a stick. I elected not to comment about that and only hoped that the shirt she appropriated was the remaining clean one from my bag. She was getting comfortable with me, too comfortable.

She had discovered where the pans and cooking implements were located. Although we had shared several meals in restaurants, I had never seen her cook anything before. I was greeted with a smile and she seemed happy to be preparing a meal.

"Good morning!" she said brightly.

"Good morning yourself, Marine," I replied resigning myself to the fact that I did not have any clean T-shirts left. Oh, well. She looked better in it than I did.

She smiled and delivered food from pans to plates. As someone who does not enjoy cooking, I am always extremely appreciative of anyone who will prepare something for me to eat. I made the right thank you comments that she accepted with more pleasure than I would have expected. An hour later we were showered, shaved, and shined. I did the dishes while she made phone calls. Marilena reappeared in time to show me the proper storage locations for the kitchen stuff. She only re-washed two items. It was ten o'clock when we left for the funeral home.

We had both dressed in casual clothes and were wearing shoes that could go the distance. In this case, the distance was eleven blocks. Franklin and Franklin, a converted brownstone was located without difficulty. Because the door was at street level, it was unlike most of the businesses now occupying a former mini-mansion. A flight of stairs, even a short one, would have made it difficult for their elderly clientele to make it to viewings. Young people, those who can handle stairs, for the most part don't go to viewings anymore. We were greeted by Oliver Franklin, fourth generation embalmer, and a cold handshake.

"Colonel Briggs?" he rhetorically asked.

"Yes. This is Miss Rigatti," I added. He actually bowed in Marilena's direction. All undertakers must belong to the same union where they ascribe to mannerisms that would be strange if affected by anyone but them.

"I am saddened to meet you in this time of personal and family sorrow," he recited his follow-up lines from well-practiced memory. Unless we behaved in some unexpected way, he could conduct our entire meeting employing a creepy autopilot.

"Let me escort you inside so we can finalize arrangements for the deceased," he said.

By referring to Ron as the "deceased," he did not have to worry about mistaking my relationship to the body — another auto-mechanism hiding the fact that this was to him just another yet-to-be-planted-corpse while feigning a personal alignment with our expected grieving.

We followed him down the hall to the "Taft Memorial Room" so identified by the well-polished engraving next to the doorway. They had prepared for the sale with practiced ease. As we walked in, we were confronted with eight caskets. All of them one-half open, showing stuffed, satin linings. They were arranged with a simpler box, albeit highly polished, at one end, progressing steadily to more and more elaborate and ornate entombments as you moved down the line. The casket at the far end was the objective of the sale. Before I let him start on the features, advantages and benefits of the different coffins, I cut him off.

"I'm not interested in caskets. Where's the body?" I asked quietly, but with an edge.

"That would be unwise at this time. Most people find it traumatic to see a loved one before we have completed our work. It is always best to wait until we have had time to dress and prepare the body. I believe that you might want to select an appropriate vessel for your loved one prior to viewing the body, which at this time, by the way, is wholly unnecessary."

"The body. Now." I glared at him. Marilena added to the heat with an unblinking frown.

"If you must," he said backing down but his tone patronizing.

I started for the door, and trying to stay in charge, he actually had to move quickly to beat me there so he could get in front and lead us. Probably the fastest six feet he had covered in fifteen years. On the way, I saddened Franklin, a rare event I believe, by informing him that my brother would be cremated: no casket required and I was not in the market for an expensive urn. His grief, genuine for once, at losing a pricey casket sale was poorly hidden.

We took an elevator down two levels. It opened into a small hallway leading to several prep rooms identified by stainless steel tables visible from the passageway. The air smelled of antiseptic and embalming fluids. Entering one of the rooms, Franklin apologized without meaning it, "We do not usually have visitors in the prep rooms because they can seem to be an uncaring place. But if you must see the body now, here is where we do our work to maintain the dignity of the remains."

The time had come. I walked up to the table where the small, pale, damaged body of an approximately 50-year-old man lay with a sheet covering him from feet to chest. The body had been partially cleaned of the blood from the injuries and the trauma of the sidewalk impact was still very visible. Two sets of eyes looked at me as I stepped up to the table. Franklin's looking for some shocked reaction so he could say "I told you so," Marilena's looking for some sign that I needed support, protection from the reality of my only brother's death. I surprised them both.

It was a body. It was just a body. It may have once been Ron, but it wasn't anymore. It held for me no source of pain. It caused no sense of loss. I was not the brother of this object, and my interests were forensic. Demonstrating this, I yanked the sheet off unceremoniously letting it fall to the floor. Two people in the room inhaled sharply as the broken body was fully exposed. I wasn't one of the two. Starting at the head, I carefully examined the damage — proof of our human frailty. Without warning, I pulled the body up into a sitting position, rigor having left the corpse days before, no resistance offered.

"Really, Colonel Briggs! Is that necessary?" Franklin demanded. I ignored him again. That was getting easier.

I looked at the back of the dead body, studying the back of the head and the areas of the torso that had absorbed almost all of the visible damage. The rib cage that normally did a superb job at protecting the organs of the stomach and chest had failed. Broken cartilage had pierced the back tearing open the skin exposing damaged inner tissue.

It was confirmation of what I had read in the crime lab's report. I had needed to see it for myself, and it was my real reason for being here, one I had not shared with Marilena. The basis for an important fact that I would tell her about later. Her lips compressed together, eyes moving back and forth between Ron's corpse and the wall to her right as she struggled between her loyalties to me, and her desire to look anywhere but at this disfigured and grotesque form. As tough as she was, this was far from a routine event and understandably disturbing to anyone of normal sensibilities. My sensibilities were abnormal. I was sorry she was here, but I could not have prevented her from coming. Easing the body back down, I continued my examination with the limbs, paying special attention to the hands and feet. She refocused on me, watching my every move, not saying anything that might jeopardize the composure she was fighting to maintain.

"Do you have the clothes that he was wearing?" I asked Franklin without looking up.

"No, this is how he came from the city people." His voice laconic and not at all upset by what I had been doing proving that his earlier outburst was just part of the show. He lived with dead bodies, and they didn't bother him in the least. As a New York operator, he had seen them folded, spindled, and mutilated. This one wasn't a big deal. At best, it had been just another body that would net a fee for services and a commission on a box. The business of death.

HEART AND SOUL

We were sitting in the bar at the Carlyle. Although I didn't tell Marilena, this was a regular stop for me, even though I had never been there during the day. It was a good place to come for a quiet conversation without being overheard. The bar seating area is extensive, yet the tables, almost all deuces with high-backed leather upholstered chairs, are separated by large plants and floor to ceiling dividers making each one an intimate setting. Small rooms flowed in several directions, each a little dark and trapping any sounds from escaping. The service is exceptional and unobtrusive. It almost makes you overlook the forty-dollar just-because-you-walked-in-the-door fee that they add to the overpriced drinks, miniature hors d'oeuvres, and automatic tip. And, I'll admit that when in the city with a date that needed a little encouragement to move the evening along, this was the place that helped me close escrow. It was classy and comfortable, guaranteed to put anyone at ease. It would give Marilena a chance to catch her breath.

After signing a cremation order, I had steered her out of the funeral parlor holding her arm, and we moved quickly out the front door to the street. I hailed a cab and instructed the driver to take us to East 76th and Madison. Marilena was slowly regaining her color but was still a little pale and uncharacteristically quiet. I stayed close in case of a misstep or a wobble.

After we got settled, she calmly ordered a glass of Chablis. It was just after noon and early for me to have a drink, but I ordered a glass of the same so Marilena would not have to drink alone. Three and a half ounces of wine would help her gather in the last of the frayed ends. Sipping, but not really drinking, would give me something to do with my hands. There would be some tense moments ahead.

"I'm sorry. I let you down," she said, surprising me for I didn't think that she had. "I don't know why I did not prepare myself better. I've seen dead bodies before. On one occasion it upset me, and I should have known that this was not going to be easy."

"Do you want to tell me about the other time, the one that upset you," I asked gently.

"I have seen several bodies as part of one investigation or another, once at the scene, the rest of the time in a hospital or morgue. With the exception of that one time, they were all what I had anticipated — cold and pale. One had an entry hole from a small caliber pistol, and the rest had not died from physical violence. I don't want to make viewing a body seem routine, it is not, but the times I had to do it, it was what I had guessed it to be. That one time it wasn't, the one time that still gives me nightmares, happened three years ago. That one surprised me, caught me off guard, like today."

"What was different about it?"

"A family of five had died in a house fire set by an arsonist," she said bitterly. "The bodies were completely burned and charred."

"You don't have to tell me anymore. I've seen it myself. It's pretty horrific if you're not used to it, if anyone could ever get used to it."

"I still have terrible nightmares that I haven't admitted to anyone. I need you to keep this between us. The Bureau would have me in front of a staff psychiatrist in an instant."

"Might not be a bad idea to talk to someone," I said carefully.

"I am. I'm talking to you."

She continued, "It was silly of me not to think that your brother's body would be horrible to see given the way he died. It caught me by surprise. Again, I am sorry. It had to be incredibly worse for you. It did not help that you had to deal with a silly girl."

"You handled it OK. The exam I did didn't help. I should have asked you to step out, or not come in at all."

"No. I wouldn't have let you do this alone. I won't let you down again." Having talked about it had already helped. Changing direction slightly, she asked, "What were you looking for?"

"What was left out of the crime lab's report. The report I was given by the crime lab did not mention injury to the limbs, the hands and the feet. There were no pictures of the limbs." She smiled for the first time, keeping the thought of any pictures out of her mind while being amused at my reference to the report as a gift.

"Why is that important?" she asked.

"Either they failed to mention injury to the limbs because there was none or because the trauma to the head and torso was so bad that it was the obvious cause of death and why waste the time on the extraneous. It turns out that there was no trauma of any significance to the arms, legs, feet, or hands."

"What does that mean to our investigation?"

"He was pushed backwards through the window," I said quietly, but with certainty.

"Please explain to me why you believe this," she said while giving me one hundred percent of her attention.

"I've jumped out of a lot of planes. I've seen the remains of those who have died from falls. The trauma to Ron's body is not consistent with that of a suicide."

She lifted both eyebrows, asking for more.

"When a skydiver goes out of a plane, he puts his body into what we call a hard arch. Both arms and both legs spread out and back. This causes you to come down face first. I'm sure you've seen this on TV or in the movies. This is important because when the time comes to deploy your parachute, it works best if it comes out of the pack that is on your back unobstructed by your body. Face up can be a mess.

"When someone commits suicide," I continued, "the person almost always goes out face first but feet down. Sometimes they will bicycle, pumping their legs all the way down. Almost always, there is considerable damage to the feet and legs and sometimes to the hands and arms as well. These are the parts of the body that strike first. Ron took it in the back. He went out the window backwards, his legs and arms trailing behind him — his body a 'U' shape, stable all the way down. It's not how he would have done it if indeed he had wanted to kill himself. He was pushed. What I don't know is why didn't the crime lab draw this conclusion?" I asked.

She thought this over trying to fit what I had said in with her specific knowledge of forensics experts with whom she had worked. I left her to her thoughts without interrupting.

She looked up at me and continued, "Forensic specialists like to make objective and quantifiable assessments like blood type, DNA analysis, a bullet's path through a body, or the identification of chemical residue. When they give expert testimony or have to defend their report, this keeps them on safe footing. It is safest for them to limit their pronouncements to cause of death and whenever possible although sometimes their hands do get forced, letting the detectives deduce the manner of death. The manner of death can require speculation and is most often impacted by other evidence at the scene."

"What's the difference between cause and manner?" I asked.

"The cause is the pathology — why the body no longer is alive. The manner is constrained to four defined states: natural, accidental, suicidal, and homicidal. How a body hits the ground after falling from twenty-four stories might lead them to believe something about the manner with a high probability of certainty, but there would be no lab test to confirm it. A sharp lawyer would make them look foolish, and they don't like that. In a case like your brother's, it's better to state that the cause of death was physical trauma due to the impact with the sidewalk and then let the police figure out how he got there — on his own or with help.

"As much as I would hope that bureau people would state facts as facts and then opinion as opinion, providing both, I would probably be disappointed. Given how you described the city crime lab, I don't think they would go out on a limb. It's good to have some physical evidence to support our position that this was a murder. I'm glad you did the examination even if I have new material for my nightmares."

She was again quiet for a few minutes. She was wrestling with whether or not to ask me a question, one that I had been expecting. I decided to give her a little push. The sooner we got this out the better.

"There is something else bothering you."

"Well, actually, I did want to ask you something."

"Then you should."

"When we were in the prep room, your behavior surprised me as much as the condition of the body. You didn't even acknowledge that it was your brother. You did not show any grief or even any emotion. Then, when you started the exam by throwing the sheet to the floor and roughly moving him so you could see those terrible things, it upset me. It wasn't the you I have come to know. I was having a very hard time reconciling these clinical and uncaring actions with the man who just last night told me so many things about the brother he loved."

"It wasn't Ron," I answered evenly, without emotion.

"What?" That wasn't your brother?" Her eyes grew wide.

"That was just a body. At one time Ron was in there but not any more."

"Is this a religious perspective? A spiritual position?" she asked.

"No. You know me well enough to know that I have no religious or metaphysical perspectives."

"That's what I thought." She looked around as if I was about to reveal one of the Universe's secrets. "You'd better explain."

"In the middle 1800s, a French physician name Broca studied the brain looking for a relationship between anatomical features and mental capabilities, specifically intelligence. He was not successful. I've seen the insides of enough craniums to understand his frustration. I don't think that is what made Ron, Ron, what makes you, you, has anything to do with the body that carried him, or carries you, around. You know that I don't subscribe to any religion and that I am certainly not some kind of deep philosopher, but I do think that what we think of as self, transcends the body. I will think that way until someone can show me the part of the brain, or whatever, that contains your essence. I don't know the answers. I'm not even sure what to call it. Is it sentience, soul, spirit, self-aware consciousness, sapience, identity? To me, it is our certain knowledge of who we are and that we exist. But, it's not the body. I wouldn't have treated Ron that way. I believe a body is like other support equipment. It's like dive gear or an astronaut's suit. What I saw was Ron's space suit that he had stepped out of. It was in a pile on a stainless steel table. I was looking for the damage that caused it to fail. Its failure caused

Ron to leave me. It's that simple for me. Being in that room with Ron's remains was an objective exercise. Ron wasn't there."

"Well, Thomas Aquinas, I'm learning more and more about you each day. The facade you maintain, Mr. Marine, is a sham. You, whether you like it or not, are a lot more complicated than you want people to think."

She smiled at me over the glass she held in two hands. She took the index finger of her right hand and rubbed it along the edge of the glass as if she could produce some musical note. She felt better. I was back in the classification of people she understood.

"Thomas, do you remember the head of the Bureau's Hostage Rescue Team, Andrew Felton? I brought him with me on a trip to Tampa."

"Vaguely."

"He observed one of the exercises that you were in — the one where your team penetrated an urban setting so you could get to a priority patient held hostage in a restaurant kitchen."

"I know the one."

"We watched from an observation tower. He was extremely surprised to learn that you were a doctor, the supposed follower who was to be delivered to the site, and not the team leader. He said you were a natural. You had the instincts and the moves. Others reacted to this and followed, looking to you. He said you were fortunate to have an outlet for what he called your bad boy behavior, the rest of us fortunate that your parents were not in the mob. That was when I decided I wanted to know you better. Sometimes, however, the funny, caring, easy-going guy I know becomes someone completely devoid of emotion and capable of whatever violence is necessary. Sometimes, the bad boy scares me a little." She paused and the smile returned, "But not enough to scare me away."

GALA PREP

We had some errands to run prior to the evening's society fund-raising gala — an event that I wasn't really looking forward to. I thought that spending a few more moments at the Carlyle was a good use of time. Marilena had her feet back under her, an interesting metaphor given that she had been and was still seated. I tried to convey verbally and with my body language that I was in no hurry at all and was perfectly happy to continue sipping the Chablis. My energy level was fully reigned in and set on simmer. Someday, she would discover that I was not a fan of white wine and take me to task about today's grape juice pretense. I'd deal with it then.

Her wobbles had been replaced with her customary self-confidence. She had not only overcome her anxieties about our stop at the funeral home but also seemed comfortable to have exposed herself to me. There was that comfort issue again. And again, too comfortable. All the same, I was glad that she was here. Her answer to my question about the crime lab demonstrated once again how little I knew about civilian police posturing and procedure. Her contribution explaining what motivates the behavior of forensics people proved again that I needed her. Her reaction at the funeral home helped delineate our roles. I'd handle the ugly; she'd guide the process and do the analysis. In the nonmilitary world of the good guys vs. bad guys, she was an excellent Sherpa.

She asked to see the suspect list that I had gotten from O'Dale. Explaining, I think unnecessarily, the color-coding while she studied the names, titles, and company affiliations. She asked me some questions about whom I knew and whom I had talked to since arriving in New York. I don't think that I was much help. She made notes and annotated the list drawing boxes around groups and adding arrows to include some outlying names into some of the boxes. She made a list of questions that had to be answered about the names on the list and wrote down the working assumptions to further reduce the number of names. She added weighting factors to her additions. She had already crossed some names off the list — I didn't know why. I could easily see her leading a team in an FBI war room complete with whiteboard walls, mapping out the plan to catch public enemy number one, her focus a little daunting. After about twenty minutes, I suggested a change of direction. She would have happily spent hours on this, planning how to eliminate names from the list, finally reducing it to the killer. I got her to relent because for the rest of the afternoon we had a challenging mission completely outside of our quest to find a murderer. We had to buy a dress — two dresses.

We both could use a break from the stress. I was glad that we had something to do that, when compared with finding Ron's murderer, was a more normal task, a fun task for the female half of the team. Marilena got a mischievous look on her face. She was planning to enjoy watching me in an uncomfortable environment and would have fun seeing me stumble through the process. She was certain that I was forcing myself to tolerate our new mission. I had other plans.

Hailing our second cab of the day was easy. Without any hesitation, I directed him to a dress shop further south on Park Avenue. Marilena was taken aback. From the name of the store, could it be that I had just given directions to a ladies boutique?

"Thomas, where are we going?" she inquired, looking a little bewildered.

"To buy you a dress — two dresses. We'll start at this shop, and if we don't see anything we like, I know of several others." I answered as if this were a question posed to me each and every day.

"Do you shop for dresses often?"

"Not often," I shrugged. "It comes up from time to time."

She looked at me, her expression mildly perplexed before continuing with, "So, tell me about this shop."

"I think you will find the selection sophisticated yet cognizant of current fashions in a subtle way," I answered as seriously as if she had asked for a surgical protocol. Her mouth fell open. This was going to be entertaining. I was, however, hoping that either the sales staff had turned over since my last visit and did not begin with "where's your girlfriend?" or that they were cool enough to help me out, taking their cues from the manager that I knew.

Playing along, while intrigued and entertained, Marilena let me take charge. She returned the faux-seriousness and said, "Well then, I shall not worry as I am in the hands of a professional."

Unlike most men, and in spite of my hunting-lodge lifestyle, I have learned to appreciate what comes your way when you help a lady pick out an outfit. It wasn't always like this because like most men, I can be dumb as a box of rocks — until someone hits me with one. My first couple of times, when forced into a lady's clothing store, I will admit that my reaction was just like all of my Neanderthal friends. Sit in the designated, uncomfortable chair outside of the dressing room, stare at the wall, make forced comments that each dress or whatever looked great and that "this is the one" while making repeated, distressed looks at my watch like we were about to miss live coverage of a major meteor impact that would end all life on Earth. And, like every other guy who displayed this sophomoric behavior, it got me nowhere.

I am, if nothing else, willing to reassess tactics in the face of abject and complete failure — especially failure that did not enamor me to an attractive lady. So, I did some research and made some allies with a couple of understanding store managers. The shop we were headed to was the one where I thought we would have the most success. The store was sophisticated in both the clothing offered and the customer service. In other words, they put on a real show. Most importantly, the manager had become a friend. At first I thought she was solely motivated by adding a wealthy client who didn't mind dropping some significant bucks on a steady procession of new girlfriends' dresses. In later conversations, she corrected my ignorant assumption. She was actually touched, in some strange female way that I will never understand, by the fact that a rough hewn, though well-off heterosexual, was sincere about picking out girl clothes. She was New York tough, but she melted over this. It seemed that I was fairly unique. She wanted me to talk to her husband. Could I run a class for the husbands and boyfriends of all of her customers?

Her assumption was as wrong as mine had been as my motives were less than pure. The fact was that you could get a lot of mileage out of this. Today my goal was not sex but rather having some fun with a friend who needed a distraction. As a bonus, I got to surprise Marilena once again about her friend the Marine, whom she had completely figured out. I'm not sure why, but I liked it.

I escorted my clothes-shopping date from the cab to the store in gentlemanly fashion. I had called Catherine, the manager, after breakfast to alert her to our upcoming visit. She saw us through the glass and hurried over to meet us coming through the door, cutting off the junior members of the staff who would normally have pulled this duty. Her greeting made us both feel like long, lost friends.

"Tom, it's so good to see you again," she said.

After making introductions, Marilena asked, "You two know each other?"

Catherine answered, "Yes. Tom is a valued client who has not been in to see us in way too long."

Very smooth, however, Marilena looked at me like she was trying to decide if Catherine was covering for me about the amount of time that had passed since my last visit. I could tell that she really didn't know. Nice.

"Tom tells me that you need an evening gown and a replacement cocktail dress for one that somehow was destroyed. I can't wait to hear how that happened. I'll bet he had something to do with it," Catherine said. Both ladies laughed; bonding had begun.

Catherine sized Marilena up and presented her with several dresses that met with enthusiastic approval. She summoned help, and we were ushered into a large alcove that was immediately closed off by a heavy curtain and a little velvet rope. Marilena was the center of attention as doting females directed by their mentor delivered gown after gown for consideration. Champagne arrived with fresh strawberries, choices were made about which dress to try on. Womanly happiness flowed in abundance.

I stood away from the activity but purposefully did not sit down. I struck a contemplative pose, one hand stroking my chin while looking at the various garments. Catherine winked at me when one particular dress was produced, spurring me into further involvement. I provided positive comments about that one and even suggested that we start with a size 4. Marilena looked at me completely surprised. Before she could comment, I moved over to a wall that I knew from a previous visit contained a sliding screen that I started to pull out. This partition could be used to provide privacy for the lady trying on clothes. Marilena watched this, and her eyes opened even wider. Catherine turned away before her knowing smile could be seen.

Getting back in the game by derailing my little charade, Marilena said, "Thomas, is that necessary?"

I should have called her bluff. She was definitely bluffing. I'm sure it was a bluff. Yeah, it had to be. Well, I think it was a bluff. Oh, boy.

A STRANGER IN A STRANGE LAND

We left the store amid a flurry of "goodbyes" and "comebacks" — Marilena and Catherine friends for life. All in all, it had gone well. Marilena had enjoyed a very pleasant time as the center of attention, and Catherine had enjoyed a very pleasant time as the center of a flow of money from me to her. A win-win for everyone important to the process. Other than funding, my importance was questionable. And even though I did enjoy seeing Marilena's reactions as she discovered that she still had a lot to learn about me, it had been a dangerous game. All I had wanted to do was to tease her a little while distracting her with girl clothes acquisition. She almost managed to use my ploy to up the ante in our relationship. I should have known better. When it came to this man-woman relationship game, whether you are trying to make a relationship or, in my case, prevent one, going up against a pro is unwise.

As it was, she seemed happy in the cab and back at the condo unwrapping boxes and hanging up new clothing treasures. We had somehow purchased more than two dresses, and I was pressed into the receiving end of another fashion show and enthusiastically thanked once more — this time I got a kiss. At the store, she had looked amazing in almost everything she had tried on. In the end, it was the black number that I had pointed out with Catherine's subtle direction that had been selected for this evening's event. I won't try to describe it in much detail as even though I have been trained a little by Catherine and her peers on girl clothes psychology, I'm still basically lost when it comes to the correct clothing construction terminology. Suffice it to say that it was floor length with lace in the right places and it was sheer, very sheer, in the right places accenting some amazing curves and flawless skin. There wasn't a lot of it up top, with two very slight straps defying the physical laws that govern the whole universe by holding the whole thing up. The other women at the event tonight were going to just hate her.

She turned her attention to me and to what I was going to wear this evening, a small but definite amount of concern in her voice. My plan had been to put on a dress uniform that I kept at Ron's. You can never go wrong with dress blues. This had been beaten into me starting as a kid in military school and from then on in one billet after another as an officer and a pretend gentleman. Also, hiding behind a uniform is always a safe place in uncomfortable surroundings. I was taking it out of the closet when she walked into my room as if letting me select suitable attire was a very risky proposition. She stepped up to the open closet and planted herself, my new clothing warden.

"You're wearing your uniform?" she asked in surprise.

"Not just any uniform. This is a top-of-the-line, military dress uniform, designed by high-paid government clothing consultants and approved by the United States Marine Corps with the advice and consent of multiple congressional subcommittees. It is suitable for all classy occasions, both foreign and domestic." I responded with strong finality — case closed.

She had completely ignored me, had not heard a single word. My well-crafted discourse guaranteed to deflect any question about what I was going to wear unheard, a waste of breath.

"What is this?" she asked reaching into the closet and pulling on the sleeve of the almost never worn tux — a tux that I had tried hard to forget.

"Haven't worn that in years. I'm sure it doesn't fit anymore."

"Try it on." Her voice carried more command than request.

"I'm really not a tuxedo guy. It was Ron's idea for me to have one. I think he got a two-for-one deal. He needed to wear a tux a lot. But like I said, it's been so long that I'm sure it doesn't fit." I was dancing.

"Try this on, please," she said again as if for the first time, no impatience in her words, certain that her request would be accommodated.

She pulled the hanger out and started to pull apart all the dumb little pieces and parts that make up a tuxedo. Tuxedo components were raining on the bed like D-Day paratroopers at Normandy. Eventually, she got down to the pants.

"Well, go on," she said. She made no signs of moving.

I was seriously hoping that somehow it had changed and wouldn't fit. The problem was that Ron had bought it for an event we had attended just two years ago, I had agonized through the alteration process, and I had not changed in size since then. She still wasn't moving. I unbuckled, dropped my trousers, and stepped into the lower half of the tux. After I got started struggling into the damn thing, she pretended to ignore me, fiddled around with the other tuxedo pieces while I was getting zipped up and somehow managed to get my uniform back into the closet. Now the case was closed.

Handing me the outer shell of the upper-half, she instructed, "Now the jacket."

I put it on. She smoothed the fabric down my shoulders, and it too fit perfectly. There was no hiding. I made one last try.

"What's wrong with my dress blues? Goes with my haircut."

"Nothing, if this were a military function. This is a society event. There is also an operational issue."

"And that is?" I inquired suspiciously.

"We need to learn more about these people. You need to fit in. In your uniform, you are not as approachable."

Maybe she had a point. I hadn't put up much of a fight. I never could with her. My look said that I acquiesced.

"Besides," she continued, springing the trap now that I had given in. "I want to have our picture taken together, I want to dance with you, and I want to be seen with an appropriate escort in my new gown, and that means you in a tuxedo, Buster."

Uh, what was that? Did she just call me Buster? Tuxedo Tommy, I thought. A stranger headed to a strange land, his date way ahead of him.

* * *

As expected, our arrival at the building lobby caused considerable commotion. The doormen, led by Caporegime Antonio himself, tripped over each other in their race to offer any doorman-type assistance to the beautiful Signora. I was physically moved aside so that she might get a professional escort front, back, left, and right all the way to Ricardo's limo. I think that if she had asked, they would have climbed in and provided a moving defensive perimeter throughout the entire evening, leaving the building to look after itself. For that matter, leaving me to look after myself as well. Antonio gave a knowing look to Ricardo that I am sure conveyed, "Do what you can — she only has him." I got a look that reminded me of the one I received from the father of my first date as we left her home so many years ago. Nothing had changed.

The Plaza was at the southeast corner of Central Park at 59th and Fifth. This would have been a walk for me, but the flimsy, yet incredibly expensive shoe selection called for wheeled transport. It amazes me that the more expensive a woman's shoe, the less utilitarian it is. There is no logic in female shoe-ware. We started off in limo-luxury for our short ride to the Plaza. Along the way, Ricardo maintained a nonstop lecture about the dangers of the city, having heard about last night's escapade. He wanted me to know, just about making me repeat the fact, that he was available at a moment's notice and would drop any other client for us. Not calling him was inexcusable. Getting a little tired of having my shining armor questioned as being a little tarnished, I decided it was time to poke back a little.

"You know, Ricardo, I have heard that those horse-drawn carriage rides around the park are a lot of fun. I think that after the event at the Plaza ends tonight, I will hire one to take us back, maybe up the middle of 5th Avenue and then across one of those park trails by the lake."

I immediately got an elbow in the ribs from my date knowing that I was just pulling his chain. It soon, however, became very apparent that Ricardo didn't know I was kidding. He abruptly stopped the limo — so much for the egg — turned back to me and said with tremendous agitation, "Please, Colonel, do not speak of this! Do not even think it! Those buggy contraptions are a death trap! A death trap I tell you! No protection at all for the lady! I will stay at the Plaza all evening so you will not have to wait a second. Please! Please do not use a horse-buggy!" I got the elbow again, this time with a glare and a small shake of the head.

"OK, OK, we will have you take us back. But you don't need to hang around all night. I'll call you twenty minutes before we need to leave."

"Ricardo, I think that we will hire you for the entire evening just in case I do not feel well and need to return unexpectedly," Marilena stated matter-of-factly, but with a smile.

I need to either carry more cash or stop playing with the pros. Fortunately, we moved on and quickly arrived at the Plaza before I could get into more trouble, cartilaginous, or financial.

We had arrived thirty minutes early by design. I knew the layout of the hotel and wanted to take advantage of the lobby bar so we could see the guests as they arrived. Ricardo helped us, I mean helped Marilena, out of the limo, and off we went without the benefit of Mafiosi protection for the first time this evening. Although I would bet that Antonio had called the Plaza and had us under the protection of another doorman syndicate as a professional courtesy, one family to another.

Up a short flight to the second floor, we stepped into a recessed, two-story bar area called the Rose Club. I steered us to a table that would be unnoticed from the foyer but offered a good view down at people coming in from the 5th Avenue entrance. We ordered drinks and settled in.

"Recon, Mr. Marine?" she asked, noticing my careful table selection.

"Stakeout, Federal Lady Police Person," I answered.

Along with those checking in, a steady stream of society partygoers mixed in with the flow, coming through the front door. You could separate them from the check-in crowd due to the women in colorful gowns and their penguin escorts. Then I remembered. God, I was a penguin, too.

While we waited and watched, Marilena filled me in on some of the research she had done on the CID Society before leaving Washington. Having the resources of the FBI made her more successful than I had been poking around the Internet.

"Although I know that good comes out of the work of the VHAs, and I am in no way trying to belittle your brother's work, the more I learn about these chronic disease advocacy groups, the less likely I am to contribute to one," she began.

"That's not completely surprising," I responded. "Ron was frustrated about his shop and told me so on several occasions."

"I asked our NFP division about the CID Society in particular and received some disturbing information from a senior agent whom I think highly of," she said carefully.

"What is the NFP division?" I asked, fearing that I already knew the answer.

"We have a small group that deals discretely with issues involving not-for-profits," she answered.

"You do?"

"Yes. They are less discrete when the NFP is a blatant sham, basically stealing from generous and well-meaning donors. They try to be more sensitive when the NFP is legitimate, and the potentially guilty parties are a small subset of the larger organization. The sad part is that more often than you would think, legitimate NFPs have some people in positions of responsibility who are plain and simply criminals. White-collar criminals, but criminals all the same."

"You said potentially guilty parties? As in plural?"

"Yes," she answered. "The bureau's involvement is because the crimes perpetrated in these NFPs are organized and cross state lines."

"What did you learn about the CID Society?" I was almost afraid to ask.

"There have been rumors and two undercover investigations. You need to keep that last part to yourself. The investigations are ongoing and involve violations of charity fund accounting."

"OK. So the crime involves multiple parties and is organized — that's why the bureau is involved. But it sounds more like some issue that a press-happy district attorney would take up on behalf of the donors who also happen to be voters, who might later make him governor."

She answered, helping me see the real issue. "It goes beyond stealing from a citizen. It is theft from charitable organizations that are tax exempt. Each donor, every donor, has the federal government as a partner because the donation reduces the donor's tax bill. Uncle Sam does not like people stealing from him and expects us to do something about it. Not-for-profits are subject to surprise audits and scrutiny because of the government's partnership with the donor base."

"How did the bureau get involved with the CID Society?"

"We were tipped off by an administrator at an academic research facility. I didn't ask which one because my source would have stopped talking to me if I had. A detail-oriented lady noticed a mismatch between money promised in a grant and money received. When she made a routine application for more money, the balance of the money granted, she was told that the grant had been reduced. Apparently, this was not the first time that this had happened with the CID but it had never happened with any other grant from any other VHA."

I considered her words and wondered what Ron would say if he were here.

We watched more people come in and head to the ballroom. I looked for Alison Montgomery but did not see her. Most of the crowd was a little senior in age, which made sense to me. Philanthropists tend to be older, having made enough money to be generous. And, trust fund babies don't go to old-people parties. I spotted Chicken Woman. She was wearing a beige dress that to me looked like an upright, ambulating tube, a bad cannoli, cut horizontally at the top and bottom. It needed to be longer as there was too much poultry exposed and about to be inflicted on an unsuspecting crowd. I had pointed her out and made my observation to Marilena.

"Thomas, that's not nice," she said, but with mock sternness.

"Yeah, to chickens."

PARTY PEOPLE

We walked through the doors of the 15,000 square foot, third-floor ballroom trying our best to slip by unnoticed. With Marilena in tow, the probability of this happening was extremely low. By moving quickly, we did manage to go through the ballroom doors and off to one side of the room without being snared into a conversation. I snatched two flutes of Champagne from a tray as it moved past us. Across the room I saw Suzie talking to a hotel employee, obviously still at work for her employer long after office hours. I knew that it wouldn't be long before she came our way. Not necessarily because of me, irresistible as I am, but because she would want to size up my date. When it comes to scoping out the opposite sex, men get all the heat and deservedly so. However, the real scrutiny that women undergo is from members of their own sex. And whereas, men tend to be generous in their assessment, especially if it has been some time since they had sex, women in my experience, can be very critical. I have learned that a woman going to an event like this one, an event where they are going to be seen by many other women, will dress and make themselves up not for their male companion, but for the other women who will be critiquing everything about them. I was fairly sure, even allowing for my personal bias, that my date was an exception. Given Marilena's level of self-confidence, I didn't think she worried too much about the more catty qualities of the sisterhood.

As predicted, Suzie appeared next to us. I made introductions, making sure that Marilena knew Suzie's business relationship to Ron. I didn't reveal that Marilena was an agent with the FBI. As I was speaking, I did notice Suzie's appraising looks at Marilena. At one point, Marilena looked away, and I got a smile along with an emphatic nod of approval from Suzie. She seemed happy for me. Go figure.

"Are you getting Ron's affairs straightened out?" Suzie asked.

"He had things pretty squared away, so for the most part it has been no problem," I answered, dodging the question.

"I was a little surprised to see you here," she continued. "You were the talk of the office all day after you left. We had seen Margaret Townsend mad before, in fact most every day, but never quite that mad and powerless to do anything about it. The entire administrative support staff was ready to marry you."

"He has that effect," Marilena said. I wasn't sure if the effect she was talking about was making women mad or making them want to marry me. Both scared me. The girls laughed. I gave them a "whatever could you be talking about" look of complete shock. They laughed some more.

"Do you know many of these people?" Suzie asked.

"I might recognize a face or two. I don't think Marilena will know anyone here." Marilena agreed with me by shaking her head. "Who is here from your office?" I asked. Marilena stopped taking in the room and focused on Suzie.

"I think that all of the senior management team will be here. That's everyone who reports directly to Alison Montgomery," Suzie spoke quietly. "There will be others from the home office but from further down the food chain. In those cases, it will be because they have some specific role to play tonight."

"Such as," Marilena asked.

"Sometimes, somebody has a presentation to make as a part of the formal program. But the most common reason that a department or program lead is at an event like this is money."

I raised my eyebrows.

She continued, "There will be targets in the crowd. People who the society are after to fund a specific program or make a family endowment." She shrugged in an apologetic way, "It's what Ron told me that he had figured out after he came to work here. Not-for-profit is a tax election, not a business model."

Her words didn't surprise Marilena in the slightest, but they made me think. I had known that Ron had become disillusioned after a year on the inside of a VHA, but I didn't think he had crossed the line into cynical. I asked myself again if he had needed me and I hadn't been listening.

I had done my time at many military formal affairs — too many. At those events, I knew what to expect as the interactions were a function of rank and unspoken role assignment, the product of generation after generation of officers forced to attend, the groupings a pyramid of authority with those in the same layers coalescing with each other. To say that those events were predictable to the point of being incredibly boring was not putting it strongly enough. Because of them, I did not attend similar functions in the civilian world unless I absolutely had to. One commonality between the military and civilian soiree is that three people trying to have a confidential and delicate conversation, whether they intend to or not, can appear to others as if they have entered the conspiracy-zone. The three of us, almost as one, recognized that this had occurred. It was comical to me that in unison, we took a ten-second conversation intermission, and purposefully looked around the room, anywhere but at each other, before resuming, hoping that others would see that we were not engaged in subversion.

I suppressed a smile when I thought that a little military social structure would help us right now. If the power players would all merge together, then we would not have had to sift through the commoners to pick them out. I missed rank insignia.

"There's someone you should know," Suzie said.

"Who," I asked.

"See the man walking in the door? The short, Middle Easterner with the neatly trimmed beard and a little too much good life around the middle. That's Omar Sayyaf. His title is Chief of Internal Operations, and he is a very sharp operator. His bio says that he is a summa cum laude Columbia grad with a graduate degree from the London School of Economics. He is the invisible hand behind a lot that happens at the society."

"Is he tight with Townsend?" I asked.

"No, I don't think that they're friends, but they have to work together. I'm sure that he gives back as good as he gets. Ron liked him a lot and told me that Omar was very smooth and great at working behind the scenes to get things done. In some ways, I think that Ron wished he had some of Omar's political skills. Also, Ron and Omar were the only two of Alison's thirteen direct reports who were men. Most of the other senior execs don't like him. Everyone down at my level thinks that it is because he actually is smart and has skills. The hen house has got to be a tough place for him. It's going to get worse unless Ron gets replaced by a man."

I was a little shocked by Suzie's gender-based attack. I would have thought that as a woman, she would have been happy that several women had made it to the top. Marilena laughed softly.

"Suzie, do you see the look of confusion on Thomas' face?"

"Yeah, he doesn't get it," Suzie replied while unsuccessfully trying to contain a growing smile.

"Thomas, let me explain," Marilena began. "Your enemies have always been men. The confrontations physical, direct, and violent. Most men seek direct remedies, even those who are not soldiers, and believe that direct confrontation is the correct course of action. Most often, by the end of the day, the combatant male parties can be found in the pub next door buying each other a drink. They punched each other, made their points, and got on with it. It's a generalization and there are exceptions, but this is the typical, simplistic male approach to dispute resolution, at least from a woman's perspective. These same traits are seen in highly successful female business people. They are driven, and there is no time in their lives for pettiness either. With some women, however, it is not this way. Because you have never had a woman as an enemy, you haven't analyzed us as potential adversaries. Again, we are talking generalizations, but most women can be far more devious than most any man. Suzie and her coworkers see it every day and recognize the behavior. There are women who never let a dispute die, and they hide their feelings and their plans with incredible duplicity, fooling their adversary into complacency. A normal male, if there is such a thing, confronted by a group of ambitious females as a peer or a subordinate, doesn't have a chance. To survive takes one with the skills that Suzie attributes to Omar. From what you have told me about Ron, he was never going to understand the sorority rules."

My thoughts about this were interrupted by Suzie.

"Look! There's Sylvia Canfield, a perfect example of what Marilena is saying," she said pointing her out with her eyes, making me leave my thoughts about complexity of the power struggle between the sexes.

A full-figured, middle-aged woman in a very bright green dress was speaking to an elderly couple while making tremendous gestures in the air with her hands. She was putting a lot of energy into conveying something to them. The hair she had piled on top of her head bobbed with each accentuated point.

"She's working the Caruthers over," said Suzie.

"Who are they," I asked.

"Their son and grandson have CID, and they're loaded. It's drilled into all of us to make the most of family members when raising money. Rich family members get big time attention from us," Suzie responded.

I guess the look I gave her was a little sharp because she followed up with, "I know. It bothers me too, sometimes. But, the society leadership tells us that if the end is curing the disease, then the means are justified, no matter what they are."

"What does Sylvia Canfield do?" Marilena asked, changing the topic of conversation.

"She is the Vice President for Chapter Relations. Kind of like a Chief Operating Officer for the external part of our organization, the chapters, and responsible for our relations with them. Did you know that we are organized into about seventy, geographically based chapters, each having its own charter, board of directors, and each organized as a separate not-for-profit entity? The chapters do most of the fund raising and interact with our constituency. This event is sponsored by one of them, the New York City Chapter, and everyone here from my office is a guest. The organization that Ron and I work for," she paused briefly with a painful look as she realized her error. "Sorry, that Ron worked for — is the umbrella organization that the chapters have joined. The chapters refer to us as 'the national.' We prefer 'the home office.' We take a share, just under half, of what the chapters raise and spend it on research, national programs, and the costs to run our offices and pay the staff. We're kind of like a clearing-house for research dollars. I think everyone agrees that it would not be efficient for each of the seventy chapters to have its own relationships with the prominent researchers."

"How do the chapters get along with the home office?"

Suzie gave us a devilish smile and said, "Not well at all. We fight back and forth all the time."

"Over what?" I asked.

"Everything. But the big issue that drives most of the underlying conflict is that they think that because they give us over a hundred million dollars, almost fifty percent of what they collect, that they should have some say about what we do with it. That we should be accountable for how we spend it. Don't tell anyone, but a lot of the rank and file at the home office agree with them, including me. The home office executives don't think that we should have to answer to them. It can get really ugly. We have more than one chapter planning to secede from the union. If one does actually leave, others will follow. It's supposed to be a secret but everyone knows."

"What do you think of Canfield?" I asked.

"I don't like her."

"Why not?"

"Because of the way she treated your brother. At first, they were close friends. Unlike his predecessor, who wouldn't travel at all, to any chapter, for any reason, Ron was always willing to help out anyone at the society. He jumped on a plane whenever he was asked to go to a chapter and explain all the good things we were doing in research and what we have learned about CID. He treated all the chapters the same. It didn't matter if they were a big money raiser or a small chapter in North Dakota. But at the end, Sylvia wanted more because she was behind the curve bringing in the money. She wanted him to ignore the smaller chapters and go only where the big money was. Worse than that, she wanted Ron to become P.T. Barnum. It was his style to deliver a balanced message about how far we had come in research but to never mislead. She wanted snake oil and was going to make him sell it or else.

"You see, it wasn't his commitment, it was his honesty. She flat out wanted him to lie about the progress being made and to make predictions about when we would have a cure. She would scream at him, and one time I overheard her yelling that he was the single biggest obstacle to the society's making its financial goals. Two weeks ago, in a senior manager's meeting where I got drafted to take minutes, she told everyone that he needed to be replaced with a team player. That until he 'retired or died' the Research and Clinical Trials Department was keeping the society from meeting its goals! She said it right in front of him! I wanted to slug her! Your brother saw how pissed I was and put his hand on my arm to keep me in my seat. He just smiled at her and didn't even respond. When I asked him later about it, he said that he hoped that everyone in the room knew the truth and that he didn't need to dignify her attack. She really hated him."

Marilena sensed my anger and warned me with a simple, "Thomas."

"I'll be good." I was going to make it a point of meeting Canfield. Marilena sighed as somehow she read my mind.

A PRESIDENTIAL PERSPECTIVE

We had avoided mingling during the entire, obligatory, thirty minute mingle period. With Suzie available to point out the various players and give us some background, the no-mingle plan had been a better option than stumbling from person to person and hoping for the best. An announcement was made that we should "Please move to our seats so that the evening's festivities could begin." Suzie launched us toward the stage at the far end of the room and in the general direction of the President's Table. She had not been to the President's Table, but she knew it would be up front, and as she put it, "a long, long, long way from us worker bees in the way, way, way back." She promised to look for us later.

Weaving our way forward with the initial influx of guests and society benefactors, we located our assigned seats at our assigned table in the area up front assigned to the overindulged pseudo-dignitaries. I felt like a sellout. I looked forward to meeting our server and telling him or her to call me by my first name. If that upset my dinner companions, then all the better, as it would reduce the odds of being invited back. The table had seats for twelve, and, surprisingly, we were almost the last to arrive whereas the tables we had passed had only begun to find their occupants. Apparently, if you are invited to sit at the President's Table, you want to make sure that you get there early lest some pesky varmint jump your claim. I wasn't sure why this was a concern as each seat had a name card. There was only one remaining seat to be had after ours. The card in front of that still empty chair simply read, "Alison Montgomery" in an oblique font; her husband, soon to be introduced to me as Mark Wilson, was already ensconced in the partner seat. He sat a little back from the table, in his place as the well-practiced subordinate, not to outdo his wife. Marilena had the seat next to him. I had not connected with Montgomery's assistant to provide Marilena's name. Her card read, "Colonel Briggs's Dinner Companion." That seemed to be the high-society equivalent of "A Player to be Named Later."

Marilena was gracious and engaging, making introductions on her side of the table while I worked mine in a less gregarious manner. As I had anticipated, Marilena's arrival had given the male guests at the table, even one octogenarian, a reason to appreciate the event. Their spouses seemed decidedly less happy, failing in their efforts to hide this behind forced smiles. One woman elected not to even go this far — no smile, but a significant glare at her husband who was intent on mentally mapping Marilena's form through the diaphanous dress. If she wore it again I should probably make it a point to keep a nitroglycerin pill or two on hand.

Marilena introduced me as *Doctor* Thomas Briggs. She was making sure that everyone understood the connection between the recently deceased Doctor Briggs and me, and, ever the sleuth, studying them with super special FBI skills as they reacted to my relationship with Ron. I have been with other dates whose motives, which I will never understand, were more along the lines of "my date is a doctor" as if she had just landed the biggest game fish on the boat. Knowing more than my share of doctors, along with the fact that had they let me in the doctor club, kept me from being quite so impressed. Marilena was certainly above that. I'm pretty sure about that. At least I think I'm pretty sure about that. Then again, before the introductions began, she had grabbed my hand and hadn't let go. Claim of title demonstrated to the other ladies — significant disappointment among the men.

The others at our table were a mixed bag. I'm sure that each one had his or her own personal story about what they had done, or more likely donated, to buy their seat at the big kid's table. I just hoped that I wasn't going to have to listen to each one of them. A waiter took an order for a round of drinks, letting me segregate my table-mates based on their selection of libation. The scale ranged from the serious drinkers and their bourbons and scotches to the frivolous imbibers ordering pina coladas, cosmopolitans, and other corny tourist tipples. A couple of the women were in category "A," giving me a reason for hope. I found it easier to remember them by their drink than by their name.

Marilena ordered sparkling water — she would not be categorized.

At present, the lights dimmed, and the orchestra that had been providing the background music broke into something dramatic and with considerably more volume. A spotlight stabbed out in the new darkness and defined a lectern on the stage less than twenty feet away. We waited for an entrance by some imposing figure, commensurate with the light and sound show. Television monitors had been set up. The lectern and the empty space above it were reproduced on two fifty-foot screens suspended in the air above the stage framing the speaker position.

The figure that rolled across the stage was a little disappointing. I was just able to determine that the movement in the still darkened areas of the stage belonged to a male human. This particular specimen was only about five feet in height. He was, however, also seemingly five feet in width. When he appeared in the spotlight, he squinted, blinded by its intensity. He looked for and found the teleprompter. He had worked up a sweat. Our speaker was round, hot, sweaty, and blind.

Mark Wilson leaned behind Marilena and over towards me. He said quietly into my ear as I bent in his direction, "That small dirigible is Woodrow Standish. He's the Chairman of the National Board and the one who led the team that selected Alison as President." I nodded, indicating that I had heard him and appreciated the help. He paused, backed away six inches, grinned, and looked into my eyes. "However, I can't help but think of him as Chubby Woody." In the low light I could see him grin widely. As his new co-conspirator, I involuntarily responded in kind. Chubby Woody, the Society "Round Boy," would forever be how I remembered him.

Chubby Woody, his eyes finally adjusting well enough to read the teleprompter, said, "On behalf of the CID Society, I would like to begin by thanking all of you for joining us tonight." He continued with the usual introductory comments about the "special evening" in this "special city," surrounded by "special people" and "coming together to fight mankind's most devastating diseases," so much for the other chronic maladies. He was long winded and liked to hear himself. He enjoyed the spotlight even if it was causing him to soak himself in even more sweat. It was, however, when he got to his real objective, introducing Alison Montgomery, that it got interesting and a little bizarre. He went beyond the normal platitudes and reminders about how fortunate we were to have Alison Montgomery as our society's president — he fawned and he gushed to the point of being inappropriate. The adjectives he used to describe Alison Montgomery quickly moved beyond those that one would use to describe a professional and became personal, just short of intimate. I could feel Wilson's body stiffen one vacant seat away from me, as Chubby Woody publicly adored his wife. Even in the dimly lit room, I could see a smirk or two at our table. A couple of people gave each other knowing looks as if sharing an inside joke, laughing at him and his fantasy. Wilson, hiding embarrassment, retreated away from me. Finally, and to the relief of many, it ended. Chubby Woody spoke her name with reverence, turned, and waddled off stage.

A new selection of music began softly and then got progressively louder, announcing the entrance of the President of the CID Society. Unlike Chubby Woody's appearance across the mostly dim stage, several banks of brilliant white lights erupted. A curtain was drawn from two sides and a gowned, regal figure in white, flaxen hair framing a tanned face, glided into view and floated at a moderate pace across the stage to the lectern. Instead of stopping behind it, she moved in front of the small speaker's stand. She must have been wired for sound as there was no microphone. From this closer vantage point, and due to the positioning of the teleprompters, it was obvious, maybe intentionally so, that she was going to speak to us extemporaneously or from a memorized set of remarks.

"We join together again," she began solemnly, both arms rising up from her sides, reaching her audience, "united by our passion and our hope. Our loved ones look to us to end their pain, their loss of humanity's most basic endowments. Driven to succeed against any obstacle, we are blessed with good fortune. To use this gift, our blessing of vitality and health for them without the slightest hesitation. And we will. Anything less is unacceptable to you, my friends and my partners in this noble quest." Her head lowered slightly, her arms returned to her sides.

Her skills at working a room of this size were impressive. Her words were visibly affecting those in the room. She had absolute dominion over her audience. I had seen this before. I don't think that it's something you can be taught — either you're born with it or you're not. It is the ability to reach each member of an audience, even in a large gathering like this, on a personal level. It is in part due to the words, but more so due to the delivery. Intense, focused passion genuinely heartfelt and delivered with laser-like accuracy. It did not allow for skeptics, enlisting the believers whose palpable reactions would drive skepticism out of anyone else's mind.

Her next message intensified the room even more as implausible as that could be.

"I think of all of you first as my friends, fellow travelers in our quest. We are conjoined by our cause, our determination, and our action. We will not be defeated.

"I want to thank all of you who have reached out to me at this time of personal pain. For those of you who have not heard, my sister's CID has worsened, and the enemy I fight with every breath, will soon take her from me."

A gasp, a collective rebuttal, filled the room.

"She asked me to share with you her love, her understanding of the tremendous work that we have accomplished knowing that when we complete our mission, AND WE WILL, it will be too late for her."

The audience became even more agitated, some in emotional distress. Glancing quickly around my table, I did not see many dry eyes with the noticeable exception of Mark Wilson; his face set in firm resolve. Now I understood her motivation, her drive to lead this fight. I had a tremendous personal experience with a sibling who had kept me in his life, dedicating his time and talents, never wavering, always there for me. Alison Montgomery, although clearly an accomplished showman, was motivated from the heart, a force not to be denied.

She continued after letting her initial words register to their full impact. "This night is a test. A test not just for me, but also for us as a family. For in addition to my personal trials, we have among us someone else who has suffered greatly and needs us, needs our strength. It was my sad duty almost ten days ago to report to you the death of a great man. A man who was a personal hero to me and to everyone who knew him. For those of you who have not been told, we have lost Dr. Ronald Briggs, the leader of the Society-initiated efforts to end CID. The authorities tell me that Ron's death was a suicide. Hearing this news, that my dear and trusted friend had taken his own life, was the worst moment of my life. When I lose Claire, my pain at that time will have had an equal predecessor. For Ron to have had problems that forced this solution upon him must have been a terrible burden beyond anything that I could have withstood. He was so strong, so resolute. I have tremendous guilt over not knowing the demons that chased him from me. I would have done anything for him. It is, however, selfish of me to make anyone think that mine is the only loss. Sitting at my table is Ron's brother, Tom. Tom is someone that Ron spoke of often, to me, to many of you. Someone that Ron was so very proud of. Someone that I very truly wanted to meet someday — just not meet on this day."

She looked my way. I felt the room share her intensity. And then, everyone else diminished until it was just me and Alison Montgomery. The only incursion, a welcome one, was Marilena's hand that had reached under the table and found mine. Her grip tightened, sensing what was to come.

As if we were the only two present, tears welling in her eyes she spoke with difficulty, "Tom, I am so sorry. I will try to be a better friend to you than I was to your brother. I failed. I failed you both."

I believed her. Everyone in the room believed her. I hadn't known about her sister. Now I understood. I understood why Ron had followed her, why he believed in her. I had an ally to help me find Ron's killer. Alison Montgomery would soon come to know what I knew — what I knew with a total and complete certainty. I would make her know. Her guilt about Ron would convert to energy. She would become the insider that Marilena and I needed.

UP CLOSE AND PERSONAL

Alison Montgomery's brief but incredibly effective address concluded. She was rewarded with applause well beyond what I would have expected from a high-society event. As the lights came up for dinner, many in the room looked in the direction of our table trying to identify me and then spoke intently to their neighbors while gesturing in my direction. Montgomery exited the stage back through the curtains and reappeared from a side door near us. She walked across the dining area to our table, pausing several times to greet someone along the way. Much to my relief, renewed focus on her made me old news.

By the time Alison Montgomery arrived, the servers had already placed small salads in front of everyone at our table. She moved next to me first. I stood, and she took my offered hand.

"Thank you again for coming tonight," she said with the sincerity motor turned to high, her expression a natural state for her, designed to make me feel special.

I responded, "Thanks for the invitation and for making room for us at your table. I'd like to introduce my date. This is Miss Marilena Rigatti. Marilena. Alison Montgomery," the last part as awkward as it was unnecessary because I didn't know her well enough to introduce her to anyone. I had used the "Miss" prefix as Marilena had asked me to do so in the past. There's no "Ms." equivalent in any of the languages, other than the "American" English that Marilena speaks. If given the slightest chance, she would tell you what she thought of "Ms." It's better not to. It's not pretty.

The two women sized each other up, both working hard at not appearing to do so, neither missing a single detail. Marilena had not risen. From her seat she held Montgomery's gaze. Speaking to the two of us, Montgomery continued, "I hope that both of you enjoy a very special evening and have the opportunity to meet many of our wonderful benefactors."

I nodded a response while planning to do anything but that. Marilena cocked her head slightly and answered in her accented voice, "It is such a lovely event in support of something so important. It must be wonderful to combine evenings like this with work that must be so personally rewarding."

Montgomery said, "Yes, I am very fortunate. But the best part of my life is that my position lets me meet so many amazing and generous people." Her emphasis to me, however, seemed to be on "her position" and not the "amazing and generous people." Or, maybe, I was just hearing her the way I wanted to, being the skeptic that I am. She returned her attention solely to me. "Tom, I am so glad that you could come tonight to see firsthand our commitment and meet some of the society's supporters. Before you leave New York, could we meet in my office? Even better, tomorrow we are having a council meeting. That's our senior management team. Ron was an integral part of that group, and I would like you to meet the people who worked closely with him leading our organization. It is very much my hope that we can maintain the strong relationship with your family that Ron brought to us." Would she be genuinely surprised to discover that I was all that was left of Ron's family?

I answered in the affirmative but with a neutral voice. We'd meet. I'd come to her council meeting. But she would learn that she wasn't the only one with an agendum. She might be a little pompous for my taste, but given her sister's affliction, I was sure that she was a true believer. I was going to use that to gain her involvement, to rid her beloved CID Society of a killer. Lacking a conscience lets me make decisions like this to use people with no loss of sleep whatsoever. She smiled and let go of my hand as she turned to the next couple. She invited us all to begin eating while she ignored the first course and spent some special time with each person at our table. I imagine that one downside of her job was that social events set around a meal might leave her hungry. The others at the table started to interact among themselves giving Montgomery, and whomever she was speaking to, a little pretend privacy as she revolved around the table. After about twenty minutes, she had completed her circumnavigation and was seated next to her husband. Salads long gone, entrée-cooling, husband bored.

The dinner was better than most of these mass-eating events. To their credit, the Plaza chefs had turned out a lot of food without making it taste institutional. WESTPAC needed to steal a couple of their guys and get things turned around at Yokosuka. Surprisingly to me, the conversations between those at my table were not about anything to do with CID. Everyone was more interested in talking about casual events in their lives and renewing acquaintances. I spoke briefly with a couple of people at the table, but for the most part, including Alison Montgomery, they seemed far more interested in Marilena than in me. If nothing else, a demonstration of good taste.

An elderly lady whose name I had already forgotten started the collective probing. I leaned back in my chair to watch the show.

"My dear, your accent is lovely. Where in Italy are you from?"

"Actually, I'm only part Italian and have spent much of my life in other parts of Europe. My paternal grandfather was from Tuscany, but he moved to the Basque area of Spain where he met and married my grandmother. My mother's family is from France, where they work hard at denying that they emigrated from Romania; rumor has it as gypsies and circus people, no less." Giving me a slightly disdainful look including a small roll of the eyes, she continued. "Thomas refers to me as a Euro-mutt." I immediately received several feigned, or maybe not so feigned, looks of disgust.

"I have offered to upgrade you to Euro-mongrel several times," I earnestly countered. Enough people laughed, including Marilena. I had avoided being drawn and quartered for the moment.

The blue-haired matron maintained her position as chief inquisitor by purposefully avoiding the laughter. She proclaimed to Marilena, "Carson and I have traveled extensively in Europe. I was having some trouble reconciling your accent with your family name. I do hear the lovely French influence intermingled with the Castilian now that I am not just listening for the Italian." Yeah, right. I was having some difficulty not laughing out loud at her sophistry. One of the little things that I had teased Marilena about was that her accent seemed to change, representing different coastal Mediterranean countries, both north and south, as it suited her or helped her work in some situation or another. She has denied this every time I bring it up, but I swear she sounds different talking to the French chargé d'affair than to a Libyan emissary.

After some additional, gentle interrogation, it was determined that my date was an exotic beauty that I did not deserve. No argument. One of the men said that she needed to "trade up" and offered to help out which earned more laughter from everyone except his wife and from Marilena, who didn't understand the colloquialism. I told her that it meant that she was extremely fortunate to have me as her escort. I was soundly rebuffed. A mob, even a small mob, can be an ugly thing.

Dessert arrived only to be overtly pushed aside by the figure-conscious ladies. I smiled at that as some of the old gals must have just this very moment given up dessert — prior to tonight it had been a staple of their diets. Good for them.

Marilena turned to me and said, "You promised me a dance. Several."

I was sure that I had not. I was even more certain that I would lose this battle. We excused ourselves and headed for the dance floor.

"Don't you think I will look insensitive dancing with you after Montgomery's public oratory about the magnitude of my recent loss?" I asked with faked sincerity.

"You will never look insensitive dancing with me. If you dance with anyone else, then you will look insensitive."

Before I could ask what that meant, we were on the floor and doing the adult slow dancing thing. At least this form of dancing offered the benefit of physical contact — a definite tactical enhancement if you are trying to move the relationship to a baser level. This was not my plan tonight so I was going to behave strictly in a brotherly kind of way. Marilena moved toward me and slipped under my arms. The adult slow dancing thing doesn't require skill or much locomotion about the dance floor. My plan was to use this to my advantage so we could talk privately. Marilena had her own plans.

"What do you think of Montgomery and her husband?" I asked.

She reached up and placed her index finger vertically on my lips. "We can talk later," she whispered and then pressed herself more closely against me, this time her head against my shoulder, taking my hands and moving them to slightly more intimate places, just this side of inappropriate. So much for my plans. She swayed slowly with me, lost in her own world. Even if I had the skill to read minds, I would have been afraid to eavesdrop on her thoughts. I had no thoughts. At least not any I would acknowledge.

Then, out of the corner of my eye, I saw her coming. It was Chicken Woman. Moving our way, a determined look — a woman on a mission. Uh oh. Not only was she focused on me, but she had also seen me recognize her. The determination modified with a large, artificial smile that required significant energy to maintain. As she got closer, she walked into better lighting. Her hair, dyed for the event, was a slightly different shade of red than before. It was now a shade of red not found anywhere in nature.

I stiffened and brought Marilena back to Earth by saying, "Trouble. Margaret Townsend, my eleven o'clock, thirty-five meters, incoming."

"Oh, she wants to talk to you, I am sure of it," Marilena said sleepily. A total lack of concern.

"Well, I want to talk to her too. But not now, not here. When I'm ready. I'll just ignore her."

"That won't work." More singsong sleepiness from my supposedly grown up date, the note of her voice rising as she spoke each word in the short sentence.

"Sure, it will."

"Thomas, is she still coming our way?"

"Yep. Right at us. I'm trying not to look."

"She plans to cut in — to dance with you. Then she can talk and you can't get away. Women do it all the time."

Holy shit! I was cornered. This was bad. "You're kidding?" I choked out. "I don't want to dance with her!" It was time to go on the offensive. I stopped moving and said with no small amount of determination, "All right then, I'll just straighten her out right now."

Marilena didn't let go. Instead, she leaned slightly away and looked up at me. "If we are going to get some cooperation from these people, it will not help to have been in a public altercation with one of their executives." Then, after a brief pause, she quietly continued, "I can prevent this. Do you want me to keep her away without making a scene in front of these very civilized society patrons?" she asked, her demeanor calm, a mildly quizzical look on her face as if she didn't care how I answered.

She was right. Starting a war wasn't going to help. If she had a way out, I was all for it.

"Yeah, sure, anything." I was desperate. It showed.

"Do you trust me?"

Strange question. "Of course. You're smoother at this stuff than I am. Do what you have to do."

"Tell me when she gets to within five meters of us," Marilena instructed, never yet having seen Chicken Woman, still so calm that she seemed barely awake. Whatever she was planning, she wasn't having any pre-combat nerves.

"Soon," I said. "Twenty feet. Now."

On cue, Marilena reached up with her right hand quickly putting it behind my neck. Without warning, she pulled my head down toward hers and before I knew what was happening, she kissed me. She kissed me hard. I think she kissed me with more intensity than anyone ever had before. She had gone from dreamy, sleepy sounding, slow moving, and too-close-dance-partner to tigress. Her entire body involved in the act. Holy shit, again! She briefly broke lip contact and implored, "You need to help," and then resumed what I hoped was an act with the same level of energy. I can be slow, but eventually I got it. I pulled her in hard and kissed her back. She ratcheted up the steam factor by opening her mouth and by sliding my left hand, the one not hidden by our bodies, up from her waist and alongside her right breast. She twisted slightly, naturally, completing the maneuver causing a more intimate contact between her insufficiently covered body and my hand. To an observer, it would look like I had made the move. Had I?

In my peripheral vision, I could see that Chicken Woman had stopped dead in her tracks. Her mouth fell open; the fixed smile gone. After about four long seconds during which her breathing seemed to have ceased, she turned quickly and marched away even faster than she had come toward us. Marilena's ploy had worked.

Marilena managed a quiet warning, "Don't stop, she might be watching." So, I didn't. And for a moment, maybe a long, long moment, I allowed myself to take a dangerous step. I enjoyed the woman, the closeness, and the intimacy of the moment. Finally we slowed down, and I worked to get my breathing under control. Marilena looked at me and laughed quietly. She said, "Thomas, I told you I could handle it." To my distress I noticed that my hand was still holding her breast. I jerked my hand quickly away. She laughed at me again.

So much for brotherly dancing.

INTRUDER

I kept my promise to Ricardo. We were headed back to the condo in limo-enabled security, the dangers of the horse-buggy death trap, successfully avoided. Between Marilena fending off unwanted dance partners and Ricardo providing secure transport, I was the safest person in Manhattan. This, however, discounted the fact that I was allowing myself to get closer to the only woman I had ever thought of as dangerous to me, to the life I had crafted and did not want to see changed. My previous relationships with every other member of the fairer sex had been on my terms — I knew that at some point I would move on. I had no worries about walking away, and with each of them I did. With Marilena, it would have been different. I had been absolutely certain about this and my opinion had not changed.

Earlier, after scaring off Townsend, she had immediately returned to her sleepy, contented dance posture as if nothing had happened. I was very aware that something had happened and could only manage two more songs on the dance floor. She had a tremendous capability to compartmentalize her life. When she was focused on some aspect of her job, there was no deterring her efforts. I'd seen it often enough. It could be intimidating to watch. But at other times, like right now, she could put all of that in a box, the lid tightly in place, personal goals having replaced professional ones.

Noticing from across the dance floor that our table was no longer occupied, our dinner companions had drifted off to mingle with others not worthy of the Presidential Table. We slipped out and linked up with Ricardo for the ride home. He didn't need a twenty-minute warning. He had stayed, on the clock with Marilena's blessing. Little was said between Marilena and me en route as neither of us wanted to start a complicated conversation and not have the time to complete it. I needed to get my mind busy with something else, even though I was putting off a problem that I knew I should address now. I copped out and rationalized that there were other, more important, tactical concerns.

During the course of the evening as dinner date and dance partner, I had managed to come in contact with most of her body, leaving very few and those very small places untouched. Where was she was hiding the Glock?

"Where is your gun?" I asked Marilena, bringing her back from wherever she was, lost in her thoughts. She turned her head and looked at me.

"Locked in my suitcase under the guest room bed."

"What?"

"You have yours," she replied, a very reasonable statement to her.

"What?" I was incredulous. "Aren't you supposed to carry at all times?"

"Yes. And tonight, I assigned that responsibility to you. If I need to shoot someone, I am sure you will do it for me. I promise, I will ask nicely."

"What?"

Ricardo pulled up in front of the condo. Antonio opened the door. It must have been his turn to work the night shift. He was most pleased that I had returned the beautiful Signora unharmed.

When we arrived at the condo door, it was time to exchange gentlemanly protocol for one mandated by security issues. Touching her arm, I indicated that she should stay behind me. I opened the door as quietly as I could and stepped inside. The rooms were well lit by several lamps. I eased the butt of the Beretta up out of its concealed location and kept my hand on it. There was no immediate threat.

Moving from the doorway, I stopped in mid step — something was wrong. I'm not sure how I knew. Maybe my subconscious had observed that some item had been disturbed; I don't know. But, I have had this experience before and have learned to trust my gut without question. Someone had been here. Someone might still be here.

Placing my finger to my lips, the international sign of, "Please keep quiet and humor your testosterone-fueled and security conscious friend — PLEASE!" and hoped that my internationally traveled friend knew the code. Moving to the center of the room, gun now in hand, I listened for movement. The code either forgotten or misunderstood, Marilena headed for the guest room, she was going to look inside, ignoring the fact that I was the only one armed on our team. I moved quickly and got between her and the open guest room doors.

"Hey, no gun, remember? Stay behind me. Please!" I whispered. She gave me a small shrug and mouthed, "OK" in what appeared to me to be a little patronizing. I was going to have to lay down the law about tactical procedures. Either she would demonstrate to me some extra sensory perception that could consistently determine the presence of threats, or I would re-sensitize her to an appropriate level of urban assault paranoia. Her life may have been a diplomatic mission, but mine had not.

Suddenly, in my peripheral vision, I saw a figure, obscured in detail due to a baggy, hooded sweat suit, dash from the den and heading fast for the front door. I dropped my gun on the couch as I passed by it, gathering speed, leading my target, legs pumping, my body leaning forward as the intercept velocity increased. I launched myself at the running body and made a mid-air tackle, my arms surrounding the intruder, shoulder driving into ribs. He was medium height and skinny. I could tell by the lack of resistance to my inertia that I had fifty pounds on him, maybe more. We hit the floor together — he took the brunt of the impact as I had planned. The reason for the physical takedown and not a gunshot was that I wanted to question this intruder more than I wanted to kill him. I could always kill him later, no gun required. It was a small risk as I had not seen a weapon and even if he had one, a running, fleeing shooter is a poor marksman against a fast-moving target. There had never been a consideration to raise my pistol and do the, "Stop or I'll shoot" thing. They didn't teach us that in the Corps. When I point a gun at someone, that person should plan on getting shot — maybe several times — cartridges are cheap, pulling the trigger easy.

Getting quickly to my feet, I was a little surprised to see that my tackling dummy had as well, but he was staggering more than standing. Adrenaline alone had gotten him off the floor. The unarmed combat the Marine Corps teaches is not fancy, not some mysterious Asian art form. It is based on boxing, street fighting, upper body strength. It is dirty, fast and effective. A quick fist, thrust hard with full-body follow-through to the gut below his sternum was all that was needed. He was lifted off his feet by my blow and sailed backwards through the air, legs trailing. He landed hard on his butt, the wind fully knocked out of him, falling backward. The final sound was his head hitting the hardwood floor.

The hood still covered his head, but I don't think it had cushioned the impact with the floor very much. I climbed on top, pinned his arms with my knees, my two hundred pounds an effective hindrance to escape. I roughly pushed the hood back away from his face only to discover that it wasn't a he but a she. My opponent was a young woman. A painful expression surrounded by blonde hair, she was in her early 20s and attractive. I frisked her for weapons without objection. She was still an enemy, gender notwithstanding.

"I'm gonna be sick," her first words, gasped while her diaphragm was attempting to rejoin the civilized world. I got up and let her roll on her side. She made good on her promise and puked, the expected reaction.

Marilena looked distressed, "Someone I should know, Thomas?"

"Maybe. I'll introduce you just as soon as I know who she is."

She was clutching her middle still in pain. "You hit me!"

"Keep your hands in sight or I'll hit you again."

Marilena went to the kitchen, got a dampened towel and a glass of water. While she did this, I retrieved my gun, but I kept my eyes on our intruder.

"Why did you hit me? I feel like my ribs are broken!"

Marilena had returned. She said, "I'm sorry, dear; his manners are terrible." Helping her sit up, she wiped the girl's face and hair with the towel and offered her the water, which she accepted. I wasn't happy about Marilena being this close to her yet. She seemed substantial enough to do some serious harm. Though thin, she was tall for a woman. Watching Marilena clean her up, I knew that mopping up the mostly liquid mess on the hardwood floor would be left to me.

"Who are you?" I asked.

"Who am I? Who are you? What are you doing here?" she replied, some anger starting to build, and then she was gripped by a coughing fit.

When she finished, I spoke again, leaving the menace in my voice. "Answer my question, little girl. You can see that I'm not constrained by old-fashioned ideas about hitting and gender restrictions." She was getting a large dose of the bad cop. Marilena said nothing; her good cop constrained to personal housekeeping.

Her eyes widened, and she answered quickly, "I'm a friend of Ron's — Dr. Briggs. He's my friend. He was my friend," she corrected. "I'm allowed to be here. I'm on the list. Who are you? Are you on the list?"

"What list?" I said, forgetting what I should have remembered.

"The list at the desk downstairs. They gave me a key. Here." She fumbled about and pulled a key out of her sweatshirt pocket. I took it from her. It was the twin to mine. I didn't return it.

"Why did you try to run?" I asked.

"I saw you from the den. You had a gun! You scared me! WHO ARE YOU?"

Marilena answered for me, "This is Thomas. He is Ron's brother."

"Thomas? You mean, Tom? You're Tom? Yeah, I can see it from all the pictures that Ron showed me. You're the Army guy, right?"

"That could get you hit again," I said.

"What?" she recoiled, fear back, displacing the anger.

Marilena said quickly, "Thomas!"

She then looked at our captive, "Don't worry, dear, he won't hurt you again. All evidence to the contrary, he's actually a very nice man — you just surprised us. Let me help you. There is a bathroom where we can finish cleaning up."

I got paper towels and spray cleaner from the kitchen and mopped up the floor while the girl stuff happened in the bathroom. Presently, they returned and sat close together on the couch. The young lady obviously still viewed me as harmful, Marilena a potential source of safety.

Marilena began, "Thomas, may I introduce April. April June."

Looking down at the young woman, I said, "April June? Don't tell me. Your middle name is May."

She answered without enthusiasm — she had heard this question before, "Yeah, actually it is. My parents were high when they named me." She was serious.

Marilena gave me a quick look — she wanted me to let her do this. OK? She looked back to April, "How did you know Ron?" She hadn't started like I would have with, "TELL ME WHAT YOU ARE DOING HERE!"

April answered, "I came to return the helicopter."

There were a lot of things that she could have said. This, however, was one that I wasn't expecting.

"The helicopter?" Marilena asked, as if she had misunderstood her words.

I had already started for the den. Marilena would keep her from running, if she tried. The empty shelf, empty no longer. A model of a Bell Jet Ranger, green and white, "Cascade Fire Fighters!" in red metallic paint, emblazoned down the tail boom, rested in its assigned place.

Taking it down carefully, I carried it to the dining room and set it on the table in view of the living room couch and the two women.

April spoke, "I had it at my place, keeping it for Ron."

I started to say something, but Marilena shot me a look — it was still her show.

She probed again, "April, he asked you to keep it? Why?"

"I don't really know. It's not like I'm into remote control planes or anything although he did take me to the park a couple of times to watch him fly the helicopters."

"Do you know why he asked you to keep it?" the same question, a police technique, but repeated in a gentle voice.

"I really don't know, but he scared me when he did. First time I ever was afraid when I was around him. I wasn't afraid of him. I was afraid for him."

"Why was that?" Marilena said in a voice a little softer with each question, pulling April in, making her comfortable, trusting.

"He told me to keep it, and if anything should happen to him that I was to give it to Tom when he came to New York." She looked at me. "He wouldn't tell me much, just to keep an eye on the condo and when you showed up to give it to you. The only other thing he said was that if something did happen to him, I was not supposed to get involved. Especially not to call the police and tell them about the helicopter. He said that I would not be in any danger if I just gave the helicopter to you and didn't tell anyone else about it. That you would know what to do! That's when I got scared. But I did it for him because of what he had done for me. I called the security desk every day after he died. Yesterday, they said that you were here, that they had given you a key. So I came over with the damn thing. If I had known that it was you coming in, I wouldn't have tried to run. All I saw was the gun, and this is New York after all."

Ron had known he was at risk. He suspected problems. He had told her that something might happen to him. What he should have done was call me. I would have set the new Tokyo to New York speed record getting here. I would have had some special friends grab Ron and keep him safe. They wouldn't even have told me where he was in case I became compromised — I wouldn't have asked. Whatever the problem, I would have dealt with it and Ron would be alive.

Marilena stepped in before I could say anything in response.

"April, what had Ron done for you?"

April looked down for a moment and then raised her eyes, not to Marilena, but to me.

"He was my friend when I needed one. It's a little embarrassing. Ron met me where I worked, where I still work but not as much."

"And dear, where was that?"

"Playoffs," she said quietly.

"Playoffs? What is Playoffs?"

I let April answer, "It's a sports bar."

I wanted to hear more about this, so I tried a softer approach. "It's a little more than that."

"I don't understand?" Marilena, for once, was behind the curve.

April looked at me, so I continued, "Well, it does have a large screen TV, and they sometimes have it tuned to a game. But that is not the principal attraction. Is it April?"

She didn't respond, so I answered for her, "It's a strip joint in midtown. I believe that our new friend is a stripper."

"It's a gentlemen's club. I — am a dancer."

In an effort to deflect my insensitivity, to keep April comfortable enough to continue, my experimental, softer approach having come and gone, Marilena looked at me and said, "Exotic dance can be quite lovely, Thomas."

"Ron met you there? I can't see it," I said, not sure if I believed this or not. I was trying not to laugh at the image of my brother, Ron, in a strip joint, and at Marilena's characterization of it as performance art.

April smiled for the first time. "It was his first, and I think, his only time in a men's club, and it definitely wasn't his idea to be there. He had been dragged along by some rich guys who were supposed to give a lot of money to the place where he worked. You know, the CID charity people. He told me about it."

"And you were the lucky lady who singled him out?" I asked with what turned out to be not enough sincerity for April. She gathered some inner resolve and defended herself and Ron, with some occasional contempt for me sprinkled in along the way.

"Lucky in more ways than you know, mister. OK, I did a couple of lap dances for him. His friends put me up to it. He figured the only way out of more of them was to pull me off of his lap and into the seat next to him. Said he wanted to talk and that he would gladly pay me each dance not to dance anymore! It was kinda cute, but at least his buddies left us alone. We talked for the next two hours, mostly me talking. He just asked questions. I told him stuff that I usually wouldn't say to a stranger. It's not easy for any of the girls who work there to trust any guy, especially right away, but it was easy to trust him, and I wasn't wrong about that. After awhile, he told me that I was wasting my life at the club. I'd heard that before, usually right before I got an offer to go home with some guy who just wanted to make my life better by marrying me, but just for the night. To make a long story short, he talked me into meeting him after work — something I could have gotten fired for. We had breakfast at three in the morning. He told me to meet him the next week at the same time in the same place. I still can't believe it, but I gave him my cell and agreed. He gave me his number, too. I mean, he was, what, thirty years older than me, maybe more, and he wasn't hitting on me and I didn't know it, but I needed a friend, and he turned out to be the best. He made me apply to get back into college — I had two years left at the time, and now I have enough credits to graduate after this semester. He paid my tuition and went with me to register. Helped me get an apartment of my own, put up the security deposit. He never wanted anything back. Never any funny stuff."

She looked at me, her teeth clenched for a moment, and then she continued, "I kind of fell in love with your brother. I would have said yes to anything, but he never made a move on me. Now, he's gone." She started to cry. Marilena put her arm around April's shoulders and began to talk quietly to her. I moved away to give them some space. I believed April. I could see Ron doing this. He didn't tell me because he was worried that I might tease him. He didn't tell me or anyone else because he didn't want to cheapen what he was doing, that anyone might think he was bragging about it.

Leaving them alone, I went back to the table and the helicopter. It looked normal, nothing special about this particular bird. But there had to be something different. What message was he trying to send me? This one had the fire suppression tank with working bomb-bay doors and a hook for an external fire water-bucket. You filled the tank with some colored water that foamed for simulated fire drops. I remembered flying it and thought back to how the flight characteristics changed when you dumped the weight of the water by radio control. I went to the den and found the controller for the model. Turning the transmitter on, I moved the lever that opened the tank belly door. An object fell out onto the table and was partially hidden by the landing skids. A USB memory stick. The girls were having a quiet conversation and had not seen this happen. I palmed the little plastic and metal rectangle and slipped it into my pocket.

BITS AND BITES

After returning the model helicopter to its shelf and listening to the conversation in the living room, I thought I wouldn't be missed if only gone for few minutes. Ron's computer was still turned on and the familiar Windows desktop was displayed on the screen. I slipped quietly into the seat, removed the USB stick from my pocket, and inserted it into one of the two available slots in the front of the computer.

I kept an ear out for approaching female voices or footsteps. The computer speaker made a bong-like sound as the operating system discovered the new hardware device. On an intellectual level, the volume of the alert was too small to be heard from the living room, yet it had surprised me when it played. To me it seemed like you could have heard it in Vermont. The USB icon appeared, and after some expected Windows sluggishness, a directory was displayed with the drive's contents.

Unlike the cryptic stuff on Ron's office computer, the names of these files were more descriptive. Included in the list were file references indicating health science research and associated notes. There were word processing files, image files, and databases that were many megabytes in size. The file titles all began with a date. The date format was one that I recognized as one that Ron had used before. It was comprised of eight digits representing YYYYMMDD. Ron had explained that if you used this format, the files would automatically sort in ascending order. One interesting file about midway down the list was titled, "CID Genesis: Out of Africa — Executive Presentation, version 3.3." That would make interesting reading. To my knowledge no one had determined how CID had gotten started.

Study of all of these in detail would come later, but for now I had to be satisfied that these data would tell me what caused Ron's fears. Fears that had made him hide these data with instructions to turn them over only to me, fears that had prompted a forecast that something bad might happen to him. Working quickly, an email with all of the files on the memory stick was forwarded to my personal email account. Given the condo's high-speed connection to the Internet, this took less than four minutes after which I shut the computer down. It would be a mistake to leave the machine running given the still unseen list of people having access to the condo. I was going to take care of that as soon as I could. After removing the USB drive and putting it back in my pocket, I returned to the living room.

Both ladies looked up at me as I approached. I didn't want to talk about the helicopter or if I had discovered anything about it, so before April could speak, I asked, "How are you feeling? How's the head?"

She reached back and felt her head. "Ouch! There's a lump. I didn't know until I felt it just now."

"Let me look at it," I said trying to use my best doctor-patient, bedside voice. Unfortunately, my bedside voice is usually directed at subordinates in the military, and I have very little practice with the more genteel portions of society.

She looked up sharply at me, still not sure if I were on the side of the angels. Knowing me better wouldn't necessarily help with that. Marilena interceded on my behalf.

"April, Thomas is a doctor, a surgeon. Let him look at you." Her words were spoken with the right mixture of urgency and sincerity. April's anxiety level decreased but only slightly.

"You're a surgeon?" she asked, incredulous that the Gorilla that had tackled her could be a doctor. "I thought you were in the military."

"Yes and yes."

Producing my ever-trusty 9-volt LED light, I turned it to its highest setting. April started to turn away from me so I could look at the back of her head — I'd get there, but not yet.

"Let me see your eyes first," I instructed.

She turned back, and I shone the light into her eyes. Her pupils were an interesting shade of green, but more importantly, they were responsive and of equal size. "Does your head hurt anywhere other than the spot where it hit the floor?"

"No, and it only hurts if I touch it."

Placing my hand on the back of her head, I gently felt the contusion. I applied a small amount of pressure, and she flinched only a little. "I think you will be OK. It will ache for a while and might hurt a little more tomorrow, along with a couple of other places where you hit the floor — sorry again. If you start to have vision problems or feel nauseous, we need to get to an emergency room. I don't think that will happen, but just to be on the safe side, why don't you stay here tonight? Marilena can check in on you from time to time," I said, offering Marilena up for night nurse duty given that April certainly trusted her more than me.

"Thomas, that is an excellent idea," Marilena added. "April, we have an ample number of guest rooms. I have not slept in mine. You can stay there."

"All right. If you think it's a good idea. I don't want to put anyone out. Thanks. I don't have to work or go to school for three days, so I can take it easy."

"What is your work schedule at Playoffs?" I asked.

"Fridays and Saturdays. The rest of the week I get to be a full-time student."

Marilena led April off to her room. I could hear their conversation although it was a little muted. Marilena was doing her best to help April feel comfortable, and I could even make out some conversation about me in an effort to improve my standing.

My cell phone rang. The number had a 617 area code indicating a Boston call. Although I did not recognize the number, our home was in Boston, so I answered in violation of my personal telephone protocol.

"Briggs," I spoke into the device.

"Are you Dr. Thomas Briggs? Ron Briggs's brother?" an abrupt, female voice asked.

"Yeah. Who wants to know?" I replied a little gruffly. After all, she had called me and had matched the number dialed to my name.

"This is Dr. Caroline Little at the Marklin Institute in Cambridge." She was not in the least put off by my blunt inquiry. Whoever she was, she didn't care how I felt about her.

"What do you want, Dr. Little?" I asked. I said it without attitude. At this point, why waste the energy?

"Dr. Briggs, I understand that you are Ron's brother? Is this correct? I got your number from that airhead Suzie at your brother's office."

"I am his brother. And, I know Suzie well enough to know that she is quite capable and doesn't deserve the name-calling. I'm getting the feeling that even though I don't know you, Little, I don't care much for you."

She continued, ignoring my remarks, "Dr. Briggs, I was your late brother's research colleague. He would have mentioned me. I am calling because of a tremendous problem that he left me with. I am hoping that you can help."

No message of condolence, just an assertion about her own importance and an accusation that Ron was the source of some problem. If I hadn't been trying to find out who killed Ron, I would have hung up on this witch. As it was, I was having difficulty keeping my tongue in check, "I don't know if I can or can't. What's the issue?" I asked using an apathetic tone.

"Your brother and I shared access to a research database that was hosted by the CID Society. He told me earlier on the day that he died that he had updated his work with key components to a CID cure based on our joint research. I have been trying to gain access to his data since then. There's nothing there. There's no update. In fact, the entire database has been deleted and all of the archives. I still have my work here, but all of his data are gone!"

"I don't see how I can help you with that. Have you spoken with the society computer people?" I asked.

"Yes, of course I have," she answered indignantly. "That's the first thing I did. Those people are morons! They say that there are no data in the directory and never have been because there is no archive from the automatic system. But I know that there was. I looked at it all the time during the last three years. I hope that he had a copy somewhere else. I need you to find it."

"Dr. Little, I can't imagine that a body of work as important as you describe was stored in only one location. If you had access to it, don't tell me that you never backed up the database at your facility?"

"Well, of course I did. I'd have been an idiot not to, given that funny farm Ron worked for."

"Then, what's the problem?"

"Dr. Briggs, you are not listening to me, and I don't need another exasperating conversation today." For someone who needed my help, she had a funny way of asking for it. "I just told you that your brother had important information to document in AN UPDATE THAT HE SAID HE MADE. Your brother could be tiresome and difficult, but he was precise. He said he made an update, an update to what I already have. But there's nothing there."

"Listen up, Little. I'm not sure what I can do for you that my tiresome and difficult, recently deceased only brother could have done," I said with a little more volume.

"Don't be so touchy, Briggs. I'm sorry he's dead, and I'm sorry for your loss. OK? But this work is more important than your feelings. I believe that he made a real breakthrough, and I can't afford to lose what he discovered."

"I tell you what. I'm headed over to his office in the morning. If I get a moment, I'll ask. I'll look around his office and here in his apartment."

"Do that. When can you call me back?"

"I'm coming to Boston tomorrow afternoon. If I find anything of interest, would you like to meet?"

"Yes, if it's a good use of my time — if you have found anything." She was a real gem.

"I'll call you from the train. Do you answer this number?" I asked.

"Yes. It's my cell. I'll expect your call. I certainly hope you understand how important this is." Her last sentence lacked any discernible degree of confidence. Not that it mattered, for she hung up, and I didn't get a chance to reply. My brother sure had a talent for surrounding himself with headstrong women. Then again, it just might be a family trait. There's a frightening thought.

Eventually, Marilena emerged from the guest room, and I was very happy to see that she had her suitcase. If she hadn't brought it out, I would have sent her back to get it. I keep track of firearm locations and had not forgotten that her Glock was in her bag. April seemed like the real deal, at least her story was believable, but I did not know her well enough yet to have her in the same condo with me while having ready access to a gun — at least not if I wanted to get any sleep. If she were something other than what she said she was, a suitcase lock would not be a deterrent.

"Is she settled in?" I asked Marilena.

"Yes. I gave her a set of my pajamas to wear and helped her into bed. She was falling asleep as I was leaving."

Thinking of my appropriated T-shirt, I said, "You had a set of pajamas?"

"Of course. Thomas, were you hoping that I did not bring something to sleep in?" Her look was pseudo-serious while failing at containing a smile. She turned and walked into my room with the suitcase. I heard it slide under the bed. Although the door didn't close, I could hear Marilena changing out of her evening gown. I got a couple of brief looks at her in various states of undress as she moved back and forth to my closet. She walked back into the living room, once again wearing my Marine Corps T-shirt, Chesty in motion with every step. It was useless to comment, so I didn't.

"Thomas," she continued in a quiet voice while steering us toward the kitchen counter stools. "I asked April some more about her relationship with your brother."

"And."

"He had been paying her rent and utilities. She had been paying her tuition and expenses. She said that Ron had offered to pay for everything but that she felt her education would mean more to her if she worked for it. I think we should stay in touch with her, make sure she is going to complete her studies and not have to work more than two nights a week."

"OK by me. Ron was a good judge of character. If he believed that our calendar girl was worth it, then she was, or rather is. Anyway, with her graduation around the corner, this particular people improvement project is about complete and might as well get finished."

She lifted an eyebrow and asked, "So, Thomas, when are you going to tell me how you know of this Playoffs nightclub and what it is like?"

"I think I should tell you about what I found in the helicopter and about a phone call I just received," I said, dodging the question.

"You found something already? Someone called?" her interest in our case temporarily displacing her desire to needle me. What is it with women and their curiosity about strip joints and what goes on inside them? Maybe I was getting better at this, and that would be the end of her asking about Playoffs. Even as this thought came to me, I was already dismissing it. She might be diverted for a little while, but eventually, the topic was sure to come up again.

I produced the memory stick and told Marilena where it had been hiding. She took it from me for a closer look and asked, "Have you looked at what it contains?" recognizing it for what it was.

"I've seen only the directory of the files. It's research stuff and won't be an easy read. I want to study it in the morning. Whatever it is, Ron was concerned enough about it to keep a secret backup copy hidden with a friend. A friend who didn't even know what she was hiding. I emailed a copy of everything to myself."

She thought about this for a moment, looked at me, gave me a knowing look, and nodded. She no doubt had come to the same conclusion about the importance of the find that I had earlier. Having a smart partner saves a lot of conversation. After a moment, she turned to more immediate concerns.

"Thomas, are you hungry?"

"Actually, I am. I didn't get to eat much of my entree before you dragged me off to the dance floor."

"Poor baby. Such a terrible experience. Go change — I will forage."

While I changed out of the tux and into gym shorts and T-shirt, silently hoping that the tux would never see the light of day again, she found some cold cuts in the fridge and a chilled bottle of white wine. As I slid onto the kitchen counter stool, I begged off on the grape juice and opted for ice water. We talked some more about April and how Ron would have taken her on as a project an opportunity to make a small improvement in humankind would have been important to him. We finished our impromptu snack and cleaned up.

"You take the bed, I'll sleep on the couch," I said. "I think there is another set of sheets in the hall closet. I'll help you make up the bed; then we can get some sleep."

"Would you not be more comfortable in Ron's room?" she asked carefully.

"I'm not ready for that yet."

"Thomas, then do not be silly. A couch is not a good bed. We are adults and I promise not to bite. Come with me."

She took my hand and led me to my room, or rather, her room. She lived up to her word and never bit me, not even once.

NIGHTMARES, BOTTLENECKS, MOTIVES

I was falling. I had the familiar sensation that everyone who has ever driven over a short, steep hill in a car knows all too well. That feeling when your stomach climbs up in your body as you experience zero Gs and become temporarily weightless. I was falling face up, my back headed to the ground. I was going to die. I was going to die just like Ron. I hit the ground expecting total blackness, death instantaneous, no time for pain.

The collision with the ground didn't kill me, but it did wake me up.

As my eyes adjusted to the very early morning light, I was able to see my surroundings. I was on the floor next to the bed looking at the ceiling. The bedside and the end table projecting above me like furniture skyscrapers — a miniature commuter's perspective. My back hurt a little from hitting the hardwood floor after falling from all of twenty-eight inches. Marilena's face, framed in disheveled, dark hair, suddenly appeared above me changing the surreal nature of the scene and bringing me back to reality. She briefly studied me and smiled, "That is one way to get out of bed. But next time, would you mind leaving me at least one blanket or maybe the sheet?"

I looked toward my feet, and I saw that I was ensnared by bedding, having taken it all with me on my unplanned trip to the floor. I can't remember the last time I fell out of a bed. I can't remember ever falling out of a bed. What could have caused me to fall out of bed? I looked up again and, just maybe, I was looking at the reason.

The night before, as we had climbed into bed Marilena reassured me again that we were adults and colleagues and that she trusted me and I trusted her and that we were working and that it was OK and that the bed would let me sleep and the couch would not and…and…and...

However, after she pulled the sheets and covers up, she reached over and took my arm, pulling me onto my side facing her. Without letting go, she rolled away from me ending up on her side and then backed up against me. She kept my arm around her, pushed back against me one more time, mumbled something about being cold, made a funny purring sound, and within moments she was asleep. I'm glad one of us found it so easy to sleep.

Finally, I drifted off, girl hair in my face and her perfume too close. I think that through the night I had backed away a little every time either of us moved only to have her move against me again. By morning, there had been no more bed left and my last, unconscious retreat had ended in an un-lover's leap.

As I pulled the blanket and sheets off, I discovered another embarrassment. I had awakened in an aroused state that was made obvious, and not just to me, but by the tent pole that had erected itself in my shorts. Not an unusual occurrence for a guy in the morning, especially given the close proximity of a beautiful woman pressed against him all night.

She laughed and said, "I'm pleased to see that all of you is up!"

I quickly sat up. That turned out to be a mistake as even though it helped me hide the undisciplined member, it brought me face to face with Marilena. She kissed me quickly without warning, rolled out of bed, stepped over me, and said as she walked away, "I'll check on April." She started for the closed bedroom door. From my position on the floor looking up at her as she walked away, I could see that panties were not a part of the Marine Corps T-shirt ensemble. I had been awake for only two minutes, and I had already experienced all the sensory overload I could take for an entire day. I really needed to talk to her before I lost control. Today — I needed to talk to her today. The view, however, had been exceptional. I wondered what I would say.

I pulled on some long pants and headed for the kitchen. Marilena and April followed me in. I poured orange juice for all.

"You were right, Tom. I do feel a little more bruised than I did last night," April said to me.

"Sorry again."

"Don't be. We'll do better next time we meet." Both ladies laughed. The odds against me were not improving.

April promised to stay in touch and everyone exchanged contact info. She dressed and left, a big hug for Marilena and a quick, little one for me.

* * *

I showered and shortened the whiskers quickly before digging into the data. Marilena had been busy making up the beds and putting things away. She followed me with her turn in the bathroom and took her time knowing that I needed to do some reading.

The data on the USB drive told the story of a collaborative research project to find the cure. The theories and discoveries were carefully documented, and significant progress had been made. Irrespective of my current attitude about Caroline Yvonne Little, Ph.D., M.D., she was smart enough to be Ron's equal partner. The recent section, the one that was probably the data that Little was missing, contained six files including the one entitled: "CID Genesis: Out of Africa." The other files described Ron's identification of the gene responsible for CID and his proof. A drug therapy to modify this gene was suggested.

I opened the "Out of Africa" files that included a written thesis and a presentation to explain the theory to a high-level audience; just enough science to provide credibility, yet still easy on the laymen while not being patronizing. Reading the thesis, I was intrigued by Ron's theory and his explanation of the genetic testing. He had convinced himself that he was right. Although not my specialty, this was pretty amazing stuff, and apparently he had kept it to himself, very atypical for my brother — my brother the team player. What could have caused him to be so secretive?

The thesis started out by summarizing what geneticists refer to as the "Out of Africa" model of human evolution. Evolutionary theorists and geneticists tell us that we evolved into hominids from predecessor primates in a specific region in eastern Africa. We then speciated, that evolutionary process by which all new biological species are formed, and moved out across the globe over many millennia becoming various *Homo sapien* varieties with interesting names like *heidelbergensis* and *neanderthalensis*. And although all of the world's people share the same genus, specie, and are all a variety of the contemporary *Homo sapien*, we don't look much alike having further evolved into races identified with geographical location.

How did this happen? If we all started in Africa sharing the same DNA, why don't we all look like indigenous Africans? Where did white people, Asians, and Latinos come from? Even within Africa, different peoples look strikingly different, and Caucasians can easily be identified as to their country of familial origin. What happened in our racial evolutionary development that caused groups of people to favor each other in ways dissimilar to other groups?

The answer lies in a bottleneck.

Prior to the Lake Toba volcanic eruption in Malaysia approximately 71,000 years ago, the *Homo sapien* population had moved out across the world in a slow and methodical manner. Most movement was very limited in distance, maybe just up the coast or down the valley. Grab some more land to hunt and gather on. Fish the coast around the next point. This is not a lightning pace of migration; however, given hundreds of thousands of years, such a dispersion rate can still cover a lot of turf.

Geneticists studying various forms of animal life have given a name to any event causing a population reduction by at least 50%. They call it a genetic bottleneck. In the case of the human population, it is a Human Bottleneck. Often, whatever event, climatological, astronomical, or otherwise affects one species, will affect many others as the environment undergoes a sudden and radical change. Several human bottlenecks occurred between 2 million and 70,000 years ago, but we know of only one that we can document with any degree of precision. It occurred about 60,000 to 70,000 years ago. For the purposes of our discussion into the latent cause of CID, let's call it the Toba Bottleneck.

There has never been an event that impacted humans like Toba. When Toba erupted and killed off over 99.5% of the human population, large gaps were created in the physical distribution of people, leaving isolated, small groups. It would not take many generations for these pockets of humans to forget their distant neighbors or even know that they had counterparts in other parts of the world. There has not been a genetic human bottleneck since the Toba Bottleneck, disproving the existence of a single breeding pair, Adam and Eve, circa 6,000 years ago. Also during the time of, and for many years after a bottleneck, evolutionary process changes from its normal path of slow and moderate adaptation and selection into something very different.

Genetic bottlenecks cause variations between these isolated groups but not within them. If indeed we are all "Out of Africa," we look different because these small, isolated groups genetically "drifted" after the bottleneck. Genetic drift is an effect that causes some biological traits to become more common or more rare over successive generations. The drift might fully remove or make universal within the group this biological trait. Genetic drift has been studied in certain animal groups in modern times. The bison was reduced in number to less than 750 in 1890. By the year 2000, it had recovered to over 360,000, allowing scientists to observe the emergence of dominant biological traits and the disappearance of others. The cheetah has been hunted to near extinction. So much so that the current population supports such a limited gene pool and so little diversity that skin grafts from one cheetah will not be rejected by any other cheetah. Beneficial traits such as this will occur within small groups in just a few generations.

Coupled with drift is "founder effect." When a new population is established by just a few individuals, the population carries only a small fraction of the original population's genetic diversity. If by chance the seed members of the isolated group contain a statistically improbable number of red-headed people, red hair will become far more prevalent in the new population.

In many ways, these effects are highly valuable to any population trying to recover from a catastrophic reduction in numbers. Many of the results of founder effect and drift help the group in evolutionary terms quickly adapt to whatever change they have confronted. Should a mating pair have a biological adaptation allowing better resistance to the recently occurring colder temperatures, this will be passed down to their children. Resistance to disease, ability to eat new and maybe the only plentiful foodstuffs, and many other biological adaptations can quickly evolve. Some side effects of founder effect and drift that may serve no known purpose can change the appearance of one group from that of another. Within the group, skin color may adapt to the lack of sunlight while in another group melanin content may climb as a result of generational exposure to solar radiation.

Unfortunately, this change machine may also bring the unwanted. In one group in Eastern Europe, founder effect caused a genetic mutation responsible for CID. CID lies dormant in the species for thousands of years until a triggering event occurred setting it free. In Ron's thesis he refers to this triggering event as "The Year Without Summer." One of the other files had a name that referenced this. Ron's work, after identifying the gene and the time of its original mutation, led to the research he was doing on drug therapy to correct the mutation.

* * *

Marilena walked into the den. I had just finished the thesis and was staring at the wall, looking at helicopters and considering what I had read.

"What have you learned, Thomas?" Her demeanor again serious.

"Ron believed that he had discovered the cause of CID, its genetic location in the human genome, and had postulated a specific drug therapy to correct the genetic mutation."

"Are you telling me that he had discovered the cure?" she asked, her words reflecting her amazement at the momentous nature of the finding.

"Yes. Or at least he got close enough that a cure would have been very probable in the near future."

"Why did this discovery motivate someone to kill him?" she asked.

She was ahead of me; I hadn't gotten there yet. I was still thinking about the science, the genetic mutation, 70,000 year-old volcanoes, and the ramifications of this discovery for people with CID. She was already looking for a connection between this discovery and a yet-to-be-discovered murderer's motivation. She was, as expected, on the right track. Motive had to be tied to his discovery. I knew of nothing else in his life that was this big, or this new, that might have upset some interpersonal relationship to the point of murder.

"Let's look at your suspect list again," she said.

I got it from the table next to the PC. She had made notes all over the list. She had drawn arrows next to a group of names.

"To begin with," she said, "I think we should focus on Ron's colleagues and, at least for the time being, ignore the employees of other companies in the building. Also, I think we should limit our working list to people near his position and not spend too much time on administrative staff. If we are looking for a motive, it will be professional jealousy, or greed, or some interaction with his peers — not a slighted mailroom worker or a chance event perpetrated by a stranger."

I looked at the list that had started with over a hundred names and let my eyes settle on the names she had marked. Fitting her criteria, the following people had been extracted from the original eleven highlighted in red and were identified by building security as having been in the society offices when Ron went out the window:

Omar Sayyaf
Jonathan Treece
Margaret Townsend
Woodrow Standish
Sylvia Canfield
Mark Wilson

and, catching me by surprise, highlighted in yellow,

Caroline Little.

A FAILURE, A SUSPECT

Seeing Caroline Little's name on the list was a surprise, and I blamed myself for the oversight. It made me painfully aware of something that I should not have missed, something that Marilena would not have missed. When Little introduced herself to me on the phone, I did not connect her name to any that I had seen intermingled with all the others, and it had no meaning to me the first time I saw it on O'Dale's list. Her reference had not earned a place in my memory. More damning was that during our phone call she had not told me that she had been at the CID offices the day that Ron died, only that he had told her about the update. My assumption was that it had been a phone conversation, given her Boston location and that her attempt to access the update had been via the Internet.

Seeing the look on my face, Marilena asked, "Is there something wrong?"

"I didn't get to tell you last night, but Caroline Little called me when you were getting April settled into the guest room."

"What did you speak about?"

"She called me from a Boston number and was a pain in the ass. She all but ordered me to find Ron's research data and give it to her. As much as I would like to find out that Margaret Townsend or Sylvia Canfield had killed Ron, I think that Little is ahead of them on points — she actually had a motive and neglected to tell me that she was at his office on the day he died."

"You think that she killed your brother so that she could take full credit for curing CID?" Marilena asked.

"It's currently my favorite hypothesis," I answered. "Winning the Nobel Prize alone beats sharing it."

"Then we need to find facts to support your favorite hypothesis. Can we meet with Dr. Little?"

"I've already set it up. We are going to Boston after our stop at the CID Society and will meet with her later this afternoon."

"You work fast. Well, at some things," she answered with a crooked smile.

"She's the only one I've met who had a motive. I want to get to her now. But first, Alison Montgomery invited me to a senior management meeting today. I want us to go there together."

She looked thoughtful for a moment and then said, "I think that we should continue to consider the others on the list. I also think that it is time to start applying some pressure. We may get a helpful reaction if the guilty party is among them."

I smiled, "I like that idea. Pressure. I'm good at pressure."

"Thomas, just a little pressure now. We will add to it later. If the killer is not Dr. Little and is one of the people here at the CID Society, we need that person to be a little nervous. Anxious people make mistakes while they attempt to keep control over a situation beginning to unravel."

"OK. What do you suggest?"

"Reveal me to them. Tell them that I am an FBI agent. That alone will turn up the heat. I'll take it from there and give them reason for concern but some hope because we will appear to be headed in the wrong direction. We need them to be concerned yet still confident in their ability to keep the truth from us. If there is a guilty party in the room, he, or maybe it is she, will not be able to keep from taking some action."

"I don't know about this," I responded, my voice concerned.

"You doubt my abilities? She asked, feigning arrogance.

I ignored the humor and got to the point. "If there is a killer here in New York, and he learns that you are more than a friend, even worse, an FBI agent, it could place you in danger. I'm not doing that."

She laughed, "You mean it could get worse than being run down in the street just because I walk next to you on the way to dinner?"

Even though she had used that incident to play it down, I considered what she had said as having merit. She was already in danger if someone came after me again. Collateral damage a real possibility.

"I just don't want you to get hurt."

She smiled. "I'm tougher than you think, and you are highly capable. If the situation calls for it, you will protect me. If you do not, I will complain to the Marine Corps and have them withhold two weeks pay."

"I'm serious, Marilena. This is not a part of your job — it's a favor. I appreciate what you are doing for me, but if I think that this is getting too deep, I'm going to put you someplace safe while I finish it. I will not be responsible for you getting hurt."

"Thomas, we are beyond that. This will almost certainly end with a simple arrest. However, if and when this becomes violent, some confrontation with your brother's killer, you will know what to do. Your probability of succeeding, however, will be much higher if I am there to watch your back. I'm not leaving you."

* * *

I packed my bag for the trip to Boston and went into the living room to wait for Marilena. It was taking her longer to get her clothes reacquainted with her suitcase than it had taken me. Then again, I am sure that when we unpack, her things will look less wrinkled than mine. I looked around and thought about when I would return here. Walking into the den, I took a last look at the helicopters. They were silly adult toys that had provided hours of fun for two brothers, brothers who while very close, were so very different. I'd like to fly them again but was not sure how much fun it would be without Ron. I made the decision to pack them up and ship them to Boston as soon as I could. I'd fly them again, but there, in Boston, not in Central Park. Not without Ron.

"Penny for your thoughts?" Marilena had come into the den. Her question was prompted by the fact that she had entered the room unnoticed — very unusual for me.

"Just thinking about what to do with this place. And, about helicopters."

"Helicopters?"

"Yeah. Come on, I'm hungry," avoiding the subject while walking past her, moving quickly back to the living room. I needed to leave the den. She hurried to catch up sensing the distress I had failed to hide.

"I want to go with you when you fly them. The helicopters," she said, hurrying after me and grabbing my arm.

She wasn't going to let me leave unsettled, angry. She waited for my answer, the first of many answers she wanted to hear.

"It takes dedication, serious commitment, to become an ace radio control helicopter pilot. Are you sure you are up to the challenge?"

"If you are willing to show me, I will do my best."

"All right." I took her hand. "I think that Ron would have approved."

She smiled. The big smile.

* * *

The bags were collected by Antonio and a helper. They took them down to the curb and loaded them into Ricardo's limo. While this was taking place, Marilena and I visited the security desk. I modified "the list" of approved people who could enter the condo. They acknowledged that I was the approved owner and controlled who was on the list. I eliminated everyone currently named and then added just three names: Marilena, Maryanne Straley, and Gus Perentanakis. Maryanne and Gus worked for our family at the house in Boston. Their help would be needed here at the condo at some time in the near future.

We walked to Arno's for breakfast, passing the sidewalk where the cab had almost run us over. The landscaping that had been uprooted had already been carried off and was being replaced, the incident erased, New York moving on.

Ricardo was waiting for us in front of Arno's for the drive across midtown to the CID Society headquarters. He helped Marilena into the limo. She was dressed in a conservative suit, the skirt a modest length. The transformation was interesting and another example of her ability to play whatever role was required.

THE COUNCIL

Arriving at the society offices, we were met in the lobby by Suzie. She had been assigned the task of delivering us to the conference room by Alison Montgomery. It seemed that Montgomery was not taking any chances on my getting detoured and having an incident similar to the one with Margaret Townsend.

"This should be good," Suzie said.

"Why's that?" I asked.

"They're only expecting you and not Marilena."

"Is that a problem?" I followed up, Marilena's face expressionless as she listened to Suzie.

"They don't like surprises. But it's not a problem for you. *You* are the gatekeeper to your family's cash. *You* can do anything *you* want." Then, with a mischievous grin, she said, "And, I am the minutes recorder, so I get to watch it all!"

We rode the elevator up and walked into the lobby. The same receptionist that I had pulled the vanishing act on was at her desk. I winked at her and got a giggle in return. Obviously, a fan of anyone who could put one over on Chicken Woman. Suzie led us down a hallway toward the society's version of Mahogany Row, that collection of expensively appointed offices that housed the senior staff. The fact that Ron's office had been in a different area and his workplace furnishings favoring function over style did not surprise me. He would have been happier near his troops and did not need to have a designer office lined up with the big dogs to support an ego. The Briggs boys had egos; it's just that they were self-supporting.

The conference room we entered was twenty by forty feet in size with a large, rectangular table dictating the room's purpose. A credenza at one end held the obligatory coffee pot and a selection of pastries that would go mostly untouched. The room was already occupied by members of the executive team, some that I already knew and a few strangers.

"Tom, thank you again for coming today," said Alison Montgomery moving toward me. Before I could get my hand out, she reached up and hugged me like a long lost and very close friend. I kind of hugged back, but without as much enthusiasm. I didn't know that we were on a hugging basis. She then turned to Marilena and without missing a beat said, "Marilena, I'm so glad you came as well." While she seemed sincere, all Marilena got was a handshake. Hugs were obviously intended for those of us higher up in the potential donor strata.

"Let me introduce you to the council," she said while turning to face the room. Starting from my left, and demonstrating her egalitarian nature, she said, "You know our indispensable Suzie, of course." She then moved on to each participant, the first being Sylvia Canfield.

Sylvia Canfield was effusive and had been waiting for this moment. "Colonel Briggs! I am so happy to finally meet you! Your brother used to tell all of us about his brother the Marine and all of the exciting things that you do. It is great to finally put a face to a name!" She was living up to her task at getting next to high net-worth donors, the enthusiasm in her words and the excitement in her body language palpable. She had a handshake that would hold up in any officers' club.

"Thanks, I'm happy to be here." My words belied my feelings about her based on what Suzie had told us.

Alison kept the intros moving along, and we shook hands with two consultants that I did not know, Barry Ledderman and Jonathan Treece. They were described by my hostess as so important to the mission that they were as much a part of he council as the rest of the senior staff. She then introduced us to two others, both new to me — Jennifer Covington, the Chief Financial Officer, and Cindy MacGuire, the Vice President of Human Resources. We reached the last one in the line, Margaret Townsend. Before she could speak, I jumped in.

"Ms. Townsend. Good to see you again!" She was on the other side of the table and a little way off for a handshake, so I gave her the friendly "I can't reach you to shake your hand so here is a wave instead." I continued, "This is my friend, Marilena Rigatti."

"It's good to see you again also, Dr. Briggs. I hope that you will forgive me for our misunderstanding when we first met. I am sorry that I did not know who you were, and I was only...."

I cut her off. "Hey, no harm, no foul." I was doing as Marilena had asked — not kicking any sleeping or mostly sleeping dogs and making everyone feel good. At the same time, I wanted to telegraph a little "even though I let you off the hook, it doesn't mean that I want to be your buddy." So I left her hanging by quickly turning away and back to Alison.

"President Montgomery, thanks again for inviting us. We don't want to hold up your meeting, so please begin."

"Thank you, Tom. For everyone else here, I invited Tom and Marilena to participate in our meeting today. I wanted them to see what we do as the organization's leaders. I hope that we can show them that we are good stewards of our donors' money and that we are dedicated to finding a cure. Given that, the reality is that we are running a large organization, and we have many challenges. I want everyone here to feel comfortable sharing the good as well as the bad. Ron, as we all know, was proud of his little brother, who by the way seems to be about a foot and a half taller than he was, and Tom as you have heard, he shared your adventures with our team, so I doubt that any problems that we are having will frighten you. I will be the first to admit that most of the things Ron told me about what you do in the military made me very concerned for your safety. Your brother was less diplomatic. He said you had caused his hair to turn white several decades before its time." This caused an appropriately conservative round of laughter.

She was very smooth, even though she bent the truth when she implied that she had invited Marilena as well as me. I smiled back and said, "Ever since I was ten years old, it was my job to worry Ron. I think that I did that very well."

Alison, with support from me, had managed to quickly get the room full of people to a comfortable place where we could interact. I had handled the exchange with Townsend and prevented a problem there. She had moved us from a business to a personal interaction by relating her experiences with Ron about me.

The agenda for the meeting covered several high-level issues about the society's direction. The only item that generated any real conversation was about the protocol for dealing with pharmaceutical companies. The position that Alison supported was that all of the pharmas had to be treated the same. No favoritism — 100% transparency. One of the consultants, Ledderman, tried to get her to bend on this. He believed that some of the pharmas rated more attention than others. His arguments made sense to me but not to Alison Montgomery. No sale.

When the call came for any new business not on the agendum, I waited a brief time for others to talk if they wanted to. Then I spoke, "Alison, I have an item of interest for your team, if you would allow me?"

"Of course, Tom," she replied but with a little concern creeping into her voice. Suzie was right — surprises were unwelcomed.

"As many of you know, a working hypothesis for the authorities has been that Ron's death was a suicide. Since my arrival in New York, I have interviewed police and crime lab personnel so that I might learn what they know. I am pleased to report that the authorities have decided to keep the investigation into Ron's death open. There has been evidence uncovered that does not support a suicide finding."

Apart from one small gasp from Sylvia Canfield, the room was silent. I was doing my best to look at as many people as possible and to discern reactions. I let only a moment pass before continuing — I did not want questions yet.

"Because of this and due to my personal desire to resolve the facts surrounding Ron's death along with my personal struggle about him ever taking his own life, I requested the help of a friend and professional acquaintance with significant criminal investigative experience." Nodding my head in Marilena's direction, I continued, "Miss Rigatti is an agent with the Federal Bureau of Investigation."

To say that I held everyone's attention was an understatement. The first to shake loose from the surprise was Omar Sayyaf.

"Miss Rigatti, you are with the FBI?"

Remembering us on the dance floor last night, Townsend spoke simultaneously, loudly, and redundantly asked, "You're an FBI agent?" her face incredulous.

"Yes, I am. I am assigned to the Washington, D.C., office." She held up the leather wallet holding her badge and I.D. card for everyone to see.

Omar was a quick study and had pushed aside surprise, "Can you tell us the status of the investigation?" His tone was that of serious interest but not concern.

"The inquiries that Colonel Briggs initiated and the forensic information he collected have reopened the case and established that Dr. Briggs did not jump to his death. He was pushed through his office window. This evaluation has been confirmed by the FBI's National Crime Laboratory and is the basis for a murder investigation."

Now she had everyone's attention. She let the words register and looked calmly at the meeting attendees as they simultaneously began to clamor for her attention: "What do you mean?" "You think he was killed by someone?" "Colonel Briggs?" "How can you know that he didn't jump?" She brushed off all of this, and when an opening in the questions came, she continued.

"The investigation into the murder of Dr. Ronald Q. Briggs is now a joint effort between the FBI and the New York City police department." Her voice was formal as if she was delivering testimony in a courtroom. "We have also determined a list of persons of interest in this case. Those individuals are located in Boston and New York. We are traveling to Boston today to continue our line of inquiry."

Omar, as expected, was the first to recover. He spoke, "You're going to Boston." A statement with an implication — not a senseless repetition of the previous statement. I was starting to like Omar, more and more. "Then you believe that your principal suspect is there?"

I won't say that there was a sudden, physical relief in the room, as if a collective mind had just realized that our investigation was headed to Boston. But you could tell that as a group, they were very focused on the fact that Boston was a better place to have a primary suspect than New York, especially because they were all in New York. Marilena had accomplished her goal of making someone think that we were headed in the wrong direction. That is, of course, if someone in the room was Ron's killer. Except for Canfield, the innocent players in this little drama wouldn't care as long as we found the killer. Innocent of murder or not, she wanted Ron out of the way. Now it was time to add a little more pressure, and Marilena did not disappoint me. Her next words hopefully the catalyst for some poorly considered move by Ron's killer.

To that end, Marilena continued. "Murder investigation is a process of elimination. If we are successful in Boston, we will report that back to you. If we determine that those in Boston of interest to us today had nothing to do with Dr. Briggs' murder, then we shall return to New York and continue our work. The identity of the person who murdered Colonel Briggs's brother will be determined."

Someone had to ask it. Everyone wanted to ask it. Omar, again, stepped up for everyone.

"Are you considering any employee of this organization as a suspect in your investigation?" His voice was even, unemotional, his inquiry professional and reasoned.

Marilena addressed the room. It must be something that they teach at the FBI academy in Quantico. She conveyed to everyone with her posture and her words total professionalism, total confidence in the ability of the FBI to uncover the truth behind any crime. The application of available talent and dependable technique would be all that was needed to solve the case. She even had an advantage beyond that of her peers at the Bureau — her accent made judging her veracity difficult, if not impossible, for her audience.

"We have not eliminated anyone, anywhere, who was associated with Dr. Briggs, as a suspect in our investigation. I am certain that we can count on all of you for your cooperation. His killer will be apprehended, tried, and convicted." Her words, statements of fact, defined the future and left no room for interpretation. Her delivery underscored the absolute certainty that those who worked in the house that J. Edgar built would always get their man.

THE THIRD OPTION

Most of the members of the council had recovered enough to wish us good luck on our trip to Boston and to offer their unconditional support. I noticed Alison Montgomery surveying her executives as they spoke. Maybe she was having the same thought that I had: In a situation like this, how do you determine if someone's behavior or facial expression is the product of an attempt to hide something or just a nervous reaction to being a suspect? I could ask Marilena; she would know. Alison probably didn't have anyone who could help her with that question. She was, however, certain to be unhappy at the thought of any of her senior team being involved in Ron's murder but was hiding her emotions behind a carefully controlled, neutral expression. As I had previously surmised, she would work hard to help me if indeed the killer was one of her employees. Her motivations were twofold: first, ridding her organization of some evil person, a killer no less, a normal protective instinct, and second, if that person did exist in her organization and she helped me find them out, then maybe I would help her minimize the public relations damage when it became generally known. She would want to have me in her debt so that when the killer was exposed, any comments sought from me would be positive about the society and limit my condemnation to one individual. Maybe I would even discredit the killer while lauding the society?

No matter what they were feeling, I was pleased. If the killer were in this room, we had poked a hornet's nest, and I was ready for the counterattack. If you're in this room, please come after me. Please.

Even though Omar had already volunteered to escort us to the lobby, Alison joined him, walking with us to the elevators. The remaining members of the council seemed to be staying in place and holding animated conversations. Nothing like being in a pool of suspected killers to provide for all the excitement anyone could ever want in a workday.

"Please call me and let me know what you discover," Alison requested.

"Sure. I hope get to the bottom of this soon."

"Nothing would make me happier," she said. And then, without missing a beat, the president of a VHA with important work to do remembered her organization and its objectives.

"When this is over, I would like you to consider joining our National Board of Directors. Not only are you the brother of someone who had dedicated his life to our cause, you are also a doctor who would lend so much to our leadership."

When she spoke, she reached you on a personal level. She was gracious yet had a fire, her eyes intense — they pulled you in. I surprised myself by not dismissing her invitation with some comment about waiting at least until we resolved Ron's death.

"This was important to Ron, and if you think I can make a contribution, well, yeah, I'll talk to you about it when I get back." Marilena looked at me, her eyes reducing to slits.

Ricardo met us at the front door on Third Avenue. We boarded the limo and pulled out into traffic for the short-by-distance, possibly long-by-time, trip to Penn Station across town. Making the next train would be close. There was another later on, but it was a local and would take longer to get to Boston.

"I can see why she is so effective in her role," Marilena said as we moved into traffic.

"Yeah?"

"She could convince almost anyone to help with her cause, even the most hard-core Marine."

"I kind of surprised myself with my answer," I offered.

"It did not surprise me. She is highly skilled."

"I wonder what she is thinking about her staff right now?"

Marilena responded, "She is working through her own list, eliminating some, giving others consideration. She will not be at ease until a killer is identified. If the killer was in that room, he or she is agitated. We were successful."

"You were pretty impressive, lady."

"I was about to complement you on your setup — very refined."

Now that was something I had never been called. Ever.

* * *

Ricardo had arranged for help with our bags, and we were met by a porter. We said our goodbyes to Ricardo and promised to see him again. I had paid him earlier in the day, and he was obviously happy with the rate and gratuity. I took an extra business card from him and told him that someone would call about engaging him in the future. He liked that idea.

I had made many trips by train between Boston and New York on both services offered by Amtrak. There is the local — it's a conventional train service that takes four hours and makes frequent stops. For a little more money, there is an express train that leaves a couple of times a day. Amtrak calls that service the Acela Express. It's worth the additional fare as it knocks off almost half the time of the local.

I knew the way from the curbside to the counter, but the porter wanted to lead the way, and I let him. I took Marilena by the hand and was happy to see that our bag pusher set a good pace — he had made it his business to be informed and knew that the departure time for the Acela to Boston was quickly approaching. He also made a good blocker with his hand truck and our luggage preceding him. We tucked in behind and made excellent time down the busy corridors. Marilena had to take two steps for each of mine and had to contend with high heels. The lady FBI agent, who had just recently commanded the attention of a room full of smart and ambitious people, now carried along in the wake of two less than sensitive males, one porting luggage, the other porting her.

When we finally arrived at the ticket counter, she blew out a big breath through pursed lips and said, "I will count that as today's exercise!"

I noticed that the porter had a very short haircut. I turned to him and asked a one-word question, "Marine?"

"Yes sir! Just discharged this summer after doing two tours in Iraq. I got accepted to NYU, and I start in January," he answered while straightening up, a reflex as he recognized me as a probable officer, my haircut and bearing all he needed to identify me as a fellow Marine.

"I figured as much. Good job getting us here double time and good luck in school. Remember what the Corps taught you — it'll help you in college." The tip I gave him made him happy, the recognition he had earned.

I purchased two tickets for seats in the first class car of the Acela that was due to leave in less than ten minutes. I carried Marilena's larger bag and pulled my smaller one on its built-in wheels. Crossing the expansive waiting area under the large departure information sign, we headed for the designated track and then down the escalator, Marilena behind me, carrying her smaller bag and a zip-up garment cover with the newly acquired dresses safely enshrouded and further protected by genetically driven, female clothing concerns.

We boarded the second car from the front. The train was OK by me, no TSA, and large luggage storage areas over the generous seats. I selected two of them at the rear of the car and intentionally maneuvered her to take the window seat. I stowed the bags in the overhead and slid into the aisle next to her. We settled in for the ride.

The car was almost empty, no one within ten rows of us — the taxpayers would be subsidizing Amtrak for a long time to come. As it was, we were alone and any conversation we had would be private.

"Thomas, how long is the ride?"

"About two and a half hours," I answered. "We can get some lunch on the train. We should be in Boston by 1 PM.

"I know that you want to talk about us, and I am going to make it easy for you."

"You are?" I asked.

"Yes. I know that you are concerned about us. About the relationship we were building, the way you set it aside, and what is happening to us now."

"Really?"

"I have thought about it and have decided that you have nothing to worry about."

"Really?" That was less than believable. Way less.

"When you said that we should stop seeing each other, your reason was that it was a problem because we worked together. That was only partly true. Your real concerns were greater and not professional."

"Really?" It seemed that my vocabulary had limited itself to one word.

She smiled at my inability to communicate. "The actual reason that you wanted to end our relationship was that you thought that I was option two."

"What?" At least I didn't say, "Really?"

"Yes. To you, women belong in one of two categories, no exceptions. The first are the little playthings that you pick up and enjoy for a brief period of time. They are easy to recognize. Very attractive, yet having an I.Q. in competition with their shoe size. Eventually, you always discard them as they quickly bore you. Bedroom activities alone, although initially an enjoyable pastime, in the long term, not enough. The second category are those women who would invade your life, make you quit your exciting and dangerous job, force you to become a husband and a father, and see to it that you mowed the lawn once a week. When a woman gets classified as category two, you run away. You thought I was a category two woman. The first couple of times that we went out, it was just to get something to eat while continuing to discuss work. After you realized that the meals had become dates, you ran away. Although I was angry at the time, I am no longer and have been waiting to talk to you so that you could understand something important about me."

"And that is?" Although I was curious about what she was about to say, I wanted to act like I had never thought about it this way. The unfortunate part was that even though I was not as articulate about the subject as she was, she was one hundred percent on the money.

"You are a lucky man, and although you have classified all women as belonging to just one of two categories, there is a third. I am the third option."

"What does that mean?"

"I am not some shiny trinket for you to pick up and play with until you tire of me. I will not permit that, and you know it. I am not category one. At the same time, I am not going to ask you to quit your exciting and dangerous job, become a husband and a father, mow the lawn, and paint the white picket fence. That would change you in ways that would make you less desirable to me. I will, however, invade your life. I want us to be close, have only each other, but I will not try to make you something that you are not. I like you just the way you are."

"Yeah? And just how do you see this working out?"

"Simple: Exclusivity, love, and excitement. Nothing less, nothing more."

BOSTON

We pulled into the South Boston train station on time. Marilena had changed the subject. She had not pushed me for an answer to her "simple" proposal. She knew that I was going to need some time to think this over, and patience was a better idea than forcing a response. That alone made her different. Every woman that I had ever met would have wanted to know immediately what my answer would be and most importantly: *Where did she stand?* For that matter, I can't think of any woman that I had ever known who could have waited this long without making her intentions not only known but also trying to find a way to make them my intentions as well. Maybe she was the third option? The third option? I wondered how many third options were out there? Had I met one before? Come back, Tommy. Focus Marine, focus.

Gus Perentanakis met us at curbside. Gus is somewhere north of sixty years old but could have passed for fifty. He had a booming voice, and his favorite expression for as long as I can remember was "B'YOOTIFUL!" It served well in two situations, ones that were actually beautiful and those that were the exact opposite. You had to listen carefully for the slight difference in inflection to know his intention. He had been in the Navy before coming to work for our family, joining his parents and becoming the second generation of the Perentanakis clan to help the Briggs get by, and by their account, we would have failed miserably without them. I had teased him that the Navy he was in used wooden ships pushed around by the wind. Ruddy complexioned, barrel-chested, and just plain big; he was the rock that Ron and I had depended on for many years. He has the look of the perpetually middle-aged prizefighter, never changing, a little too old to compete, too young to retire. Calling him from the train to make arrangements to meet us, I told him I was bringing a guest, a lady guest, who would be staying with us. He must have heard something in my voice and believed that a good impression was in order because he showed up in the dark blue, 7 Series BMW, four-door sedan that he and Ron had selected two years ago. I knew that somehow, through some business interest or another, we had paid for it, but he protects it like it is his own, and it doesn't venture out without good reason. No one gets to drive it except him and sometimes, rarely, me. Ron had given up trying to get the keys away from him. I'm sure that when I am out driving it, he's still worried about what I may do to his baby. An immediate and complete inspection of the vehicle follows my return. Subsequent comments can be heard about the dirty footprints on the driver's side. If I had arrived at the train station alone, he would have driven our pickup truck. I would have been fine with that, and he knew it. That says a lot about our history. He had been a great surrogate dad.

"Marilena, this is Gus. He's responsible for all of my bad habits. Each and every one of them."

"What? Tommy! Say it ain't so!" The words delivered in his loud, Boston brogue, might have indicated some unhappiness with me, but the big grin I got was followed by the look he was giving Marilena made me know that he was in the process of forgetting everything I had said.

"Hello, Gus!" she said brightly while moving towards him. He got the 1,000-watt smile and both hands from her to place in his. "Don't pay any attention to him." Ignoring the car but making a point of looking him up and down, she said, "I can already tell that you are a gentleman. Maybe some of it will rub off on Thomas?"

"I'd like to think so, Miss. I've been trying for a lot of years, but, well, you know. I mean, look at him. It's kinda sad."

"There's still hope. We can work on improving him together!"

"B'YOOTIFUL!"

They laughed. I shook my head, outgunned again. The founding member of the Marilena Fan Club, Boston Chapter, had just signed up and accepted a lifetime appointment as president. The newsletter wouldn't even mention me.

Gus got a serious look on his face and turned to me. "Hey Pal. About Ronny. Real sorry. Ya got no idea." The last part delivered in a quiet, seldom used voice.

"Thanks, Gus. I know. Actually, we're here because we might learn something more about his murder from a colleague of his at the Marklin."

"Murder? You mean it wasn't a suicide?" His eyes turned cold as they looked into me, wanting more. "I knew it! I knew it all along! You boys have been like my own, and I know you both too well. Ronny never killed himself — never! It never happened! Couldn't have!"

"I agree. More importantly, Marilena agrees. Marilena is an FBI Special Agent. We are going to find out what happened and who killed him." I wish that I felt as confident as I sounded.

"What can I do? I can help. Anything! Anything for Ronny!" His voice a mixture of emotions: relief, anger, resolve.

We settled into the back seat. I was getting more than my share of time in row number two. Driving, or at least riding shotgun, was more of what I am used to. Marilena was looking out the window as we pulled out of the station headed for Beacon Hill. She was happiest in row two.

"I've never been to this city," she said. "It's quite lovely."

"Boston is a great town. Lot's to do, great restaurants, amazing architecture, and if you're interested, the history connecting the city and the Revolutionary War is very interesting. There are also some of the finest colleges in the country all within walking distance. The best, of course, being B.C."

"B.C.?"

"Boston College."

"Ah, might that be the college you attended."

"How did you know?"

"Lucky guess."

"Across the river from here is Cambridge, home of the Marklin Institute. That's where we'll meet Caroline Little."

"Have you been there before?" she asked.

"Yep. The Marklin Institute had a grand opening, and Ron and I went to it. Ron made a donation in our family name, and we were invited. As usual, I wasn't excited about going, you know, the tuxedo thing. But when I got there, I was glad that I did. It's a very impressive place. Ron said that the gear was the best; the people that they had convinced to work there were the best in their fields."

"You sound impressed. And, by the way, I am impressed to learn that you have multiple tuxedos." I should have kept that part to myself.

"I'm sure that by now that tux has been donated to some worthy cause." Getting back to the important issue and hopefully leaving formal wear behind, I said, "The other thing about the Marklin is that the quality of their science is fantastic. They have selected real and difficult issues to work on. The Boston area is home to many fine research institutes but also to some that are not so fine."

"What do you mean?"

"The BioTech industry is primarily located here and in Northern California. The founders of these companies were often educated, or worked as researchers, in these two parts of the country. There is also a very talented pool of potential employees available, as well as investors who understand the risks of biotechnology. Many of these BioTech companies have discovered amazing compounds that they have made into pharmaceutical products, either on their own or through a partnership with one of the big pharma guys. Some of them, however, seem to be fronts for marketing firms and make me wonder how far we have actually come from snake oil and patent medicine."

"Really?" She was starting to sound like me. It was becoming obvious that a lot of our communication was based on this one word. If she could teach me the translation in three or four foreign languages, I could fake any conversation.

"Have you noticed that during the last couple of years, television commercials have been teaching, or rather preaching to us, about new maladies and syndromes. A practice that is legal only here in the U.S. and in New Zealand. The rest of the world considers it so contrary to the common good and it's a crime. We have "Chronic This" and "Irritable That." In the hotel in Los Angeles on the way to New York, I saw a commercial for a new restless limb disorder. Many of them get catchy acronyms to help us remember them. You don't learn about any of this stuff in medical school because it's made up by marketing firms. These companies have acquired some intellectual property that may have failed as a therapy for some targeted, real disease, but it showed a side effect that in some remotely arguable way is beneficial to someone. Then, they turned their unscrupulous lawyers loose on the FDA, and, low and behold, we have a new disease and coincidentally the perfect drug to combat it. Ask your doctor! Do you have restless limb disorder? Should you be taking Supernewdrugthatendsinexium?"

"Quite a soapbox, Thomas." She laughed and continued with, "I don't remember ever seeing you this worried about the population at large being hoodwinked by big business."

"I'm a fan of big business. All business — big, small, and those in the middle. I just don't know what I like less, stupid people or people preying on stupid people. And, it eventually all becomes the basis for the excuse: I can't do this, I can't learn that, I can't go to work — I have this terrible disorder. It explains everything, and I didn't even know I had it. You know, the one on TV? I'm on The Little Purple Pill."

"Thomas, such bedside manner! I can see why you have stayed away from private practice."

"I'd be the best thing to ever hit private practice," I countered, causing us both to laugh at the absurdity of that statement. "My patients would get a full dose of, 'I'll tell you what drugs you need, not some actor!' To hell with the 'The Little Purple Pill!' Drop and give me twenty!"

Abandoning my rant-voice for a more serious one, I said, "You know the world would view me as one of the big three."

"The big three?"

"Yeah, Mother Theresa, Desmond Tutu, and me."

From the front seat, we could hear, "Oh, God! Every time he comes home, I hope that he'd have changed! But no, he still suffers from being a Marine!"

"Hey, retired Navy, who asked you?" I countered.

"That's the best thing about me, Marilena. You never have to ask for my opinion. I'll always make sure that you get it! It's why I'm here. Ask Tommy. Always here for you, Kid!"

"I wish there was a drug for 'Lack of Marine Corps Respect Syndrome.' I'd buy it in case lots!"

Gus solemnly answered back, "I'm sure it's one of those drugs that I'd be allergic to!"

We pulled through the brick arch into the compound. It's what I always thought of it as — the compound. Ron had called it our home, and it was. But, it was also a big, big, brick and block house surrounded by a collection of smaller brick and block buildings, surrounded by a brick and block wall. A compound, a large expensive piece of real estate, in an expensive part of town.

Gus stopped under a portico at the front door. The remaining staff, all eleven of them, were lined up to greet us. They had been magically alerted as to our impending arrival — I hated this. They weren't troops for me to review, and I wasn't anyone's general. Besides that, I had either grown up with them or at the very least known them for over a decade. They were more friends than servants. Some of them had been more parents than friends. I didn't want any one of them to run to the door just because I had arrived. It was unnatural for me, and for Ron before me, to have grown into some kind of Lord and Master. At least Gus didn't take me too seriously. I wished that the rest of them would follow his lead — I didn't want to be the spoiled, over indulged, rich kid who grew up to be imperious and insufferable.

I jumped out of the car, pulling Marilena out behind me before Gus could get to the door and made sure that all knew that I was happy to see them again and glad to be home. Not being a normally effusive kind of guy, I had to work at it, hoping that it would come off naturally. They knew this. Each one acknowledged Ron's death in some way, and I was genuinely appreciative because the way that they felt about him was real, not just a show for the boss — the new boss. Oh, God, that was me.

Marilena had patiently waited off to one side letting me deal with the staff one at a time, recognizing what was happening and not wanting to intrude. After an individual exchange with each of them, I introduced them all to Marilena, from groundskeepers to housekeeping staff, and told her some little story or fact about each one and their relationship to Ron and me. I could tell that she was working hard to memorize their names and the facts about them. Little did they know that they too would soon be members of the fan club. It was only a matter of time before there would again be talk of her "trading up!"

We walked through the foyer and up the main staircase that curved up past large windows and was illuminated by a massive crystal chandelier. The chandelier was amazing in its size and quality. It was never dusty, yet I had never seen anyone clean it. I had decided that I would never know how they did that. Gus was directing suitcase flow. He forwarded mine to my room, where it would be searched for dirty clothes and removed of such, posthaste. He personally accompanied Marilena and her nicer looking luggage to the guest room down the hall. I imagined a velvet rope on brass floor stands being set up around her bags.

* * *

While Marilena unpacked, with considerable attention from two of the ladies who worked for us, I went back downstairs to the room I liked the most on the first floor. There were several formal living rooms, entertaining areas, and dining rooms on the ground level. I seldom went into any of them. The room I went to was different. It was tucked around back and adjoined the kitchen, a place that I learned as a kid was where tasty things originated that would be delivered by wonderful ladies to little, and later big, Tommy. It had floor-to-ceiling glass looking out onto a garden and the lawn beyond. I sat at a small table and looked at the package of paperwork that had been delivered by our law firm. Almost immediately, food and drink appeared. Dependable magic.

Most of the paperwork required my signature to become the principal family representative replacing Ron. I signed my name about two million times and made notes on a few things that I would ask the attorneys about. There were notices of board meetings with notes from our lead (and most expensive) attorney, about which ones I could ditch and which ones I couldn't. I'd talk to him about relaxing his definitions and moving some of the category B meetings to category A. It reminded me about my last conversation with Alison Montgomery. Was my life going to become an endless series of board meetings? The last document in the pile was a letter to me from a probate lawyer at the same firm explaining the basics of Ron's will. The original was attached for my review and returned to a place far safer it seemed than my personal possession. It was shorter than I would have guessed it would have been. The letter, and my reading of the will, seemed to agree that everything that was Ron's was now mine. The will didn't need to be long. The letter also assured me that the probate period would be as brief as possible — my mighty legal team was working diligently to move things along with tremendous efficiency. I wondered what the efficiency would cost?

Marilena entered the room. She must have been told where I was because you could spend considerable time searching the four-story house looking for someone if you didn't get pointed in the right direction. I'm sure that she saw that I was reading a will, and it did not take a lot of FBI detective smarts to figure out whose it was. Instead of asking me about it, she started out with something that I am sure was designed to take my mind off of wills and lawyers.

"Thomas, this home of yours is amazing! I've seen only a small part of it, and I don't know quite what to say."

"It was definitely a different way to grow up. When I was a kid, Hide n' Seek with my buddies required a map and compass. It seems strange that I am the only one left of the Briggs clan to enjoy it."

"The people who work for you are wonderful. However, I can tell that they are concerned about what you plan to do with the house. They are too polite and considerate to ask you about it."

"No. No one will say anything to me. They would see it as putting their problems ahead of the guy who just lost his only brother. A guy they cared for, too. Most of the relationship that we have was Ron's doing. He never made them feel like just the help."

"You have that same quality. They are very comfortable with you and respect you at the same time." This observation surprised me. I hoped she was right.

"I'll let Gus know to pass the word that I'm not changing anything. I'll also let him know that I will try to be home more often. Tell everyone that I have decided that someday I'll retire here. Nobody needs to worry."

Marilena smiled at me and said, "I think that you should call them all together and tell them everything yourself. They need to hear it from you."

"You think?"

"Yes. Occasionally. And what is this about retirement? You? Hmm, there's an unlikely image. Well, if you feel that you must, when the time comes, this would be a great way to spend one's reclining years. Might there be room for a very deserving, retired federal agent who has unselfishly risked her life on countless occasions for the good of the country?"

"I don't know. What does she look like?"

"Is that all that is important to you?" she said, faking insult.

"Pretty much."

THE MARKLIN

Dr. Caroline Little was a surprise, a physical specimen that was unexpected. Her features, while plain, were not unattractive. They were just delivered in extreme measure. Little was a poor moniker for the middle-aged woman standing three inches taller than I at somewhere near six and a half feet. And it wasn't just her height; her frame was as impressive, imposing. She had to weigh over two hundred pounds, and it looked like it was mostly muscle. Her shoulders were almost as wide as mine, and her hands were large and muscular. She knew her way around the gym. I couldn't help myself. My first thought was that in addition to her having a motive, she had the physical ability to toss most people out of any window regardless of the height of the sill. With a little guy like Ron, she wouldn't have broken a sweat. As we entered her lab, she spoke first, handshaking superfluous.

"Well?" she demanded. "Did you find his update?"

"It's nice to meet you too, Little." I didn't get the expected warning look from my FBI partner. She stared at Little, her expression businesslike.

"Jeez, for a big boy, you sure are sensitive," she shot back irritably. Marilena choked back a laugh at the thought of someone confusing me as sensitive, a quick departure from the stern look. This caused Little to focus on her, noting the conservative businesswoman's suit — out of place in the lab.

"Is this funny? What are you supposed to be anyway, Sweetie?"

"It's not Sweetie. It's Special Agent Rigatti, FBI." Marilena produced her ID without taking her eyes from Little. Her demeanor had returned to dead serious, her voice one of someone to be reckoned with.

"When will you have the update?" Little continued, pointedly ignoring Marilena. Oh, boy, that was a mistake.

Marilena spoke forcefully, not to be dismissed. "Dr. Little, I am responsible for the investigation into the murder of Dr. Ronald Briggs, *your* professional associate. You are a person of interest in that investigation. I have questions for you that you will answer. When I am satisfied, Colonel Briggs may indulge you. That is up to him, but only when I am finished. If you would prefer, I can arrange for an arrest warrant, and we can continue our conversation in less comfortable surroundings. It is your choice." Marilena had been staring into Little's face during her lecture. Now she adopted a bored expression and began to examine her nails as if patiently waiting for the answer from a child who had just gotten reprimanded.

Little transformed from tough gal, very big tough gal, to helpful, though still sarcastic, citizen. "OK, OK. We can talk now. Whatever. I'm not surprised that he was murdered. What do you want to know?"

"To begin with, why are you not surprised that his death was a murder?" she asked.

"Easy — I never believed it. For all the pain in the ass that he was, he was a brilliant scientist, a great collaborator, and I respected him. We were close to finding out the genetic basis for CID. A cure might come quickly after that. He wouldn't have bailed on me now. I needed him and he knew it. I know that my reaction to his death is not all touchy-feely like most people. I'm not that kind of gal. I'm not a girly-girl like you. I get by with what I got. Ron would understand. Ron knew me. I'm going to miss the little twerp for his mind and his contribution to our work. He made me think and wasn't afraid to disagree with me like most people are. It pissed me off sometimes, especially because he was always so nice about it, but it was good for me all the same. I never told him that. I didn't have to; he knew it."

"Why didn't you tell me that you were at the CID offices when Ron died?" I asked, closing my last open switch.

"Because I wasn't there, I had already left. I left the building about ten minutes before he died."

"I can't tell when you left. The security log showed that you never signed out."

"Because I didn't, I never do. I just walked out. Doesn't everyone? Ask that shrew, Margaret Townsend."

"Townsend?" I asked.

"She was with me in the elevator and left at the same time I did."

This made no sense. The security system that registered her RFID tag didn't show her leaving before the system reset at midnight. I assumed that she had been there with the police until after that.

"Did you notice if Townsend went back upstairs?"

"No, I know that she didn't."

"How do you know this?" Marilena joined the conversation.

"Townsend told me that she left her purse upstairs and didn't have cab fare on her. She didn't want to go back up for it because her security tag thingy was in it, and the guards would make her fill out some long form and have to accompany her upstairs as if they didn't know her. She said she'd deal with that tomorrow and asked if we could share a cab, with me paying, of course. I agreed just so she'd stop yakking about it, and we detoured out of the way to take her home. We were together in the cab when Ron died."

She hesitated for a moment, thinking hard and then coming to a decision. Marilena remained quiet knowing more was coming.

"Let me show you something." She walked to her desk and opened a drawer. My hand moved to my gun, just in case. Marilena saw my action, yet her hands remained at her sides. Little consulted a list, maybe a directory of some kind, from the open drawer and then poked awkwardly at her keyboard. A printer next to her desk started up. She took the printed page out and handed it to us. Marilena read it while I watched Little. When she finished, she passed the page to me. With a nod in Little's direction, I passed observational responsibility back to Marilena and looked at the paper. It was a letter to her board. I read the first two paragraphs where she informed them about the status of her work and the fact that the critical elements to her collaborative effort with Dr. Briggs were his discoveries, not hers, and that the Marklin was in the society's debt. Her writing was sincere and artful. Caroline Little had more than one side to her personality.

When I looked up from the letter, I was sure that my face registered some surprise, surprise noted by Dr. Little who was still seated, not moving from her desk chair.

"I needed your brother's help. I made sure that everyone knew what he had contributed and not just for his sake, either. The man simply didn't care who got credit; he just wanted to end CID. If it's possible, I may be a bigger pain in the ass than he was, but I wasn't going to let him duck the credit he was due. He deserved it, and I also wanted others to know that despite rumors to the contrary, it is possible to work with me. A great man, Ron Briggs, had worked with me. It would have been stupid to send this letter, letting everyone know that he was key to our work, and then kill him to be the sole researcher on the project. You can check my board; they got this letter last week."

She had a point.

"I know that I am not an easy person to get along with, but I'm good at my job and so was Ron. We were a good team in other ways also. Well, he was better for me than I was for him, I guess. I could call and yell at him to blow off some steam after some piss ant here got me wound up. I would yell at him and call him terrible things, and he just ignored all of the crap, knowing that he was helping."

She paused again, looked at me and continued, "I wish he were alive so that I could call him all the same terrible things all over again." Then, the large, strong, offensive woman started to lose control. Her eyes began to fill up, and her lower lip was quivering. She was fighting hard to keep it together.

It's never easy for me to watch anyone whose emotions have taken over. This comes from being someone whose feelings are kept inside and not on display except as an intentional part of some communication, like yelling at a new recruit, something a Marine does well. Fortunately, Marilena was more evolved and better equipped. She pulled a chair over to Little's and sat next to her. For some measured period, based on what I don't know, she was quiet but letting Caroline Little, Ph.D., M.D., know by her closeness that she was not alone. Then she started talking to her softly, calmly, a different kind of outlet for Little than Ron had been, but one just as important. It appeared that a recovery was underway and an embarrassing moment was to be avoided. I hoped that I would be as much comfort when I sent her the data from the USB stick. She may be different, but she didn't kill my brother.

I walked away. Caroline Little and I had something in common. My emotions about Ron's death were also very near the surface.

* * *

We had a tail. It was more than a feeling — I had spotted the car. I was sitting in row two again and had turned sideways to face Marilena. My position allowed me to face her as we talked about Caroline Little but also let me look out the rear window from time to time. She knew what I was doing, what I had been doing since we left to see Dr. Little, and wasn't offended by my divided attention. I figured that if anyone were interested in us, he would pick us up as we left the compound, and I had been vigilant ever since. I hadn't told anyone at the society that we were traveling by train, so the earlier ride from the station was probably without unwanted company. As we had hoped to evoke a reaction, it was time to become more careful. The near miss with the cab in Manhattan had almost eliminated the remaining Briggs brother, not to mention his pretty girlfriend.

"Gus. We're being followed." Marilena heard me but continued to look forward, not wanting to alert our follower with a sudden look behind us. For someone whose assignment was mostly diplomatic, she had good fieldcraft instincts.

"The green Merc two cars back?" Gus asked. "I saw him get in line behind us when we left home. Some coincidence that he's still back there after your meeting."

"That's the car, and it's no coincidence," I said.

"He's not being very careful. Jumping out right behind us when we left was kinda obvious. Must think we're idiots."

"He, or she, is an amateur." Marilena nodded, acknowledging the reference to our tail as a possible "she."

Gus asked, "Ya want me to lose him."

"Just the opposite. Make it easy for him to stay with us."

"Are you planning something, Thomas?" she asked.

"I think I should meet our new friend." I pulled the Beretta out of its holster and checked the safety. I looked up and to my complete surprise, I saw the Glock in her hands, her high-heels slipping off of her feet.

"We should do it at the next light," she calmly stated.

I don't know why this came as a surprise. She was an agent with the nation's most respected police organization. She had been trained to deal with situations involving violence and wasn't going to sit on the sidelines. My personal feelings notwithstanding, I couldn't make some scene about her staying out of the way in the middle of a developing action. The opportunity to park her out of harm's way for the trip to the Marklin ended when we got in the car at the house.

"It's a one-way street. When we go out, cross to the far side and use the parked cars as cover. Stay low and move fast."

She nodded her agreement. At least she would take orders from me while in a tactical situation.

"Gus, we're going to rush the car following us. No matter what, don't let it get past you. Use the car as a ram if you have to."

He put aside any issue with his baby getting smashed and said, "He ain't getting by me." He wouldn't.

The Beemer braked, and we popped the doors simultaneously. I was low and running back to the Mercury. Marilena had made it to the other side of the street, was moving in parallel and a little behind me. I made myself accept the fact that she was an asset for me to use, had to use. I had to keep personal concern out of my mind. Having both of us confront the car at the same instant, weapons drawn, would have the greatest effect. If the driver was armed and started shooting at one of us, the other could return fire. As we were separated, running us both down was not possible. I just hoped that Marilena would do her part from behind some protective cover.

I still couldn't make out the driver of the Mercury. Between tinted windows and the large sunglasses, I could just barely see that the driver appeared to be female — no surprise there. Whoever it was, she had seen us and was panicked — the gearshift jammed into reverse, the accelerator stomped on. Tires squealed, smoked, and finally grabbed. Backing up and rapidly accelerating, the once pursuing, though now fleeing, automobile was out of control. It careened off of cars parked on both sides of the street as it over-corrected in an effort to escape. Backing up at high speed is an acquired talent. Stunt drivers in the movies make it seem effortless, especially when they execute the fish-tailing one-hundred eighty degree sliding turn, off and on the brakes at just the right moment causing the tires to lose adhesion and then retake it. From the way this driver was coping, there wouldn't be any fancy Hollywood maneuvers.

She emerged from the crowded street and into the intersection at well over sixty miles per hour. Her speed did not give the driver of the large dump truck crossing at right angles with a green light the opportunity to stop. Although he was traveling at less than half of her velocity, he had more momentum due to the weight of his load. To the truck's driver, her car appeared out of nowhere. His left front fender struck the left rear fender of her car. Her motion was instantaneously slowed to zero as her car oil-canned into the heavier vehicle and spun ninety degrees ending up in line with and in front of the truck. The truck's speed didn't reduce by a single mile per hour — he just was too heavy. Momentum is the product of mass and velocity. It doesn't take a lot of speed when you have that much weight on your side. The truck continued over the car, crushing it underfoot with little effort, the truck driver doing his best to stop the onslaught without success.

I was the first to reach her, not that she could notice. She'd never notice anything again. Marilena ran up next to me, stocking feet having served her well. It was just becoming dark enough in the evening twilight that seeing through the front window into the car was difficult. I pulled out the 9-volt light and flicked it on.

There she was, or rather, there it was. The airbag had been no match for the crushing weight of the truck as it tried to prevent the steering wheel from dividing her into two unequal parts, her neck the line of division. Her decapitated head, now illuminated in the light, had been separated from her body and was pushed forward, still upright, onto the dash, her blood pooling around the neck, a sticky red lake hiding the torn flesh and bone while supporting a pale face under a tangled forest of obscenely red hair. Her eyes were still open, attacking, and accusing the world at large, her style in life following her into her death, though now, unfocused, no one accosted. Margaret Townsend was dead, Chicken Woman no more.

RULES OF ENGAGEMENT

Slightly winded, Gus arrived next to me having abandoned his beloved Beemer and run the length of the block to the intersection where Margaret Townsend had died. Still, I'd bet that the doors on the car had been locked and the alarm set before he left. A man has to have priorities.

After noting that we were unharmed, Gus looked at the detached head on the car's dash like he saw this every day. Having quickly gotten his breathing back to normal, he calmly asked, "Who lost her head?"

"She was a senior staff member where Ron worked," I replied, emphasizing the word "was."

"Not anymore," he observed, matter-of-factly.

"What should we tell the local law when they arrive?" I asked Marilena, the sirens already in earshot.

"Yeah, what ya want me to say?" Gus followed up.

I looked at Marilena; it was her call. We had been passing ourselves off in not one, but two states, as representatives of an officially sanctioned, multi-jurisdictional investigation, and I didn't want to cause her any intramural problems — the FBI and local law enforcement didn't always get along.

She answered simply, "The truth. I've handled the inter-departmental issues already." I should have known.

The driver of the truck, a young black man with a baseball cap on backwards, had finally come down from the cab. He stared open-mouthed at Townsend's head, the object of our discussion. Then he turned, stumbled away, bent over, and puked in the gutter. He wiped his mouth on his sleeve, turned to look back at me, and said, "The city don't pay me enough for this shit." He was right.

* * *

I was worried that the next several hours would be full of hurry-up-and-wait, good cop, bad cop, holding cells, summoning lawyers, and frustrating interrogation. Marilena identified herself to uniforms first to arrive on the scene and immediately started giving orders. Fifteen minutes later, a precinct lieutenant arrived, certainly because of the FBI involvement and the fact that Marilena had taken charge. He and Marilena spoke while Gus and I waited off to one side. Their conversation seemed amicable. After about ten minutes, she signaled us to join them.

"Thomas, Gus, would you both please give this officer your driver's licenses so that he can make note of your identification."

We pulled out the plastic IDs showing us to be local citizens entitled to operate motor vehicles and to be willing organ donors upon death. It became obvious that the precinct lieutenant who was supervising had already been informed by Marilena who and what I was. He was especially polite.

"Colonel Briggs, thanks for waiting and for your cooperation."

I had waited only a little and had not cooperated with anyone or anything, at least not yet. It didn't seem wise to point that out, so instead I offered, "No problem. Anything we can do to help." I was still a little concerned. It didn't matter that he was being a nice guy right now — that could change quickly. My concern quickly vanished when he addressed Gus.

"And you, you drunken, low-rent, Greek reprobate? What ya got to say for yourself?"

"This one wasn't my fault, Kev. Honest! I figured that it was just another crazy broad trying to get my eye! You know, like always!" They each laughed and shook hands — friends from some part of Gus's life that I knew nothing about. My personal relief coefficient was climbing steadily.

The lieutenant looked back at me while shaking his head sadly and said, "Colonel, you should be careful about who you associate with. This guy is trouble. A word to the wise: Never let him keep score when you're bowling!"

"I'll keep that in mind, lieutenant. He's shifty, eh?"

"Let's just say that his arithmetic is frequently faulty, though consistently favorable to him. He says it's age!" Gus assumed a wounded expression that wasn't fooling anyone.

Marilena smiled and spoke, employing her diplomatic skill set, "Lieutenant O'Shanlon has offered to let you both come to the station tomorrow to make your statements. I have assured him that you will both do so. Because of his consideration, we can leave now. Thank you again, Kevin." She smiled sweetly in his direction, and he turned a shade of pink that I am sure was unnatural for him. Whatever she had said to him, and whatever she had done back channel, had worked. My worry that this was going to become an all-night tangle in local law enforcement bureaucracy ended in short order. That is exactly what would have happened if I had been on my own. Sherpa Marilena had come through again.

* * *

Gus had kept the household staff informed of our slightly delayed arrival time. He told us that a special dinner was being prepared to celebrate my homecoming, and that for the first time ever, I had brought home an attractive dinner date worthy of the staff's combined efforts.

Marilena, once again comfortably ensconced in the back of the Beemer, and looking for a way to lighten the mood, perked up at this. She spoke loudly enough for Gus to hear, "Very nice, Thomas. Beautiful car, talented, intelligent and handsome chauffeur, wonderful people who are cooking a 'special dinner' for you. Very nice, indeed."

"Did you hear that, Tommy? *Talented, intelligent, and handsome — B'YOOTIFUL!*"

"Oh God," my only response.

"Marilena, keep reminding him about how lucky he is. OK?" Gus was really enjoying this. "The Marine Corps must be some amazing place to be. Even better than his life here at home in Boston among the talented, intelligent, and handsome!"

"Or the company of an attractive dinner date, Gus. He hurts my feelings all of the time," she said and then stuck her lower lip out slightly for his inspection in the rear view mirror.

"Do I need to straighten him out, Miss? It would be a privilege!" Gus volunteered.

"Would you do that for me?" She asked hopefully. "It might become necessary," her voice emphasizing the false gravity of the situation. Then the two conspirators laughed. It was going to be a long visit.

Arriving back at the compound, I was pleased to see that the formal receiving line was nowhere in sight. We walked inside, and while I cleaned up in one of the first floor bathrooms, excuse me, powder rooms, Marilena went directly to the kitchen. I heard complimentary and happy women sounds as I came out of the washroom, or whatever it's called. Somewhere after the salad and before the entree, I turned the conversation away from the meal we were enjoying and back to our case.

"Well, I'm turning out to be a pretty poor detective."

"Why do you think that?" she asked.

"Let's see. Item one, I have gone from 'favorite working hypothesis' that Caroline Little was our killer only to discover in less than twenty-four hours that she was not. Item two, my fall-back position, that it was Margaret Townsend, got shot down when we learned that she had left the building with Little before Ron was killed. I'll bet that when we check with the cab company, it will confirm Little's statements. Item three, Townsend's behavior following us today is a total mystery. If she wasn't the killer, then what was she doing? See what I mean? I don't have a clue. Is there a detective school that I can go to? Maybe a correspondence course or something on the Internet?"

"Why does this disappoint you? It should not," she said, honestly surprised at my personal indictment. "I think that you have done very well. Two prominent figures have been eliminated from suspicion of having killed your brother. One of them, unfortunately only because we can't question her, is dead and remains as an accessory, possibly before and definitely after the fact. To have accomplished this in the twenty-four hours you speak of is excellent progress. An FBI team with dedicated support staff doing research would be very pleased."

"We're doing well?"

"Better than I would have forecast. Tomorrow, we will meet with the police and see what they have learned about

Townsend, if she planned to meet someone else here, what was in the car with her and anything else they have learned. If there is anything to follow up on from that, we will do so and then go back to New York. Townsend's death will be causing someone to be very concerned right now."

I thought about what she had said. It made sense. It was just a new world to me. Marilena was right that we were quickly eliminating people on the list of suspects. In Townsend's case, the elimination was permanent although that wasn't going to keep me up nights.

Marilena continued, "Our working assumption remains unchanged, Ron's killer is on the suspect list. A suspect list now reduced. We will announce to those remaining on our list that the focus is no longer Boston. The good news for us is the killer's bad news; the list is shorter, and he or she is still on it. I think that we can further assume that Townsend is, or was, in league with the killer. Her presence here is proof that the killer is incapable of simply doing nothing. Townsend had an assignment; we just don't know what it was. Townsend's failure, her death, and the soon to be announced elimination of Dr. Little as a suspect have changed the rules of engagement in a way that will be very disturbing to the killer. This should make you happy — the pressure factor has just increased. Congratulations, not recriminations are in order."

* * *

I was in my room upstairs. My bedroom had been updated when I graduated from college. It no longer reflected the likes and dislikes of a teenage boy. The furnishings were contemporary, a decorator's attempt to make me sophisticated. Like Ron's, the bedroom had a large, attached workroom area that had originally been designed, though never used, as a sitting room. We had each used this space the same way — it was where we hid from the world's noise and studied something of interest or something mandatory, each in our own private sanctuary. There were floor-to-ceiling bookshelves on each wall everywhere there wasn't a window. A desk and several worktables were arranged in no particular order. The shelves were full of textbooks from the schools and universities I had attended, course material from a wide variety of military training, and other books that I had acquired in support of outside hobbies and interests. A walk around the room would tell you a lot about me, if you cared to look. Very few had ever done that — none of them had been women. Off to one side was a comfortable, over-stuffed easy chair with a reading lamp next to it. I had planted myself there to read the final documents from the stack I had started on earlier. I heard a soft knock at the door, it opened, and Marilena walked in.

"Thomas, can I come in?"

"Sure." I didn't mention that she already had. "I'm finished with this stuff for the night."

"Learning the family business?" she asked.

"Yeah. Ron sure took care of a lot of things for me. I really had no idea."

"Is there anything I can help you with?"

"Yeah, but not about this. It can wait." I paused and looked intently at her. "I have only one question."

"And that is?" she asked softly, knowing that the topic of conversation was about to become more important to her than my family administrivia.

I had considered this carefully. I knew that we had to come to an understanding about us, and we had to do it soon. I needed to get out of this ambiguous world about us that we were in. Whatever course we took, it had to be determined, not accidental.

"I heard what you said earlier, about us. I have only one concern."

She waited, not interrupting.

"What if, after we start down this road, you change your mind? I mean, what you defined is not the norm for a couple as their relationship grows. What happens if our rules, our rules of engagement, stop working for you? Someday, you might not want to be involved with someone who is gone much of the time, who has a sometimes hazardous job? What if you decide that you want a more conventional life with two point one kids and the white picket fence? You know I can't do that. What if you change your mind?"

"That's it? That is your only concern? That I might change the rules — the rules of engagement?" She looked relieved and smiled at the reference.

"Uh, yeah. That's really it. For me, it's a big one. The big one."

"Then, I want you to know, that what I have promised is not just a promise. It is what I want as well. What I want will not change, so I don't have to worry about going back on my promise because I know myself well. Think about it from my perspective. I don't want to become involved with someone who wants me to leave the FBI. To give up all of the things that make me who I am. I want three things: Exclusivity, love, and excitement. It's simple."

I looked at her standing in front of me. "There are a lot of little things that make up a relationship that you haven't addressed."

"We will work them out. There is no guarantee that this will work. But I want to try." And a little more softly, "Do you?"

She was still wearing the business attire but without the jacket: silk blouse, skirt, stockings, and heels. Her eyes were partially closed to slits that studied me, looking for my next step. Standing up, I moved toward her. It was because I believed her that it was time for me to lead, for me to take the next step, not her. I reached my arms around her, she thought for an embrace, but instead, I found the little zipper in back that held her skirt together. I slid it down; her skirt fell to the floor. I brought my hands around to the front of her blouse and began to unbutton it from top to bottom. I eased the blouse off of her shoulders, and it joined the skirt. She looked at me — her growing smile and her widely open eyes, questioning and hopeful.

"Thomas, this is different. As much as I appreciate your assistance in helping me remove my clothing, I am confused by this change in your behavior. Should I be reading into this that you have accepted my proposal?"

"Yep."

I took her by the hand and led her back toward the bed. She stopped me when we crossed the room. Up until now, her flirting, her teasing, and tempting were to keep my attention, to keep me focused on something very important to her, to decide one way or another, were we going to be together, a couple? And, for the first time, the confidence, the playfulness, the certain knowledge that she was in complete control, evaporated. It was her turn to be concerned — I had given her the answer to her question, the question.

With an uncharacteristically shaky sound in her voice, she said, "Thomas, I need to hear you say it. I need to hear that you accept, that you want to do this, that you want me."

"Option three — oh, yeah. I accept. Completely. Absolutely. I want you. No more questions. The answer is yes. Committed, one hundred percent. I'm in."

And then I was.

TRENDY LAWYERS

I awoke to the familiar surroundings of my own bedroom and to the only recently recurring experience of not being alone with the sunrise. This had never happened before at home as I had always kept that part of my life removed from the curious eyes of our family's staff — there are some things they just don't need to know, much less tease me about later.

Although I had enjoyed adult bedroom activity many times and in many locations — a personal objective never far removed from my mind — I rarely actually slept with my temporary partner. I always found a reason, admittedly an excuse, to move on after the fun, but always before the sleep. I knew that I had done this intentionally — an admission that, in many cases, the thought of interacting with the selected young lady who although pretty and willing to accommodate my immediate needs, was something I didn't want. I had no desire to be her soul mate for a morning-after conversation. I won't deny it. I am scum.

Marilena was lying on her side and pressed against me. I sensed her becoming awake. "Good morning, Darling," she said. It seemed that in my brave new world, I had acquired a new title.

"Seems like you're awake," I answered.

"Yes, and we need to get going. We have a full agenda, and I would like to exercise before we start out." She was kind enough not to mention that on a previous occasion, my exercise had been limited to falling out of bed. At least I hadn't done that again.

"We have a nicely equipped facility," I said.

"Why does that not surprise me?" She gave me a knowing smile. Escaping from my grasp before I could implement my rather obvious plan for the morning, she said, "I will go put on something appropriate for your nicely equipped facility." Then she slid naked out from the sheets. The room never looked so good. I could get used to this. She pulled the top sheet off of the bed and fashioned it without difficulty into an off the shoulder, emergency-use toga. Had she done this before? She stepped over her clothes, opened and walked out the door and in the direction of her room — another guest room that she would not sleep in.

From outside my door and to my horror, I heard Marilena say brightly and without even the hint of any awkwardness, "Good morning, Maryanne!" Marilena then paused and began a conversation with our housekeeper while completely relaxed about having been seen coming from my room wrapped in the sheet from my bed. Not a care in the world.

"Would you do something for me, dear? I left some clothes in Thomas' room. I'm sure he will not know what to do with them, and if you would be so kind?"

"Of course. I'll take care of it when I make up his room. Will you want breakfast?" Maryanne was playing along as if seeing Marilena come from my bed was completely expected.

Marilena answered, "Thank you so much. Yes, we're going to exercise for a little while first. Something light after that would be very nice."

"I'll let everyone know." Yeah, I'll bet she will.

* * *

We arrived at the pricey home of the Central New England Group, LLC on the top floor of a downtown office building. CNEG was one of the first and most successful private equity groups in the country. The letters were always pronounced individually: See — Ehn — Eee — Gee, never See-NEG for obvious reasons. Even some business illiterate like me, who manages somehow to get by without memorizing the *Wall Street Journal* each and every day, had heard of them, and knew of their impressive track record. Their investments made the news as they always involved large companies and often merged ferocious competitors, domestically and abroad. The returns to their secretive clients, some of whom had recently been revealed to be nefarious international players, were consistently impressive. I found this amusing because I knew that we were clients as well.

If my boss, General F., ever discovered this, I'd get gutted, filleted, and fried.

Yesterday, while on the train, I had called the partner who had cultivated Ron as an investor and had set up a meeting for this morning. I was starting to enjoy the power that I had as the controller of our family's fortune. It didn't seem to matter whether the cash flow was philanthropic or selfish — I was the guy everyone wanted as a friend. My new friend today would soon discover that if necessary, I would employ some of that power to find out about a past partner at CNEG.

We were escorted to the offices of William Heget by a very serious young man. After the intros, expressions of remorse about Ron and offers of coffee, we settled in to talk. I introduced Marilena as a friend helping me in my new role as family head, not as an FBI agent. Heget began by describing the preparations he had made for our meeting.

"Colonel, I've prepared a summary and an analysis of your family's holdings, specific investments in our partner ventures, and the returns to date. I can explain them to you now, or if you like, you can read this, and we can get back together in person or by phone at your convenience. My partners and I strongly hope that we can continue to serve and to provide the excellent return on investment that you have enjoyed."

Although his words were self-serving, I liked his approach. No nonsense — we had a deal, and his team had been living up to its end. The message being, "Let's keep doing just that." Given the numbers I was seeing while rifling through the data and the associated color graphs, I was OK with a continued relationship. I wasn't even sure of how difficult it would be to disassociate us. Our initial investment had grown to somewhere near ten million dollars at current value. It was a small enough percentage of the whole portfolio (God, I was sounding like a finance geek) that I wasn't worried about the speculative nature of what PE firms did, not that I fully understood whatever that was. I passed the file to Marilena, helping maintain her role as adviser. She set it on her lap but did not look at the contents.

"Mr. Heget, as you might guess, all of this is new to me. Ron made my life easy by taking care of the family business, so I do appreciate your time. I will read your package and with some help (nodding in Marilena's direction) do my best to understand everything. I am sure that I will take you up on your offer to call back."

"By all means, please do. And if you like, your brother and I had become on good enough terms to use first names."

"All the better by me," I answered. "I go by Tom."

"I'm Bill, but a couple of times when Ron and I had too much to drink after a dinner meeting, I somehow had been Billy. No one else ever called me that." He looked off at the window, obviously remembering good times with my brother.

I thought it best to be as straightforward with him as he had been with me. "Bill, we have reason to believe that he did not commit suicide."

"What?" he spoke the word softly, without emotion. "Are you sure? Can I help?" his voice sincere. Once again, Ron's impact on others was making it easy to get their cooperation.

"I don't know if you saw the news yet about your former partner, Margaret Townsend?"

His face took on a grimace. "Yes, I saw that she died yesterday. Here in town."

"We were there when she died."

"You were? Why?"

"Yes. We recognized her driving a car that was following us on the way back from an appointment in Cambridge. When we stopped and got out of our car to talk to her, to see if she needed anything, she quickly backed up away from us and caused the accident that killed her."

"Any reason why she did that?"

"No. She was, however, a person of interest to the police authorities, but it has been determined that she was not physically near Ron when he died and could not have been his killer. I don't know if she was following us or, for that matter, why she would have followed us here to Boston and then tailed us around town. Do you know if she had an appointment here? Maybe seeing us was just a coincidence."

"Funny you should ask. This morning when the news broke here, one of the partners asked around if she had an appointment with any of us. He checked with everyone and she didn't. So, she wasn't here to see us, and, in any case, since she left the firm, I can't remember her ever having come back. I'll level with you because of my relationship with Ron. She didn't have friends in Boston to my knowledge — just the opposite."

"The opposite?"

Marilena was letting me run with it, not wanting the purpose of our visit to become official. She played the attractive girlfriend well, showing just the right amount of interest.

"Yeah, well, Margaret is, was, a bit of an embarrassment for me. I was the one who brought her on, pushed the others to start her as a partner, and then had to deal with the mess that it became."

"I'll admit that I don't know many people who are in the private equity world, but when I met her in New York, she didn't seem like someone I would invest my money with," I prodded, gently.

He nodded back at me and then said, "About ten years ago, we were getting beat up in the press as being a boys' club, one of many in our business. One of the first and largest PE firms had been started out in the lobby of a midtown Manhattan hotel in a casual meeting between a couple of guys. Since then, our industry has had the image of businessmen, emphasis on men, meeting in smoke-filled bars and hotels, no women allowed. I started out as a securities lawyer and know how fickle big investors can be. Their investment criteria are not always objective. The issue of gender bias might get some pillow talk going, and some client's wife might keep us from working for them. Because of this, we decided to add some women to the team. One of them worked out great, but one of them, the one person I found and pushed for, didn't. Margaret was a nightmare. Within a month of getting started here, we learned two things about her: in spite of her degree in finance and work experience, she didn't know much about deal valuation or investment analysis, and, even worse because we couldn't hide this, she was a bitch on wheels. Within two months, everyone in the building hated her, even people who worked for other companies whose only interaction with her was passing her in the hallway. Several of us tried to talk to her, to get her to fit in, to lighten up. It only got worse. Eventually, we struck a deal to get rid of her — an expensive deal. She was promoted to partner and retired from the firm on the same day. Walked out with over a million bucks for less than five months' work where she basically did nothing except screw up one of my projects. Part of the deal was that we had to publicly attribute the success of one of our largest investments to her when in fact she had nothing to do with it. Her lawyer said that it would reduce the damage to her reputation that we would have to pay for in addition to the seven-figure settlement. I understand that one of my partners had to be a reference for her to help her get the job at the CID charity where Ron worked. Ron was decent enough not to ever bring her up although I am sure that he knew our role in getting her hired. I don't know the makeup of the senior team where Ron worked. Maybe they were under some pressure to balance the team with some ladies. The cost of being trendy."

I thought about the CID senior team and smiled. No one would ever accuse Alison Montgomery of not hiring enough women. But trendy, she did trendy well.

* * *

Our next stop was at the police station. Gus went in with us, and he and I each wrote out a statement. Marilena went off with O'Shanlon to meet the precinct commander and talk police talk. They let me borrow a computer so I could type my statement out. I had told them that my handwriting started out bad, and then I became a doctor. They understood.

After we finished, Marilena read our reports and suggested some changes. The locals didn't seem to mind this, which I found strange. She had worked out some very close interdepartmental cooperation. We signed our statements and were led to a conference room. Lieutenant O'Shanlon was waiting for us and had brought a bag marked "Evidence."

"We can't find any reason for Margaret Townsend to come to Boston. There is no record of an appointment with anyone whom we have uncovered, and she sold her home here when she moved to New York. That doesn't mean that she didn't have a reason to come here; we just can't find one."

He turned to an evidence bag on the conference room table. He surprised us by producing a gun from the pouch. It was a revolver, a thirty-eight Smith with a shrouded hammer. A five-shot, aluminum-framed hand blaster that wouldn't hang up when you yanked it out of a pocket. I asked if I could see the ammo in the plastic bag. They were .38 plus P rounds and as hot as that gun could handle. She had been planning some serious damage. Well, as serious as her pistol could inflict.

"She had this in the front seat with her. Did she have motive to kill you?" O'Shanlon asked.

"We still don't know what her plans were or her role in Dr. Briggs's murder," Marilena answered.

"Seems like pretty poor planning, just riding around behind us hoping to get an opportunity to drop us all without getting noticed," I offered.

"Yeah — not bright," O'Shanlon said. "Although, every time I try to credit a criminal with some intelligence, I'm wrong. Also, the more desperate the crook, the more crazy they get."

I didn't say the words, but in my mind I heard, "We're counting on that."

* * *

Our last stop of the day was a meeting with our family lawyers. This had nothing to do with the case, but they were clamoring to meet with me. Their stated motivation was to educate me; a second one was to begin developing a relationship with me like the one they had with Ron.

Gus took us to a seafood restaurant for lunch that had a view of the harbor. He regaled Marilena with a series of embarrassing stories about my childhood. She pushed for more, and he promised that later he would get out some photo albums and fill in the rest of my ill-spent youth. She thought that this was a fantastic idea. I considered joining the French Foreign Legion.

I took Marilena in with me to meet Jason Inch, our senior partner at Keeson, Inch, Merrimack and Wynters, an erudite collection of barristers, I'm sure. I had met Jason about a dozen times, mostly when my signature was needed and Ron took advantage of the request to expose me to some of the family business issues. I remembered that Jason always wore the latest GQ fashions, something that Ron would bring to my attention later with a little laugh. Another trendy lawyer.

He asked Marilena's standing with me or the family, prompting her to offer to excuse herself so we could meet in private. I didn't know whether I should feel awkward about this or whether I should decline her offer or what I should do when she said, "Listen to your lawyer. These are confidential matters. I'm sure there is somewhere here where I can use a telephone?"

Jason was relieved and made immediate arrangements for a comfortable office with refreshments. He then led me through a two-hour presentation of my business interests and my new role as head of the family. Most of it I had heard something about before and had only one real surprise. It turned out that we were being sued in two separate actions. Jason assured me that it was nothing to worry about — we were always being sued! A fact of life for a wealthy family but not of any concern because he and his team of legal pit bulls handled them all to a satisfactory conclusion. I wasn't too worried. I knew I had talented help, and they would work me into everything, keeping me from screwing up too badly, and they would be paid excessively. What amazed me about all of this was that when Ron was about half my age, he had taken on this same role.

We finished up and went together to collect Marilena. While I left them for a visit to the restroom, she began a conversation with Jason. My return five minutes later provided me with another surprise.

Jason spoke first. He was very pleased about something. "Tom, Marilena has made an excellent suggestion that we should act on. It is very considerate and understanding on her part."

"Yeah, what's that?" I said, having absolutely no clue as to what he was talking about.

"She has asked me to create an agreement, a palimony agreement, between the two of you and specifically directed me to state that irrespective of the nature of your relationship, or how long your relationship lasts, even if it's forever, she will have no claim against your personal or your family's financial interests."

I stared at the two of them. "Palimony? What's that?"

Marilena smiled at Jason and said, "Jason, you had better make it bilateral. I can't have this sophisticated legal scoundrel fleecing me in some moment of female weakness!" They both laughed out loud. I was lost.

"Bilateral?"

MANHATTAN WORRIES, MANHATTAN BOUND

We were back in row two of the Beemer with Gus once again in the pilot's seat, threading our way home through the Boston rush hour. I noticed that Marilena was more relaxed and had been sitting closer to me today than she had yesterday. She had also abandoned the sideways seating position that had allowed her to look directly at me when we talked. Instead, she had slid over in my direction and leaned against me when it suited her. Intimacy had replaced scrutiny.

Even though our personal relationship had moved to a new level, her attention to our case had not slipped away. "Thomas, I have called April twice without success. She hasn't returned my calls. I'm becoming concerned."

"She's a young girl and she's a student and she has a very strange job. Who knows what hours she's keeping or how often she checks her messages?"

"I will keep trying. I will feel better when I have spoken with her."

"You don't think she's in any danger, do you?" I asked.

"I'm not sure." She looked pensive, too serious. She didn't like being unsure of anything.

I had a different issue on my mind. I said, "Not meaning to change the subject, but I will anyway. Who's your favorite on our reduced list of five suspects? Canfield, Sayyaf, Wilson, Treece or Standish?"

"I will let you know my favorite when we eliminate four more of them," her answer a foretelling of the future. I know that she is one hundred percent European, but as a detective, she had an inscrutable side. A female Charlie Chan.

* * *

The trip home via Boston's wide avenues and back streets was thankfully uneventful. No maniacal drivers attempted vehicular manslaughter — no crazed women lost their heads. I was happy to contain today's surprises to small business issues and palimony agreements, whatever they were. Even though today's curious events were lower on the excitement scale, they were more numerous and kept coming.

We went upstairs, and, on the way to my room, were intercepted by Maryanne, coming down the hall.

"We finished with your laundry and dry cleaning," she said to Marilena. No surprise there. She continued, "I moved all of your clothes into Tom's room. He had an extra closet that was almost empty. Let me know if you need anything else." Big surprise there.

As my mouth was probably hanging open, Marilena had to respond for both of us, "Thank you so much, Maryanne. That was very thoughtful and makes everything more convenient. Did Gus talk to you about dinner?"

"Yes. We are both looking forward to it!" Maryanne said.

Huh?

I decided that the best course was the course of least resistance. I followed Marilena's lead and began changing into more casual clothes. Whatever was going on, she was calling the shots.

We went down to the first floor where I discovered the dining room table set for five. Marilena disappeared into the kitchen, leaving me alone to look at the newspaper I found in the hallway.

In short order, food started to emerge through the swinging door separating the kitchen from the dining room. Marilena and Maryanne, with Gus bringing up the rear, carried platters and serving dishes to the table. The ladies were chatting between themselves like old friends. Gus looked as befuddled as I was but seemed to be taking orders without complaint.

"Thomas, I thought that you should have some time with Maryanne and Gus before we leave. I asked them to have dinner with us."

"Good idea. Whose the fifth?" I asked, nodding at the table set for five.

Gus answered, "Katie Rice from Jason Inch's office. You've met her. She keeps the papers flowing and pays the bills. Maryanne and I talk to her all the time. While you were meeting with Jason, Marilena asked me who had that job figuring it was someone from Jason's office. I told her, and she went and found her and invited her to dinner."

Right on time, the doorbell rang, and Gus went to let Katie in.

"Hi everyone! Hi Marilena! Hi Colonel Briggs! She was a petite young lady with long brown hair. Her face was partially hidden by an impressively large pair of glasses with dark plastic frames. From the thickness of the lenses, I could tell that without them, I would be reduced to a bug on a far wall.

"Hello, Katie. Your timing is perfect," Marilena said, as we all returned Katie's greetings and moved to the table.

I was steered to the head of the table by Marilena to Dad's and then Ron's old seat — an unwelcomed procession. Marilena sat on my right with Maryanne next to her. Katie sat next to me on my left with Gus next to her further down the table.

The food was, as always, excellent. I told myself to enjoy it while I could. There were certain to be more military commissaries and cafeterias in my future. Marilena gently directed the conversation and kept it centered on my three, full-time family helpers, making them feel comfortable as they got to know her, and in Katie's case, got to know me a little better. At some point she even convinced Katie to stop calling me Colonel. Gus regaled us all with more stories about my growing up, and, as promised, had brought a photo album. He had marked several pages that I had assumed would contain embarrassing pictures of me as an awkward kid. I turned out to be wrong. I was in all of the shots, and they were ones of Ron and me growing up. They brought back some good memories. He even had some I had never seen of us with our parents before they died and some later ones of the two brothers growing into young men interacting with Gus while he stepped in as surrogate dad. As he described the photos, there was pride in his voice replacing the normal gruff persona.

Somewhere during the main course, we got around to talking about how the household responsibilities were divided up and how they had kept Ron informed of issues that needed his input. Fortunately, there were not many of those. However, this now had to shift to me and was going to be more of a challenge.

"Most of the time, I am easy to find by either cell or email," I said. "Also, I plan to come here more often. But sometimes, the military sends me places where I can't be reached for days or even weeks. That could be a problem."

Gus jumped in with a suggestion that I would have made if I had had the opportunity to discuss it with Marilena beforehand and in private. Apparently, he didn't feel constrained in any way and didn't need to check with her prior to asking, "Well, when the Marines have you off beyond civilization somewhere, can we call Marilena? I'll bet you can't hide from her! B'YOOTIFUL!"

She smiled. Her liaison duties had just expanded.

* * *

The next morning we found ourselves back on the Acela Express, this time headed to New York. The evening before had ended well with everyone pleased about the fact that operationally nothing had changed. People don't like change. A different Briggs was in charge, but like his predecessor, he had the common sense to empower those who looked after him. The only real piece of business to take place was that Katie reminded me that she had check signing authority for up to $5,000. Jason could add his signature and take it up to $50,000. I had wondered how my American Express bill got paid? Beyond that, they had to find me and get an original scribble. She wanted to know if I was OK with the way it was set up, or did I want to change anything? I instructed her to keep it the way it was and said that we would quickly get as comfortable working together as she and Ron had been. She also left me with a copy of the previous month's ledger of money in and out as she had always done for Ron. She promised to email it to me each month along with the family financial statements that someone else in the firm created and for me to call if I had questions. Marilena remembered to thank everyone for everything each one did to keep me out of trouble.

The morning routine was significantly changed in that for the first time, we shared a bathroom. This was more unsettling to me than sharing a bed for purposes of sleep. My procedure for getting ready is executed with military precision, and I move quickly. It takes me twenty-one minutes to shower, shave, and do everything necessary to take on the world. This changes, however, when you have to work around a female attempting the same. We didn't set any records; we occasionally collided. She laughed at my attempts to stay out of her way. The house has countless bathrooms, but before I could suggest that one of us take advantage of that, she informed me that sharing a bathroom was an important part of growing together. I had plans to expand her definition of sharing as both of us using the same bathroom, just not at the same time. Girl preparations can be scary.

* * *

"Thomas?"

"Yes."

We were on the train. She was sitting in the window seat next to me and reading some papers that she had printed before we left the house. Like the last trip, we were in a mostly empty passenger car. She did not look up when she said, "I want you to know that I am aware of how difficult the changes that you are going through have been for you. And, that I think you are doing extremely well for a regimented male not having the benefit of a woman's sensitivity and perspective."

"Thanks — I think. Somehow I'll get used to being the responsible member of the Briggs household even though I only have one 'X' chromosome to guide me."

The smile disappeared and she turned serious. "It's more than that — you will learn your new administrative tasks without difficulty," she replied, this time looking at me. "You are, however, dealing with several personal and highly emotional issues all at the same time. Besides losing the most important person in the world to you, you are taking on new responsibilities while undertaking a murder investigation. That's a lot, especially for someone like you."

"How's that?" I asked, still a little confused about how she was segregating my new responsibilities.

"Thomas, I'm not being insulting. In your professional life, you are highly trained in several challenging areas. You are a surgeon who lives in a dangerous and exciting world full of the military's best people routinely doing things that would terrify the average man. You know this, and it makes you confident about everything around you. You give orders, you take charge, you expect a positive outcome, you don't expect failure — you will not allow it. Discovering that you, a Marine Corps officer no less, who takes direct and decisive action about everything has had some lesser person take away his brother and then discover that you were unprepared to investigate a murder had to be unsettling, upsetting, and frustrating. Add to that, the two of us working together while resolving our personal issues, and you have been on a wild ride, Darling. The responsibilities that I referred to earlier are not the family business issues. You will learn how to interact with the lawyers and the bankers without problems. You will even go to board meetings and make the other children nervous. The bigger issues for you will be those dealing with your employees and their lives, because who you really are is someone who takes charge, forcing a favorable situation for those that you are responsible for. I want you to know that what is happening to us is not an additional responsibility for you alone to bear. We have a responsibility to each other, and I plan to give more than I take. For me, discovering your personal financial situation added some difficulty. I want you irrespective of your financial resources. I would have been perfectly pleased sharing my life with a lieutenant colonel. That is why I asked Jason for this."

She signed the agreement that, unknown to me, Jason had immediately prepared. She folded it carefully and put it into an envelope previously addressed to Jason's office. He had even pre-metered the envelope with postage. Had he been here, he would have made seventeen copies and mailed them all to different, secure locations.

MISSING MONTHS

Ricardo met us outside of Penn Station at 2 PM. We had been gone only two days, but so much had happened that it seemed like longer.

"Colonel Briggs! Beautiful Signora! My heart was glad when I learned that you return so quickly! Colonel Briggs, your Mr. Gus is a good man I think, but I think he a little crazy. He call me and we meet first time on the phone. He said he would come to New York soon and show me around. Show me? But I live here, I tell him. He say that don't matter. He show me around! I don't understand? He say I am beautiful. He say it twice and very loud. Why would he say that? Is he, you know, funny?"

"Ricardo, you are in over your head. Just go with the flow."

"With the flow? What is the flow?"

For once someone besides me was in the dark.

When we arrived at the condo, Antonio and his assistant Consiglieri's descended on us in a mob action of Italian-flourish and Italian-speak, none of which was for my benefit. I let Antonio precede me into the apartment. He had made enough noise that if anyone was inside who shouldn't be, the person would have had plenty of time to hide. After he left, I checked each room. We were alone. While I was looking in closets and checking under beds, Marilena had been on the phone talking insistently with someone.

"Thomas, I am now very concerned about April. I feel that something bad has happened. I am afraid that we made a mistake by not taking her with us to Boston," she said.

"It was difficult enough explaining you. If I had shown up with each of you hanging onto an arm, Gus and company would have truly had a field day."

Marilena ignored my reply. Our calendar girl's radio silence was really bothering her. "We need to find her. I was just on the telephone with the local FBI office. I was trying to see whom they could speak to with the local police on our behalf to find April. Apparently, your relations with Captain O'Dale are superior to what we enjoy between the bureau and the NYPD. Can you call him and ask him to help us find April?"

From her attitude, I could tell that there was more to this story, but it would have to wait until I made the call. I pulled out my cell and dialed the 17th Precinct from the list of previously called numbers faithfully stored by the phone. O'Dale's admin immediately remembered me and said that her instructions, if I called, were to find him. His schedule for the rest of the day didn't include any mandatory meetings, and she suggested that I either call back or come by in person. I opted for the face-to-face and asked her to warn him.

Marilena had listened to my half of the call and nodded approvingly. Without saying anything else about the subject, she turned and walked into the guest room that we had shared, this annoying subject closed. She needed something to do and started to unpack, hanging her clothes and mine in the closets. She looked back at me and said, "We might as well get settled in. I think we will be here for several days."

"It's kinda funny," I said without hiding a growing smile as I walked in behind her.

"What is funny?" she said in a tone that revealed her frustration with her counterpart at the New York FBI office here had not fully departed and the fact that I wasn't going to pass up this opportunity.

"Oh, that my casually developed relationship with O'Dale might get us someplace where the official FBI-NYPD conduit can't."

Surprisingly, she didn't push back at my juvenile behavior and acquiesced instead. She compressed her lips, dropped her shoulders, and said, "If you must know, I was speaking with a special agent that I know — a woman. She is insufferable and causes many male agents to think less of the rest of the female agents. It gets worse. Her liaison with the local police is unfortunately another woman who, unlike me, doesn't have to put up with her."

"Ah, not a sterling example of the FBI sisterhood? Have you ever met her in person?"

"Yes, unfortunately. Several times."

"Can you see any evidence of residual ancestral poultry in her features? Have you ever noticed if she is uncomfortable eating eggs?"

"What? Whatever are you talking about?"

This day was getting better and better.

* * *

It was good to see Jim O'Dale again. He hit it off with Marilena right away. I didn't think that it was because he was in love with the FBI. For her, however, he would overlook who employed her. He even mentioned that he was glad to see that I had enlisted the right talent. She gave him the big smile, and he melted a little more — so much for tough, New York precinct commanders.

We brought him up to speed on what had transpired since he and I met. He nodded approvingly at the right places and was appropriately, though only mildly, shocked at the more violent episodes. He smiled at the references to my meeting with Michaelson and about how we met April June, even guessing her middle name. We discussed the reduced lists of suspects with him.

"This one guy, this Wilson. President Montgomery's husband, right? Do you really think that he could be a suspect?" O'Dale asked.

"It would be nice, maybe even easy, to eliminate him," I answered.

"I would like to know why he was there and his wife was not?" Marilena asked. "Does he work for the society? He was marked as an employee."

"Those are a couple of good questions," O'Dale said.

"There is a more pressing question," Marilena replied.

"Yeah, what's that?" he asked her back.

"We have lost contact with April. She hasn't returned my calls. I am concerned."

He paused for a moment while he looked at her, one pro assessing another. I've gotten the same looks from other docs after speculating about a diagnosis. He knew that she was going on her gut and nothing more, but it was still important. A seasoned cop understanding that another seasoned cop *just had a feeling* was not something you dismissed. "Do you want me to put out the word?" he asked carefully.

"That would be very helpful," she said, appreciating his understanding.

He nodded and then, offering some common sense advice of his own, said, "Of course, the best way to find her is to go to her job. Given what she does for a living, I would recommend that you send Tom instead of having me send a uniform. Our guys have a way of putting a chill on a room like that, and people become not as forthcoming real fast."

This day was definitely getting better and better. Marilena had just been told that the best way to find April was to send me to a strip joint, albeit an upscale strip joint, but a strip joint all the same. O'Dale winked at her, and Marilena answered his challenge head on.

"Jim, I was thinking exactly the same thing with one small enhancement," she said. "I am sure that the ladies who work there would be even more relaxed and forthcoming if I went with Thomas, as well. I'm sure that Thomas knows where it is. He can escort me there this evening."

The day had just stopped getting better and better.

* * *

We had dinner at a small Italian restaurant on the East side in the 50s that I liked and that Ricardo approved of. I had invited O'Dale, but he had another engagement so he declined.

After getting settled at a table, I said, "Do you really want to go with me tonight? It's not your kind of place."

"Why is that?"

"Well, you know."

"No, tell me."

"Listen, it's not the kind of place I would choose to take you."

"I will be fine. We are just going find out if any of her coworkers have seen April."

"That's not all you are going to see."

She smiled, "Thomas, I have seen naked women before. I see one in the mirror every morning. I will survive. Besides, I think that it will be highly entertaining because of how awkward it will be for you to see me, seeing you see all the naked ladies. See what I mean?"

"What?"

* * *

Playoffs wasn't far from the restaurant. Marilena saved me some grief by telling Ricardo our destination and asking him to take us there. She didn't tell him why we were going, leaving him hanging, and the obvious question unasked. After he helped her into the car, he looked at me still standing on the curb.

He leaned over, now a fellow male conspirator, and said quietly but with obvious enthusiasm, "Colonel, you are a lucky man! Dinner with the lovely Signora, and then she takes you to the rich-man's stripper club!"

Oh, boy.

We walked up to the front door at Playoffs. Two bouncers in tuxedos quickly opened the door for us. They were both impressed with my date more than they were with me. Coming back to Earth, the one closer to me said, "Sir. Don't forget that there is no cover when you bring a lady in with you!"

"Do you see, Thomas? I am already being beneficial to our visit."

The cover charge could have been any amount, and I would have paid it to avoid this. Stay focused, Tommy. Just get in, get the intel, and get out as fast as you can.

We entered the club and walked past the cashier who, without Marilena, would have clipped me for a twenty. The cashier was dressed in a slinky sequined affair with a considerable plunge to the neckline. She appraised Marilena and called another bouncer over, giving him instructions to help us find a seat.

The room we entered was about one hundred feet long by seventy-five feet wide and was dimly lit except for the stages. There was a center stage and another behind the bar with tables and booths throughout the room. The chairs at the tables were high-backed with wings providing a lot of tableside privacy. Both stages were occupied by young women in various stages of undress moving haphazardly to the music. The room was about two-thirds occupied. I told the bouncer to put us in one of the round booths along the back wall.

There were about thirty dancers who were working the room, their turns on stage either having come and gone or yet to come. By working the room, I mean that they were moving casually from table to table trying to get a patron to buy a dance from them. They made their real money on the floor, not from tips while up on the stage. About ten of the ladies had managed this and were performing solo acts of stripping and then draping themselves on top of the customer for the duration of one song played by the DJ. There was a lot of body-to-body and hand-to-body contact going on, and like my palimony agreement, it was bilateral. O'Dale was right, with a uniform in the room the uninhibited environment would have changed — bilaterally.

A provocatively dressed waitress appeared at our booth and placed paper napkins on the small round table in front of us. She took our order and left. I made sure that we had both ordered alcoholic beverages so that the word would pass that we were not cops. I explained this to Marilena.

"Thomas, your understanding of the subtleties here is impressive."

I had decided that the way to handle this was denial, basic, and broad-spectrum denial, denial by absurdity, in spite of the fact that both parties knew better.

"I was in a place just like this once."

"Just once?"

"Yeah, I was eighteen and my buddies forced me to go. I really didn't want to. To make a long story short, a stripper promised to marry me. She broke my heart, and I have never been back to one since. Honest." I gave her my best innocent puppy dog look.

"Of course you haven't. Even though it has been decades since your last and only visit, your memory of the correct protocols is very impressive." She had a hard time getting this out while laughing at the same time.

"Well, given my still-working memory for how these places work, why don't you let me take the lead?" If I stayed in control, I could make this short and sweet, and we could get out quick.

"If you believe that your memory is good enough, given how long it has been since you have been in a strip club, excuse me, adult artistic theater, then I, and probably soon, one of the dancers will be in your hands. Lead on, McDuff."

My objective was twofold: Get any info on April as quickly as possible and get out without providing Marilena any ammunition for future tormenting sessions. Looking at her, I could see that we were operating at cross-purposes. She had leaned back against the couch, was in no hurry at all, and was casually collecting as much blackmail material as she could. I was definitely in the danger zone. Still, if she knew everything that had ever happened in the seat she now occupied, she would have thought of our booth as a biological danger zone and not been quite so comfortable.

Pushing ahead, my objectives at the forefront of my mind, I got busy. In a men's club you can get more real intelligence from the drink pushers than from the strippers. Our drinks arrived, and my twenty-dollar tip got our waitress's attention. The servers, though usually just as cute and as provocatively dressed as the dancers, are generally ignored while the guys leer at the stage. Any customer who focuses on his waitress and not the entertainment is welcome.

I began with an earnest approach, "Hi, I'm Tom, and this is Marilena."

"I'm Sindy with an Ess," she said. "You guys been here before?"

"First time."

"Oh, I think you'll like it here. A lot of couples come in. They always have a good time!"

I motioned to the one chair at our table and said, "Can we buy you a drink?"

"That would be great! Let me go get it and come back. Is a Jager OK? Maybe a double?"

"Whatever you want," I agreed.

She left to get her drink, a new bounce to her step, which had until now been lethargic. Another night schlepping drinks to guys there to see the girls who took off their clothes. While she was gone, Marilena was taking in the room and the various activities happening around us like side shows at an adult circus.

"Thomas, can she drink while working?" Marilena asked.

"I've never been in, I mean, I've never heard of one of these places where they couldn't."

Sindy with an Ess returned with her drink, dropped into the chair, offered her thanks, and then drained the double in one gulp. It was not the first drink of her life.

"Thanks, man. I needed that!"

"Sure. How long have you worked here?" I asked.

"About two years."

"Do you like it?"

"Well, the money's good enough so I can share a place in the city. I mean, it's not as good as what the dancers make, but I get by."

"Thought about dancing?" My question got me a not-so-nice look from Marilena that was unnoticed by Sindy.

"Yeah. Once, on my birthday, I got on stage. I was drunk and don't remember much. The dancers were nice to me and made sure all the guys tipped me. I woke up the next morning at home but in someone else's clothes. I think I'll stick to being a waitress."

"Do you know many of the other girls here?"

"Oh, yeah. Almost all of them. Are you looking for someone to play with?"

"Not yet. Maybe later," I said. Marilena's eyebrows headed toward her hairline.

"Just let me know. I can tell you who the good ones are so you don't waste your money on some cock-tease, or worse, a dyke. You know, I'll get you one of the good ones who, uh, well, someone a little more adventurous, especially with a couple."

"Actually, I do know one of the ladies who works here. She is a friend of my brother's."

Between the double Jagermeister and putting her at ease with the small talk, she wasn't suspicious. "Who is that? Maybe she's here, and I can get her for you?"

"Her real name is April, but I don't know her stage name." This got me another look from Marilena as I revealed more of what I knew — this time about stripper naming practices. I described April until Sindy made the connection.

"Oh, April May June! Her dancer name is Mercedes."

"You know her?"

"Sure, everyone here does. She is so nice and has it together. You know, going to college and everything, but not acting all superior. I haven't seen her tonight. Let me go check the schedule in the DJ booth and see if she's coming in."

Off she went. Marilena looked at me and said, "I am going to tell everyone at the FBI to call you first if an undercover operation is required at a gentlemen's club."

"Gee, thanks."

Sindy came back. "She's not coming in tonight. I asked Mikey, the DJ, and he said that she was on the schedule last night and didn't show. She's never done that before. He was real surprised."

"Does she have any close friends here?" I asked.

"Yeah, Katrina, I mean Porsche. They hang out together sometimes. Let me go find her. I know she's here tonight. I saw her a little while ago."

"Thomas — Mercedes and Porsche? Is it customary for the girls to assume automobile names?"

"The automobile model name association is one that is currently popular," I said with professorial diction. "Recently published studies indicate that current dancer names tend to come from a small number of categories. There are the exotic car girls like April, there are those named after primitive emotions like 'Passion' and 'Fury,' there are some named after gemstones like 'Diamond,' 'Ruby' and 'Sapphire,' there are the small animal girls like 'Bambi' and 'Thumper,' and so it goes. Some future anthropologist will, no doubt, be able to provide a complete taxonomy of stripper naming conventions." Then, dropping the fake college lecturer voice, I added defensively, "Of course, that's just what the guys in the office tell me. I really wouldn't know personally."

"Of course. Still, you are a wealth of information!"

Sindy returned with a tall, very attractive young blonde with Slavic features. She was wearing a tiny "G" string on the bottom and a miniscule piece of lingerie, completely transparent on top. Sindy pushed the new girl towards me. As was the custom here, without any warning and catching me completely off guard even though I should have been expecting it — she sat in my lap. OK, I'll admit that this had happened to me before, maybe several times. I just wasn't expecting it tonight. I had brought along my own date and foolishly thought that this would certainly deter any of the girls from just dropping into my lap.

Before I could object, slip out from under her, or do anything to extricate myself, Sindy said, "This is Porsche. K, these are friends of April's."

"Hi." Even the one syllable, though spoken shyly, was accented but accompanied with a small smile.

"Dear, where are you from?" Marilena asked, pretending to ignore the fact that the voluptuous, ninety-eight percent naked blonde was sitting on my lap.

"The Czech Republic. I am two years here."

Marilena immediately broke into a language entirely unknown to me. I guessed that it was whatever they spoke where Katrina was from. Whatever it was, Katrina lit up like a Roman candle. She responded in her country's language, both of them speaking rapidly, starting to laugh, leaning toward each other almost not noticing that I was in the way. Marilena's hand reached out to rest on Katrina's wrist. I was still trying to think of a way to escape, maybe slide Katrina between Marilena and me, except that Marilena had closed that off by sliding next to me in order to be closer to Katrina. This was not going according to my plan.

Sindy leaned over and whispered to me, "I'll be back. I have to check on some of my other tables. Remember, don't pick out a dancer for a lap dance unless you check with me first!"

I promised not to. I had no plans to pick out a dancer, approved or not, for anything. Sindy left, Marilena and Katrina didn't notice her departure. I had no idea what they were talking about, and although there were a couple of what seemed to be serious moments, Katrina was fully engaged and obviously pleased to meet someone who spoke the mother tongue.

Eventually, and only after repeated prayers to my very own personal God, Katrina smiled at me as if noticing me for the first time, got up, and left. My particular lap was vacated at last, obviously just another in a long night of laps.

Marilena continued, but now with a more serious tone, "She knows where April is and is getting the address for us now. Katrina has spoken to her today, and April is safe. Katrina also said that April was not feeling well and just taking some time off."

"Then let's get the address and get going." This was a plan I could get behind.

"Don't worry, Thomas. There does not seem to be any reason to hurry. Katrina will be right back, and I will have her sit on your lap again." She was having way too much fun. This was not going well. Not well at all.

FRUSTRATIONS, LIMITATIONS, COMPLICATIONS

When Katrina returned I made sure that she sat in the booth seat between Marilena and me and not in my lap. Marilena continued to smile at my discomfort but said nothing to Katrina who would have been amazed that I had any problem with her seat selection. After all, she was doing her part as expected, and if I were uncomfortable with it, why had I come in? After collecting the note with the address and phone number where April was hiding out, I got up, pulling Marilena to her feet. This little circus would soon be behind me. I pushed three one hundred dollar bills into Katrina's hand, and we headed for the door. Along the way, we were stopped by the manager.

"Are you folk's leaving us?" he asked, disappointment in his voice.

"Yeah. Afraid so. We have an early morning," I answered back looking for a quick and affable way around him.

He shifted his focus from me to Marilena and said, "You know, if you ever want to work at a club, we're the best, and I'll always have a place for you here, sweet thing. I don't know what you do now, but the money here would be absolutely amazing for a gal with your looks."

"What do you think, Thomas?" she asked me while lifting an eyebrow and cocking her head to one side. Falling for her act, the sleaze ball manager immediately looked at me as if only my permission stood between him and his ability to land this incredibly sexy woman as a new and serious moneymaker. His expression was very hopeful. If I waited ten seconds, actual drooling would commence.

I moved forward, glared down at him while speaking in a calm yet unmistakably displeased voice, "She would need a different boyfriend. The one she's with now is prone to violence —

especially when other guys get too close to what's his." A path to the door magically opened up.

I had sent Ricardo home because we hadn't known how long it was going to take us to find someone who knew where April might be. The club had a limo, and the manager directed someone to give us a ride. Not my first choice, but better than hailing a cab. The manager was keeping the door open for Marilena in case her personal situation changed.

I gave the driver a Central Park West intersection about two blocks from the condo. I was not at all interested in having them report back our home address to Sleaze Ball, Inc. On the way, our very friendly and talkative driver shared stories with us about famous people who had been at the club and then in the limo and what they were like. As we got close to our destination, he also told us that many of the dancers were available for entertainment outside of the club, entertainment of a very personal nature. He could set it up, and it was really not that expensive. I declined.

Upstairs and again behind the door with all of the locks, Marilena asked me, "Thomas, was the driver offering the dancers out for sex?"

"Yep. I'm sure that several of them have let it be known that they wouldn't mind making a little more cash after their shift ends."

"Well, I am proud of you for not engaging a private dancer for entertainment of a very personal nature!" she said with mock seriousness.

"As much as I was tempted, I'm fairly certain that it would have been a violation of part one of the bilateral agreement that you proposed and I accepted. That exclusivity thing, remember? And, as far as your employment in a strip joint is concerned, fantasy or otherwise, that same part one of our arrangement has reduced the number of laps that you may sit upon and squirm around on to just one. Besides, I brought home the only woman I saw tonight who lights me up."

She laughed and moved into my arms, "Although I doubt that I am unique in having the ability to excite you, thank you for saying it. In fact, kind sir, your endearing words and your earlier revelation of jealousy, buys you enough credit with me, while on the only lap that I am now allowed to sit upon and squirm around on, to entertain you for a long time."

And then she did. The club manager had been right. She could make a fortune.

* * *

We slept in a little later than normal the next morning due to the late return from Playoffs and our pre-sleep playtime that lasted into the middle of the night. We were getting better at the bathroom routine and made up a little time as we coordinated showering, exfoliating, hot combing, brushing, nail polishing, face painting, and shaving. Even though the preponderance of those activities was hers, she managed to work it out so that we finished at about the same time.

The day's schedule was in flux until we made some phone calls. Marilena called April while I sat in the den and thought about where we stood finding Ron's killer and about what Marilena had said about the changes that I was going through.

I hadn't had time yet to think about everything she had said, but one point she had made was true, I was struggling with my role as murder investigator. She was right. I was finding this to be surprisingly different from the world where my training and experience had value, and it was extremely frustrating. When I had first decided that I would determine if Ron was murdered and if so, find his killer, I had foolishly believed that I had at least some of the skills required. With help from a pro filling in the rest, I would be successful. In fact, I had further deluded myself that I was way better equipped than the average guy to work with a civilian investigator because I had extensive military combat training. Training that included urban threat assessment and assault techniques. I was very wrong. The sad fact was I did not have the skills that you need to catch a killer — far from it.

Looking back on this, I was amazed at how incredibly dumb I had been — there was no other way to put it, my arrogance seemed to have no limit. As a Marine I had been trained in physical combat and was very good at it. I had learned logistics and tactics and how to employ them as a leader of a platoon. My enemies would attempt to evade or overwhelm my team and me.

But I knew if we got to grips, we would succeed, and they would die. No doubt. Not for a minute. On top of all of this, I had become a doctor, a surgeon no less, adding even more to my inflated assessment of my lofty level of smarts. This investigation had been a humbling experience for me, and I didn't like that at all. A Marine Corps Force Recon gunslinger and military surgeon who specialized in very hazardous insertions into enemy country just doesn't do humbling experiences well. What could there ever be about any enemy action for which I was not prepared? However, this enemy was in hiding, hiding behind lies and duplicity and a pretense of civilization that I could not see through. All of my ability to defeat an opponent was of little value if I couldn't tell who my opponent was. So far, my investigative technique was limited to blindly antagonizing and then reacting after, and only after, the enemy made a move.

My enemy was in control, and my only advancements had come when he, or more recently she, made a mistake. Marilena was not sharing my frustrations and completely surprised me when she repeatedly told me we were making good progress. She had the skills that, when coupled with enough interaction with our suspects, could discern who was lying to us, and she had the patience to wait for the opposition to move and make mistakes. She lived in this Machiavellian chess game knowing that people are duplicitous, hiding their intentions and actions with deceit. My world was simple. The bad guys had different uniforms, and all I had to do was beat them in a stand-up fight. I didn't have to talk to them or figure out if their words were the truth or lies. All I had to do was kill them. I was going to have to start respecting a lot of people who weren't Marines. I didn't like that either.

I didn't mind the fact that Marilena walked in and interrupted my damning self-assessment — I was getting depressed.

"Thomas, I talked to April."

"Great! Is she OK?"

"Yes. She is better now."

"Now?"

"She believed that she was being followed, and her apartment was broken into. She decided that she needed to go into hiding for a while. At least until she talked to us."

"But she didn't call you or return your calls."

"She fled her apartment and came here as quickly as she could. She left so fast that she forgot her cell phone. When she got here, she was no longer on the approved visitor list, and they wouldn't give her a key or let her in. Not knowing where to go and being afraid to go back to her apartment, she went to a girlfriend's loft on the West side down near the old meat packing district. Her friend is traveling but always leaves a key under the doormat. We will see April tonight. I'd like to bring her back here."

"Do you think she's safe? Should we go get her now?"

"If someone was trying to find her and has not been able to do so in the last two days, then she is OK where she is. It will be safe for her to come here but only when we can be with her. This is a known location to all of our suspects. We have to go to the CID Society today, and I don't want to leave her alone. Not here."

"OK, I see your point."

I called Jim O'Dale and told him to save some taxpayer money by calling off the search — we had found April and would see her later tonight. He asked me where she was — wanting to know in case something happened to us today. He laughed and said that I was a lightning rod for hazardous events. I read him the address from Katrina's note.

After calling O'Dale, I dialed Alison Montgomery's cell. She agreed to meet with us at 2 PM and invited me to her national board meeting at 3 PM. I agreed with her plan. I spent the rest of the morning reading more of Ron's research while Marilena made phone calls to friends at the FBI.

Ricardo drove us to a restaurant near the CID offices on 2nd where we ate lunch and planned our conversation with Alison Montgomery. We still needed her help to stay close to the remaining suspects. Lunch was close enough to the CID headquarters that we could walk to it so I had dismissed Ricardo. In short order, we found ourselves in Alison's office.

"I'm still in shock over Margaret's death," she said painfully, the hurt evident in her eyes. "She worked here for several years and although she could sometimes be abrasive, she had high energy and was committed to our cause. I thought I really knew her. I'm not sure what is more shocking, her death or that she was involved in Ron's death. Do you really think she had something to do with it?"

"Yes. We believe that we will connect her with the murderer," Marilena answered.

"But, she was not the killer? You are certain?" Alison asked.

"We do not believe that she was in the building when Thomas's brother was killed. We are confirming that now."

"What do you think her relationship was to the killer?"

"We will discover that soon," Marilena spoke with the authority of an oracle.

I interjected, "Alison, it's not over yet. Townsend was in league with Ron's killer, and we will find out who and why. Your help is of paramount importance."

"Of course you have it, Tom. I won't rest until we find out who it was. The fact that it was probably another member of my senior team is so devastating to me and to our cause that I can't eat or sleep. We need to end this as soon as we can so the society can move on."

"We will, Alison. And, in return for your support, we will portray this as some twisted issue between individuals and not associate it with the work the society is doing."

"Oh, thank you, Tom. We need that. No matter what has happened, we have a higher responsibility to those with this disease. Your brother would agree."

"I know he would."

"What can I do?"

Marilena answered, "Continuing to involve us with activities and events with the remaining suspects is very helpful. Thank you for allowing us to attend your board meeting this afternoon. We need to make the killer believe that we are pleased with our progress and have no concerns about discovering Ron's killer. Eventually, he or she will become panicked enough to take some rash action."

Alison responded to her request. "Tom, I want to finish this, and then I want you to take your brother's place on our board. I want your help to find a cure. Nothing else matters."

"There could be good news on that front. We have come into possession of Ron's recent research data that not only indicate that he has discovered the genetic basis for CID but also that he had even proposed a therapy to cure those afflicted and to prevent the onset for those having the genetic marker. We need to validate this information, and if I can help I will. This was Ron's final gift, and that makes it important to me. You can count on my involvement and our family's continued financial support."

"This is wonderful news! With everything else going on, I can't believe it, but you have made me very happy. I believe more than ever that we will win. *We will defeat CID!*" Her words were not just spoken. They were delivered with a certainty, an intensity that made you believe right along with her. "Let's go to the meeting so I can tell everyone about your commitment to move ahead with us. As for these new discoveries, a potential cure, and Ron's research findings, I agree that we need to validate his research as soon as possible. In the meantime, however, let's not speak to anyone about that until we are sure. Revealing it now would get everyone's hopes up, and even if we asked the hundred or so people in the boardroom to keep it a secret, it would be all over the world thirty minutes after we adjourn. If it turns out not to be the road to a cure, we would lose a lot of credibility."

"It's your call, Alison, and I agree with your concern. We won't say anything about it yet."

"Are the data safe?" she asked.

"Yes, Ron placed a copy with a trusted friend. She gave it to me, and I have made one backup copy in addition to the original."

"So, it hasn't been distributed to anyone and has only been in your possession and that of Ron's friend?"

"Yeah, we're good."

"OK, I'll make some calls to scientists whom Ron respected and line them up to analyze the data. I'll let you know tomorrow what our next steps should be."

* * *

We entered the boardroom on Alison's heels. She spoke with someone who rearranged the name cards at the table to make room for me. There appeared to be about thirty-five board members making it a very large board. From what I knew, it was populated by business people and scientists. Marilena discretely moved to one side of the room and sat in a chair along the wall with others who were not board members.

The meeting came to order, a quorum achieved. Alison began by announcing a change to the agenda that had been distributed. She then proceeded to introduce me to the other board members, many of whom made appreciative comments about my new participation as a board member and expressed condolences. A couple of the male members sitting near me stood up and leaned my way to shake my hand.

The first two orders of business, while being supported by the board, were identified as ones that would considerably upset the part of the chapter leadership in the field. It had been proposed to reduce the number of chapters from sixty to about twelve. A committee had been examining just how to do this and what the remaining chapters should look like. The principal reason for this move was cost reduction that would come from consolidation. There were going to be a lot of chapter presidents out of a job and unhappy — very unhappy.

The second issue that was causing angst among the field troops was the home office's move to consolidate the chapter donor databases into one physical location. This would allow the home office to solicit funds based on nationwide programs. The chapters were upset over losing control of major donors that they had cultivated over many years.

I didn't know enough about either of these issues to comment, but the field concerns, the chapter concerns, seemed reasonable, at least about the competing donor solicitations. Maybe the chapter consolidation objections were simply people worried about having a job. What came next, however, I understood completely and was absolutely stunned at what I heard. So totally blown away that I would forget to leave the message that we were making progress in our investigation and Ron's murderer would soon be uncovered.

A young lady sitting at the end of the table away from Alison and me had been introduced to us as Lindy Price. Even though she wasn't a board member, she, like me, had been granted a seat at the big kid's table. Lindy had CID and was a fundraiser — a significant fundraiser. She sponsored events in New York raising, by Alison's very complimentary statements, over five hundred thousand dollars each summer. The unspoken problem was that she donated her funds directly to the National Institutes of Health and not to the CID Society. Alison had invited her to the board meeting most likely as a first step in getting her to play ball and funnel her money through the society. Alison's efforts were about to be squashed. Squashed by Chubby Woody.

Chubby Woody had been sitting about three seats away from me and had not been as effusive as the others when Alison introduced me. He flowed out of his chair on three sides with only the back preventing it from being four, a human sphere. He was sitting slightly away from the table and was reading some paperwork during the conversation so far. This abruptly changed and not for the better.

"Miss Price. My name is Woodrow Standish — you probably have heard of me and my role in building this organization. I know that you think that having CID and your five-hundred thousand a year is a big deal, but compared to the twenty years of my life that I have dedicated to finding a cure for this disease that afflicts millions of people and not just you, it really isn't so much. Please try to keep this in mind and keep your efforts in perspective."

Whoa! What had he just said? Did I hear it right? I looked at Marilena, whose face was registering total surprise. Lindy Price was taken aback and looked like someone had just hit her with a baseball bat. Quickly, her surprise was replaced with anger.

"Mr. Standish, thank you for helping me see how insignificant my accomplishments are." And with that, she got up and left. I looked at Alison. Her head was tilted forward, and she was studying her hands. She made no effort to respond or placate Lindy Price. Many of the board members physically shrank back in their seats, obviously wishing they were anywhere but here, not surprised at Chubby Woody's stupidity and complete lack of sensitivity. Amazing — simply amazing. What kind of an organization had I just joined?

The meeting ended on that discordant note. Alison quickly left the room, I'm sure so she wouldn't have to deal with the Standish-Price fallout. As for Chubby Woody, he was feeling very happy with himself even though he was bemoaning the fact that it was always up to him to straighten out those upstarts who didn't appreciate his leadership and years of effort.

I was quickly on my feet and was going to do some straightening out myself, in person and right now. Marilena, knowing what I was thinking, had moved more quickly than I would have imagined and intercepted me before I took two steps.

"No, Thomas. We have a more important responsibility than taking that pompous ass apart." Wow, she had cursed. It was definitely for effect, and it worked. Her hand on my arm further anchored me in place while I worked at reducing my blood pressure and to remove the image of Chubby Woody hanging from the chandelier by his tongue.

It was at that moment that Omar Sayyaf walked up to us. "We need to talk. It's important. Can you join me for dinner?"

DISEASED ADVOCACY

The board meeting's abrupt ending was no more bizarre than the way the board members and staff quickly removed themselves from the scene of Chubby Woody's despicable verbal attack. Admittedly, my experience with board meetings was limited to Ron's painful description of them, but even remembering his dislike for the tedium and back-stabbing behavior, this had to have been surprising for even the most tough-skinned business executives like some on the society's board. Taking their queue from Alison Montgomery, the meeting's participants did their best to exit without being entrapped in an embarrassing conversation about what had just happened. Sylvia Canfield had fled after Lindy Price in a belated effort to repair the damage. I doubted that she would be successful. She would probably agree with me.

Omar steered us out the door and toward the elevators. We were met by Barry Ledderman, one of the two outside consultants hired by the society.

"I asked Barry to join us, if that's all right with you?" Omar asked.

"Sure," I said as I shook Ledderman's hand. Although his greeting was polite, his expression was hard and angry, telling us his feelings about the board meeting. I noticed that the other consultant, Jonathan Treece, had walked up behind Omar and was listening to our conversation. "We have to meet someone later tonight at her apartment in the old meat packing district. Can we eat near there?" I asked Omar.

"Maybe I can be of assistance," this from Treece interrupting as he stepped forward. "I live in that area. Where do you need to be after dinner?" I told him the address where April was hiding out, which by now I had memorized. He nodded and said, "There is an excellent restaurant, very new and less than two blocks from there on Little West 12th Street. I highly recommend it." He told us the name, said he would be happy to make reservations, and declined to join us as he had another engagement. I didn't remember inviting him, but I appreciated the help.

Our trip to the restaurant utilized two taxis with Omar and Barry leading the way in first cab and me next to Marilena in the second.

"Between the two of us, you probably know a lot more about board meetings than I do. Was that surprising to you?" I asked my very sophisticated girlfriend."

"That man, that tubby buffoon, was offensive and insulting beyond measure in the way he spoke to that young lady! If we did not have a more important issue to address with these people, I would have let you pound that insufferable idiot senseless. I think that several others would have helped you, including me!" Sophistication was taking a temporary vacation.

"Why didn't Alison stop him?"

"She is either indebted to him or afraid of him."

We arrived at a restaurant only recently opened. It was a very high-end eatery that was part restaurant and part nightclub. After helping Marilena through the entry, we were coolly received, I won't say greeted, by a fashion plate who dutifully led us to our table. I wondered how someone so young and whose only claim to fame was seating people to eat could have already become such an arrogant pain in the ass.

We arranged ourselves and ordered drinks. Omar remarked that he had been told by several friends that this restaurant was worth a try. He only hoped that the food was more appealing than the attitude of the hostess. Drinks arrived and after hearing the litany of not specials, but "off-the-menu chef's exclusives," we ordered.

Omar began, "Thank you again for meeting with us. We need to talk. I asked Barry to join us because he, your brother Ron, and I were collaborating to make changes at the society. If indeed you plan to join the board and make an impact on the society, we would like to share with you our concerns and what we had been doing with Ron's help to make changes."

"Barry, help me understand your area of expertise and your role with the society." Marilena asked Ledderman.

"I am a business and technology consultant. My little firm — I own the company, there are only five of us — helps large organizations acquire business entities and technology in strategic transactions. We have worked for the society for over ten years, due mostly to Alison Montgomery's predecessor. Working for a charity is not our company's primary business, but we do have skills that are not found inside the society, and we do all we can to help. The president before Montgomery was a retired admiral who was truly a great man. Working for him was a pleasure even though he was a taskmaster. He put the mission of the society in the forefront of everything."

"Barry and his team have helped us in countless ways from negotiating on our behalf with our vendors and assisting us with technology implementation in order to help us develop our venture philanthropy program."

"Venture philanthropy?" I asked.

"It'll be great but only if we can keep Alison Montgomery from screwing it up," Ledderman said with a little disgust creeping into his voice.

Omar jumped in to keep the conversation on track. "You need to understand a little of our traditional business model to see how exciting venture philanthropy is."

"How would you describe your business model?" I asked.

"Archaic, frustrating, and quite frankly, in the way of finding a cure for CID. Don't get me entirely wrong. Most of the other health-focused charities suffer in the same way in spite of the fact that many very good people work for them. Charities that are not in the chronic disease arena and have a focus on some non-health related cause have far better business people than we do and have been very successful."

"Give me an example," I said.

"The NRA or the AARP come to mind," Omar said. "They support a parochial issue; they are not embarrassed about it, are professionally managed, and are operated like real businesses that drive for results without apology. In comparison, our successes, even given the considerable sums we raise, are miniscule. If our constituencies, those either having CID or having a loved one with it, fully know how inept we were when compared with an organization promoting gun owner rights, they would be incensed and rightfully so. After all, our mission isn't a political cause like lobbying the congress for some group of farmers. We are fighting a life-robbing disease that afflicts innocent sufferers. Our cause is unimpeachable. We have the moral high ground. The problem is that due to our arrogance we are largely ineffective."

"How and why do you see the society as arrogant?" I asked.

"I believe that it is the combination of two things. First, our mission is one based on science with very smart scientists in our midst. And, second, as I said before, we are morally superior. The two together put us in a place where we certainly can't learn anything from mere business people who can't be as smart as our scientists and certainly are not as trustworthy being the greedy business types that they are." A smile formed on Omar's face as he said this last part, and he looked at Barry. "Barry, here, is a perfect example. He's made a tremendous amount of money, but it is not due to his intelligence. It is because society's misguided principles financially reward the for-profit sector even though they aren't as smart or as principled as we superior humanitarians! It's just not fair!" His words were cynical, his jabs at his friend understood by Ledderman knowing that Omar was in reality stating that the organization he worked for had little to base any arrogance upon.

"Get back to your business model," I said.

"Oh, yes. I'm sorry. My current personal dislike for my organization can get in the way. Our business model is simple. We send children out to play in traffic. Many, many do so, and their very numbers insure two things: fifty-cents and a dollar per mile sponsorship adds up to a lot of money, and sadly one or two of them will die each year supporting our cause."

"What do you mean?" asked Marilena in some shock at Omar's statements.

"We run hundreds of walk and bike fundraising events each year. Our average donor, our bread and butter, is not the big society type writing us a check for a hundred grand but rather a neighbor of little Kathy or little Jimmy sponsoring the child's bike ride in the name of our cause. The neighbors' check will average fifteen dollars. We just get lots and lots and lots of them. Hundreds of millions of dollars."

"You said some die?" I asked.

"Yes. Each year, one or two people will get struck by a car or truck while participating in an event. This last year was especially difficult. We lost two children at two separate events but on the same day, both in plain view of their parents who were also participating. What I am saying is that given the hard work, and in some cases the ultimate sacrifices of our donors, we should be better stewards of the money entrusted to us."

"And you are not?" Marilena said with more surprise.

"We spend the minority of what we take in on research. The rest gets mysteriously spent in what is called in fund accounting, program-related costs, and administration. We live life well. Salaries are high, some executives travel first class, we stay at very expensive hotels, and even our research dollars are suspect. Let's begin with the research spending. The money is handed out to educational centers in the form of research grants. It is mostly an institutionalized program to keep graduate students employed. Very little actual research into CID actually gets accomplished. Even worse, if you were to go to a premier research facility like the Marklin and ask them to comment on the research work being sponsored by our grant, they would tell you that all too often, the science is bad science. The bottom third of our grant money is easily wasted on science that the rest of the medical community will not only ignore but distance itself from. Putting it simply, the traditional grant model spends a lot of money and in return, we get papers, not therapies. And if the papers are of such value, why is there no mechanism for promoting them to other researchers? There isn't even a database available that tells you what papers have been written with our grant money and a synopsis of their findings. That's because little of it has actual value. We report the number of papers written, not discoveries made that will help find a cure for CID."

"That's pretty damning," I said quietly while thinking of the money our family has donated to healthcare advocacies.

Ledderman joined the conversation with, "That's what we have been trying to fix with venture philanthropy."

"How does that work?" again from Marilena, who, like me, was both fascinated and distressed by what we were hearing.

Ledderman continued, "It's a simple, yet powerful departure from the academic grant model. We take donor money and invest it in commercial initiatives developing therapies or diagnostic tools for people with CID. Our money has real and tremendous impact. For example, there are over fifty compounds that show promise for someone with CID that are languishing on the shelf with early stage pharma companies because they lack the resources to do clinical trials. In over sixty years since the society was formed, we have seen the delivery of only five drugs that are approved for people with CID. None of them is a cure. They treat only some symptoms, and the side effects can be worse than the disease. Over half of our constituency doesn't take any of them."

"I don't understand. What's the hold up? Why don't you do more of the venture philanthropy? Get the trials started for the other compounds?" I was sure that I was missing something simple.

"Like all organizations, we resist change. There are departments staffed with well-paid people administering those grants. Diverting their grant money diminishes their departments' worth and political clout. Their arguments are fallacious," Omar continued. "The society response to venture philanthropy has been that it too closely aligns greedy commercial business with donor money. Let's stick with a model that isn't working instead of making a change to something that may make us look like a partner to a commercial venture."

"You're kidding?"

Omar looked at me and said seriously, "I only wish I were."

"What is Alison's take on this?"

Omar's lips compressed into thin lines while Ledderman exhaled in open disgust. Omar said, "This is a place where Barry and I disagree. I believe that Alison just doesn't understand the issue and is being manipulated by those in the society who have built empires around the current programs. Barry thinks that she knows exactly what the issue is and for some unknown reason is fighting us."

Marilena said, "That is actually promising that you have differing views and you debate them. Barry, what are your reasons for suspecting Alison of any malfeasance?"

Omar nodded and said, "Telling them about it is a good idea, Barry. We're among friends. Tell Tom and Marilena what has been bugging you. Although I haven't yet decided that Alison is anything more than incredibly naive, there are some things that I have seen lately that trouble me."

Ledderman looked down at his drink, gathered his thoughts and began, "Ever since we lost the Admiral, the society has made decisions that I don't understand. We make mistakes, and instead of fixing them in the open, as he would have, we hide them. We are no longer the central organization directing the resources delivered by the chapters on their behalf. We are taking and reorganizing to control more money without seeming concerned about fighting the disease. Omar is on the fence about whether it is the executive team's inexperience or whether they know what they are doing, and that is for some reason not in support of the mission. I'm not on the fence, at least not anymore. Let me give you some examples of what is going on at the CID Society.

"Last year the home office fought a war with the chapters to have them move their donor databases into a national repository for safe keeping. The chapters, by and large, are as sophisticated or even more so than the national about data management. There was no risk. It was a plain and simple grab at the contact info for the donors. The national now mails them directly soliciting their money.

"Montgomery, the least qualified senior executive in existence today, routinely makes really bad decisions. Two months ago, she decided to take the three largest bike event fundraisers on a reward trip. Where did she decide to take them along with her friends on the senior staff? Italy! Two weeks in first class accommodations! If that ever got out, it would look really bad. Imagine if your child had died raising money that was spent on an Italian boondoggle.

"We have several items that we are working to hide because of the bad press they would generate. A former employee in our office has stolen over one hundred and fifty thousand dollars of donor money over the last two years. We fired her but neglected to get her building pass. She has been coming in every Saturday and going through the mail that the mailman leaves at our office door and pulling out the checks. She has even been sending them back thank you letters so they don't follow up! After discovering this, the energy was put into keeping it a secret and not fixing the problem with new protocols and safeguards.

"Then, there's that idiot Treece. He's mister touchy-feely consultant for Montgomery; one of those soft science guys whose work can't be objectively measured — a modern day shaman. He does the love-in meetings where people get to describe what cartoon characters the society reminds them of and to have their personalities profiled so that the others can better understand them. He's a fruitcake. Last week I had to sit in one of his group gropes because Montgomery believed it would bring us together. What a load of crap.

"But the part I really don't understand is why Montgomery's two most influential staff members are such evil bitches, and she sees them as key to the society's success! Well, one still is; the other just died."

"I take it you mean Townsend. Who is the other?" I asked guessing that I already knew.

"Canfield is the other and is just as bad as Townsend was, only she is sneakier and not as in-your-face. And then on top of that, what is the deal with that butterball Standish? You heard that bullshit in the meeting with Lindy Price? And Montgomery did nothing. What's he got on her?"

At that moment my cell phone rang. I looked at it, and it was Jim O'Dale. I thought it best if I took this one, opened the thing, and spoke into it, "Hi, Jim."

"Tom, where are you?" His voice had an anxious note that I had not heard before.

"We're at dinner at a restaurant in the meat packing district."

"Then you're near the address you gave me earlier?" he asked.

"Yeah, just around the corner. What's up?"

"After you called me today, I started having second thoughts about April's safety. So, I called my counterpart at the precinct you're in right now. I told him the background and asked him to have a couple of uniforms drop by the apartment and keep an eye on her until you got there."

"And?" I quickly asked, not liking where this was going.

"They've been there twice in the last hour and knocked on the door several times with no answer. They don't have a court order or probable cause to bust in. They called it in and headed back out on patrol, figuring they'd stop by again later. I got that uneasy feeling in my gut, and I'm in my car headed there now."

"I'm two blocks away. I'll be there in less than five." I hung up.

The issue of whether Alison Montgomery, albeit an inspirational and charismatic personality, was fundamentally naive and possibly never capable of filling an executive role or just inexperienced and needing some time and a lot of support to grow into her position would have to be left for a later conversation. Either was disconcerting, neither mattered. O'Dale's news couldn't be ignored.

SAVING ANGELS AND FLYING DEMONS

"That was Jim O'Dale. He had some patrol cops go to April's. She's not there and he's worried. So am I." Building in my gut was one of those feelings that could not be ignored.

"What about April?" Ledderman asked having only partially understood what I had quickly said. He was still seated along with Omar and Marilena at our dinner table. Well, they had been anticipating dinner and were about to find out that it would be delayed.

I was already on my feet and yelling to them, "Come on! April is just around the corner. We need to move out now!"

"OK, I'm lost. April's six months from now." Ledderman said in resigned voice. I didn't have time to explain. He'd find out soon enough.

I pulled a C note bill from my billfold, crumpled it into a ball and pitched it at the waiter who was returning with a second round of drinks. Between strip joints and aborted dinners, hundred dollar bills were leaving me at a faster than normal rate. The Benjamin hit him in the face and bounced to his tray, landing in a glass containing an amber liquid — most likely Omar's beer. Grabbing Marilena by the hand and leading the others, we moved quickly to the door. I ignored the soulless hostess, and she ignored us as we hurried out the door. As we moved outside, I retrieved Katrina's note and glanced at the address to confirm my memory.

Turning right at the sidewalk, I took off, part walking, part running, still keeping Marilena's hand tightly in mine. I was moving as fast as I could without losing my three companions: Marilena trying her best to keep her high-heeled feet under her as I pulled her behind me, Omar and Barry huffing and puffing with each step as they tried to keep pace. We were so close that if I left them and ran ahead, I would only beat them to the address where

April was hiding by twenty or thirty seconds, and that was only if I could find it right away. It was better to keep together.

"April was a friend of Ron's, and she may be in danger! We need to find her now!" I yelled this at Omar and Barry as I made the first right at Greenwich Street and headed south. The door I was looking for was less than one hundred feet ahead and on our side of the street. My small expeditionary force was too winded to express their happiness at having arrived. Their exertions, however, were not over yet.

The door was not locked, and I pushed my way through it. April's address indicated a unit on the fourth floor, and it was a walk-up. Not waiting to hear any complaining, I started up the stairs taking them two at a time. The others fell in behind. Reaching the third floor landing while the others were just arriving at the second, I slowed and took the last two half-flights as quietly, but as quickly as I could. You could only turn left out of the staircase and down the hall. The hallway was dimly lit with low-wattage light fixtures every twenty feet or so. April's door was the third on the right.

I stood at the door and pressed my ear to the wood, ignoring the rough and splintered texture. The building didn't get the maintenance attention that Ron's did. I couldn't hear anything inside the unit. Marilena arrived with the boys behind her. She signaled them to be quiet.

"Can you tell if she is in there?" she asked me softly, her lips next to my ear. Marilena's attention to exercise had paid off. She was the only one of the three whose breathing was back under control.

"Can't tell. All quiet."

She put her hand on the knob and carefully tested it. It was locked. Reaching into her purse, she quickly pulled out a small leather envelope about the size of a fat playing card. I was going to have to give her more credit about her purse content retrieval capabilities. Opening the flap, she selected two small hand tools, each a slender pick, one having a bend at the very end. Slipping them into the lock, she quietly worked them back and forth, rotating one while pulling the other back against some obstacle. The lock omitted an occasional click as some part of the mechanism fell into place. It seemed that my new girlfriend could pick a lock. I doubt that I will forget that.

When the lock finally yielded to Marilena's deft manipulation, I turned the knob, pushed the door open quietly and entered the room, the Beretta in my hand although I don't remember pulling it from its holster. The small living area with sparse furnishings was empty. A window was open, and the evening breeze moved a sheer curtain slowly back and forth. There was only one doorway out of the room, and I walked quickly to it. I looked into a small bedroom only to discover that it too was empty. The closet and the area under the bed were full of clutter but no April.

"Tom, come quick," Omar said to me. "Marilena just went out the window!"

I ran to the window, stuck my head, out and found a fire escape. Marilena's shapely lower half was in view and already ascending.

Omar and Barry were still catching their breath, and the thought of more stairs probably unappealing. I pushed the curtain aside and stepped out onto the fire escape landing. Unlike the movies where the characters spent considerable amounts of their evening hours perched on a fire escape that was large and secure, this metal contraption was both small and it wobbled side to side. I climbed the escape stairs up one short flight before getting to a rusty iron ladder secured to the side of the building. Going up the ladder required that I replace the gun in its holster. At the top of the ladder, I slowly peered over the top of the building wall and out on a roof littered with pipes and ventilators. Marilena was stooped low, looking around a ventilator with her gun drawn.

The sky was overcast, but the glow from the windows of taller buildings dimly lit the scene in front of me. About fifty feet from my vantage point was a clear area near the far side of the building. Sylvia Canfield stood behind April — they both faced away from me looking over the edge of the old building. She had her left arm around April's upper body and was holding a knife in her right hand, its blade tip pointed at April's right temple. The breeze that had moved the curtain was just loud enough so that I could not hear what Canfield was saying to April.

I looked down at Barry and Omar and motioned for them to be stay put. Slipping over the top of the ladder and onto the roof, I moved past Marilena, heading for Canfield and April as quietly as I could. I had the gun back in my hand, the center of Canfield's back now a backdrop for the front sight. If they hadn't been so close to the edge, I might have fired. I was confident that I would not hit April. But given where they were standing, I didn't want the kinetic energy of the bullet to knock Canfield forward over the edge taking April with her. I kept moving.

I could hear Canfield now as she threatened April.

"Do you think I'm stupid? Don't tell me he didn't give you a copy! I want his research data! He must have given you a disk, a CD, something! Where have you hidden it? Tell me, or I will cut your brain out, you little slut!"

"He only gave me the helicopter! It's the truth! Just the helicopter!"

"What? What do you mean? Did you say helicopter?"

It was at that moment when I was within fifteen feet of them that Omar stepped off the ladder and onto the roof next to Ledderman. Marilena was five steps behind me, her gun in her hand. Omar slipped and fell face forward. The noise alerted Canfield. She spun around, still holding April. Her face combined anger with the shock at recognizing the four of us.

"Stay away! Stay back! I'll cut her throat! I swear to you, I'll kill her!" She moved the knife from April's head where from my closer vantage point I could see that she had pushed the knife into her temple. A rivulet of blood driven by an unseen pulse had coursed its way down the side of her neck. Blood had saturated the right shoulder of April's blouse. Canfield held the blade across April's throat, pressing the edge into her skin. A red line appeared and blood welled up along the blade. April inhaled sharply from the pain of the surprise incision.

Assuming a balanced stance, I held my gun in both hands and slowly, carefully, aimed it at Canfield's head, the only part of her body not hidden by April. I still did not want to shoot. I was certain I could hit her in the center of her face and not shoot April, but if she went backwards off the building and managed to hold onto her hostage, they would both die. I put my right thumb on the hammer and pulled it back. It made a satisfying click, a click heard by Canfield.

"I'm not joking, Briggs! I'll kill your brother's little bitch!"

I held the hammer back by not taking my thumb from it. I pulled the trigger, it clicked, and Canfield's expression changed from defiance to, for the first time, fear. The hammer did not fall on the cartridge when the trigger mechanism released it — it was still retained by my thumb.

"I've pulled the trigger," the words came out calmly as I stepped closer and closer. "The only thing keeping you from getting a new and very large hole in your head is my thumb holding the hammer back. When it slips out, I won't be able to stop it. This gun will fire, and you will die."

"I'll kill her," she said, but this time much less convincingly. I had moved to within three feet of them and stopped.

"I can't help that. I am going to keep this gun pointed at your head. Sooner or later, my thumb will tire, and you will die. I can already feel my thumb starting to weaken against the hammer spring. It's getting a little sweaty. It's funny, I can't tell you how long I can hold it. I can't tell you when you will die. I can only promise that unless I ease the hammer down, you will die."

Sylvia Canfield was out of options, and she knew it. She closed her eyes. Without warning, she pushed April at me, turned and stepped off the roof.

I gently set the hammer down preventing the gun from firing and caught April, setting her down as quickly as I could. Marilena was there to catch her head; April was fading fast. I handed my gun to Marilena, who instinctively took it without questioning why.

Racing to the roof edge, I looked down and to my surprise there was Canfield about ten feet below me on a sharply inclined portion of roof that I didn't know was there. This small abutment was covered in corrugated tin, had at least a forty-degree down angle, and had several pipes protruding up through it. She had managed to fall without impaling herself on any of them. As it was, she was slipping and clawing at the tin as she slid down the sloping metal. I could see no more outcropped roof sections to stop her from going the rest of the way to the ground.

I moved back three steps and then pumped hard, running to the edge of the roof. Marilena screamed, "Thomas! No! No!" I disappeared from her view as I went over the side.

My short run had propelled me far enough out so that I landed on my butt next to Canfield fifteen feet from the building's edge where she was still in a slow motion slide to a final fall. We were quickly approaching the edge in our parallel slide. I rolled to my side and hooked a pipe with my arm as we passed by it. With my free hand, I grabbed for Canfield. Her arm flailed back and forth finally managing to make contact with my hand. I grabbed her wrist and locked on. Canfield's arm stretched out as she continued to slide off the edge. Her body went over the side; my grip on her wrist remained. Her arm broke as it bent backwards at the elbow. She screamed in sudden agony. Her weight pulled me further to the edge, my face ending up over the edge looking down at her.

"Hold on. I'll get you up!" I yelled at her.

"Don't drop me! Oh God, it hurts!"

"I'm not going to drop you! Hold on!"

"You can't do it! I feel my elbow tearing out! God! Oh, God! It hurts!" her words punctuated by screams, excruciating shrieks that filled the night air.

We hung there for a minute or two, Canfield screaming in pain, me concentrating on not letting go. I saw Marilena's face over the building edge, her look one of terror. She vanished out of sight.

"Agent Rigatti is getting help! Just hold on! Your arm won't tear in half! It's tougher than you think!"

Marilena reappeared above me looking down at us. She was joined by Omar and Barry. Her voice was loud, but it trembled as she said, "The fire department is coming! They will have a rope! Thomas! Please don't fall!"

Canfield had stopped screaming, suddenly quiet except for deep and labored breaths. She looked up at me, her face pale and glistening with sweat. She was barely lucid, her body going into shock.

"I didn't do it."

"What? Just hold on! The rescue team is on the way!" I wondered how much longer I could maintain my grip. They had better hurry.

"I didn't kill your brother!" she said, passing in and out of consciousness, tears streaming down her face. "I didn't do it!"

It was the reason that I had jumped down to her, risking my life to save hers would not alone have been enough for me to take this risk. I needed to know. I had to know. "Who killed him?" I demanded. "Tell me!"

She answered me immediately and said as forcefully as she could, her voice rasping, "It was Townsend! Margaret Townsend!"

And with that, as I accepted the accusation with little surprise, a lie, another attempt to misdirect, the pipe I was holding onto broke off at its base, and we fell together three stories to the alleyway below. The only sound I heard as we plummeted toward the ground was Marilena's scream.

Canfield was under me and hit some barrier, taking it in the small of her back. Instantaneously, I fell into her, was deflected to one side, twisted and crashed face up into a pile of wooden crates. I still had her wrist locked in my hand and had unknowingly pulled her on top of me. I looked at her head and shoulders lying across my chest and then up at what had originally stopped her fall. It was a wrought iron fence with closely spaced decorative spikes pointing skyward blocking access to the alley. The fence had pierced her along her waist and cut her in a jagged laceration, the force of the fall and my hold on her arm separating her into two pieces. Only the upper half of Sylvia Canfield had followed me onto the crates beside the fence. I couldn't see the other half. It seemed I was developing a trend. When I suspected someone of killing my brother, the person soon died, and the cause of death was the body separating into two pieces.

AFTERMATH

I had been smart enough to remain completely still after I had landed until professional help could arrive to assess my condition. My body was covered in blood, and as much as I hoped it was all Canfield's, there was no way to be sure. Even though I had not lost consciousness from the collision with the ground and felt alert, the impact had rung my bell pretty good making me a poor evaluator of my condition.

Having raced down ladders and stairs, Marilena had been the first to get to me. Given the darkened location of the alley and the fact that no one had been nearby when we landed, our incident was still a private one. As she was alone, my guess was that Omar and Barry had been left in charge of April, no doubt with explicit, yet rapidly delivered, instructions.

"Thomas! Thomas!" she had yelled to me while running up to the alleyway fence. She stopped in disbelief at the macabre tableau — me looking up at her while covered in the blood of a deranged killer whose upper torso and head constituted the only visible remains. She turned pale and fought an internal war between an almost uncontrollable need to look away and her just as strong requirement to determine my condition. Her concern for me won out, but just barely. Had our dinner not been an aborted affair, the gruesome mess that I had become would have gotten worse. Given the events of the last few days, her relationship with me would either toughen her up or drive her away.

"Oh, God! There's so much blood! Please tell me that all of it is hers and not yours!"

"I'm not absolutely positive, but I don't think that I'm leaking. I'm not moving because I don't want to alter the crime scene."

"To hell with the scene! You're alive, and she is dead! Saving your life is more important than the forensics! I need to see how badly you're hurt!"

"Easy, Baby. We need to take this by the numbers. The troops are on the way. I really don't think I am bleeding out." And, at that moment we heard the first siren. Marilena might have been a little relieved, but it wasn't registering on her face. She ran to the end of the alley where it dumped out onto the street and waved excitedly at the oncoming rescue wagon. For my part, they couldn't get here soon enough. I was starting to coagulate.

The EMT guys arrived, and even though they were tough skinned, New York ambulance jocks, the site of Canfield's upper half hemorrhaging blood and damaged tissue all over me did cause the two of them, one male and one female, to lose a little color. The calm delivery of my end of our conversation with them further added to the surreal nature of the emergency call. Jim O'Dale's car pulled up next to the oversized ambulance having found us easily, the previously dark alley now a strobe light show. He jumped out of the driver's seat and trotted over to me. Unlike Marilena and the EMTs, he briefly looked at me and the half-body of Canfield as if he had seen something just like this thousands of times before. He joined the discussion about how to handle the very unusual situation.

The EMTs and O'Dale agreed with Marilena, who was barely hanging onto a professional demeanor and offering little chance that they could successfully object, that ascertaining my condition trumped evidence preservation. This was fine by me. It only mattered that someone else make that decision and then be around to tell the world that I had not tampered with evidence. As there was no protocol for pulling a live body out from under the partial remains of a dead one, we had to improvise. They slid Canfield's upper half off of me and onto a plastic sheet without difficulty due to the slippery puddle I had become all the while trying to keep her from changing position. The arrival of a fire engine at the scene provided the help we needed for the next step. The only way we were going to see what had happened to me was to get rid of the muck. A water line was rigged up to the pumper truck and necked down from a large diameter fire hose to something more resembling a common garden hose in both flow rate and pressure. Carefully, but with water about the temperature of an Alpine lake, they hosed me off — a river of red headed to a nearby storm sewer. I had often wondered why the fire department would send a fire truck to a medical emergency call, and now I knew — you might just need to hose the victim down, and the pumper carried several hundred gallons of water. I mentioned this to Marilena attempting to lighten her mood a little. She was not amused in the least. A quick injury check confirmed that I wasn't the major contributor to the mess — my leakage fairly limited. I had Marilena take charge of my watch and billfold; my clothes had been cut off of me and stuffed into a plastic bag. Even though the onsite exam didn't indicate any spinal damage, they slid a backboard under me for transport. I approved. O'Dale told Marilena to ride in the wagon with me to the hospital and cleared it with the EMTs, whose protocol allowed only immediate family in the rig.

As they prepared to load me into the back of the oversized ambulance, Jim told Marilena that they needed to stay connected by cell throughout the night so they could tag team the local precinct. She agreed but was not focused on his words as she tried to hurry the techs along. O'Dale turned to me, rocked back and forth on his heels, and said, "Well, here's another fine mess you've gotten me into!"

I answered back, "I believe that the actual quote was 'another *nice* mess' but it got screwed up by the papers." He and I laughed.

"Would you two please shut up?" This, from my now fully exasperated girlfriend who obviously did not appreciate the sophisticated musings of Oliver Hardy. We'd have to work on that.

* * *

"Seven stitches? That's it?"

"Yep," I answered back. "Told you I was OK."

It had been ten hours since I had fallen from the roof with Canfield. The hospital had x-rayed and CAT-scanned me looking for unseen trauma finding nothing. Marilena looked at me in disbelief, her head slowly moving back and forth in wonderment. It was about 6 AM, and she was standing next to the hospital bed in the emergency room where I had been treated. I am certain that I had annoyed the ER docs and nurses by providing, well maybe providing is not a strong enough word, supervisory services with respect to my case. After completing their work, they had vanished. Marilena had been with me most of the night, leaving only once to bounce back and forth between the apartment where April had been hiding out, the alley, the local police headquarters, Ron's condo, and then back to the hospital where April and I were being treated. O'Dale had tried hard to minimize her involvement, so she could stay with me. He was mostly successful. I was happy that she had called Ricardo and not been in and out of cabs in the middle of the night. I had overheard the hospital staff comment on her frequent calls to inquire about me during the brief time she was gone. When she returned, I didn't know if she had flashed her badge to get past the visitor's area, or if the help just didn't care who came to see me after my un-requested insertion into their management chain. Some people just don't appreciate me.

I continued, "The wooden crates and pallets were great at providing an energy absorbing landing, you know, crunch, crunch, crunch, but a couple of slats stuck me when they broke."

"Where?"

"My butt, left side. Made it difficult to direct the suturing. I made them rig up two mirrors."

"They didn't mind doing that?"

"I didn't say that."

The hospital docs wanted to admit me. Not because the scans and images showed damage but simply due to the fact that I had fallen almost thirty feet, and I should have been hurt worse than I was. I refused. I had been very, very lucky.

Marilena had brought clothes for me from the condo. The residual pain and bruising in multiple places did thwart my plan to jump out of the hospital bed and pull on the clothes without assistance. I got un-requested girlfriend help getting dressed. Although I was moving a little slower than normal, nobody besides Marilena seemed to notice, and I was allowed to walk out of the place after signing multiple documents releasing the hospital from liability, real or imagined.

Marilena had also arranged for April to be released after a night of examination, minor repair, and observation. She helped

April sign out and wheeled her to the curb where I was waiting. April gave me a brave smile, and I returned one of my own.

Ricardo had been again summoned by Marilena and provided the ride to Central Park West. After arriving, we had to undergo the doorman circus. Antonio made it clear that he was posting a guard at the door, and we would be accompanied wherever we went, as we couldn't be trusted without adult supervision. I was relieved when I finally dropped onto the couch in the living room. Marilena walked April into the guest room and helped her into bed.

"You need to get some sleep," I said as she returned and sat down beside me. She should have gone to the bedroom.

"I intend to," she replied and promptly leaned back on the couch and then over against me. I looked down at her. She smiled up at me, squeezed my arm, closed her eyes and in less than twenty seconds was out.

I had been up all night as well, and even though I had a lot to think about, sleep was not far off for me either. The big question was whether or not it was all over? I hoped it was. I was sure that Canfield had killed Ron and that Townsend had been involved in some way. I still had some open switches to consider. The biggest issue in my mind was if there were others in league with them? Right behind this question was accepting that Canfield's dislike for Ron was strong enough to be a motive for murder? Even as interesting was why Townsend had helped, what was behind her relationship with Canfield and what had her involvement been? I believed that when both Canfield and Townsend had been fully investigated, answers to these questions would come out. Between now and then, I would be limited to speculation and that was really of little value.

I slid Marilena down so that her head was in my lap, pulled the sofa quilt over her, leaned back, and closed my eyes.

INTROSPECTION

Three days had passed since my impromptu flight off the rooftop with Sylvia Canfield. Marilena wanted some downtime to spend with April, who remained our houseguest, and she got it. At first, their time together was quiet and behind closed doors. Since yesterday afternoon, however, April had reemerged with a cautiously happy disposition and had even become comfortable, well a little more comfortable, around me. Marilena had worked her magic. The three of us were sitting on the couch, April between us — another dinner delivered by Antonio and company. Tonight it was Chinese.

"Thanks again for coming after me the way you did. Marilena told me how you raced to the apartment dragging everyone out of the restaurant. I remember you on the roof standing up to that evil crazy woman. You made her believe that you would shoot her in the head. I believed it too! It made her let me go. And then, when you jumped off the building, I didn't know what to think! Either you could fly, or you know something about gravity that I don't! Remember, she had me at the edge of the roof and was going to push me off. I was terrified! But you, you didn't even hesitate — you just jumped! Anyway, after that, I just closed my eyes and tried not to think about anything. I'm really glad you're OK."

"You wouldn't have been in that situation at all if it weren't for your relationship with the Briggs brothers. I'm sorry — again." As she listened to me, Marilena smiled softly looking across at April.

April began to speak again. "Don't be. I'd go through worse to have Ron back." She meant it. I was seeing the person that Ron thought was worth saving. She continued, "Ron was right about you, though."

"Yeah, how's that?" I asked.

April thought for a minute, and I knew I was in for another stream-of-consciousness jag like she had the day I met her, and she defended Ron to me. I braced myself not to take what she was about to say too seriously.

"He talked about you a lot. It was almost always about your career and the crazy military stuff you did. He was proud, really proud, of what you had become, you know, doctor and all, but he was more amazed by the other stuff. What he was right about, like I was saying, was that you are two different guys in the same body. There's you, Mr. Civilized Doctor, and then there is some completely different guy who only comes out when it gets dangerous. One time, it was only once, after he had talked to you on the phone, he got kind of thoughtful, and he told me about when you guys were together and some other men tried to get tough and mess with you. He said it was in Florida. He told me that you grabbed a guy off of a motorcycle and threw him into a brick wall and then left his two buddies in a pile, knocked out cold with broken bones. He said that you handled it real calm, like you were bored and totally without any emotion, and that you wouldn't talk about it later, kind of pretending it didn't even happen. I know what he was talking about now. There is another you; I've seen him."

Marilena had listened intently during April's little discourse. She looked at April and carefully said, "April, because of his work in the military, Thomas, even more so than the average soldier, lives in a violent world. What Ron knew, what I know, and what you must also know is that for Thomas to survive that world, he must divorce himself from normal sensitivities, seeming to you and to me to become cold and detached. Sometimes it can be disconcerting to watch, but you shouldn't be afraid."

"I'm not. Well, not anymore." April looked at me and smiled. "You didn't scare Ron, you don't scare Marilena, so I won't let you scare me." She leaned over to me and put her arms around me. "Just, well, thanks again."

"The two of you are way too deep for me!" I said trying to make light of the situation and get out of the psychoanalysis session.

"And, just like before with Ron, you don't want to talk about it," April said without letting go. "I'm just glad that you're on my side!" I got a quick kiss on the cheek.

* * *

Later that night after April had turned in, Marilena and I were alone for the first time today, side by side and facing each other in bed. Since returning to the condo three days ago, we had been together just about twenty-four hours a day with the only exception being the time she had spent alone with April. She had not brought up the subject of my leap off the roof to get to Canfield. I had not been on the receiving end of any lecture about my foolish disregard for my personal safety and how getting hurt would hurt her and so on. She was living up to her end of the deal and had not harassed me about the dangerous things I do and that I had to consider her and us and grow up. Maybe she was the third option.

"Someday, you need to tell me about what happened in Florida," she said quietly.

"OK. Someday."

"I meant what I said," she whispered.

"What's that?"

"I know who you are." She closed her eyes.

I hoped she did. Someday, maybe she would tell me.

* * *

I called Billy Sanchez on his sat phone. Billy was still at Yokosuka, and my call arrived at around 2:30 AM his time. Regardless of the late hour, I knew he would answer the phone. It wasn't his choice; it was his department sat phone.

"What? Who is this?"

"Is that any way to answer your sat phone? I could have been General F." I said.

"Who the hell is this?" he said, still waking up. "Is that you Briggs? Where the hell are you? Why are you calling me in the middle of the night?" He was coming to and, as usual, full of himself.

"I'm on the other side of the world."

Becoming even more awake and remembering my current circumstance, he put aside his normal, full-time acerbic wit, paused for a moment and then asked, "Hey Tom, you OK?"

"Yeah. I'm dealing."

"Is Marilena with you?" he asked, proving again that as cool as she and I had been, no secret could be kept in our small group.

"She's here."

"Good, good. What do you need?" His gruffness gone, a pro and a friend stood ready, as I knew he would. As I would have done for him.

"I need a lesson in geophysics."

"Hey, I'm not a miracle worker. I mean you're a Marine after all!"

"Use small words."

"OK. What do you need to know about geophysics?"

"Volcano eruptions. I need to know about sulfuric acid formation and how an eruption reduces the Earth's temperature. I thought that all the carbon gas an eruption put into the atmosphere would enhance greenhouse effects."

"It's not the carbon dioxide, even though a volcano can spit out a ton of the shit, it's the sulfur dioxide gas that causes the cooling. You get a lot of it."

"What does the sulfur dioxide do?" Ron's work talked about sulfuric acid, not sulfur dioxide.

"Well, first the ash column must be high enough to get above the troposphere and into the stratosphere. In the stratosphere, the sulfur dioxide from the volcano becomes sulfuric acid. It exists as a sulfate aerosol and raises the Earth's albedo." He knew that I had been in enough chemistry classes that he didn't need to diagram the chemical transformation from sulfur dioxide to sulfuric acid. All he needed to do was tell me the compounds.

"What's with the albedo?"

"The reflectivity of the Earth. It's whiteness, like you white boy, and unlike me, a properly pigmented Hispanic gentlemen. You have a higher albedo than me. A high albedo causes the Sun's radiation to reflect back into space. More reflectivity means less photons absorbed, less heat. A volcanic eruption, again if it's big enough to get the sulfur dioxide into the stratosphere, will shield the planet from a lot of the sun's heat."

I thought about this for a moment. I was at a place in Ron's writings where he was describing CID's triggering event. Like the genetic basis for the disease, it was linked to a volcanic eruption. I had been surprised that an eruption could cool the planet, not add to the greenhouse effect. I needed to know the mechanics. Ron believed, however, that it wasn't the cooling of the planet that triggered CID, but the effect of the sulfuric acid on some part of the population in Eastern Europe that trigged CID. I needed Billy to explain how that happened.

"Does the sulfuric acid get back to the ground?"

"Sure does. It drifts all the way down, and if along the way it comes in contact with condensing water, you get acid rain. What's this all about, Tom?" His use of my first name another indication that he was trying to be a friend.

"My brother was working on a theory about the genesis of a neurological disease, and the trigger was volcano dispersal of sulfuric acid."

"The big one for sulfur dioxide was Mount Tambora in the early 1800s. Although, one of the concerns about Mount Pinatubo, the one that just uncorked in the Philippines, was that it was a big sulfur generator, and the plume made it way up into the Stratosphere. We don't know the effects yet on people, but it's not good."

* * *

Marilena had spoken several times with the local police. We went through the statement thing again. And again, she provided direction. We signed forms, and a uniform picked them up. I faxed a copy to Jason Inch. He was apoplectic when he called and pleaded with me to stay out of trouble.

We were visited by Jim O'Dale on the fourth day of our confinement. He had been interceding on our behalf, even though the event had occurred outside of his precinct. I was pretty sure that the district attorney's lack of interest in me was due to Jim and Marilena.

After we were seated around the dining room table, he said, "You guys don't look any worse for the wear!" He laughed as he said to me, "Although I did hear that you got jabbed in a delicate area."

"My ass hurts," I said.

"Has anyone told you yet how dumb it was to jump off that building after Canfield?"

"We are doing very well, Captain. Thank you for your concern." Marilena had answered him, answering him as if she hadn't heard his question. April just smiled.

"Well then, let me fill you in on a couple of things we have learned about Canfield and Townsend. It is becoming clear that they were responsible for your brother's death. We have learned enough about each of them to establish motive, not only for Ron's death but also for the attacks on the three of you. We have not discovered anyone else aligned with them and think that your ordeal is over."

"That's good news!" This from April. Marilena was quiet, and I definitely wanted to hear more before totally buying into this.

"First let me tell you about Townsend. It seems that in her previous job at the PE firm in Boston and in her position at the CID Society, no one bothered to do a background check before hiring her. My guys did some digging into her past and discovered that Townsend had something to hide. Something pretty big. About twenty-five years ago, she was living in the Washington, D.C. suburbs where she had a baby out of wedlock. She abused the infant, and it died. Even worse, she tried to hide the corpse in a freezer at her home. She delayed a felony conviction by accepting institutionalization at a mental health facility. After being there for less than a week, there was a fire at the hospital, and she escaped by walking right out the front door. In the resulting chaos, her case was not returned to the court system. If she were exposed today, the district attorney would have re-opened the case. And this is where Sylvia Canfield enters the picture.

"Canfield apparently is pretty good at digging into people's pasts. She would routinely check out a potential donor to uncover the asset picture and anything personal that she could use to get a contribution to the society. She sounded like a real arm-twister, and I wouldn't be surprised if some of her donors were the victims of extortion. At some point, and for some reason we don't know, she decided to check out Townsend and discovered her secret. You can actually get an Internet hit on Townsend as a patient missing after the fire at the mental institution. It's a link to a newspaper article that was digitized and put up on a web server about five years ago. Running down the reason for her incarceration takes a couple of phone calls. My detective, Sento, called the hospital and got the names of the administrator at the time of the fire. I sent him to Maryland to interview the guy. He remembered Townsend, why she was at the hospital, and even remarked that a woman had called him about two years ago asking the same questions. He thought she was still a fugitive. We're sure that Canfield held this over Townsend to get her to do whatever she wanted."

"So, it was Canfield who called the shots?" I asked.

"I think so. We have interviewed just about everyone at the society a second time. Other than one outburst at a staff meeting where Canfield blasted your brother for not supporting her fund raising efforts and wanting him gone, there were no overt or obvious actions or statements on her part about Ron. With some careful questioning, however, we pieced together a genuine hatred that she held for Ron. She had an upcoming event with some serious potential donors where Ron was scheduled to deliver the status on the search for a cure. In Canfield's office, we found an agendum for the event with one of Ron's subordinates slated to give the pitch instead of Ron. This was news to everyone, and it would have only happened if Ron couldn't make it. The subordinate, from what we have learned, was more amenable to selling the story the way Canfield wanted it. There was even a memo in his personnel file from Ron reprimanding him and directing him to be conservative and tell only the facts in any public or private forum about CID. The clincher for us was the bonus plan that Canfield was paid on. She was close to meeting a fundraising threshold that would have paid her a significant bonus. We think she needed the money. When we searched her apartment we discovered evidence supporting a serious drug habit. She was into Oxycontin and Vicodin in a big way. She may have even been blackmailing Townsend for money for all I know."

Marilena had been quiet, taking in the information and in her own way, categorizing and assigning importance to each piece. I'd get her take on all of this later in private. She asked Jim, "How did Canfield find out where April was hiding?"

Jim paused for a moment and said, "I got to be honest with you, I don't know. We don't have all the pieces tied up yet. We know she was looking for April. It may have been through someone where April went to school or where she worked, just like they way you did it. We may never know."

"So who tried to run Marilena and me down? Who came up with the cab?" I asked.

"We are pretty sure it was Townsend. Canfield was in Denver, and Townsend was unaccounted for when you were attacked. Getting a beater car, in this case an old cab, from a junkyard would not have been difficult. We think that Canfield sent Townsend to kill you in Boston as well."

"When I was holding onto Canfield, before the pipe broke and we fell, she tried very hard to convince me that she didn't kill Ron — that it was Townsend. From what we discovered, Townsend was out of the building when Ron died. What do you make of that?"

He answered, "I'd like a nickel for every criminal who has lied about their crime right up to the last minute. I wouldn't give her denial much weight." I had thought as much, but still, it bothered me. Well, it didn't matter anymore. Her lies were just a small part of a disturbing life.

"So it was as simple as money for drugs," I said to Jim, my voice depressed. I had lost Ron so someone could make a bonus so drugs could be bought.

"Unfortunately, that's the way it looks."

"What's Alison Montgomery's take on all of this?" Marilena asked.

"She's devastated. She thought she knew her staff. She told me that she is almost ashamed to call you."

"I'll call her. It wasn't her fault. No one can fully know what subordinates are all about no matter how long they work together," I responded.

"Do you have the data she told me about? Is it safe?" he asked.

I got up and went to the den. I returned with the USB stick. "This is where April got involved," I said.

April looked at the little piece of plastic and said to me, "I never saw this before."

"It was in the helicopter."

Jim's face got a puzzled look, and he asked, "What helicopter?"

"Ron had April keep one of his radio controlled helicopters. He told her to give it to me if something happened to him. The memory stick was in a firefighting, water-drop bomb bay. April didn't know about it. Canfield must have learned of Ron's discovery and wanted the data so badly that she almost killed April to get that information. It would have made it difficult to get donations if the word got out about a cure. If she could have prevented the return of the data by killing the three of us, and possibly securing the only copy, then she could go on raising money and getting her share. A cure would have put her out of a job."

O'Dale's eyes opened wider, and his mouth hung open. After a moment he put into words something no one wanted to speak much less believe, "It's pretty disgusting that someone working to cure a horrible disease would prevent the cure for personal gain. Jesus Christ, just when I think I've seen and heard it all!"

INVITATION

After O'Dale left, I called Alison. She answered her cell phone on the second ring.

"Hello."

"Alison, it's Tom Briggs."

"Oh, Tom. I'm glad you called. I have so wanted to talk to you but am incredibly ashamed about what two members of my staff have done to your family that I have actually dreaded speaking with you!"

"I don't see how any of this is your fault."

"I can't tell you how much it means that you are not angry with me."

"Alison, again, there is no reason to be. Now that this is over, we need to meet and talk about how to handle Ron's research data. I'm tempted to just send it to Caroline Little at the Marklin. She seemed to be on the ball, and her shop is very impressive."

"Oh, no. That would be a mistake. We need to disseminate it to a wider audience after we complete some preparatory work. It is imperative that we don't offend any of the academic research facilities. We don't want enemies."

"What are you worried about?" I asked, thinking that we were about to make Caroline Little an enemy.

"Have you ever read about the how the cure for polio came about? About the rivalry between Jonas Salk and Albert Sabin?"

"No."

"You must. There is a book about it called *Polio: An American Story,* and it will make you sick about how close we came to not having a cure for polio. The medical and scientific community must be properly managed, or all of Ron's work will be for nothing! This is something I am very familiar with, and you need to trust me."

"OK. What do you want to do?"

"I have been preparing the research community, using our own research advisory board since you told me of Ron's findings. This is important. Have you given the data to anyone else?"

"No. I have the only copy."

"Excellent. Let's keep it that way. I'm very anxious to see it. And speaking of that, I would like to extend an invitation to you and Marilena. I absolutely must get out of New York and imagine that you may feel the same way. I have access to a wealthy donor's vacation villa in Barbados. How would you feel about joining me there for some rest and relaxation? I've been there many times before. It's a fantastic place right on the beach with a big sport fishing yacht and a pool and all the luxuries you could imagine. There is no house staff, but the kitchen is always well stocked, and there are great restaurants nearby if we get tired of grilling steaks. I think that some undisturbed time to talk about Ron's work and a plan to continue his work would be the best for everyone. Also, I understand that there was a young lady who was injured by Sylvia. According to Captain O'Dale, she was terrified and was almost killed. Please extend an invitation to her to join us. Some beach time might help her recover as well. The society will pay for her travel expenses."

"OK. I'm in, and I'll talk to the ladies. If they agree, we'll come down in the next day or two. I'll email you our travel info."

* * *

Two days later we traveled to Teterboro airport in northern New Jersey. I had made arrangements for us to fly to Barbados in a private business jet. Ricardo dropped us off at a hanger where the air taxi operator had his business.

"I could get used to this," Marilena commented with a smile as she looked at the mid-sized jet, in this case a Hawker 800XP.

After a little paperwork with the manager, we were led to the aircraft. Our bags had vanished, taken by helpful people as we climbed a short flight of stairs into the plane. Four of the suitcases were new and contained clothing that Marilena had described as resort-wear for ladies. The bags and their contents had been acquired yesterday in a shopping spree that I had managed to avoid, having the legitimate excuse that I needed to finish reading Ron's research. My singular suitcase remained unchanged and without new apparel. My boring khaki trunks and Marine Corps t-shirts would suffice. We each had a small carry on, mine containing my normal traveling doctor gear. My Beretta and spare clips were in a side pocket. I assumed that Marilena's Glock was in her bag, but with her you just never knew. Once inside, we met the flight attendant, who showed us to our seats. The seating was arranged more like a living room than the typical row-by-row seats in commercial aircraft.

April's eyes were wide open as she looked around. "Wow. I mean really wow!" she said as she settled into a recliner that faced a plasma screen television. My reaction was more reserved as I had been in private jets many times, using them whenever I could because no matter how good first class is, this is better. Marilena sat next to me, cocked her head to one side, and studied her surroundings.

We were briefed on the safety equipment and procedures as the plane was towed out of the hanger. After startup and taxi, we were shortly airborne for our direct, six-hour flight to the southeastern Caribbean.

"You know, this indulgent and luxurious life could be habit forming," Marilena said. I could see April listening in. She had become more and more curious about our relationship. Marilena told me it was a girl thing.

I looked back at Marilena and said, "It's been a habit for me for a long time. I was just keeping it a secret being the humble guy that I am." April rolled her eyes and leaned over, not missing a word.

"Well, it's a secret no more. Never let it be said that I can't pick a boyfriend. Boston mansion, Central Park West condo, luxury jets, designer clothes from trendy dress shops. You actually do know how to treat a girl!"

"Let's not forget, run down by crazed killers pretending to be cabbies, cheap pizzas in lieu of fancy dinners, boring, high-society fund raisers, pompous charity board meetings, and late night rooftop interventions with more crazed killers."

"All such little things that I will gladly endure to be with you. By the way, anytime you want company while being forced to endure a flight somewhere in one of these, will you remember to invite me, your lowly civil-servant girlfriend whose employer pays only for discount airfare?"

"You and no one else." This got me the big smile.

"You guys are so cute!" This from April. Marilena laughed. I grimaced and stuck my head in a newspaper. Having a girlfriend was tough enough. I didn't need her to have an irritating little sister.

* * *

After eating an exceptional lunch, April drifted off to sleep. I used our temporary privacy to talk about a couple of items that had been bothering me.

"I'm still not sure about what to do with the society?"

"What do you mean?" she asked.

"No matter how well meaning Alison is, she runs a screwed up organization. I'm torn between supporting a cause that was important to Ron without saying anything and demanding that some changes get made or we turn off the tap."

"I think you need to talk to Alison about that. I'm just glad she's out of the country."

"Oh? Why is that?" I asked, my internal alarm bell started to rattle, not quite ringing, but getting ready to.

"Something's not finished about this. If there is another player in this multi-murderer game, Alison could be in danger."

I hadn't thought about that.

TRIGGERS

I estimated from the amount of time that we had been airborne that we had flown south of Florida and were well into the Caribbean; still over a thousand miles to go as Barbados was way south, just northeast of Granada and almost to South America. We had finished lunch served by our own personal flight attendant, whose duties were limited to all of three passengers. Our young and female flight attendant had very nice legs that emerged from a very short skirt. I worked hard at ignoring them. Marilena pointedly ignored my less than successful efforts at visual restraint.

After lunch, while April explored the programming offered on the television, Marilena reviewed the PowerPoint presentation and the executive summary that Ron had written on the genetic basis for CID. She closed the binder holding the documents that I had assembled, looked down at the closed tome on her lap and sighed, "A lot of this was over my head. I know it's stereotypical, but this girl avoided science and math classes. I would hate to have to read the material not intended for executives allegedly as science-challenged as I. I looked at a couple of the documents that you had read, the ones you made notes on. Now I know how people feel when I speak with someone else in a foreign language. I still need to fill in some blanks. Maybe you can help me? Let's see if you can focus in light of the exceptional visual stimuli present."

"If I can. Don't be surprised if what was over your head has me standing on my toes. Ron was the geneticist. I had to work at a lot of this and do some research along the way to stay in the game."

Marilena began with, "OK, Ron believed that CID had two parts: a genetic change that happened 70,000 years ago to some people in Eastern Europe and then a triggering action more recently. I understand a little about the first event and the Out of Africa model causing, what was it? Genetic drift?"

"That's right. The bottleneck causes genetic drift and founder effect. At some place in Eastern Europe, a change took place in *Homo sapien* DNA that was a time bomb waiting to be triggered."

"I haven't gotten to the triggering event yet," she said, "and I don't know if I'm up to another fifty pages of this. Have you read that part yet?"

"Yes. I've finished a first pass at everything and studied some of it in depth."

"Then please, do your girlfriend, who by the way is far sexier than that child serving us, a favor and summarize the triggering event. I will see to it that you are properly rewarded."

"I think that would disturb April."

"Down boy!" she said quietly but with a smile. "Educate me now. I will entertain you later."

Suddenly and sufficiently motivated, I organized my thoughts and began, "Volcanoes played a big part in Ron's understanding of CID. You read about the DNA groundwork that was laid because of the genetic bottleneck caused by the Lake Toba eruption 70,000 years ago."

"Yes."

"Well, Ron believed that a second eruption in 1815 indirectly triggered CID the following year. A year that was known as *The Year Without Summer*."

"Did this Year Without Summer affect Europe? I've never heard of it," she said with surprise.

"Yes, it did and in a big way. The year after the eruption, 1816, was also known as the last great subsistence crisis in the Western world. Civilization as a whole had a tough time with the basics like eating. The days were dark, the temperature dropped, and the crops failed."

"This lasted for a whole year?" she asked.

"Actually a little longer."

I started in on my hastily crafted lecture about CID's triggering event, the pieces of which had only just settled in my mind.

"At the time, no one knew what was going on with the weather and the reduced amount of sunlight. Some people blamed Benjamin Franklin because it was popularly known that he was experimenting with lightning and electricity. Maybe he had screwed up the atmosphere. He was bailed out by an American climatologist William Humphreys. Humphreys was the first guy to figure out what happened, but unfortunately for Franklin, who continued to get heat, it wasn't until 1920. Humphreys postulated that The Year Without a Summer may have been caused by volcanic activity and the ejecta pumped into the air by an eruption. Ironically, his work was somewhat based on a paper written by none other than Benjamin Franklin. Franklin's premise was that the cold weather and gloomy days in 1816 were the result of a volcanic eruption in Iceland in 1783. Wrong year, wrong volcano, but Ben was on the right track.

"What caused The Year Without a Summer was the eruption of Mount Tambora on the island of Sumbawa in what is now Malaysia from April 5 to April 15, 1816. Like the Lake Toba eruption 70,000 years earlier, it generated tremendous amounts of ejecta — the stuff the volcano spits out. The chemicals inserted into the upper atmosphere by the Mount Tambora volcano caused much of the sun's light to be reflected back into space.

"Tambora was a huge event with four times the energy of Krakatoa with tsunamis and an ash column over 140,000 feet high reaching well into the stratosphere. Some 10,000 people on Sumbawa died in the pyroclastic flows with another 50,000 dying from starvation and disease in the months to follow. Mount Tambora's eruption also carried into the higher parts of the atmosphere a tremendous amount of sulfur. Tens of millions of tons of aerosolized sulfur dioxide. This caused a global climate anomaly because it reflected light from the sun back into space reducing both daytime light and temperatures. I won't bore you with the chemistry, but the sulfur dioxide became sulfuric acid, and this fell to the ground and on the people. This was CID's trigger. Ron believed that the conditions and the genetics were just right in an area just north of the Balkan Peninsula for the CID monster to be unleashed. There is historical evidence of brown snow falling to the ground in Hungary during 1816."

"It is amazing," she said quietly, "that people have forgotten this."

"Besides the CID kick start, a couple of other interesting things happened in 1816."

"Such as?" she asked politely.

"Mary Shelley was vacationing in Switzerland and due to the conditions, stayed indoors and joined a writing competition with some friends. She wrote *Frankenstein*. The book is full of scenes with terrible weather and cold.

"The crummy weather also motivated the rapid settlement of the American Midwest. There was a considerable famine in New England. The family of Joseph Smith, the eventual founder of the Mormon Church, moved from Sharon, Vermont, to Palmyra, New York, after several crop failures. It was there that he claims to have experienced events that led to the founding of the Latter Day Saints church."

"Do Mormons appreciate the impact of this one particular volcano on their religion?" she asked with fake seriousness.

"Probably not. It wasn't much better in Europe. The countries there were still suffering from the aftereffects of the Napoleonic Wars, and the food shortages were especially unwelcome. Food shortages in Switzerland caused a lot of violence, and the government declared a national emergency.

"And don't forget, in Eastern Europe, the snow is brown colored as it falls from the sky. Many Hungarians experience illness from exposure to sulfuric acid and were unknowingly the progenitors of CID. The next generations of Hungarians reported symptoms consistent with CID."

* * *

Two hours later, we landed at the island's international airport and reluctantly moved ourselves from the luxury of the Hawker to the Barbados equivalent of a limousine. I transferred my pistol from the bag to its holster inside the waistband of my pants. Some habits are hard to break, and collecting my bags when arriving at an airport always reminds me of this one. A twenty-minute drive on the left hand side of the road from the airport to the west and more developed coast of the island delivered us to our vacation home, courtesy of Alison Montgomery and an unknown CID benefactor.

We rang the bell and were met at the door by Alison Montgomery's husband, Mark Wilson. "About time you got here!" he said. "Come on in. Leave your bags just inside the door, and we can schlep them to your rooms later." We followed him into the house stopping in a great room just off the foyer. Wilson called for his wife, and he turned to another entrance into the room from the rear part of the house. Through this passageway, you could see the ocean through the windows at the far end of the house. In walked Montgomery. Stepping in next to her was Jonathan Treece, who must have been out by the pool because he was in trunks and a flowered shirt. He had a beach towel over his arm. I was a little surprised to see Treece. Montgomery had not mentioned that he would be joining us.

"Tom, you look surprised," she observed the obvious. And then with a voice that was hard, devoid of emotion, "Well, you should be used to surprises by now. Throughout this entire affair, you have been sadly ignorant of just about everything." With that, Treece quickly produced from under the towel a small caliber automatic and pointed it at my face, his finger on the trigger.

EVIL ADVOCATE

Demonstrating far more intelligence than his wife, Mark Wilson moved off to my right, taking himself out of the line of fire that existed between Treece and me. Marilena slowly started after him, moving sideways while facing the front of the room, trying to go unnoticed, pretending to be focused on Montgomery and not Wilson. April was behind me and a little to one side. The shock of the situation had more than likely anchored her in place. Even though Treece had managed to get the gun lined up on me, and Montgomery had successfully recited her practiced words, working very hard to be cool, they were amateurs, and that was my biggest concern. At least with a pro, the weapon doesn't go off accidentally. She was a pretender, a poser. She had seen too many TV shows and movies. The shiny automatic pistol with the long barrel in her partner's hand guaranteed her total authority. Or so she thought.

The tactical situation was pretty straightforward, and the best course of action was counterattacking immediately — a move the amateurs would find incredulous given their current frame of mind. Right now, Montgomery was confident that she was in control and, more importantly, she believed that I would have agreed with her. By the time she figured out that I didn't share her conviction, it would be too late for Treece to shoot me. I knew this, and Marilena knew it as well. The reason she was still slowly moving toward Wilson was she planned to take him down when I went after Treece and his target pistol. She was still ten feet from Wilson, who had stood next to a fireplace. He reached for a fireplace poker from a stand and hefted it. I guess he believed the poker to be a better weapon than either the brush or the shovel. That answered my question about whether or not he was armed with a gun.

The reason I hadn't acted was that I wanted answers. This was selfish on my part. Maybe it made me as much an amateur as

Montgomery, my unnecessary need to know, as it added risk to Marilena and to April. But as long as Montgomery believed she had the upper hand, I could get her to talk. That would be easy. I probably couldn't prevent it. Her only words so far, about me being obtuse, had tagged her as an amateur. When the time comes to pull out a gun and point it at someone, a pro doesn't play games, just puts the weapon to use and kills. Montgomery wasn't a pro, and lacking that, she had a different plan. She was dying to tell me how smart she was. Even if she planned to kill us, which she undoubtedly did, she would first satiate a need to gloat and enjoy the moment to be relived over and over again.

The second indication that no matter what they thought of themselves, they were no match for anyone experienced in this type of gunplay, was that they should have selected a gun with some real stopping power. Treece held a Ruger Competition Mark II. He probably didn't know that it was a gun used mostly in target ranges — the round was small, a .22 caliber, and inexpensive. I looked at the gun a little more, making them think that I was fixated on the source of their control. I had to be appear to be concerned, worried about the weapon pointed at me, when most likely, the only way that gun would fire would be by accident. I wanted them confident, no accidents. The gun was very clean, but it didn't shine from any oily reflection. My only real surprise would be if the pistol had ever been fired. It sure hadn't been maintained. I wondered if they had loaded it correctly. The magazine that holds the small rounds is prone to feed jams when new and requires some extra attention. Getting shot at by Treece was probably not an issue. Even if he intentionally got one off, hitting me was iffy. I was close and would be moving fast. Getting hit by the small caliber bullet would probably not be fatal. There was always the chance of what pilots call the "Golden BB," that lucky round that hits some small and vital component bringing the aircraft down. A round through my eye and into my brain, no matter how small the caliber, would most likely be fatal — a Golden BB. But unless he got really lucky, I could absorb several body shots and still kill him. I knew these things while Treece and Montgomery did not. I had shot people — they hadn't. I had removed lead from battlefield casualties — they hadn't.

The third and most telling indication of Montgomery and company's amateur status was the absolutely amazing fact that they hadn't immediately checked Marilena or me for weapons. I had never let on to Montgomery, Wilson, or Treece that I was anything other than a military doctor, and in their world, docs didn't carry. But they knew that Marilena was an FBI agent and must have known that an agent has a gun. A pro would have checked us both, very carefully, and April too, just to be sure.

As I predicted, it didn't take long for Montgomery to take the stage, "I still have the same problem that I thought I had fixed when I killed your brother." Her words, her tone, and her look let me know that she enjoyed telling me that she had killed Ron. "The cure that ends my little empire didn't disappear with him. It was passed to you. But no further, I think. And that is good news." She smiled as she spoke, a cat playing with her meal before killing it.

"You killed him?" I asked quietly ignoring her other comments and with just enough intentionally added emotion, implied sadness, to make her think she was hurting me.

"It was easy. He was such a coward. Backing up to the window and almost falling through it himself. He even closed his eyes. All I had to do was push, just a little, and out he went. It just came to me. A suicide solved all my problems." She paused for a moment, "You're his brother. I half expected you to shut your eyes the moment Jonathan pointed the gun at you."

"Maybe I'm too tired to care. One disappointment too many." I let my shoulders drop, doing all I could to assume a defeated posture.

"The condemned man should know all of his mistakes. Would you like to know the rest of them before I have you killed?" True to form, she was enjoying the drama way too much to let it end quickly.

"How did you get Canfield and Townsend to do your dirty work?"

She laughed again, "That was easy. By now that imbecile O'Dale has told you about Margaret's little secret and the fact that Sylvia was blackmailing her. It took him long enough to discover it. Margaret's hidden past proved useful to me because I controlled Sylvia, and I could use Margaret through her. Margaret never knew that most of what Sylvia made her do was actually for me." She was on a roll, and I didn't stop her. "I actually put Margaret up for our Core Values Award to solidify her position with the society. Kind of ironic, don't you think, a baby killer exemplifying our core values? And speaking of Margaret, it was time to remove her, and you were such a help."

"What do you mean?"

"Margaret was getting out of control. She really was disturbed. Still, I needed Sylvia to send her to Boston. She had a friend there, a former coworker, who knew that your family had invested in SynapTherapies. I was concerned that Ron may have shared his data with them. Margaret met with her contact outside of the office. She was not well liked there. In fact, her mentor, the man who hired her, disliked her so much that he had instructed everyone at the firm to avoid her. She did find out that Ron had not spoken with SynapTherapies, and that was a relief. Sylvia also told her to follow you, and if the opportunity presented itself, to finish what she had attempted with the cab in Manhattan. Her death, even accidental as she fled from you, not only got rid of her as a growing problem but pointed the finger at her as a suspect in your brother's death in case the police ever gave up on the suicide theory."

"What did you have on Canfield?"

"She was stealing from the society. I set her up. I put her in a place where the internal safeguards appeared to be lax enough that she could divert donor money into her own pocket. She took the bait."

"I don't understand how that helped you?"

"I let her go on stealing donor money for several months, all the while being observed and videotaped by Jonathan, I called her in to my office. I showed her the evidence. At first she panicked — that was fun to watch. She thought I was going to fire her and press charges. Imagine her relief when I explained an alternative plan. I made it possible for her to take even more money, some for her but much more for me. I made her pay me in cash. All of the paper trail had her name on it, so she couldn't do to me what I was doing to her. Not that it ever became an issue. She was happy with the arrangement. She got more than enough money to pay for her lifestyle, which included the drugs she planted at Margaret's."

"Sorry you lost such a valuable confederate," I said with just a little sarcasm.

Not wanting me to win even a small victory, Montgomery shook her head and blinked her eyes as if preparing to lecture a small boy. "You are so naive when it comes to the base-level human condition. Getting someone to take Sylvia's place is easy. I already have him in mind. Your brother had a subordinate who is very pliable, and I've learned that he likes to gamble. Allowing him to supplement his income will be as easy as it was with Sylvia. I've already proven that the steps are easy: first you tempt, then you catch, then you own. I am already looking forward to our meeting after he spends a few months believing with total certainty that he will never get caught!"

"Why did Canfield tell me that Townsend had killed Ron?"

"Because I told Sylvia that I believed she did. That she had lost control over her. I told Margaret that I believed that Sylvia had killed him. If this were ever to move from a suicide to a murder, I wanted the police to have both of them pointing their fingers at each other. Pretty smooth, eh?"

I didn't think it was smooth at all. Her logic proved again that she was an amateur. O'Dale and his guys would have asked both women why they thought the other was the murderer, and eventually they would implicate Montgomery as the source of their suspicions. Her ploy, however, had caused Canfield to tell me in her last moments that Townsend had killed Ron. She hadn't had the time to tell me that Montgomery had told her that and I had erroneously assumed that it was just the two thieves falling out. Who knew who was lying? And, I had mistakenly bought into a scenario limited to Canfield and Townsend.

"How did you get in the office building without showing up on the RFID security system?"

"Simple. I went in with Mark who had a tag. The silly thing clicked, and the guards assumed it had recorded both of us. We went out the same way. Kept me off of your precious list and let you chase everyone else."

"Why do you put up with Standish?"

"That fat pig," she said disgustedly. "He controls the board, at least for a while, and I work for them. Soon that will change. In the meantime, I have to put up with his slobbering, lecherous behavior. Although leading him on and letting him think that someday he could have me was kind of fun. The fact that that human fat factory could ever believe that I was interested in him defied any logic. I mean look at him and then look at me. Really. Well, no matter, that will end soon enough and so will he."

"How did Canfield find out where April was hiding?"

"You told us."

"I did?" How could that have been? Then it hit me. Outside the elevator with Omar getting the restaurant recommendation. Treece had asked the address where we needed to get to later in the evening. He had passed it along to Montgomery, who told Canfield."

"Why was it so important to find April? How did you even know about her?" I asked.

Montgomery laughed and said, "You men can be so easy — especially a church mouse like your late brother. I was hoping to get some leverage over him. The owner of this house helped me out. He forced Ron to go to a strip club one evening. He watched him connect with one of the dancers, but true to form, the great Dr. Briggs never took advantage of the situation, at least not that we could tell in all the time we had them under observation. How altruistic making her go back to college. What a sap!" Montgomery never acknowledged April as the subject of her words. April was beneath her. "Then, we had to make sure that his little project girl wasn't holding another copy of the research data. All of this is rather obvious, isn't it?" She looked at me, her face continued to display pleasure, but her eyes revealed annoyance. She was annoyed not to be facing a better opponent. I was a little annoyed by that myself.

She didn't disappoint me when she said, "You are more unaware than I thought. Eliminating the three of you will wrap this up nicely."

"I really need to hear you say it. To tell me that you killed my brother, that you have prevented a cure to a horrible disease, the focus of your organization, one that your own sister has, just for money."

"Yes, I'm sorry to disappoint you that there's no more to it than that. I need money. I like money. More than the pittance that my position pays which is considerably less than I am worth." I thought about her three hundred fifty thousand dollar salary and the honoraria bringing in another quarter mil. She again let out another small, superior laugh and then said, "You must know by now. Surely you've figured it out. Especially since I've told you about the personal financial improvement plan that Sylvia and I — well, Sylvia, Jonathan, Mark and I — have been on. Money. I like it and need lots of it. Curing CID would have ended a lifestyle that I wasn't willing to give up."

"But, your own sister?"

Alison immediately interrupted me, "My sister never had CID." She turned and looked at the unknown woman who had followed her into the room. "This is my sister, Caitlin."

The younger woman certainly looked healthy enough. Tall and slim with long brown hair, she only favored Montgomery in the face. She had the same duplicitous smile.

"Someday, someone will find this out," I said.

"I doubt that. Caitlin and Mark are going away. A beautiful island in the South Pacific. They are well funded due to our little endeavor and will live very nicely. And, I think they like this idea, as they have grown very fond of each other. Very fond."

This gave me the excuse to look over at Wilson. He was smiling while brandishing the fireplace poker. I looked at him and tried not to let my face telegraph my certain knowledge that Montgomery wouldn't let him or her sister exist as a liability. Looking back at her, I could see it on her face as for the first time she couldn't hold eye contact with me. Her sister and Wilson would soon die.

Montgomery spoke again. With regained authority she said, "Enough of this. We are all going to take a ride on the boat behind the house. You know, that nice big one, the one that I promised to take you out on to go fishing. Unfortunately for you, my plans have changed. Let's go. Jonathan, watch them!"

I let out a small sigh, capitulation communicated. I stepped meekly forward as if to follow Montgomery out of the room. I knew that I couldn't get to my gun without being noticed so I had to get in close. Walking past Treece, I coughed once twisting slightly to face him and raised my left hand as if to cover my mouth. He bought my subterfuge. He lived in a civilized world and people cover their mouths when they cough — I guess even those heading to their execution. My world lacks such civility. Simultaneously, I slammed my left hand down deflecting the gun barrel to the floor while the open palm of my right hand rammed up and into his face. I drove the heel of my hand with everything I had into his nose actually lifting his body off of the ground. I felt the cartilage break and be driven into the frontal lobe of his brain. Treece died instantly.

Grabbing the gun before he fell, I turned toward Marilena and Wilson. Waiting for me to make my move, she had rushed him the moment I struck. I watched him stiff-arm her away, almost knocking her down. Before she could react, and as I was about halfway to them, he swung the poker down on her, striking her left collarbone. I heard it crack and she fell to her knees and then the floor. Wilson's focus had been on her, and he never saw me coming at him. I dropped Treece's probably useless gun so I could grab his arm that had cocked back with the poker. He was going to take another swing at Marilena. I stopped his arm just before it could start forward again. Twisting him around so his back was to me, I pulled the poker with both hands across in front of him at neck level and yanked back hard smashing the iron rod sideways against his neck. While choking from the assault on his trachea, he tried unsuccessfully to get his hands under the poker to stop me. As Marilena rolled over in pain and looked up at me, I let one hand go from the iron rod and grabbed the back of his neck. I swept a leg under him and pushed his head down to the floor while his feet were flying upwards as hard and as fast as I could. I never let go. I let my knees buckle and followed him all the way to the hard tile floor. His forehead made a very satisfactory cracking sound and due to the angle of his head with the rest of his body and the force that I had used to cause his cranium to floor connection, his neck snapped just above the shoulders. Just like it was supposed to.

Quickly standing up, I turned back to Montgomery. Her sister ran from the room. She had witnessed two brutal deaths and didn't want to be the third. Montgomery, however, was standing her ground as she fumbled in her pocket and pulled out a small frame aluminum revolver. It was either a Colt or a Smith and Wesson, a .38 and unlike the larger but less deadly gun that Treece had used, this one could do some damage. Having her produce a pistol was not a total surprise, but I did have to deal with it now before she could point it at me and pull the trigger. I was ten feet from her and needed to buy some time to get my gun out. I still had the poker in my left hand. I quickly transferred it to my right hand, just as quickly wound up like a baseball pitcher and threw it at her as hard as I could.

I wasn't going to need my gun. The pointed end of the poker hit her mid torso and fully penetrated her body. She dropped the revolver and slumped, twisting to the floor as I ran to her. The tip of the poker was visible where it had exited her back. She grabbed the poker shaft in front of her for just a moment. She felt her own blood, warm to the touch, and she screamed. I knelt next to her, not a surgeon with skills that she desperately needed, but a brother of a great man that she had murdered in cold blood. I grabbed her head and looked into her eyes. Weeks of anger had welled into hatred. My control was slipping away from me for the first time in my life. I wanted her to see me, to see her executioner.

"You murdered my brother! Now you're going to hell!"

"Thomas! Stop! No! Please!" All of this quickly from Marilena, who had fought past the pain of a broken collarbone and gotten to her feet. I could see her in my peripheral vision as she came to me as fast as she could, her face pale with pain, shouting panicked words. Her voice though, was barely registering, a distant and failed intervention.

I squeezed Montgomery's head between my hands and told my arms to twist her head, to twist it until her neck snapped! At exactly that moment, Marilena stumbled on top of me, her body hitting mine, and her right arm encircling me as she slid to the floor. Her remaining usable hand found one of mine still holding Montgomery's head; her left arm dangled uselessly from her shoulder. Her touch, her right hand on mine, somehow stopped me. Amazingly, my arms and hands failed to follow my brain's orders. I let go and sat back. Marilena gripped me tighter and looked into my eyes.

She spoke softly and held my gaze. "You are not a murderer. You are not her. Remember Ron. Just do what's right. Let the world work out the rest."

Her words, Ron's words, hit me like a physical blow. I pulled us away from Montgomery, away from evil, and held

Marilena in both arms dropping to the floor so I could better support her left arm and protect her. She clenched her teeth, containing her pain.

I had killed many times in the line of duty, I had killed to defend my friends while in battle, but she was right. Marilena was right. She had stopped me just in time. I did not want to be a murderer.

Looking around the room, I made eye contact with April who looked like she hadn't breathed since Treece pulled the gun. She fainted.

QUOD ERAT DEMONSTRANDUM

The days immediately following Montgomery's failed attempt to kill us were difficult. I called for emergency services from the house, pleasantly surprised to see that 911 worked in Barbados but not so happy about the response time of the EMTs. Surprisingly, Montgomery survived. I later found out that the poker had passed between major organs and had only damaged some parts of her small intestine. I didn't volunteer to do the gut surgery to repair the damage. She no longer mattered. I didn't care if she lived or died. My second call was to Jim O'Dale. I didn't have a clue who to turn to in Barbados given that I had just killed two people and the count could rise to three. I got him on his cell and gave him the short version. He told me to keep the faith and hung up. Finally, I heard sirens in the background.

My focus was on Marilena and, to a slightly lesser extent, April. I supervised, again without being requested to do so, the emergency room docs in evaluation and treatment of Marilena's broken clavicle. Not sure of April's state and not wanting her to wander off, I kept her close by. Very rarely is surgery required to fix a broken collarbone and, in Marilena's case like most, it wasn't. The sling that the hospital finally provided was not much of an improvement on the one I had improvised at the villa. Her recovery would take as much as twelve weeks during which her left arm would be immobilized as much as possible. I knew that I would be pressed into becoming a personal assistant for my temporarily, one-armed girlfriend. April was bouncing back pretty quickly. I co-opted her as assistant's assistant. I didn't think that she had gotten used to the violence that had recently become a part of her life because of the Briggs brothers, but being able to focus on helping Marilena gave her something else to think about.

Barbados was considerably more laid back than the U.S., where I would have been hauled off to a jail pending charge. The police escorted us to the hospital, and after we arrived, we were closely watched by four uniformed officers. Their lieutenant departed with our passports. We had been instructed not to leave the island, and I assured the authorities that we wouldn't. I made reservations at a resort hotel on the southwest coast and passed that along to the uniforms. I was very relieved when, less than ten hours after calling him, Jim O'Dale walked into the emergency room just as we were about to sign Marilena out. He had been accompanied by two FBI people and an assistant district attorney for the State of New York. They interviewed each of us and headed back out to confer with their Barbadian counterparts. I had tried to pin O'Dale down about our prospects as foreigners in the Barbados court system. All I got back was a grin and instructions to sit tight and try not to kill anyone else.

During the next three days, Jim and his hastily assembled team traveled back and forth to the resort, sometimes with local law enforcement types, sometimes alone. At the end of the third day, he appeared by himself and announced that we could leave the island. The Barbadians had been convinced that a trial would be expensive, and more importantly, would damage the tourist trade. No Caribbean island wanted press like that in Aruba over the Holloway disappearance. Basically, it was a matter for the New York district attorney's office representatives who were conveniently here to escort us back to the U.S. I invited Jim and his friends to accompany us back home on the Hawker. He assured me that by doing so I had reduced the probability of our arrest back in New York. The assistant district attorney had also worked out Montgomery's return at a later date when it would become safe for her to travel. The local police promised not to let her out of their sight until she was fit to leave. I didn't volunteer to send a jet for her.

* * *

Four months had passed since Barbados. Four months that continued to bring changes to my life, changes that had been set in motion since the day Alison Montgomery murdered my only brother.

The Marine Corps extended my leave of absence and the FBI did the same for Marilena. We needed the time to get our legal problems, problems that had transplanted themselves from Barbados to New York resolved, to help the CID Society with an unplanned transition in the light of very bad publicity, and most importantly to me, for Marilena to heal.

The three of us stayed once again at the condo in New York. It was the first time that I had thought of it as just the condo, and not Ron's condo. I promised both ladies a return to the Caribbean under better circumstances. We visited April's university and with some help from the FBI, who had written April a "Letter of Appreciation," got them to waive the last two weeks of school that she had missed. She took her finals and graduated. Helping her study during the evenings gave us something to do after long days working with the police and FBI wrapping up the Montgomery affair.

The CID Society had taken a serious hit due to the press about Alison Montgomery, Margaret Townsend, Sylvia Canfield, Mark Wilson, Caitlin Montgomery, and Jonathan Treece. I met with the board, and we acted to get things turned around. Marilena and I had a quiet conversation with Chubby Woody about how awkward it would be for his romantic feelings about Alison to become widely known and come to the attention of the FBI. We assured him that if we wanted to, we could have the district attorney make their relationship a part of his examination of Montgomery while on the stand. The court reporters would find that juicy grist for the mill — his wife would probably not understand. He quietly resigned as board chair. Probably the first time he had ever done anything quietly. A replacement was selected, and the board moved quickly to install Omar Sayyaf as the new President and Barry Ledderman as the new Chief Operating Officer. I was asked to join the board as Vice Chair. Omar had a private conversation with a former subordinate of Ron's, the one who had a gambling problem. He resigned as well.

Caroline Little had validated Ron's work and was in close contact with two pharmaceutical companies that were involved with clinical trials and testing for a new CID therapy. Both companies called me repeatedly, pleading with me to control the "Wild Woman at the Marklin." I told them they were on their own. Omar, Barry, and I put a new face on the CID Society. We launched a major publicity campaign positioning the society as the enabler of the now discovered cure. Omar restructured the

CID Society in preparation for this, and there were many personnel and program changes. As a team, we twisted some arms and with seed money from the Briggs family; a trust was established to make the cure available for free to anyone with CID. Caroline Little, true to Ron's memory, produced a documentary about how the cure for CID had been discovered. The show aired repeatedly on educational cable channels. She sent me a very kind note and a copy of the show on DVD along with copies of her letters to the scientific community maximizing Ron's involvement while minimizing hers. The woman is still an enigma to me. She kidded me about how I would have to go to Stockholm to get the Nobel Prize on Ron's behalf. I told her we would go together. For a second time, I heard her struggle with her emotions. She told me again how she wished that Ron were alive so that she could yell at him some more.

Alison Montgomery returned four weeks after us to face trial for Ron's murder and a multitude of other crimes. The FBI task force was fighting the New York district attorney's office over jurisdiction. No matter, we had been told that irrespective of who got it, the case against her was rock solid. I hoped so. Jurisprudence in America seems to me to be anything but predictable and often not just.

True to her word, Marilena involved herself in my life in a big way. She became the de-facto head of the Briggs's compound in Boston much to my relief and that of my staff who had all joined her fan club — the Boston Chapter. She remodeled the New York condo combining Ron's bedroom with one of the guest rooms and rearranging enough of it so that we could sleep in what was his old room. I didn't question her excuses for the remodel. We needed more room and a bigger bathroom, but we both knew the real reason for the floor plan upheaval. We cleaned up the den, and it became, once again, just a den. Given the time that we would spend in New York, it made sense to keep the place. Marilena stopped her lease on her one-bedroom apartment in Washington, D.C., near Cleveland Park. We selected a large condo just around the corner from the George Washington University, and she furnished it. I read about it in the monthly financial statement. She had exercised little restraint.

She moved April to Boston, and we helped her enroll in law school. April would live at the compound and commute to school. Jason Inch offered her a part time job in their law library after a visit from Marilena. Gus, with Maryanne's help, was keeping an eye on her and promised me that he would chase off any guys who showed up to date her if they didn't pass muster. April thought that was cute. Where was he when she was working at Playoffs?

Marilena and I would divide our time between D.C. and Boston with an occasional trip for me to my seldom-visited office in Tampa Bay. I purchased a fractional share arrangement to make frequent use of private jets for the interstate commuting. Marilena added the concierge number for fractional jet provider to her speed dial on her office, cell, and home phones. Of all the perks that came with putting up with me, this one would make up for all of my less desirable traits. She never did give me my Marine Corps t-shirt back although it did periodically reappear, animation included.

As for me, I reflected on my efforts as a detective and decided that I shouldn't give up my day job. I had bluffed and blundered my way through the entire affair. If it had been left to Marilena and others like her, I believe that the truth would have been eventually discovered and the bad guys caught. The only difference would have been fewer bodies littering the landscape. Marilena was kind enough not to agree with me.

* * *

It was a quiet Sunday afternoon in Boston. Summer was just weeks away, and the weather guessers said it would be a hot one. Considering this, and knowing that much of the next few months would be in the great air conditioned indoors, I asked Marilena if she would go out with me.

"Of course. Thomas, where are we going?"

"Humor me. I need you and Gus to help me with something."

Gus met us outside and held the rear door of the BMW open for Marilena. She smiled at him but didn't ask anything knowing by our conspiratorial behavior that he wouldn't tell. She settled patiently into row two.

We drove to a park by the water that Ron and Gus had taken me to shortly after our parents had died. On that day, we had flown a kite and tossed a football back and forth — the formation of a new family

I helped her out of the car. Gus went to the trunk and opened it. I reached in and pulled out the radio control helicopter that had held the USB stick, the green and white one with "Cascade Fire Fighters" on the tail boom. The same one that April had kept for Ron. Marilena's eyes opened wide.

"Is it the same one?" Marilena asked.

"Yeah. I had Antonio ship it back."

"Are you going to fly it?"

"That's why we're here."

"Do you want to be alone?" she asked quietly.

"No. I want you and Gus with me. We have something important to do."

I had discussed my plan with Gus, and he had been all for it. We had prepped the model a week before checking out the motor and all the systems. I had even made a short flight in the backyard while Marilena and April had been out of the house. Gus removed a small plastic bottle from a case in the trunk. The bottle was small, holding only two or three of ounces of ash. Gus helped me turn the bird upside down. I moved the lever on the control box and opened the water bomb-bay doors and then carefully poured the ash into the compartment, protecting it from the wind with a cupped hand. I moved the lever again and closed the doors.

"Thomas. Are those Ron's ashes?" Marilena asked, knowing it was a redundant question.

"A little from the urn at the house. Not all, but enough."

Gus helped me start up the helicopter. We backed away and I picked up the control box. I manipulated the controls and the model lifted off of the ground. For the next several minutes, I flew the toy, a toy that had brought a lot of good times for two grown up brothers, back and forth in front of us, sweeping turns over the ocean and then back to land. I then positioned the helicopter further away, over the water and hovered about twenty-five feet in the air. I knew that I had to finish this soon as for some reason it was getting difficult to see clearly. Must have been some salt spray from the ocean blowing in my eyes. I looked over at the man who had been our surrogate father and the woman who now meant so much to me.

They both nodded, not trusting their voices. I focused on the older man, my stand-in father and said, "I want you to help me with this. He became your son as much as he was my brother." Marilena's face lit up and she enthusiastically added, "Gus, yes! Ron was your family too!"

Gus looked at me and said, "Pal, I may have helped raise you when you were little, but since you've grown up, you needed Ronny more than me. Hell, I'm terrified every time you're out of my sight. You still need someone keeping you in line and she's right here!" He looked over at Marilena. His face had left behind its serious demeanor, and a big smile had spread across it while he spoke.

I motioned her to me with a small movement of my head. She looked from him to me, her look one of total surprise. My girlfriend, usually a lightning quick study, was for once the one behind the curve.

"Thomas, are you sure?"

"Yes."

She moved over to me, lifted her hand to the control box and moved her index finger to the lever she had seen me use. Then she hesitated, looked up at me, and then over to Gus, "No. I can't do this without some help. Gus. Please?"

I noticed that the big Greek, the older man who never aged, never changed, had been studying his shoes. He looked up hearing her ask for him, his earlier smile slowly returning. Gus walked up and with that, he took her hand and guided her finger back to the same lever. He didn't let go of her hand. "It's this one," he said softly, knowing she didn't need his direction.

"Now?" she asked, worried that she might make a mistake, no matter how small.

"Now is good," I answered.

Together, they moved the switch that opened the bomb bay doors and the gray and white ash exploded out into the vortex of air under the bird, settling onto the ocean swells below. Goodbye big brother.

As I brought the helicopter back and set it down, Gus wrapped Marilena up in a hug. He towered over her, like I did.

He kissed her on the top of her head. She hugged him back tighter when he did. She knew she was family.

EPILOGUE

Her name was Betsy McClure, or as she was currently known, Federal Corrections Employee No. 427734. She found her badge number comforting. The last four digits, 7734, had been the last four digits of her daughter Rebecca's social security number. Betsy often ran her fingers over these special numbers, her only remaining physical connection to Becca. She had refused to bring any pictures of her to the prison, to decorate her locker, to look back at her when she put on her uniform. A beautiful child's image did not belong in such a hate-filled place. Betsy's arrival had added to the hate.

She thought about Becca all the time. Her daughter was the most loving and kind child Betsy had ever known, that anyone in Four Points County, Texas, had ever known. She was a friend to everyone, and all the neighbor ladies in their rural community said that she had a "heart bigger than all outdoors!" But Becca was gone now, struck down while working to help others. Stolen from her single mom while Becca undertook an act of selflessness.

Becca had a friend at school with a terrible disease; a poor little child named Connie. Connie had CID, and it caused her nerves not to work the way they were supposed to. Becca didn't know why, but others did. Connie's mom had taken Connie to New York to see a special doctor who knew about CID.

After returning home from New York, their school had received a DVD with a call to help from a wonderful lady named Alison Montgomery. Ms. Montgomery led an amazing organization in New York City dedicated to ending CID. The doctor who diagnosed Connie worked for these people. Ms. Montgomery was going to beat CID, but to do so she needed everyone's help. Watching the DVD, Becca thought that Ms. Montgomery was looking right at her! A brave and beautiful angel who could help Connie! So, when the school sponsored a bike riding team to raise money for the fight against CID, a fight that would be won by that wonderful Ms. Montgomery, Becca was committed to do her part. She scoured the economically depressed county getting just about everyone to sponsor her bike ride. Ten cents, twenty-five cents, sometimes even fifty cents a mile, people made their pledge and wished Becca well. Becca would not let Connie down. She would not let Ms. Montgomery down. She would raise a lot of money for Ms. Montgomery! For Connie!

At 3:14 PM on the rainy Saturday afternoon of the fund-raising bike ride, at the junction of Farm to Market 1924 and State Highway 116, Becca's bike was hit by a panel van delivering packages tied up in brown paper from all over the country. Becca died at the scene. Her small but energetic body no match for the truck's steel and the inertia of undelivered packages. It was an accident in the truest sense of the word. The driver hadn't been drinking, he hadn't been speeding, he had a long record as a safe deliveryman — he just hadn't seen the little bicyclist pumping hard for her friend. He had kids of his own and had to be restrained by onlookers as he tried to lift the large truck off the small child all by himself — his life forever changed.

Betsy arrived at the hospital only to identify a small, crushed little girl now hidden under a single white sheet. Betsy's world had ended.

Two weeks later, the news of Alison Montgomery's crimes and evil life had become the main story on the evening news. Betsy came to know that her daughter had died in vain. At the time of her daughter's death, a cure was already known though suppressed by the murder of Montgomery's lead researcher, a man named Dr. Briggs, a doctor Montgomery had murdered for money. The same doctor who had seen Connie in New York. Montgomery hadn't needed Becca's help. Becca's death, all the more senseless. Montgomery was an evil person, whose greed had killed her daughter.

Betsy quit her job keeping books for the grain silo company in town. Her boss, old Mr. Kincaid, told her to come back after she had some time to think. She would always have a place at Wilkerson Silo and Grain. Betsy knew she was leaving for good, that soon others would not let her come back.

She had done her homework. She had studied the Montgomery trials and followed the news of her incarceration. Betsy applied to work at the same correctional facility on the plains of Nebraska over a thousand miles from the home she had kept with pride. Betsy had no experience in law enforcement, so the only position that she could apply for was in the infirmary as a very-part-time orderly and most-of-the-time cleaning woman. She had been on the job for the last three weeks and had unpacked only one of the two suitcases in the second-floor room that she rented by the week.

Betsy worked the 4 PM till 1 AM shift. The full-time nurse worked only days, and the doctor visited only on Mondays and Thursdays. Betsy was mostly alone and filled her evenings remembering her daughter while sharpening a piece of metal strap that she had pried off of a bunk in the small medical ward. She couldn't take home the steel strap that was soon to be a blade, as the metal detectors would find it. For a first-time prison shank maker, she had done a very credible job, scraping the metal back and forth over the rough concrete floor forming a two-inch long blade with a sharp point. She had finished the knife earlier today. Tonight she would put it to work. Sitting up behind the admitting desk, she watched down the corridor. Her patience was soon rewarded. Just as she had almost every evening since Betsy had arrived, Alison Montgomery, her face devoid of emotion, walked past her to the showers. Montgomery never noticed or acknowledged her. It was if Betsy was just another inmate, her office just another cell locking in just another tormented soul. Betsy would have agreed with the description.

Betsy stepped out in the corridor and with a smile on her face, the first in months, quietly followed Alison Montgomery. The shank was hidden in her shirt. The cool metal against her skin a comfort to a mother whose heart had been needlessly broken. Broken by one who almost was the death of a cure.

ABOUT THE AUTHOR

For more than twenty-five years Steve Jackson has worked as a management and technology consultant assisting organizations of all sizes with the evaluation and assimilation of new technology and the outsourcing of non-core competencies. As an internationally recognized expert in several areas of high technology and their marketplaces, Mr. Jackson has provided business leaders with the insight necessary to acquire and integrate complementary technology and its supporting organization. He has also assisted Fortune 100 companies in the analysis of emerging technologies helping them to make strategic decisions.

He continues to advise industry in both a consulting capacity and as an authority on strategic growth through acquisition, divestiture, and outsourcing both domestically and abroad.

Mr. Jackson lives with his wife in Florida, where he is currently working on his next Thomas Briggs novel.

Visit his website at http://www.stevenhjackson.com